A Royal
Mess

INCLUDES *DUELING PRINCES*
AND *DUMPING PRINCES*

TYNE O'CONNELL

NEW YORK BERLIN LONDON SYDNEY

Dueling Princes

To my daughter and muse, Her Royal Stunningness, Cordelia O'Connell, and my son, the most distressingly fit boy to ever wield a sabre, Zad Santospirito. I kiss my blade and salute you both.

Dumping Princes

To my muses, Her Royal Magnifiqueness, the stylish Cordelia O'Connell, and my worshipfully clever Santospirito sons, Zad and Kajj, who brought Italy and Windsor to life for me.

Dueling Princes first published in Great Britain by Piccadilly Press in 2005;
published in the United States of America by Bloomsbury Publishing in 2005
Dumping Princes first published in the United States of America by Bloomsbury U.S.A. Children's Books in 2006
This edition published by Bloomsbury Books for Young Readers in October 2011
www.bloomsburyteens.com

For information about permission to reproduce selections from this book, write to Permissions, Bloomsbury BFYR, 175 Fifth Avenue, New York, New York 10010

LCCN: 2011934595
ISBN: 978-1-59990-888-5

Typeset by Hewer Text UK Ltd, Edinburgh
Printed in the U.S.A. by Quad/Graphics, Fairfield, Pennsylvania
1 3 5 7 9 10 8 6 4 2

All papers used by Bloomsbury Publishing, Inc., are natural, recyclable products made from wood grown in well-managed forests. The manufacturing processes conform to the environmental regulations of the country of origin.

Dueling Princes

• • •

If I were the only girl in the world, and

you were the only prince . . . (ribbit)!

ONE

Doing the KR with My Posse

I had my head out the window of the cab and my hair was blowing about my face – only not so much as to blow my tiara off – as we cabbed it down the Kings Road. We were en route to Waterloo for the train, which would take us back to Saint Augustine's.

'This has officially been *the* most awesome half-term break in the history of half-term breaks,' Georgina declared with that grand English drawl of hers that had once so intimidated me as she gave my hand a squeeze.

We'd bought said tiara for two pounds at Ad Hoc for a laugh in the morning. Immediately after that we piled into the photo booth at the Virgin Mega Store Centre, where havoc and mayhem ensued. This mood had carried us up and down the KR all day, and Indie and I had even been approached by model scouts. She had her security followers politely decline on her behalf. Indie's security guys are meant to look inconspicuous and follow at a discreet distance, but the art of blending in seems to elude them. Their idea of a discreet distance and Indie's are about ten yards apart. Indie is a *real* princess, with her own kingdom, personal zoo and everything, but she's not a bit affected. 'They approach me all the time, darling,' she groaned as the nice model scout was being despatched. 'They can be soooo annoying, don't you think?' she asked, grabbing my arm before it had a chance to greedily snatch at the business cards the model scout was begging us to take 'just in case.'

I rolled my eyes as if I knew exactly what she meant when inside I was thinking, a real model scout just approached me and said I had the look they were looking for!

I'm not surprised they approach Indie all the time. She is the most beautiful girl I know. She looks like a young Naomi Campbell. I suppose Indie is right, though; the last thing I would want to be is a model because it means basing your entire life on your body image. Plus the camera puts ten pounds on you. And then one day when you don't have 'the look' anymore, your body image must go to pot.

Indie had bought the tiara for me as I was paying for a pair of gorgeous green sequined slippers, turned up at the toe, to replace my Hello Kitty ones. Yes, I had reached that benchmark point when it was time to say a fond farewell to my Hello Kitty stage and leave that innocent babyish period of my life behind. Of course there would be a certain amount of regret and there would always be a place in my heart for Hello Kitty. I would never give up my Hello Kitty toaster back at home in LA because it toasts little Hello Kitty faces on your bread. It was just that at fifteen – well, two months off anyway – I felt it was time to feng shui my life. To make way for more, well, for more grown-up-ish pursuits. Like boys.

'Now that you've pulled your prince you'll be needing a crown, darling,' Indie had teased in a nice piss-take of my American accent, plonking the ghastly purple paste tiara on my head. Once I would have been too embarrassed to walk the street in a paste tiara. Even when I was a little girl playing fairies, dressing up always embarrassed me, mostly because my parents had this little stage built in the living room with curtains and all the trimmings. I'd have to give performances for my two adoring fans who cheered and carried on like I was a superstar.

Can I just say, and I think I speak for a lot of only children here, it's really, really hard being the object of all that parental love. Bob, that's what my father likes me to call him, explained he was only trying to support my creative endeavours. Given that my creative endeavours at age five were, for the most part, focused on trying to get my mud pies to taste like chocolate and to defy gravity and fly, all the stages and curtains in the world weren't going to help me, were they? When I have children, I'll be much more restrained than Sarah and Bob are with me. I'll be reasonable and sane and let my children call me Mummy or Mom, like normal children. Mind you, I am soooo glad that I am NOT a grown-up, because as far as I can tell being a grown-up sucks big-time.

Anyway, while I didn't say anything to my friends, I couldn't help this feeling that I had finally arrived. Okay, so I wasn't a Trustafarian, or a real princess, and the car packed with security guys discreetly following us wasn't for *my* protection, but I was here. I was on the Kings Road, that HQ of Sloaneishness where all public school girls and boys go to burn Daddy's plastic, parade with their posses, and meet one another.

By the way, public schools in England are the opposite of public schools in America. They are ancient grand places where the great and the good parents send their children from age eleven (or seven even) to learn what it is to be great and good. My parents are good but not what you'd call great. They packed me off at age eleven to Saint Augustine's School for Young Ladies because my mom, Sarah, went there and said it was super. My father's American, but he always goes along with whatever Sarah thinks – actually I think they think with one mind, they are such clones of one another. My first three years at public school in England really sucked (apart from having Star as a best friend). But since working out how the system operates and pulling boys (well, one boy in particular, Prince Freddie, heir to the throne of Great Britain) my life has really been looking up.

If you ever want to go public school spotting, the Kings Road is *the* place to go. You can do the Ken High

(Kensington High Street) as well, but it's not quite in the same league. The long, narrow traffic-choked street of mostly Georgian buildings that runs from Sloane Square to World's End, with its boutique shops and chichi High Street brands, is a Mecca for public school spotting. 'Well,' as Star says, 'we need some sort of meeting place when we're locked up in our boarding schools like prisoners most of the year, don't we?'

The last time I'd done the KR with Georgina and Star, I still hadn't shaken my insecurities about being an American outsider taking an illicit peek at a parallel universe. A universe of privileged girls and boys, their names all listed in *Debrett's Peerage and Baronetage* or, if European, the *Almanach de Gotha* – proving they are someone. You can scan yourself blind poring over *Debrett's* and the *Almanach*, but you won't find a Calypso Kelly listed. But these girls and boys, armed with their Trustafarian credentials, rule this part of London, ever mindful that one day they would in all likelihood rule the world.

As Star has always opined in a wonderful piss-take of her own class, 'Their sort always travel in packs, darling. *Quelle horreur!* that a posh teen be seen out on her own. No, no, no. You never go anywhere without your posse, daaarling.' Star is rock-star royalty, which is virtually the same as real royalty these days. But even if she weren't royal, Star is bursting with an energy and self-assurance that doesn't acknowledge obstacles.

You can always recognise the public school tribes by

their clothes: pashminas, short skirts or jeans, and long, glossy designer-blonde tresses for the girls. Ralph Lauren shirts, thin jumpers, and chinos or Levi's for the boys. Sunglasses, if worn, are sported on the back of the head, darling, not the front. The girls will all be calling one another daaarling as they air-kiss members of their extended circle in greeting, or furiously text the friends they are already with on their mobile phones. The boys will be laughing loudly with their mateage, listening to their iPods and flicking butts. For some reason they always smoke their cigarettes right down to the filter, if not beyond.

I've watched these tribes since I first came to England – the way an anthropologist might observe another culture – and even though I would never have admitted it until a year ago, I had longed more than anything to be like them. Up until last summer, that had seemed an utterly impossible task for an American Freak brim full of insecurities and paranoia like me. But that was then. It seemed a long, long time ago too, because now I *am* one of them. Properly one of them. I had scaled the castle walls (only not literally, because I'm rubbish at climbing and scared of heights) and pulled one of their own; the heir to the British throne, Prince Freddie. Freds to me. *My* Freds. Just thinking about him made me glow.

In fact, apart from the Daddy's plastic issue – my daddy doesn't believe in plastic – you couldn't tell me apart from the rest of the KR Sloanes on parade that day, and believe me they were all out in force because it was the last day of half term. I was there with my own posse, Georgina (George), Star, Indie and the rabbit George and I own together, Dorothy Parker. We'd been very popular strolling down the KR with our bunny, who is breathtakingly cute. Everyone we met stopped us to chat and stroke her, apart from the horrible people in Pizza Express Pheasantry, who wouldn't let us in even with her in her pet carrier bag! The pimply maître d' had muttered something lame about health and safety regulations but was totally rinsed by Star before the word 'safety' was safely out of his prissy mouth.

'How *dare* you,' Star had railed. 'There's more intelligence in this rabbit's ear than all your pizza dough brains put together!'

Indie, George and I managed to calm her down and drag her off before she could throw the maître d' in the pizza oven. Star can get very passionate about things, which is one of the million reasons she's my best friend. Apart from Pizza Express, though, all the other non-food shops had insisted we let Dorothy have a little hop on the counter and asked to stroke her and ooohed and aaahed.

'She's got star quality,' Indie explained earnestly as she twisted one of her braids seductively at this fit guy who worked in the magic shop where we all had our astrology charts done. You could tell the guy was mesmerised by her beauty; even I was mesmerised by it.

When he told us that her Jupiter was trined with her

Mercury or something mad like that, Star announced in a bored sort of way, 'I always suspected that, daaarling!' and even the fit astrology guy laughed.

Seriously, it was a perfect day, just like in that song by that . . . that person, you know, thingamee whatsit, the one who sang that song, 'It's Such a Perfect Day.' I just couldn't wipe the smile off my soul as the cab edged its way slowly from light to light. I arranged my tiara and wondered what Freds was doing before stopping myself. I am determined to be one of those wildly cool girls who doesn't scramble her brains, txt-ing and obsessing about her boyfriend all the time and neglecting her schoolwork and her fencing. Especially my fencing, because I have *five* tournaments coming up where FIE judges, BFA scouts and other important people of the fencing world will be watching my every move with eagle eyes.

No. As lovely and princely as Freddie is, I was going to be madly cool and mentally collected about our relationship. Even though that would be very difficult because my lips were still quite puffy from all the kissing we'd been doing yesterday, and he is the most distressingly fit boy in all the world. Oh, the bliss! When we weren't quad bike riding around Star's estate, we had barely drawn breath. Not just because of all our kissing but because we couldn't stop talking. I find everything about him interesting and extraordinary, and here's the maddest thing of all: he says the same about me! On Tuesday he said I was the most exotic creature he'd ever met. That was soooo cool that I was quite literally gob-smacked, meaning I couldn't even blurt something stupid back like I normally would.

Yesterday, he went back home to Balmoral or one of his other famous ancient castles. I wasn't really paying attention to what he was saying, it was just so mesmerising watching the way his lips moved when he spoke. And what are words to soul mates anyway?

It's true, apart from being the fittest boy God ever breathed life into, Freddie kisses like, well . . . like a very good kisser. In America we say hot! Thank goodness he isn't like those sloppy kissers you see on movies that look like they want to swallow one another's faces and make slurpy slushy noises with their saliva. Star had a sloppy kisser at her house party. I think he was from the village. Clemmie pulled him and then regretted it because his lips roamed all over her face. Luckily Star spotted him and pulled him off to her father's chill room, where Jim Beam poured out of an angel of death fountain onto a Japanese rock pool.

Star's father being a madly famous rock star has made their whole house an homage to the rock-and-roll lifestyle as seen on MTV's *Cribs*. I love staying with Star, and even my stricter-than-thou parents are cool with it on account of how Bob is a huge fan of Dirge – that's Tiger's band. Tiger is Star's father, and even though he's perpetually stoned and calls everyone 'man' and goes into unconscious stupors on the floor so that you have to step over him to get your breakfast, he's wildly cool. As Star says, 'He's incredibly bright and wise occasionally, you know, when he's more or less conscious.'

But back to Freddie, he of the glossy, short sticky-up black hair that doesn't need gel or mousse to make it gorgeous. Freddie of the smooth, long-fingered hands and soft lips – well, you get the picture, FIT – although I explained to my mother that he was HOT in fear of her thinking he was some sort of exercise steroid-taking freak. Even though he will one day be the King of England, he's not in the least bit grand or pretentious about it. He sends me lovely txt messages all the time, and although he hasn't said anything official, I just know he's serious by the way he supports my neck when he kisses me and smells all lemony.

After living in England for four years I am fully aware that the term 'dating' is considered gauche by the English, and to use it would make one the object of derision and disgust. No one here does dates. They catch up, meet up, see one another and pull – pull like no other nation on earth. But the word 'dating' isn't in their lexicon. So while Freds and I are not actually 'dating,' it's sort of understood that we are boyfriend and girlfriend – I especially after the half-term week which we spent quad biking around Star's enormous Derbyshire estate, pulling one another's lips off and micro-studying one another's backgrounds.

And even though half term had now sadly come to an end, Star, George, Indie and I were going out on a high.

Or at least we were until Star spotted Ed, the boy Indie had pulled at Star's house party, talking to some girls from Cheltenham. We could tell they were from Cheltenham because . . . well . . . because of the subtle tribal things that suggested it.

'Darling, check out Eds and his mateage,' yelled Star as we were stalled at the lights. 'Who *are* those Cheltenham slappers he's talking to?'

Without anything needing to be said, we all stuck our heads out the window and hissed and jeered. Then, just as Eds turned around, we bobbed on the floor of the cab so he wouldn't see us. We hated Cheltenham girls, for, erm, well, because they are . . . okay, for no particular reason whatsoever, actually. Apart from the fact that they aren't Saint Augustine girls. And how dare they fraternise with Eds, whom the most stunning girl in our year had pulled and txt-flirted with relentlessly all break!

Indie was txt-ing furiously before we'd even wound the window up, which we did because it was autumn and bloody freezing and we were all wearing the skimpiest clothes we could feasibly get away with without dying of hypothermia. 'How *dare* he!' she said with a fearsome amount of feeling. 'Bloody boys. I am soooo never, never, never . . . ,' she ranted before running out of steam.

'What are you going to say to him?' Star asked, looking slightly worried. Indie can get quite hotheaded – just like Star, really.

'Who the hell are you talking to and why the fruup

didn't you tell me you were on the KR?' she replied, holding up her phone so we could read the words for ourselves. Then she pressed 'Send' before we could discuss the matter further.

'But he might know them!' I blurted. That's what I do; blurt things like that when emotions are running high and the last thing people want to hear is my blurt, even if it is vaguely reasonable. I don't know why I do it. Bob, who is soooo PC and wholemeal it's a wonder he hasn't turned into a bowl of granola, says I need to be more grounded. He's very big on grounding, is Bob, bless him. But seriously, for all their mad liberal ideas, I really do love my parents and miss them dreadfully when I'm over here at school.

I'd sent Bob and Sarah loads of e-mails during half-term break, but I hadn't heard much back, which was unusual because they are normally delirious e-mailers. For all their foibles and mad LA theories, I am rather proud of my parents for being so kind and lovely and obsessed with me. Of course we've had our ups and downs, but compared to lots of my friend's parents, like poor Georgina, whose father ran off with someone called Koo-Koo and barely ever sees her, Bob and Sarah are totally cool. And more important, they are always there for me.

'Well he can bloody well *un*-know them,' Indie said, replying to my reasonable suggestion about Eds – only she was smiling as she said it. Indie is fearsome when she's cross. Thank goodness she's never been cross with me. Yet.

'Well, I didn't like the look of them,' Star told her supportively as we climbed off the floor of the cab and sat back up on the seats. 'They looked very slutty to me.'

'Nor did Dorothy,' added Georgina. 'Madly unimpressed,' she told us as she held Dorothy up so we could inspect her unimpressed expression. I suspect Dorothy was just cross because she hates going in cars, but Indie was sold. She rubbed her nose against Dorothy's. 'Dorothy, you are soooo wise. If you say I should dump Eds here and now, I will. Wiggle your nose for "no" and flap your ears for "yes," okay?'

Dorothy wiggled her nose, but actually I don't think she's ever flapped her floppity ears in all her life, and I think Indie knows that very well.

A txt alert sounded, but it wasn't Indie's, so a mad scramble through tiny handbags for still tinier mobiles ensued, which resulted in all our handbags being emptied on the floor of the cab.

It was mine.

missing u alrdy. I've got a gorg photo of u on my laptop. U R distressingly stunning Kelly. No wonder scouts R after U! Freds xxx

How sweet and psychic was that? I bet our planets were trined. I'd only seen him, well, yesterday, actually, and already he was missing me. He had to go to some shoot thingamee. Most of my friends like shooting things, apart from Star. She's a mad *anti*, only she can get away with it because she's a proper rock royalty eccentric. Unlike me, who's just an opinionated PC liberal American with misguided opinions about field sports and country pursuits, which is what the English call killing foxes, grouse, deer and pheasants.

Freddie had been very sweet when I'd lectured him about the killing of things wild and winged. He ruffled my hair and kissed my nose and promised to try and aim poorly. I hope he'd just aimed poorly, remembered me, and sent me the txt. How wildly romantic would that be!

I had the best boyfriend in the world. I had to keep pinching myself to stop screaming it out loud at the top of my lungs for all the world to hear.

Missing you too, xxxx C I typed into my mobile before thinking better of it and changing the four x's to three.

Missing you too, xxx C – yes, that was much better. If he sent me three kisses, I should follow suit. I didn't want him to think I was planning our wedding or something tragic like that.

Then I added a PS: hope you are missing all things winged too!

His response was immediate. Want to meet up in Windsor on Sat? F xxx

I didn't need to even think about my answer.

Defs! xxx C

TWO

'Rental Meltdown

Back at school we all clambered up the narrow, dimly lit ancient stairs of the main building of Saint Augustine's. I was rushing a bit, keen to get back to my own dorm room to catch up with my roommate Portia, so we could stress out and strategise about our upcoming fencing tournaments.

Portia and I have had our ups and downs, but the downs were mostly my fault, like, well, erm, wrongfully accusing her of trying to steal Freds. I know now that my suspicions were mad, especially as she was actually pulling Billy. But we'd made up and were now very much on an up. Portia was as keen as me to distinguish herself at the Nationals, but before that, we had our regional and three other tournaments to place second or first in. For the next six weeks we'd have to have our sabres practically glued to our hands.

I heard voices in my room, which made me curious, as apart from Lady Portia Herrington Briggs (not that she was so tragic as to use her title), my only other roomie was the Honorable Honey O'Hare (who has her title written on her stationery). Portia and Honey barely maintain civilities. But as I entered the room I had a hallucination and completely missed my bed, falling instead in a heap on the floor.

'Whoops-a-daisy,' my mother, Sarah, said in a baby voice and laughed.

Yes, my mother. Sarah Kelly, who should have been tucked up in Hollywood with my father, Bob, eating granola, reading *Variety* magazine and bemoaning the lack of art house and foreign movies up for awards these days. I wish it had been a hallucination, but no, it really *was* my mother, in all her wholemeal glory, sitting on my bed as large as life.

'Come and give your mumsy-wumsy a huggle, Boojie.' Her accent was halfway between Freddie's mother's and Hillary Clinton – a bit like Madonna used to sound when she was going through her Anglophile stage.

And what was with the baby talk?

Honey, who was pretending innocently to listen to her iPod, started making the noise she makes when she laughs, sort of like a hog snuffling through rubbish. She can't actually laugh because she's had soooo much Botox she's running a serious risk of botulism poisoning.

'What are you doing here, Sarah?' I demanded, climbing off the floor.

'I've run away,' she said, as if she really were a little girl who'd run away.

'Run away? Run away from what?' I felt like adding 'at your age?' but I held back.

'Rents are such hypocrites – if I were to run away, they'd track me down, probably with tracker dogs and social workers, and lecture me from here to eternity. I felt like giving Sarah a lecture and telling her what a naughty madam she was and how she was going to be grounded for life – only not here in my dorm, obviously. They don't condone the presence of parents at Saint Augustine's apart from speech day or Sunday Mass.

I gave her a very, very, very stern look before realising I was still wearing my tiara. I chucked it on my bedside table. I needed to be taken seriously, and a purple tiara would limit my aspirations in that department.

'What do you mean, "run away"? You can't run away, Sarah. What will Bob do without you?'

'Humph!' was her response to that. 'It's your father I've run away from, Calypso.'

'What about my father?' I asked, realising this was bad. Sarah has never called Bob 'your father.' That's how divorced parents talk in movies. But then I guess my parents do live in Hollywood.

'Yes, your father. Bob and his Big One. Oh, Calypso, I've had it up to here with his Big One!' she cried, holding her hand several inches above her head to demonstrate.

More smirks from Honey.

'You know what he's like. All he's gone on about these past two years is his Big One. I supported him all this time in his creative endeavour, but the last month has been intolerable. He's barely surfaced from his study. And then when I told him I'd had it up to here!' – she held her hand above her head again – 'he asked me if I wanted him to trade his soul for an unfulfilling job on some godawful soap like me! Well that's it! Finito! My godawful soap has supported us all these years, so I told him to take his Big One and shove it where the sun don't shine.'

I looked over at Portia. Her inscrutable dark long-lashed eyes were bug-eyed with horror – only I couldn't be sure what she was horrified by exactly.

'It's his script,' I explained hastily, lest she think my father's Big One was, well, you know what. 'He's writing his Big One, the script that will carve his name in cinematic history.'

'And currently brings in no money,' Sarah added pointedly. 'Can you believe it, girls?' Sarah asked, playing to her audience. 'Well that was the last straw. I packed my bags and decided to come where I was appreciated – here.'

'But you can't stay here, Sarah!' I told her, horrified.

All the girls looked at one another, no doubt embarrassed for me. Parents in England don't share their problems with their offspring – well, not in my world. But Sarah was oblivious to her audience's discomfort as she wiped a tear from her eye.

'I mean, they don't let grown-ups stay in dorms,' I said.

'I don't mean *here*. I mean the land of my birth.'

'But Sarah, are you sure? I mean, Bob can't pack in a

script he's been working on for so long. He told me he had almost finished it, and besides, he does get *some* money from the Writers' Guild, and you *were* the one who insisted he chuck his perfectly good job and focus his genius on his creative endeavours,' I reminded her.

'Yes, well that was before I knew his creative endeavours were going to take so long. No, I discussed it with Bunny. And last week I made the decision I should have made years ago and put my plan to leave into action. I've come home to London to be with you!'

Okay, this was officially serious. Images of a frantic Bob pacing madly in search of his other half flashed through my mind. And who was Bunny? 'Did you tell him you were leaving?' I asked, my voice showing my panic. 'He's probably beside himself with worry!'

'Huh!' Sarah brushed this idea aside with a wave of her hand. I noticed she was still wearing her wedding ring at least. 'He probably hasn't even noticed I've gone. Last time I saw him he was head bent over his laptop waving away the dim sum I'd brought him for supper, you know the ones he loves with the . . .' And that was when it got seriously scary. Her lower lip wobbled, she stretched out her arms for me to fall into and, reverting back to baby talk, added, 'Bunny's right. At least I'll get to spend more quality time with my Boojie-woojems.'

'Boojie-woojems,' Honey mimicked. This time she *did* laugh, and her collagen-enhanced lips looked ready to explode with the mirth of it all.

See, this proves the absurdity of 'rentals. You love them, you put up with their unreasonable demands, you patiently endure their weird food fads and cultural oddities. For years, you even obey them slavishly and look up to them like they're veritable gods, but ultimately you start seeing through the disguise, right into the insanity and hypocrisy of who they *really* are.

For starters, it was Sarah's idea to pack me off to boarding school when I was eleven, promising me how it would be 'super' and how 'you'll make friends for life' when for three and a half years it wasn't a bit 'super.' It was a nightmare. And now that I actually *was* having a 'super' time and making friends for life, my mother pitches up and calls me a name she hasn't called me since I was five and starts ranting about my father's Big One. It's perverse, that's what it is. Even all this guff about Bob and his Big One, that was her idea too! She was the one who persuaded him to chuck his perfectly decent job at Warner and concentrate on his script. Okay, it was taking him a lot longer than she'd probably imagined, but still!

Portia was looking at me sympathetically, or perhaps it was a look of helpless pity, the sort of look you give to mad teachers.

'But surely you and Bob will work this out? You love each other. Who'll finish off Bob's sentences if you're not there?' I reasoned, stroking her hair like she was the child and I was the grown-up. 'And who is Bunny?'

'Oh, Boojie . . . ,' she said in a slightly hysterical baby voice as she attempted to wrap me in a cuddle.

I wriggled away from her. 'Can you stop calling me *that*!' I snapped.

Sarah looked as if I'd struck her, and I immediately felt bad.

The room fell silent for a bit. I could hear the *tap, tap, tap* of our House Spinster Miss Bibsmore's stick as she wandered down the corridor on her rounds, when suddenly Sarah began to sob, big heart-wrenching sobs. Portia gave her a tissue and I wrapped my mother in a big daughterly cuddle.

'Bob's Big One, what a joke!' my mother remarked sarcastically.

'Sarah, you've soooo got to stop saying that,' I pleaded with her under my breath, handing her another tissue.

'Saying what?' she asked innocently as she dabbed at her mascara-daubed panda eyes.

'Well . . . you know, Bob's Big One. People might think, well they might get the wrong idea about what the Big One *is*, if you see what I mean.'

'You mean the big earthquake? Well they'd be right, because this all feels pretty damn cataclysmic to me.'

I didn't know what she was talking about for a minute, but then I remembered that Los Angeles is on a fault line.

'I thought you left him because his penis is too small, darling,' Honey said, fluttering her eyelashes, which were almost long enough to do herself an injury.

Sarah looked momentarily horrified by what Honey had just said, but then she started to cry again, not in a sobbing, wrenching way, though, but more in a crumpled little girl sort of way, which made me feel even more helpless. Honey started dialling someone on her phone. 'Oh my gawd, darling, you have got to get down here and fast. The American Freak's mother's turned up. She's a bigger freak than *her*. She's clearly from a long line of ancestral freakage. . . .' This was rich coming from a girl who only two weeks ago was gadding about with an iron beak on her nose.

I grabbed her phone and threw it across the room. 'Get out,' I told her with an authority I barely knew I had off the fencing piste.

'*You* can't talk to *me* like that!' she shrieked, flicking her long, blonde expensively streaked and straightened hair over her skinny tanned shoulders.

'Just leave now,' Portia added in her grandly aloof way, and Honey, seeing herself outnumbered, retrieved her phone and sauntered into the corridor, checking her reflection in her Chanel compact as if it had been her own idea to ban herself from her own dorm room. For those of you who've not met Honey, she's not the sort of girl to miss a scandal – she's the sort of girl to start one.

'Look, I'm sure it's just a bit of a tiff,' I soothed, rubbing her back, unsure of what to do or say. I gave her a cuddle, and as I wrapped my arms around her I noticed some strands of grey hair mixed in with her lovely natural fair hair.

She struggled free. 'A tiff? A tiff? Is that what you think this is? Do you think I'm so shallow that I'd walk out on the man I love over a tiff?'

Stupid, stupid, stupid Calypso! Why did I blurt that stupid word 'tiff'? It sounded like a cleaning product. I slapped my forehead. 'Sorry, I didn't mean to say that. But if you love him, why –'

But Sarah was on a roll. 'You try living with a man who's self-absorbed in an ever-growing mountain of script. I hardly ever see him. And he's making *no* money, as I was just explaining to Portia earlier. *I'm* holding everything together.'

'Well, you can't hold things together if you're here, though, can you?' I reasoned.

'Yes, I can. Remember I am still a British citizen,' she said, holding herself upright in an imperious sort of way. For a moment I feared she was about to burst into a chorus of 'God Save the Queen.' 'I've got a job on *Gladesdale* in fact.'

'*Gladesdale*?' *Gladesdale* was probably the chaviest program on television, a sort of bad soap opera for teens.

'And taken a house in Clapham.'

'Clapham!' I yelped. Clapham, was *not* the place girls from Saint Augustine's spoke of. Clapham was where people who couldn't afford a big house in Chelsea lived in delusional gentrification and, more important, it was south of the river, and south of the river soooo wasn't part of my friends' world. Between *Gladesdale* and Clapham, I was going to be massacred.

I could hear Honey giggling in the corridor. She shrieked out the words 'Clapham' and '*Gladesdale*' with the relish of a hound dog baying for blood. The writing was already on the wall for me now. From this moment forth I would be known as the Girl from Clapham, or probably the Clap, for short. And just when things were going so well.

Sarah hugged me to her tiny bosom. 'Won't it be lovely to see more of one another, darling? You can have sleep-over parties with your friends. I can buy marshmallows and fish and chips.'

I tried to smile back. 'Sarah, I'm not five anymore, and the next six weeks are really, really busy for me. I've got the Nationals and before that the Regionals and as well as that I've got three other tournaments. And GCSEs to study for.'

Miss Bibsmore's *tap, tap, tap*ping was drawing closer.

'Oh, I see. So what you're saying is, you'd rather I go back to Bob and his Big One and live in a perpetual twilight of unhappiness?' my mother asked as a solitary tear ran down her mascara-stained cheek.

'Yes,' I blurted before I had time to shove my pillow in my mouth. 'No, of course not. I meant no. No, that is, I don't want you to live in a perpetual twilight of unhappiness, but, well, I don't want you and Bob to break up, do I? You guys love each other. You said so yourself.'

'Ha!' my mother scoffed. 'Callow youth. What do you know about love?'

I managed to stop myself from saying, 'Well, quite a lot, actually.'

But I did say, 'Sarah, for the last time, will you stop calling his script the Big One! Just call it his, erm, Opus or something.'

'Oh, an' wot 'ave we got 'ere then, eh?' Miss Bibsmore asked, her odd little form leaning on the doorframe, looking none too pleased at the sight of my mother sprawled on the bed.

'Miss Bibsmore, this is my mother. She's, erm, she's visiting from America.'

Miss Bibsmore took in the scene. The panda-eyed, tear-streaked face of my mother, the looks of worry and concern on the faces of Portia and myself, and the shadowy presence of Honey peering in from the corridor. 'Well, I'm pleased to meet you an' all, I'm sure, Mrs Kelly. Miss Kelly 'ere is a good girl, no trouble from her. Not like some,' she added darkly, turning to eye up Honey. 'Always polite is Miss Kelly.'

'How kind of you to say,' my mother replied. 'We tried to teach her manners and, well, I'm an old girl myself, actually.'

Miss Bibsmore put her hands on her hips. 'I'm not old! What do mean coming in 'ere and calling me *old*. I'm in my prime I am, an' all. "Old" indeed!'

'No, no, no, you misunderstood me, Miss Bibsmore,' Sarah said. 'I was a Saint Augustine's girl myself many years ago.'

Miss Bibsmore humphed. 'All the same, be that as it may, it's time for visitors to be off innit. Parents or no parents. Old girl or not. Rules is rules.'

My mother nodded obediently and gathered up her large handbag and a pale blue pashmina I'd never seen. As she kissed both cheeks she said, 'I'll call you on your cell, but if you need me, this is my number.' She passed across a card with an address and phone number on it.

She already had a card? This was serious. Sarah really *had* left Bob!

She didn't look at me as I took the card, and I felt that I'd failed her somehow. Maybe I should have joined her in attacking Bob and his Big One, but the truth was I just didn't believe something like this could happen to my parents. I gave her a proper cuddle, and the familiar smell of her musky Keils perfume made me feel like crying myself. She seemed so small and I felt so strong and tall as I stroked her hair the way she used to stroke mine.

How could this be happening? How could my good, decent, liberal, loving parents have come to this? Bob and Sarah? Sarah and Bob? Even their names sounded right together. They thought with one mind, their hearts beat to the same political ideological pulse, and they backed one another's madness to the hilt. If that isn't love, I don't know what is.

But now here we were, Bob on one side of the world and Sarah, living in Clapham, of all places. I couldn't begin to imagine what Bob was going through. I mean, he can barely pour his own granola without Sarah. I imagined him lying in a heap of despair, living under piles of pizza boxes, too weak to work, too despondent to go on. Surely he'd be on a plane begging her forgiveness and tearing his script to shreds. Okay, so there'd be a back-up copy on his Zip drive, but at least it would be a gesture.

Sarah was the love of his life. He was always saying that (much to my embarrassment). He'd even told my headmistress, Sister Constance. Surely he'd be on the first plane over. But what if Sarah was right? Maybe he *hadn't* noticed she'd even gone, buried as he was under his, erm, Opus.

Before Sarah left, I agreed to go and see the house in Clapham with her on Saturday. It was the least I could do. It was only after she had said her tearful good-bye that I remembered I'd agreed to see Freds on Saturday. And then I felt conflicted. Was it really shallow of me to put the joy of meeting my boyfriend above spending time with my mother in her time of need? I was pretty sure the answer was yes.

I would have to txt Fred, although maybe calling him would be better. I was sure he'd be sympathetic, or was it too early in our relationship for me to start burdening him with personal problems? Oh God, it was all so complicated.

Portia came over and sat on my bed with me. 'I'm really sorry about your parents, Calypso. But I've seen Bob and Sarah together, when they came to the school after Honey sold those photographs of you and Freddie to the tabloids, and –'

'I did *not* sell them,' Honey snapped indignantly, stepping back into the room. 'I just gave them to them. There is a difference you know, it's not as if I needed the money –'

'Oh shut up, Honey. No one was talking to you,' Portia said calmly. 'Seriously, Calypso I'm sure they'll work it out. . . .'

I nodded, because in the summer, Portia had watched her mother killed by a car on Sloane Street, and I knew she wasn't just offering polite words of comfort.

'Yes, poor Boojie. But at least you'll have your mumsy close by you in lovely gentrified Clapham,' said Honey as she admired her false talons. 'But just think of all the sleepover parties you can have in *Clapham*. Won't it just be super, darling!' she squealed, in a scarily good piss-take of my mother's accent as she clapped her hands with fake glee. 'I wish I could be more like you, Boojie,' she taunted me.

'Well, why don't you start by helping yourself to a little less Botox – it's clearly gone to your brain,' Star sneered as she entered the room with Indie. 'It's about time you started showing Calypso some respect. She's probably the most talented person you know. She's going to be a writer, and the pen is mightier than the post code. Apart from writing the lyrics for our album' – she looked over at Indie and put her finger to her lips – 'she's entering the Interschool Essay Competition. She'll definitely win it,' Star announced with enormous authority. 'They're publishing the best three in the *Telegraph*, Honey.'

'So, why would I care about a sorry little essay?' Honey asked with a little less bravado.

'Because the sorry little essay has to depict personal suffering, and I'd say Calypso has been through quite a lot of personal suffering at your hands, wouldn't you, Honey?'

Honey was uncharacteristically quiet.

It was the first I'd heard about either lyric writing or essay competitions, but I trusted Star and loved the way it had shut Honey up, so I nodded with smug vigour.

Later that night, I crept into Star's room to ask about the competition. She dug about in her drawer and found a pamphlet advertising a £1,000 prize for the best essay. I read and reread the rules. The essay, which had to be 3,000 words in length, was to be an autobiographical account of the most painful experience of a teenager's life. The traumas suggested were growing up as a victim of abuse, coming from a broken or violent home, bullying and the struggles of being an immigrant.

I might not be the richest girl in my privileged world, but it *was* a privileged world. And while I was American, I didn't think the judges would rank me as a struggling asylum seeker. True, I had faced the toxic trauma of living with Honey, but would Post-it notes slapped on my back classify as serious abuse? Was there anything in my decent dull life that would bring a tear to the eyes of the judges? No, was the answer.

It was soooo not a competition for me.

But Star was insistent. 'Of course it is. Your writing is brilliant, Calypso.'

'But I've never suffered, well, not in that sort of way,' I told her, pointing to the pamphlet. Then I thought about the problems I was facing. Saturday for example, and how I'd told Freds I'd meet him and how now I was going to have to tell him that my mother had left my father, which would make me the Complicated Girlfriend even if he was really sympathetic. Oh god. Maybe I should think up some elaborate lie about not being able to make it to Windsor.

Star interrupted my problem-solving plans. 'Darling, we've all suffered. Even me, even Honey. Anyway, you do actually come from a broken home now, remember?'

'But I don't want to come from a broken home, Star,' I suddenly cried. And then the floodgates opened, and I couldn't stop crying. 'I don't want Bob and Sarah to split up!'

'It's okay, darling,' she soothed. 'We'll fix it. I promise. Bob and Sarah were made for each other. Even a fool like Honey can see that.'

THREE

The Fascism of Creative Endeavours

On Star's suggestion, I fired off an absolute stinker of an e-mail to Bob. She was of a mind that the short, sharp shock worked best with men. 'Stick it to him,' she told me. 'Make him writhe with guilt.' I was inclined to trust Star on these matters.

Whenever her father went off the rails, her mother wasted no time pulling him into line. 'Men are blameless, brainless creatures, darling. In my opinion, Sarah's only come out here to frighten the bejesus out of Bob. You Americans love all that shock-and-awe business. Sarah's probably counting the minutes until Bob turns up in England on his white charger and carries her back to Hollywood. But the truth is that men are like quad bikes – they need to be driven.

I decided on a formal tone, which would leave him in no doubt as to what he needed to do.

Dear Bob,

I am forced to write this unpleasant e-mail because you don't 'believe' in snail mail (although that would have taken longer anyway, and this is an emergency). But I think not believing in snail mail points to a madness within you because snail mail (like plastic) blatantly does exist. All my school life spent over here I have watched the other girls receive post from their parents and lovingly pin it to the pin boards above their beds as a statement to all that their madres and padres love them.

But I digress. The real reason I am writing to you is to insisit that you stop this macho obsession you have with writing the Big One and get yourself a nice soul-destroying job like Sarah and the rest of the world have to put up with.

Creative endeavours are all well and good, but not when they come at the cost of the people you love, e.g., Sarah and your daughter (me). Also, I know you wouldn't want to tear asunder what God glued together the day you wed Sarah on that beach in Hawaii. Nor do I mean to sound selfish, but this marital drama has come at a very inconvenient time for me (yes, me, your little girl whom you said you loved more than life itself). In case you have forgotten, I am trying out for the Nationals, which you once said was all you lived for!

And poor Sarah is beside herself. She thinks you care more about your script than her! I know that isn't true. I know you love her and this is all just a gigantic misunderstanding. I know what you are like when you write. You go into your own world, but in the process you've made Sarah feel like you don't care about her. Also, this script is taking an awfully long time. I'm sure it will be very good and meaningful and you MIGHT even sell it for loads of money, but maybe you should take a break for the sake of your marriage and come to England to show Sarah how much you love her? It is blatantly obvious to everyone that you are made for one another. The point is you need to nip this in the bud before it goes any further. Sarah has already got a job and is renting a house in CLAPHAM, which, in case you don't know, is where 'the clap' comes from due to the density of prostitutes that once lived there. At least that's what Honey told me, and although she's a compulsive liar, you told me even liars tell the truth sometimes.

Is this what you really want for the mother of your child? Is this what you want for your wife – working on some plebbie show she really, really hates! Burying *her* creative yearnings alive. [I'd made this bit up, as we hadn't actually spoken about her new gig on *Gladesdale* or her creative yearnings, but I felt it might strike a chord just the same.] Maybe to prove you love her you will have to go back to your old job writing dramadies like *I Hear Laughter*, which I actually think was very good, even though it did win the Worst Dramady

Award three seasons running. So just get a job for a bit and make things right with Sarah so she can go home. You must be wondering where the granola is kept by now anyway.
Your loving daughter,
Calypso

I was very pleased with my e-mail. I was convinced it had been both sympathetic and insistent. Star agreed. We had no doubt that Bob would be charging off to his agents to discuss getting back on a new show as a staff writer before he even read my sign-off.

Instead, I'd hardly pressed 'Send' when he e-mailed a response.

Dearest Calypso,
I am shocked by your narrow-minded determination to cast me as the demon in all this. Sarah knows she can come back any time she chooses to. If your mother really loved me she would respect my need to express myself creatively, as she promised to when we made our marriage vows on that beach in Hawaii. I hope you are eating well and working hard. Maybe she just wants to be near *you* for a bit, have you thought of that!
Love, Bob

I was gutted. How could he be so obtuse? While I never really thought of my parents as one of the great love stories of our time, I had always imagined that when I grew up and got married I would want a marriage like Sarah and Bob's. Also, I really didn't want to come from a broken home!

My friends were all brilliantly supportive. The next morning at breakfast as we dunked our croissants and slurped our cereal, Star was still working on me to enter the essay competition. But honestly, my plate was already full with fencing and GCSEs, I told her, and besides, my plan was to get Sarah and Bob back together, which would mean there wouldn't be an essay of heartfelt loss and suffering to write.

'What essay?' Indie asked.

'Calypso's entering an essay-writing competition about the agonies of coming from a broken home,' Star announced to the table at large.

I tried to kick her under the table, missed and knocked my shin on the table leg.

'Wow, that is soooo cool,' Indie said.

I glared at Star as I rubbed my shin, but she smiled at me sweetly and said, 'Darling, don't get your knickers in a twist. You just said your e-mail didn't work, so maybe the essay-writing competition will be the thing that actually brings Bob and Sarah back together. Imagine how Bob will feel when he reads of the pain his creative endeavours have wrought on his daughter. He'll drop his Big One like a lead balloon and propose to Sarah all over again.'

'Are you really entering that competition, Calypso?'

Portia asked as she sat down. 'We're going to have soooo much going on with the Nationals coming up.'

Sometimes I could strangle Star. But then she somehow always redeems herself. She tossed a croissant at me. 'Don't worry, Calypso. I'm sure this break won't stick. Honestly, grown-ups are such drama queens, and I should know. My parents break up all the time. Mummy even has her own suite at Claridges for her fortnightly bolt. She's always leaving Daddy, hoping that it will make him give up weed.' Star shrugged, as one resigned to her parents' foibles. 'But she always comes back or he always goes to fetch her because they both know no one else is going to put up with either of them. Bob and Sarah are the same.'

'That's true. Bob and Sarah have never had an individual thought. They're like one being. You can't have a Bob without a Sarah, it would be like . . . well, like a Siegfried without the Roy.'

'Like toast without marmalade?' Arabella suggested, spreading a large portion of marmalade on her croissant.

'Quite,' agreed Georgina. 'Like Tobias without my vodka stash.'

We all laughed at that, remembering the debacle of a few weeks back when Star's snake, Brian, had tried to swallow Georgina's teddy, Tobias – who, by the way, is a full fee-paying student with the same rights and responsibilities as other students. Anyway, in the process, Brian tore Tobias apart, exposing the stash of vodka Georgina had concealed inside his stuffing. Tobias had been suspended for a week for drinking. Since then Tobias has been seen by teachers and students alike as a bit of a drunk. Georgina had to promise Sister Constance that she would give him a really stern talking to.

'Poor Sarah. I think your father is being absolutely bloody about this Big One,' Indie added, piling the sugar into her tea. 'How long has he been working on it?'

'About two years,' I told her, cringing that I had been responsible for bringing the term 'Big One' into my friends' lexicon. Surely it was worse than 'dating' even? 'But it was Sarah who insisted he pursue his creative endeavour to write his, erm, Opus,' I justified, feeling suddenly defensive on Bob's behalf. He was soooo passionate about his script, and even though it was taking forever to write, I really did admire him for being so committed.

'Well, personally, I think he should toss this madness. I think we should all be supportive of Sarah. It must be ghastly for her to be all alone, starting a new job, living in Clapham.' Indie's lovely model-like features shivered at the very thought.

'Yes, but Bob wants her back,' I told her. 'He thinks she's being unfair to him when he's so close to finishing it,' I explained, paraphrasing Bob's e-mail.

'Piffle,' Indie scoffed.

'Sarah *did* say she'd like you to have a sleepover party,' Portia reminded me. 'That would cheer her up, having a house full of marauding teenagers.'

I gulped my hot chocolate at the thought and started choking, knowing that (in Sarah's mind) a sleepover meant something very different than what it meant to my friends. Sarah would probably bake chocolate biscuits and have us all sitting in a circle, chatting about our innermost thoughts – with her. Unlike the other girls' parents, who all lived in a different wing of their houses, Sarah would want to spend every moment of the night with us.

'So? Let's all go?' piped up Clemmie, who adores parties almost as much as Tobias.

'I'm in,' agreed Arabella. 'Where did you say she was living?'

'Clapham,' Honey announced loudly, slamming her tray down at our table. She made the word 'Clapham' sound like something a dog might cough up.

'Clapham it is, then,' Georgina declared. 'Arabella? Clems? Indie? Star? Portia?'

'Clapham it is,' they all agreed.

'Oh all right, then,' sighed Honey. 'Clapham it is,' she conceded as if she'd even been invited or something.

'I'll see you in class,' Portia said, unfolding her impossibly long legs and standing beside me. 'And I'll meet you during break in the salle, Calypso, yaah?' she confirmed.

'Yaah,' I agreed. 'I hope Bell End is up for getting us into shape,' I mused.

Portia leant over and lightly kissed my cheek. 'Don't worry, darling. It's Bell End's glory and reputation on the line as much as ours. And don't worry about your parents. I'm sure it's all going to be fine. They're sooo obviously the perfect couple.'

I smiled and said, 'of course,' because that's what you have to do when people reassure you – make them feel that they've really helped. Especially after everything Portia had been through. Just the same, Bob's e-mail hadn't exactly encouraged me. What if Sarah wasn't overreacting? What if Bob really was being insensitive? It happens to artists. Only a few weeks ago I felt Star was putting her music before me, but then again I am prone to extreme bouts of insecurity. The truth was, I couldn't have felt less confident, but I hoped against hope that Portia was right.

I was just about to say my own laters to the group when my txt alert sounded.

Wish it was Sat 2day! Freds xxx

Oh the joy of having a boyfriend to distract you from the horrors and madness of 'rental separations! Suddenly, Bob and his Big One and Sarah's flight to Clapham were the last things on my mind. The 'rentals would just have to grow up and look after themselves. I couldn't be responsible for them *all* my life. Also, I had far more pressing matters to deal with, like registration, clearing up my room, chapel, lessons, fencing and most of all, my lovely, lovely Freds.

There was no way I could enter an essay-writing

competition about my personal pain after his txt. I was walking on air. And then I remembered I had agreed to meet Sarah *and* Freds on Saturday. Star, who had leaned over to read my txt, gave me a look of sympathy because she knew I'd agreed to go to the house with Sarah on Saturday.

'What are you going to do?' she asked.

'Be in two places at once,' I joked, but actually there was nothing funny about it. Whatever I did, two people were going to be hurt – one of them me. The essay suddenly seemed like an increasingly less absurd idea.

FOUR

Bell End Goes Double Bonkers!

Bell End had taken over for Professor Sullivan while he took his sabbatical. We'd had our doubts about him initially, just, well, because he was as different from our suave and debonair professor as it is possible to be. His name wasn't really Bell End, it was Mr Wellend, but because he was a bit of an idiot, Portia and I had started calling him Bell End – which in England is the name for the end of a boy's whatsit. He was loud, brash, coarse and South African, but there was no doubting his determination to whip us into shape. As the only two serious sabreurs, Portia and I were his big hope. At least that was Portia's reasoning.

We entered the salle at lunch to find it empty, though.

'You don't think he's forgotten us?' I asked, plonking myself on a bench. If he didn't turn up, we wouldn't even be able to practise, such is the policing of the British

Fencing Association. The school would be fined thousands of pounds.

'We only spoke to him at break, and he was madly wound up about it. We've already got a tournament this Saturday in Sheffield and he said he'd drive us.'

'Oh, that's brilliant!' I squealed with excitement, jumping up and down on the spot. Sarah definitely wouldn't want me to miss a tournament, and Freds would be there too! All my problems would be solved.

'God, no nerves on your side, then?' Portia said, surprised by the level of my excitement.

'Oh God, no, I will be nervous, It's just that, well, we'll get to see Billy and Freds now.'

'Billy definitely,' she agreed, grinning from ear to ear at the prospect of seeing her boyfriend. 'I spoke to him earlier. But I got the impression from him that Freds wasn't going. You know how he loves to visit his gran whenever he can. And with his security situation, Billy reckons Freds might figure it's not worth it. I mean, the tournaments are more preparatory than essential. Also, Sheffield is like a four-hour drive, and while girls are seeded out by three thirty or so, the boys sometimes don't finish until seven or even later.'

My face fell.

'But darling, don't worry. It will still be a fantastic day out for Sarah.'

'What?'

'Sarah. You had planned to check out her new house in

Clapham,' Portia reminded me. 'But she's sure to want to come to the tournament, isn't she?'

I nodded, trying not to betray myself, but there was no more speculation, as that was when we heard Bell End enter the salle. He was laughing like a, well, like a bit of a maniac actually.

'Come on, then, you big girls' blouses (his favourite term for us), git out here and let's see what you're made of,' he called out to us.

We scrambled into our fencing gear and rushed out to the salle, and without a word being spoken, we got straight onto our stretches.

While we stretched and lunged and lunged some more, Bell End (in full fencing gear) roamed the salle, slashing the air with his sabre. His muscular little body was as stiff as a board as he muttered to himself about new world orders and standards being set and met. Portia and I did our best to stop giggling, but we weren't entirely successful.

Then after ten minutes he suddenly yelled out, 'Jerzy Pawlowski!' His voice bounced off the walls.

Portia and I stopped our lunges and looked around the salle, expecting to see some crony of Bell End's entering. But no, it was just Bell End being mad.

We went back to our lunges.

'Jerzy Pawlowski! He yelled again – only louder this time, so that his voice bounced around the walls for a good while longer. 'Greatest sabreur that ever lived!' he yelled so loudly the words echoed back.

It's best to ignore teachers when they start cracking up, otherwise you can end up being showered in blues, or questioned by therapists, or involved in an investigation after they cart them off to the loony bin. I moved on to my supermans, as did Portia.

'Won the world title outright three years in a row, he did! In 1957, '58 and '59. Took the gold in '68 at the Olympics, and with the Polish team he took gold from the Hungarians in '61, '62 and '63.'

I looked at Portia and she looked at me. Our warm-ups were done, and we were awaiting instructions, but all Bell End did was repeat the name 'Jerzy Pawlowski!' over and over again.

It was going to be a bloody nuisance if our fencing master chose now to crack up. We'd never get through to the Nationals. Ignoring Bell End, Portia and I stood quietly, waiting for him to finish.

'Hungary still hasn't recovered.'

'Heavens,' said Portia just so he knew we were listening.

Bell End humphed. 'How many ways of moving forward do you think Jerzy had, eh?'

'Erm . . . one, sir,' I hazarded. I mean, as a sabreur you spend your life practising moving forward. It's the most repetitive exercise you do. Moving forward and then moving forward over and over again. It doesn't take a genius to work out that there's only one way of moving forward . . . and that's, well . . . it's moving forward, basically.

Portia looked at me and raised one eyebrow in that special aristocratic way she has.

'Eight!' Bell End yelled, slashing the air with his sabre. Again, his voice bounced around the salle. His face had gone purple too, like he might, be about to have an apoplectic fit. I wasn't sure about Portia, but I was crap at first aid.

'Eight different ways of moving forward,' Bell End declared in his booming South African voice. 'Footwork of a dancer and every way of moving forward cunningly calculated to provoke a different reaction from his opponent, eh? Eh? Eh?'

Clearly a response was required. 'Eight, you say?' I replied in an upbeat, interested sort of way. Nutters like Bell End like you taking an interest in their mad rants. 'Heck, that is a lot, isn't it, sir?'

'Yes, blast you!' he yelled, fiercely slashing his blade in fury. 'It is impressive. More than impressive, even. Man was a genius! A genius! Eight. Think about it, eh? One, two, three, four, five, six, seven, EIGHT!' He punctuated each number with a forward lunge – each looked pretty similar to me.

'Oh,' I said quietly. 'So he was quite, erm, prolific, then?' I added, showing him I was all ears and keen as mustard on this Jerzy chap.

Bell End glared at me and pressed the point of his sabre into the floor to flex it. I began to feel afraid.

'Sabre is like poker –' he started, but like the mad blurter

I am, I interjected. 'Professor Sullivan said it was a physical game of chess.'

'I'm talking about *bluff*, girl. Bluff. Bluff, damn you! Go on, say the word!'

I looked at Portia and Portia looked at me, and we both knew what had to be done. 'Erm, bluff, sir,' we muttered.

This seemed to pacify him, though. He began to speak to us more gently. 'You're both excellent bloody fencers. Excellent for interschool matches, that is, but you're playing tournament now.' And then he started yelling again. 'Tournament! Do you *really* know what that means? It's not like a cosy friendly between schools with cheerful salutes and etiquette, followed by finger sandwiches and tea.'

I didn't interrupt, but in all my time at interschool fencing matches I'd never been offered a single finger sandwich. A glass of juice and some crisps were as good as it ever got.

Bell End was on a roll, though. 'No, you've got tantrums, threats, bullying, and more important, the bloody-minded focus of girls who have been waiting their whole life to rip you to shreds and dance on your entrails. And on top of that you've got all those scouts and FIE spies, wandering about, lurking, spooking. Then, of course, there's the fan clubs.'

'Fan clubs?' I blurted as an image of cheerleaders like we have in the States popped into my mind. Pom-poms, cheers of support as they cried:

'Give me C!' '*C!*'

'Give me an A!' '*A!*'

'Give me an L!' '*L!*'

'Give me a Y!' '*Y!*'

'Give me a P!' '*P!*'

'Give me an S!' '*S!*'

'Give me an O!' '*O!*'

'What does it spell?'

'*CALYPSO! Yaaaaah!*'

It seemed very unlikely in England.

'You mean fans for the fencers, Mr Wellend?' Because however unlikely cheerleaders might be, I was quite excited about the idea of a fan club. I'd never imagined fencers to have fan clubs. I know polo players and footballers have them, but fencing had always seemed to me like the chess club of sports. I wondered if they'd write me fan letters.

But Bell End brought me crashing back down to reality with a thud. 'Yes, fan clubs. I'm not talking about girls like *you*, but mark my words, weak, gutless fencers get their families and friends to come to cheer them on in the hope of intimidating their opponents.'

'Oh my God!' I cried, suddenly envisioning Sarah running up and down the piste crying out, 'Go Boojie! Go Boojie!'

'And presumably you both have aspirations for the Nationals, and to make that you've got to place third at the very least. The very least. And let me pop another of your girlish little dream bubbles. All the competition you'll be up against are going to be as good as, if not better than, you.'

I was a bit insulted by that little girlish-dream-bubble remark and almost blurted an objection, but Portia nudged me.

'And make no mistake, it is in my interest as much as yours that you succeed in your goals to make it to the Nationals. When I take you up to Sheffield on Saturday, all the other masters will be looking at *me*, yes, *me*. They'll be looking to see what I've done with you. How well I've whipped you into shape and trained you up. And I don't want to be a laughingstock. Which is why I'll be teaching you on a one-to-one every day on top of your regular classes.'

'Thank you, Bell End, I mean Mr Wellend,' I said quickly.

'And I've got another surprise for you too, girlies.'

Something about the glint in his eye made me suspect it wasn't going to be a nice surprise – like a finger sandwich, for example.

'I'll be using two sabres to fence you!'

'Sir?' Portia questioned.

'One in each hand. Double the challenge, double the lesson. We can't afford to waste time, Briggs. Now grab your weapon, you're up first. Kelly, wire her up.'

I did as I was told, as Bell End grabbed another sabre off the wall of the salle and wired himself up. Then I sat on the bench for what would be the most incredible lesson in sabre tactics I had ever witnessed.

Bell End was shorter than Portia, but with the two sabres in his hand he cut an imposing, if not terrifying, figure. Sort of like the Incredible Hulk with elegance. His gruff ways off the piste didn't match the grace and speed he displayed thereon. He was lightning fast and had the supreme footwork of a dancer. As much as I love taking the piss out of poor old Bell End, I had to admit I was spellbound.

I watched Portia too as she was forced to fence on a different level than I'd seen her fence before. She advanced and retreated with such control that her torso didn't even seem to be moving, and the speed of her sword and Bell End's two weapons was so fast, I didn't know what was going on. The buzzers and lights of the recording box just kept buzzing and flashing.

After their bout, Portia took her mask off and shook out her hair. Instead of her usual perfect hair-commercial coif, which I had always been so envious of, a spray of sweat such as I'd never seen shot out of her hair for a metre or more.

'See what I mean, Briggs? You were forced to up your game. Well done. Now, Kelly, git up here. Briggs, wire her up.'

Having had the advantage of watching Portia, I knew what I was in for. With two blades coming at me simultaneously, I realised how lethal the combination of wrist action, speed and surprise can be. What really struck me, though, was the simplicity of Bell End's actions. For the first time in my fencing life, I could see the vital importance of drawing my opponent with bluffs. Of course I'd bluffed before – it's the nature of the game – but with two sabres coming at me I had to let go of preplanned strategies and trust my instinct.

I took a lot of hits, but I struck a few of my own as well, and when we took our masks off, Bell End did the most extraordinary thing. He bowed. Yes, he bowed at *me*, Calypso Kelly, and it was a low, graceful, princely bow too.

Portia was clapping.

'Miss Kelly, I honour you. You're a bloody fine little fencer girl, and you'll see the Olympics if I have any control over it, mark my words. And we men from Capers don't make idle threats.'

I was wet with sweat and slightly dazed by exhaustion and what Bell End had just told me. In the next minute Portia swept me up in a hug and spun me around. 'Do you know how amazing you are?' she asked, laughing.

'I only know something amazing has just happened,' I told her, laughing in what I believe is termed a giddy way.

Neither Portia nor I could come down to earth after what had happened. The rest of the day's lessons passed in a blur. I was probably going to fail all my GCSEs, but I felt like I'd taken a leap into another part of my body and my life. I felt that new vistas awaited me, new exhilarating possibilities were beckoning.

Mad, mad, mad, fantastic fencing class today. Will tell all later. Are you going to Sheffield Saturday? Please say yes xxxxxxx C.

(For once I was too exhilarated to hold back on my kisses and just pressed 'Send.')

NO! 2 busy hanging out with u in Windsor REMEMBER! Freds xx

Whoops!

Actually, I am going to the fencing tournament in Sheffield, thought you would be too? x Calypso

(I limited myself to one kiss to make up for my earlier effusiveness.)

No, just doing the regionals and nationals. But good luck. Let's make it Sunday, OK? Freds xxx

Deal! xxx Calypso

Did I mention that I have the most understanding and wise boyfriend in *all* of Christendom and beyond? Well, I have. My spirits soared once more. Even when Honey started making some poisonous jibe about my plebeian mother and Clapham, I riposted with a pretty sharp comeback of my own. 'Oh, bugger off, Honey.'

Sadly, Sarah was neither as wise nor as understanding as my boyfriend. She called me soon after and rattled on for what seemed like forever about how she was going to pick me up after classes on Saturday and take me back to London to see the house in Clapham. 'Oh, Mumsy can't wait for her Boojems to see the house.'

'But Mumsy, I mean Sarah, there's a really important fencing tournament in Sheffield on Saturday, which means we'll be heading off at six in the morning and won't be back until the evening. So you see –'

'Oh, wonderful. I'll come and watch.'

Again I felt horrible as I lied – but I still did. 'That would be great, but the thing is they don't let observers come. It's a real shame. I was really looking forward to seeing the house.'

'No, no, no, of course it's more important that you attend this tournament. You know how much I support your fencing. Never mind. I'll pick you up Sunday, darling. We'll have a . . .'

I didn't listen to the rest of her baby-talk babblings. I was just too wildly depressed. I mean I love Sarah and I wanted to support her over her midlife crisis with Bob but, well, I was soooo looking forward to seeing Freddie on Sunday that . . . oh, I don't know, it was all a mess!

When I told my friends about my dilemma over brown slops in the refractory at dinner, though, Star said, 'Just explain to Sarah you're meeting Freddie on Sunday. Parents hate thinking they're inhibiting your social life.'

'Exactly, darling,' Indie agreed. 'All 'rents are terrified that if they get in the way of your social life, you'll become a friendless nobody.'

Everyone nodded knowingly.

'Just explain about how exhausted you'll be from the tournament and suggest lunch in Windsor instead. After lunch, simply say you've got to meet up with your boyfriend. She'll understand,' Indie naively reasoned.

If I knew Sarah as well as I thought I did – though lately she'd been rather odd – it would take more than straitjackets, armed police and attack dogs to prevent Sarah from meeting Freddie. You see, in my friends' privileged world of Daddy's plastic and Mummy's contacts, freedom, like status, was taken for granted. And it was no use trying to explain to my friends that Sarah would see it as a mother's duty to meet her daughter's first boyfriend. And that's without even taking into account that he was heir to the throne of Britain. No, Sarah would want to interview him and take photographs and everything.

As I looked around at my friends' supportive faces, I knew they could never comprehend that Sarah might not be convinced to blithely say ta-ta and wave me off to meet up with my first official boyfriend. My friends' parents would be mortified at the prospect of being seen as interfering or overprotective. Of course they want their children to be safe and well, but they figure by age four, any intelligent child (and of course with their genes their children are all wildly intelligent – NOT) can sort out their own social lives. They had been serving alcohol at meals to their children since they were out of their high chairs and all thought it perfectly natural for them to help themselves to the cocktail shaker when at home. If you treat your children like civilised adults, they'll behave like civilised adults went the philosophy. I was on the wrong side of a cultural barrier that would take a lifetime to explain. So I didn't even try.

Indie called over to one of her bodyguards and as I observed him do his duty, piling the remainder of Indie's brown slops into the pocket of his jacket, I suddenly thought, what if Sarah called me Boojie in front of Freds? *Quelle horreur!*

Everyone knows that princes are renowned for their understanding and wisdom, but still, even princes must have their limits.

FIVE

My Knickers Were in a Right Twist

Later in the afternoon, I received an e-mail from Sarah which sent my spirits plummeting like a dead dove to the ground.

> My Darling Boojie [what was it with this constant use of her old baby name for me, a name I had rejoiced at never hearing again after age five!],
> I have arranged with Sister Constance to take you out on Sunday after Mass as we discussed. Just the two of us, won't that be super?
> Love,
> Mumsy xxxxxx

My knickers were in a right twist now! The situation was far, far graver than I had first thought – and that was pretty grave indeed. My mother was regressing, or was it reverting? I'd read about this reverting business in the

Dummy's Guide to Psycho Babble only recently. According to the book, baby talk in adults is the final stage before dribbling, incontinence and compulsive thumb sucking set in. Any idea I had entertained about explaining my parents' split to Freds were splattered like road kill now.

And then I realised that *Gladesdale* would hardly be thrilled about having a dribbling, nappy-wearing baby talker on their writing team, however lowbrow their show might be.

Ipso facto, the wise men and women of *Gladesdale* might well give Sarah her marching orders – or at least call for a pram to take her away. And as Bob earned, let me see, about, oh, nada, this would mean Sarah couldn't pay my school fees. Had this been the case even a year ago, I would have worn bells on my ankles and bounced about like a folk dancer at a village fair. But now it was an entirely different story. I adored Saint Augustine's, I adored my friends. I adored my life – even with my nemesis Honey plonked right in the middle of it.

I had to take decisive action. There would be no more messing about or talk of 'creative endeavours.' Bob would simply have to give up the madness of his Big One and take Sarah back to LA for clinical treatment. Preferably before Sunday.

Dear Daddy [I wasn't going to 'Bob' him anymore. He needed to be reminded of his parental and husbandly duties.],

The situation is far graver than I first led you to believe. Come IMMEDIATELY, before *Gladesdale* calls for a pram to take Mummy off to the loony asylum for reverting. She's not quite in diapers yet, but it's only a matter of time, and then who will pay my fees? I'll have to go to one of those Hollywood schools you've always hated so much. No, dearest padre, now is not the time for creative endeavours. Your wife is on the verge of requiring potty training and your daughter will be school-less! Tell me your flight times.

Your loving daughter,

Calypso

PS: please make sure you come BEFORE SUNDAY! URGENT! BEFORE SUNDAY!

I swear he must have been at his laptop because he fired off his response with lightning speed.

Dearest Daughter [Daughter indeed, how droll! Well if he thought drollness would make things right, he was very much mistaken],

You have begged me for years to go to a 'normal school.' Consider this your Big Break. Besides, I love and trust Sarah enough to know that you are exaggerating her mental state. You weren't awarded the title Queen of the Doomsday Prophesies for nothing. I am working night and day to get this script finished so that I can give Sarah (and you) the life she deserves. I haven't slept since Sarah left, and a bit of support from my own daughter would be much appreciated. In the meantime, enjoy your mother's company and stop whining.

Your loving father,

Bob xxx

PS: It is ALWAYS the time for creative endeavors, Calypso! You of all people should know that.

If it wasn't a sin to dishonour your parents, I would have told him to bugger off and boil his head in his Big One. Instead I held fire and shared my despair with Portia, Georgina, Indie, Clemmie, Arabella and Star over a pile of tuck and a sip or two from our Body Shop Specials. Honey was there too, stretched out like a lioness on her bed. I had reached the stage with Honey where I was pretty much able to pretend that she didn't exist.

'I feel soooo disloyal about Sarah. I mean, I know she's distressed and upset and I *do* want to see her Sunday, I *do*! But I want to see Freddie as well, and believe me, I know my mad madre will not just say ta-ta and wave me off. It's not the American way,' I explained as I took a sip of the vodka that Star passed me.

'Darling, you could always combine the two,' Star suggested. 'I'm sure Freddie would *love* to meet Sarah. I think she's cool. Totally bonkers obviously, but cool.'

'Well, yes, but –'

'Though Calypso can hardly pull Freds with Sarah

looking on,' Georgina reminded her. Finally, some sanity from my posse!

I didn't say anything, but the last thing I wanted was my baby-talking-reverting mother scaring Freds off. Is that evil? I think it probably is.

'Could you ask for some alone time with Sarah? Suggest she come to chapel, and then the two of you have a lovely mother-daughter lunch somewhere fabulous in Windsor and duck off to meet Freddie afterwards?'

'But you understand, Sarah will want to come,' I insisted.

'Not if you suggest to Sarah that she might like to meet him on another more formal occasion, like a proper lunch the next weekend? Apart from anything else, she might be feeling a bit stronger by then,' Portia suggested as she unwound the towel turban her hair had been drying in. Her idea was pure genius. I wanted to hug her but settled for passing her the vodka.

'Brilliant,' George agreed. ''Rents love it when you suggest things they think they'll have to force you to do.'

'Is Boojie-Woojie ashamed of her mumsy, then?' asked Honey in a baby voice.

I threw a Jelly Baby at her but unfortunately she caught it adroitly on her serpent-like tongue. 'And I thought you PC Americans were soooo keen on the Christian values of honouring your folks?' She said all this in a bad attempt at a piss-take of a southern accent. I think it is the only American accent she knows how to do.

'Oh, and what might we have here?' demanded Miss Bibsmore, suddenly appearing in our doorway.

All of us sat there on the floor looking dumbstruck. None of us had heard her stick coming down the corridor, and as I looked down, I saw why. She'd wrapped the bottom of her stick in duct tape.

'Just a little chat, Miss Bibsmore. Would you like a sweet?' Portia asked casually, offering up a bag of marshmallows.

'No, I would not like a sweet, thank you, Briggsie, but I would like to smell what it is you've been drinking from that shampoo bottle.'

You could hear the collective gulp of our room as Star passed up the Body Shop bottle to Miss Bibsmore.

Miss Bibsmore sniffed it, wrinkled her nose and then stuffed one of her stumpy old fingers in it. Licking her finger, she pronounced, 'Vodka.'

'Yes, it's a special, erm, shampoo they're doing this season, Miss Bibsmore,' I blurted. 'It makes your hair wildly glossy and, well, lovely and soft. Portia's just used some on her hair . . .' I pointed to Portia's lovely freshly washed glossy hair.

Miss Bibsmore ignored my mad rant. 'I'll hazard it's yours, Miss O'Hare,' she said, turning her attention to Honey.

'You'll hazard no such thing, you mad old witch. Why would it be mine?'

'Oh, I got my eye on you, madam.'

'A blind eye, maybe,' Honey sneered, her collagen pumped-up lips blistering with derision.

'Well, evidence would suggest that as I don't see young Mr Tobias in the room, you are the most likely suspect an' all.'

'What's Tobias got to do with it? He's a soft toy!' Honey argued, bug-eyed with the horror that she was being so unfairly persecuted. In Honey's mind, she had the patent on unfair persecution. I almost felt a bit sorry for her, although she was only making matters worse for herself by referring to Tobias as a 'soft toy.' I mean, we are talking about a bear with his own custom-made LVT trunk and designer outfits.

'How dare you!' Georgina spat, diving off the floor and looming over Honey's bed, her eyes flashing with fury.

Miss Bibsmore interjected, placing her stick between Georgina and Honey. 'Soft toy or no, he's a full fee-paying student at this school and the only other student, apart from you, Miss O'Hare, in my dormitory what 'as a drinking problem.'

'Tobias has given up drinking,' Georgina assured Miss Bibsmore earnestly. 'He took himself off to detox over half term.'

Miss Bibsmore thought about this and nodded. 'Well, I hope the treatment sticks an' all, Miss Castle Orpington, and that's genuine, that is. But Mr Tobias isn't my concern on this occasion. So, Miss O'Hare, you can come down with me to Sister Constance.'

'This is outrageous. You have singled me out for persecution since you first laid eyes on me.'

I could relate to that, as that was exactly what Honey had done to me.

Miss Bibsmore cackled. 'Well, you were the one wot told me that you sued the last person what treated you like everyone else.'

'Ugh!' Honey grunted as she started punching numbers into her phone. 'Well I'm calling my lawyers! There are witnesses here who have just heard you admit you're singling me out –'

Miss Bibsmore swooped on the little gem-like phone and pocketed it. 'You can call your lawyers after you've spoken to Sister. Now up you get, one, two, three.'

The rest of us sat in stunned silence as Miss Bibsmore bustled the loudly protesting Honey from the room. We waited all of a minute before bursting into raucous laughter.

The maddest thing was that we still had the rest of our Body Shop Specials piled amongst our tuck feast.

SIX

Be Warned! Life's NOT All Nicey-Nicey

Naturally, I couldn't follow the advice of my friends to overlap my meeting with Sarah with my meeting with Freddie. After careful thought I decided even Portia's flawless plan left room for random 'rental disobedience. I knew how much Sarah was longing to meet Freds. Formal lunches sounded all well and good, but formality and Sarah were just not a natural fit. I had no choice. Imagine Freds, heir to the throne of England, meeting my baby-talking-reverting mother? He'd run a mile – with Sarah following him in hot pursuit.

No, as dismal a prospect as it was, I would have to put Sarah first and cancel Freds. I tried and tried to think of an alternative, but I owed it to Sarah to be there for her in her time of need. There was no way out. As I composed the txt the next evening, little tears banked up behind my eyes at the thought that I wasn't going to see Freds on Sunday and feel his lovely lips on mine, or smell the lovely lemony smell of his neck.

> Soz, but Sunday isn't go to work, the madres in town and wants me all to herself. Next Saturday though promise. xxxx Calypso

I watched the screen of my mobile for what seemed like an eternity, but there was no response, and eventually I had to go off to study period. I told myself that he was obviously wildly busy . . . either that or furious and planning to dump me.

By Saturday morning at 5:00 a.m., when my alarm woke us for our drive up to the tournament in Sheffield, Freds *still* hadn't responded to my txts. Yes, tragic as it sounds, I'd sent several txts because each time I told myself he was probably in divs (that's what they call lessons at Eades) or chapel, or well, just very, very busy loading up his iPod. After my recent phone txt face-off with Freddie before half-term – which turned out to be all Honey's fault – I wasn't going to let any sort of misunderstanding between us happen again.

After Freds' reaction to Honey selling that mobile phone snap to the tabloids, Star has always thought Freddie was overly keen on himself. She's always telling me I'm too good for him, but then she's so fiercely loyal she doesn't think any boy is good enough for me. I hadn't told Star that I had chucked meeting Freds on Sunday altogether because I didn't want him to meet my regressing madre. She would not have been impressed by that, nor, deep down, was, I, but . . . well, I could hardly have Sarah baby talking to the heir to the throne, could I? In the past three days she'd called me diddums, like, nine times! Diddums? What was I, a cat?

On Saturday morning, Portia and I dressed in our jeans and hoodies in the en suite so as not to wake Honey, who was snoring so loudly, I swear, it's a miracle she doesn't ever wake herself up. Then we rushed down the stairs with our torches and out across the damp lawn to the nun's house, where the tiny little form of Sister Regina was already at the door waiting for us in an overexcited state. She was hopping from one foot to the other.

It had been decided by Sister Constance that one of the nuns should chaperone us to the tournament, and so they'd had a raffle and the lucky winner was Sister Regina. After a lot of nun-ish clucking and cuddling and telling us how all the other nuns were sick with jealously, she led us into the kitchen of the convent, which hadn't been updated since the fifties.

She'd cooked us a full English breakfast, bless her. 'Well, you'll need the nutrition with all that swordplay you'll be doing. And I've packed tuna sandwiches for the journey!'

'Oh, that's really sweet, Sister,' Portia and I told her.

'Only, don't say a word to Sister Michael, because it was her tin of tuna I stole.'

'Sister!' we chastised.

'Oh, stop. We each get a little treat in the weekly shop, see, only I always choose cigarettes,' she explained, dropping her voice to a low whisper.

'Sister, that's very, very naughty. Now we'll feel guilty,' Portia teased. 'Poor Sister Michael.'

'Oh, shush,' she said, cackling wickedly as she bustled busily about the kitchen, dishing out the eggs, bacon, sausages, toast and baked beans onto the old, chipped green plates. 'Sister Michael won't even remember she ordered it. She's about to reach her century in another month, she is.'

'Wow!' I exclaimed. 'That's . . . totally cool.'

'Yes, and they'll be a big tea with scones and cream and cucumber *and* tuna sandwiches. We're all looking forward to it, but while the body may be strong, the mind's not all it could be in Sister Michael's case, bless her. Last night when we were playing animal snap, she didn't get *one* hand in. Even the chicken had her flummoxed and she always gets the chicken – always. Anyway, she wouldn't mind. Truth is, all of us nuns are very proud of you, and I'm sure no one could begrudge two lovely girls like you a little tuna. Now eat up and stop fussing.'

We were just scraping our plates when we heard Bell End knocking on the door of the cottage. It was only six o'clock now and still dark, so all four of us used our torches to make our way to the school mini-bus. Bell End gallantly led Sister Regina through the wet grass. 'Isn't this exciting, girls?' she kept exclaiming. 'Oh, Mr Wellend, I do hope they do well.'

Bell End had already packed our kit. 'Can't trust you bloody girls to remember your own heads,' he'd insisted when we'd offered to help the day before. 'No, leave it to the master; at least that way I'll know everything's in order.'

Sister Regina sat up front with Bell End and took control of the radio, which she set to Radio One and started singing along to an old Britney Spears song. When I say singing along, I mean 'nun-singing,' because obviously she didn't get to hear that many pop songs in the convent, so she just sang 'la-la-la-diddlie-dah' to the tune.

Bell End had brought along a few cushions to prop her up on, so she could see over the dashboard. Portia nudged me, 'Do you think he might be a big softy after all?' she whispered.

'No!' I told her firmly, rubbing my arm, which was still bruised from yesterday's training session with our two-sabre-wielding maniac of a fencing master.

Most of the journey, Bell End prepared us for what awaited us at the other end. 'It's not all nicey-nicey like interschool. You've got to expect all sorts. You've got those that play dirty and those that play clean in a nasty sort of way. Just like in poker, they'll use anything but skill to bluff or intimidate as they see fit. And another thing, you've got to ignore the Great Badger Rapists.'

'Sir?' I asked.

'Them pratts with GBR written on their backs.'

'But why?' I asked, because, truly, that was all I dreamed of, being one of those pratts with KELLY GBR (Great Britain) emblazoned across *my* back.

'Because you only get that honour if you've made the National Squad and are fencing internationally,' explained Bell End. 'Only there are some that award themselves the honour. I keep telling you, fencing's not all nicey-nicey.'

'But that's cheating!' I cried out indignantly over the top of Sister Regina's la-la-diddlie-dahing.

'Pathetic, that's what it is. These pratts get themselves colours made up for tournament intimidation. They figure it'll scare the bejesus out of you.'

'How elaborate,' Portia remarked. 'Elaborate' was Portia's ultimate toff put down. By elaborate she meant, scheming, low-life, social-climbing pond scum.

'That's one word for it, Briggs,' Bell End chuckled. I think he was starting to pick up on Portia's aristocratic codes, Mistress of the Understatement that she was.

'Then of course they'll have their fan clubs, you know, family, friends and the like. Mates from school, anyone they can dig up. Some of them even pay groupies to cheer them on. Even the bravest sabreur can be thrown when their opponent's end of the piste is full of a cheering squad yelling for blood, and your end's empty,' he said as if speaking from personal experience. 'You girls will be right today with Sister here and me, but there will be times when the lonely fear hits you, when you don't even have someone to plug in your body wire and they've got people chanting, 'Cut the guts out of the South African wanker! Only being South African he pronounced it *winker*.'

Luckily Sister was loudly diddle-dee-deeing to a song, so she didn't hear the profanity. Portia and I looked at one another. Clearly Bell End had had some painful personal experience in this area.

He elaborated a bit more about the abuse we could expect. Portia and I both sneered though at the thought of such obvious and puerile intimidation tactics. Star and the others had *begged* to come and watch us, but we agreed that we'd be too stressed out and that, if anything, it might put us off.

I'd taken the precaution of telling Sarah that they didn't allow anyone to watch, because the thought of her running around the piste crying out 'Go, Boojie!' was too much even for the most dutiful daughter.

'So, you've got to shut down emotionally. Understood? Think with your brain, move with your body, slam 'em with your blade,' Bell End insisted. 'That's your business. Your *only* business. The rest of the carry-on, the taunting of the opponents' fans, the verbal abuse they'll sling at you – none of that matters. Just GFTB, git it? Go for the Bollocks! Let that be your battle cry.'

Since Bell End's arrival at Saint Augustine's, GFTB had slipped into our everyday speech. Portia and I often giggled when Bell End shouted it out at us when it was just the two of us fencing. For a start, as girls we didn't have bollocks. Also, I don't think Sister Constance or our parents would appreciate our young minds being exposed to such obscenities. We, after all, were the crème de la crème of teenage girls.

Sister Regina, who'd happily been la-la-la-diddlie-dah-ing to a heavy rap song, was horrified. 'Oooh, Mr Well-end, language.'

'Sorry, Sister,' he apologised, his face red with embarrassment. Actually, the song Sister had been nun-singing along to was positively littered with obscenities, all of which celebrated the joys of sinning.

'And don't forget, girls,' Sister shouted out over another filthy rap song about gunning down rivals, 'I'll be there, praying for you. A decade of the rosary is worth a thousand fan clubs. All this artifice that Mr Wellend has warned you about will melt away under the divine intervention of Our Lady, girls. *Always* remember that.'

'Yes, Sister,' we agreed.

'And if they get too crude, I shall wave my rosary at them in defiance, I will.'

'That should have them trembling in their boots,' Bell End muttered under his breath.

'But honestly, Mr Wellend, I hope you won't mind if I call out a little *hoorah*! now and then if the girls get a particularly good goal or such like?'

Bless. I could have reached over and cuddled her. Nuns are so sweetly unworldly.

'No, I'm sure that would be most appropriate, Sister . . .'

I think even Bell End was a bit choked up by her innocence.

'Good, because I do like a nice little cheer, Mr Wellend. Revs up the engines, it does.'

We made good time and arrived at the BFA Sheffield Open venue a little earlier than planned. But there were already dozens of other vehicles there; some of them like ours, with their school motifs on them, others just random cars and mini-buses, which had presumably transported the dreaded fan clubs. Bell End pointed out that most people would have come by train. That meant there was going to be a *lot* of people at the tournament. I think that's when it really hit me just how defining an event this was going to be in my fencing career.

Portia and I pulled our heavy kits out of the mini-bus while Bell End lifted our little nun out of the car. At four foot nothing, she was like a doll. One that was becoming increasingly wound up with excitement!

And that was when all Bell End's pep talks turned into a worthless heap of rubbish.

Because that was when I heard the word 'Boojie!' as my mother appeared out of nowhere, just as we entered the building. 'Isn't this exciting? Oh, let me look at you,' she cried, grabbing my cheeks and pinching them. 'You'll knock them dead!' She was incandescent with pride.

I, on the other hand, was incandescent with quite another emotion altogether.

SEVEN

My Tragic Fan Club

It was difficult to make it even to the table near the entrance, where we had to have our names ticked off for the pools. Apart from the crowds, Sarah was wrapped around my body like a limpet, and Sister Regina was hanging off my fencing kit, chirping, 'Just wait till I tell all the other nuns about this. I know it's sinful, but I'll revel in their envy, I will.'

Portia managed to have her name ticked off and made her way imperiously through the throngs of people, many of whom we'd soon be slamming with our blades. Everyone was just mingling and chatting amicably, which made me doubt Bell End's fearsome stories of what we'd be up against, although I did see a few fencers with GBR on their backs wandering about the hall. Bell End nudged me. 'See what I mean? GBR my arse, they're Great Badger Rapists, you mark my words. But they think if you see that you'll be intimidated.'

'Pathetic,' I agreed as I finally made it to the desk, weighed down with the twin burden of my mother and my dread of what she might do to embarrass me. Bell End slapped my back. I think he was being supportive but, unaware of his own strength, he winded me, and I fell onto the book with all the names written on it.

'Christ Almighty, look what we've got here,' some Hoorah Henry joked to his mateage, and they all laughed loudly.

'Don't you get cheeky, gentlemen, or I'll have your master on to you, I will,' Sister Regina threatened, raising herself up to her full four feet. Nuns can be surprisingly imperious and menacing, especially where boys are concerned. They reddened at her threat and muttered, 'Sorry, Sister.'

Any menace her threat may have held, however, was immediately dissolved by Sarah, who threw her arms around me and told them to leave me alone. 'Big bullies!'

I unwound her arms from around my neck and looked her in the eye. 'Look, Sarah, seriously, you can't do that here. I'm not five anymore.'

'You'll always be my little, widdle girl, Calypso,' she promised me with another cheek pinch – as if this might actually cheer me up.

After finally having my name ticked off, I chased after Portia, who was already nearing the changing rooms.

'See you later, widdle, widdle girl,' the Hoorah Henrys called after me. Sarah, who was tagging along, didn't say anything, but I think she knew she'd landed me in it.

It was all I could do to shake her off at the changing

rooms. Fortunately, Sister Regina had already been seduced by the tea table. If you ever wanted to kidnap a nun, all you'd have do is to offer them a nice cup of tea and they'd go anywhere.

'You sure you don't want me to help you change into your fencing outfit, darling?' Sarah asked at the changing rooms.

I shut the door on her with a firm 'No, thank you.'

'I take it you weren't expecting Sarah?' Portia put it to me. She didn't look too happy about it, either.

'Of course not. I told her they didn't allow non-fencers, but, well, she's lived in America for a long time. Mothers sort of learn how to push pretty hard over there, you see.'

'I know it sounds horrible, but I am sooo glad we didn't bring a fan club. I would be ten times more nervous with Star and the others watching us.'

I agreed.

There was a crowd of other girls kitting up, so we let the conversation drop. No one spoke to us, and we didn't attempt to speak to them. Portia and I didn't need to say anything to one another, either. It was quite clear that we were both scared out of our wits.

Once we were kitted up we wandered back out into the maelstrom of the hall, which had twice the number of people crowded into it compared to when we'd first arrived.

We couldn't see Bell End, although I spotted Sarah chatting to Sister Regina by the tea table. Portia and I looked about to see what we should be doing, but everything was utter chaos. There were loads of random announcements coming over the loudspeaker, which further added to the confusion.

'If there are any qualified presidents in the hall today who have not volunteered, could they please come forward, as we are short of referees today.'

Bell End suddenly appeared out of nowhere and sprinted swiftly towards the other end of the hall like he was about to receive another Olympic medal. Sister Regina started to clap and cheer him on. Sarah, looking a little dazed, joined her.

'Let's do some stretches,' I suggested to Portia in the hope that in doing a few low lunges, Sarah wouldn't be able to spot us.

'Can Simon Tyler please report to sign in, as you have not yet registered?' blared a voice over the loudspeaker.

'Everything seems so disorganised,' Portia remarked as people stepped over us. 'I don't have a clue what we're meant to be doing. There's no boards about pools or where we're meant to be fencing, nothing.'

'Attention!' the announcer called over the loudspeaker. 'The girls' pools will be starting shortly. And I repeat, Simon Tyler, report to registration, NOW!' Then the names for the girls' pools were rattled off.

'This is it,' I said to Portia as several names were called and asked to assemble at piste 5. Portia's name came up in the next lot of pools being held on piste 6. My name was called to the pools being held at piste 7.

'Well, should we shake hands or something, do you think?' I blurted in that special idiotic way I have.

I was feeling the adrenaline begin to course through my veins as the calls for Simon Tyler to come to registration became increasingly threatening.

'No, I think we should hug,' Portia insisted. And so we did.

Of course, my mother and Sister Regina had also heard our names called and were waiting for me at piste 7 with a banner they'd cobbled together out of a stolen tablecloth. They were clutching it with the pride of two women who've just knitted a quilt.

It read – and this causes me some agony to relay – 'Go Boojie! Go!' The words were written in jam.

And then out of the blue I wished Bob were there. He'd know just what to say – even if it was one of his stupid gridiron football chants from his college years. Also, Bob actually did know quite a bit about fencing, whereas Sarah's support was purely emotional.

The other girls assembled at my piste began to giggle as I approached and Sarah and Sister Regina began to chant, 'Go Boojie! Go!' Unfortunately I don't think anyone was in any doubt as to who Boojie was.

Bell End strode over to our piste in a very authoritative manner with a referee's clipboard. As he was to preside over our bouts, he didn't make eye contact with me.

He had an officious air about him as he said, 'Right, first up, Kelly and Rogers-Staughten-Bowhip. And ladies,' he added, looking over at Sister and Sarah sternly, 'I think we can dispense with the banner for the pools.'

'Boooooh!' Sister and Sarah called out. 'Spoilsport!'

It was conflicting on so many levels. Part of me was relieved and the other part felt sorry for the sweet effort Sister and Sarah had put into their banner, even if it was a banner of shame. Also, I just knew that if Bob were here he would have stuck up for their right to express themselves.

Rogers-Staughten-bloody-Bowhip wasn't conflicted, though. She was in spasms of laughter as she shook my hand. But then another random girl hooked me up from the back, which made me feel like maybe I wasn't the total object of ridicule I imagined.

Rogers-Staughten-Bowhip was practically choking on her own mirth during the salute, and I caught a look in Bell End's eye. It was just a glance, but he seemed to be reminding me of what I was there for. If Rogers-Staughten-Bowhip thought she could intimidate me over a banner crafted of jam by a four foot nun and a regressing runaway mother, she was about to discover that she was very much mistaken.

From the moment 'play' was called, I could already taste victory. 'You are Jerzy Pawlowski,' I told myself. Rogers-Staughten-Bowhip's ridicule was to cost her dearly, because all my emotions fell away. As I advanced down the piste, I was thinking with my head, moving with my body and, within seconds, slamming her with my blade. I took all five points and the game was mine.

It had been a ridiculously easy victory, but I wasn't kidding myself that the day was mine. We hadn't even started the direct elimination, which was where things would get ugly.

But Sarah and Sister were thrilled and tried to pick me up and carry me on their shoulders, a manoeuvre that all went horribly wrong as I became entangled in my own body wire.

'Git off the bloody piste, yer idiots!' Bell End yelled, and they dropped me on their banner, leaving me smeared in jam.

Over at the tea table, I bumped into Billy.

'Bit of a bloody one, I see?' he teased, pointing at the jam on my *lamé*.

'Oh yaah, killer of a match.' I shrugged, in faux boast.

'But you triumphed?'

'You should see my opponent.'

'You pulped her?'

'And then some.'

Billy laughed, but our lovely banter was halted by Rogers-Staughten-Bowhip, who clearly hadn't been humbled enough en piste because she sidled up and said, 'Good game, *Boojie*.' The derisive emphasis she put on the word 'Boojie' made me want to kick her.

'Boojie?' Billy repeated, looking understandably confused.

'Don't ask,' I replied. 'All you need to know is that it involves a nun, a regressing mother and my opponent here, a wannabe that isn't.' Then I stormed off because I could see Sarah and Sister Regina coming towards me.

Back in the changing rooms, I checked my mobile, still vainly hoping that Freddie might ultimately forgive me for chucking him two dates running. I didn't really think he would, but I needed a sign from God at this point that all was not lost. And there it was.

Soz about being a dick. Thinking of you, missing you. Call me when you're done rinsing them all, Freds xxx

EIGHT

She Who Would Valiant Be

It turned out that Bell End wasn't exaggerating about the intimidation and cheap-trick tactics of tournaments. I had made it through four gruelling rounds of direct elimination, and now I was at the finals.

Yes, the finals. Now it was just down to me and Jenny Frogmorten. Freddie's txt had given me all the confidence I needed to play my best. Also, Bell End's pep talk *had* actually helped me keep my focus as my opponent's fan club did everything they could to humiliate and undermine me. As I was being wired up they were already calling me an 'F – g sad case.' It was lucky Bob wasn't here. He'd go ballistic if he heard that sort of language yelled at his daughter.

'Jenny's going to kill you, Kelly!' my opponent's boyfriend yelled while the rest of her fan club hissed.

'Whatever!' I yelled back as if I were bored rather than terrified.

I wasn't fazed. All their taunts couldn't demoralise me, because apart from getting used to the abuse, I now knew that Freds loved me. Well, he'd sent me a txt that was loving. Also, four years of being Honey's torture toy had immunised me to ugly taunts and filthy abuse.

In each bout, I was down my end with Sarah and Sister Regina. And while they may have embarrassed me in the pools with their jam-smeared banner, now I saw no difference in their madness and that of the hordes of filthy-mouthed barbarians up the other end of the piste, cheering on my opponents and abusing me.

In fact I had become rather proud of my posse. Portia had been knocked out in semi-finals, which still meant she'd placed highly. But while she had been fencing, Sister and Sarah had valiantly run from piste to piste to support each of us through our matches. Now their attention was firmly fixed on moi, as was Bell End's, whose presidential duties were done for the day. Portia was over at another end of the hall cheering on Billy as she should, given she was his girlfriend. But still, I missed her, because as this was the last game for the girls that day, my opponent now had practically every other person in the hall backing her. My backup was very thin, but then they say it's quality not quantity that counts.

'GFTB, Kelly,' Bell End whispered in my ear as he wired me up. 'I'm right here behind you, and I have to warn you, I plan on making a lot of noise.'

'Okay,' I replied, figuring he meant cheering.

'Some of what I may yell admittedly isn't fit for poor Sister Regina's ears, but this is war. I intend to throw back the abuse those ratbags are hurling at you, only ten times over and then some. Git it?'

Okay, now I was nervous. 'I'm not sure I understand, Mr Wellend?'

'You don't need to understand, girl. Close your ears to what I yell at them. Your job is to slice that little piece of meat up the other end of the piste to ribbons. So ignore me, it's not for your benefit but for those scum suckers up there,' he said, indicating the opposing fan club, some of whom were giving me the finger and others who were pep-talking Jenny.

'Okay,' I told him. 'So you're going to give as good as we get in terms of abuse?'

'I'm going to give a damn sight better. They're baying for your blood, Kelly, and there are near to a hundred of them. I'm going to bay for Jenny's blood.' Then he pushed me onto the piste.

As I shook my opponent's hand, she leaned in and said, 'Like the banner, Kelly,' only not in a totally unfriendly way.

I probably should explain that said banner *had* deteriorated somewhat during its arduous day. The words now read 'Oo Booo Oo.' But Sarah and Sister weren't giving up on it. They clutched both ends of it, jumping up and down with endless energy.

'Thanks,' I said to my opponent. 'So do I; they made it with jam.'

'Jam?' she asked, looking at me as if I were demented.

'It looked better earlier in the day,' I told her, more than happy for her to underestimate me.

The niceties ended there, though. From the moment 'Play' was called, I heard Bell End yelling the abuse he had hinted at earlier. But all the warnings in the world could never have prepared me for, 'Gut the little slag! Gut her like a fish!'

It was hard to ignore, especially with Sarah and Sister singing along to Bell End's chants, converting them all to the tune of 'He Who Would Valiant Be': 'Gut Her! Gut Her! Gut Her Like a Fish!' one of my favourite hymns as it happens – well, at least it was.

But I couldn't focus on Bell End or Sister and Sarah's 'hymn.' Jenny was my target. I'd watched her win one of her earlier bouts and I knew she had a penchant for cuts to the wrist and a weakness when it came to defending her mask. It's not unusual for someone with a strength for making cuts to the hand to have a weakness at defending their mask, because their sword arm hangs slightly lower, ready to make their favourite cut.

I therefore resolved to begin my attack in *quinte*. A successful manoeuvre – I won the point – but I knew I couldn't repeat my advantage too frequently or she'd be on to me.

All the while, Bell End was yelling behind me, 'Slice

off her ugly head, Kelly, and feed it to the dogs behind her!'

Even the sad cases standing behind my opponent looked shocked by the vitriol of Bell End's verbal abuse, or maybe it was just shock at hearing a sacred hymn profaned by a nun and a reverting mother.

My opponent's fan club's cries of 'Go for her, Jenny!' and 'Go for the kill!' seemed outclassed somehow by Bell End yelling, 'Rip the rodent's throat open and spit down the little weasel's mouth, Kelly.'

After my second point, Jenny's fans upped their ante, adding a few lame profanities of their own, which sadly lacked any of the originality or imaginative forensic detail of Bell End's.

The first three hits had been mine, but I knew I'd have to diversify my approach if I was to maintain my lead, because Jenny now knew what I knew. Sure enough, she scored the next hit on my mask after perfectly riposting my attack to *quinte*.

She was fast and she was smart. That's why she'd made it to the finals.

Somewhere in the background I could hear Bell End up his ante in a vitriolic personal attack on the remainder of Jenny's fan club. Detailing what he was going to do to them after the competition and mentioning he had ways of finding out where they lived and finding their loved ones, whom he planned to mete out similar vengeful bloody justice to.

'And mete out vengeful justice,' sang Sister and Sarah sweetly to the tune of a hymn I would never be able to sing with the same sense of piety again.

The stream of abuse carried me through to match point fourteen, which meant everything hinged on the final point. Bell End fell silent, although Sister and Sarah valiantly kept up their Pilgrim's Progress of Filth, undeterred by the yellow card the president had threatened them with earlier.

And then suddenly, out of the silence – because Jenny's fan club was now for the most part engaged in studying their shoes – Bell End yelled, 'Jerzy Pawlowski! Eight ways of moving forward! How many have you got, Kelly? You big girl's blouse! Daisy-chain fairy! Girlie wimp!' he taunted me.

It was as if with that taunt, time stopped just for a millionth of a second, time enough for the talent of Jerzy Pawlowski to well up within me and carry me forward into a flawless advance which was *almost* too late into Jenny's counterattack. It was in that *almost*, though, that everything happened.

Suspended in that moment, my mind stopped. The world off the piste ceased to exist. I pivoted my body and blade a fraction of a centimetre from Jenny's counter attack with the elegance of a dancer. Her blade missed me so narrowly, I could hear it *whoosh* past my ear.

In the second it took her to realise that her *flawless* counterattack had been flawed, I had already snapped my arm into a blinding riposte. Feeling the satisfying *thwack* as my blade made contact on her *lamé,* I heard the hit registering the electronic buzz that proclaimed my victory.

NINE

Even Toxic Psycho Toffs Can Talk Sense, Occasionally

The first thing I wanted to do as the victory light buzzed above my head – apart from taking off my mask – was txt Freds. Sister Regina, Sarah and Bell End were a compelling fan club, but it was Freds I wanted to scoop me up into his arms – after a shower anyway.

Over the deafening roar of the crowd because now EVERYONE was cheering *me*, I looked around and saw it might be a while before I was left alone long enough with my mobile to txt Freds. I think Bell End was even more thrilled by my victory than I was. Jenny was very sweet too, even when Bell End pushed her away like a stray dog and attempted a non-sexual manly hug with me. With Sister Regina and Sarah hanging off him, though, things didn't go as planned, and we all landed in a tangled heap on the floor.

'Need a hand, darling?' Portia asked, bemused.

'My guardian angel,' I said, reaching my hand out to her.

'Me? I saw the last bit, darling, and believe me, you do *not* need an angel to protect you.' She was laughing as she pulled me out of the tangle of bodies, nun habits and banners and hugged my sweaty head. 'And what was Bell End on?' she asked. 'We could hear him over at the boy's end. Incredible. I'm sure poor Sister didn't have a clue what she was singing. At least I hope not?'

I spotted Billy standing behind her, grinning madly. 'Bloody brilliant, Kelly. Where'd you learn to do that?'

'Jerzy Pawlowski,' I explained in a South African accent, but only Portia got the joke.

'Best bloody sabreur that ever lived!' Bell End announced with a slight wobble in his voice. I watched him affectionately as he roughly wiped away a tear trickling down his cheek. 'That's my girl!' he told me gruffly as he stood up and squeezed my shoulder. 'That's my bloody girl! I'll make an Olympian of you, girl. I'll get you gold.'

Sister and Sarah had helped one another up, and Sister was marvelling at what the power of prayer could do. 'Not that you weren't a terrific little swordplayer, Calypso, but heavens, well, simply remarkable! The other nuns will eat their habits when I regale them with the events of today.'

Sarah hugged me as well and told me how proud she was – without reverting to baby talk – and then she pinched my cheeks really, really hard. It was mortifying, having my mad madre gripping my cheeks while all around people snickered. One moment the champion, the next a figure of fun.

I was rescued by Bell End, who took me aside briefly. 'And don't think it's only me who noticed your talent today, girl,' he whispered darkly. Then he pointed around the hall. 'Spies and scouts are everywhere.'

I looked around the hall where the girls and their fans were gathering their gear and preparing to leave and the boys were still fencing. 'That's why I want to get going quickly, before they can get to you,' he said, tapping his nose.

'But why do they want to get to me? What do they want?'

'You, Kelly. You, damn it. You might be a remarkable sabreur, but you're not the sharpest tool in the box, are you, Kelly?'

'But what do they want me for?' I asked, confused.

'Sponsorship deals, advertising. But don't worry, they're not going to get you. At least not today,' he explained darkly, tapping the side of his nose again. 'We've whet their appetite, though, haven't we, Kelly?'

'Yes, sir,' I agreed, putting his madness down to a long and exhaustive bout of inflicting abuse on poor Jenny and her fans.

'We've whet their appetites good and proper.' Then he threw his head back and laughed like a lunatic. He really had lost his marbles, poor man.

On the journey going back everyone chatted excitedly about the tournament. Bell End was especially proud of his spine-chilling attack on Jenny and her fans. He kept asking questions like, 'And did you see their faces when I yelled, "Spit down the little weasel's throat!"'

'Oh yes, Mr Wellend, you're imaginative *bon mots* really seemed to discourage the other side,' agreed Sister.

'Well, I had a fantastic back-up chorus,' he said, giving Sister and Sarah their due. Even Portia was unusually chatty as she shared the details of her own victories and defeats. Although I had won the tournament, Portia had distinguished herself sufficiently to give rise to Bell End's hopes that she'd also make it to the Nationals.

Our excitement levels hadn't dropped when we finally got the chance to tell our friends about the day. After we returned from supper slops, Star insisted that we have a tuck fest to celebrate, and Portia and I were happy to repeat our tales of victory once more. Even Portia was animated beyond her usual regal demeanour and acted out some of Sister Regina and my mother's maddest antics. We were high on the whole adventure, and with a pile of sweets on the floor nothing was likely to bring us down anytime soon. Even Honey – who sat by the window smoking cigarette after cigarette – couldn't dent my excitement.

'We're definitely coming to the next tournament,' Star insisted firmly.

'Definitely,' agreed the others – even Honey.

Indie laughed. 'Sorry, I keep thinking of your mother and Sister Regina and that banner. We'll have to make our own banner!'

Portia and I looked across at one another in solidarity. The fact of the matter was, Bell End, Sarah and Sister Regina had actually done us proud.

'Yes, let's all go,' Honey added in syrupy tones, stubbing out her cigarette on the window sill and spraying the room with Febreze. 'It sounds like fun. I want to be there next time to see you rinse the competition. And Bell End sounds hilarious. We could all join him in insulting your competition.'

'I think he's got that side of things under control,' Portia said as she suppressed a smile.

Honey continued. 'It must have felt fantastic, Calypso, winning the tournament like that. I'm seriously impressed. You and Portia deserved to win.'

'Thanks, Honey,' I replied, surprised by the genuine warmth in her congratulations.

'Although with all this time you're putting into your sabre, it's natural that your other subjects *will* suffer.' She flopped onto her bed, grabbed her *Tatler* and pretended to be absorbed by an article.

Once again I'd been too hasty in thanking her for her warm wishes.

'Not that failing GCSEs matters, darling, well, not to the rest of us,' she added, without looking up from her magazine. 'Between Daddy's plastic and Mummy's contacts, we'll all be fine,' she assured me. Then she looked up at me through the curtain of her implausibly long lashes and added, 'But you don't have a trust fund of your own do you, Calypso?' Her collagen-inflated lower lip wobbled as if she were truly moved by the pathos of my plight. As if she really were about to burst into tears at my lack of plastic and contacts.

Once again, Star came to my rescue. This time with a bag of sugared almonds. 'Almond?' she offered Honey sweetly, holding out a pink coated nut, knowing full well that Honey was allergic to nuts. Once the 'idiot chavs in the kitchen' had added nuts to a pudding, and she'd had to be rushed to hospital and been kept in for a week on a drip. The school was forced to sack all the 'idiot chavs in the kitchen' for fear of a legal suit. That was back in the days when Honey was still sticking Post-it notes on my back declaring me an American Freak.

Honey shoved away the proffered nut. 'But perhaps money doesn't matter to an American wild child like you, Calypso?' she continued, looking innocently into my eyes. 'You can always make Freddie pay your way, can't you?'

'Pack it in, Honey,' Portia warned.

'Yes, once Calypso wins the essay-writing competition, she'll get a book deal. Unlike you, she doesn't need to rely on Daddy's plastic and Mummy's contacts. She's got something you don't even understand. Talent,' Star said.

As if set off by satanic forces, my txt alert sounded.

Congrats on your victory. F

Merde! I hadn't rung Freddie! Billy must have told him about my victory. All I could think of as I read and reread the message – apart from what a horrible girlfriend I was – was the distinct lack of kisses. I should have been the one to tell him. Billy would have told him about Sarah too, and about the madness of the 'Go Boojie! Go!' banner. Fantastic. Just fantastic.

Star and Indie, who were sitting on either side of me, looked at the message. Arabella and Clemmie clambered over to have a look too.

'No kisses,' Arabella noted.

I showed Portia, who grimaced. 'You should have txt-ed him immediately. Billy would have told him as soon as he got back.'

I was already punching in a reply.

Cheers, we just got back. I tried to txt earlier but no signal, soz. xxx C

Before pressing 'Send,' I held the message up for a group opinion.

Star shook her head. 'Too lame,' she announced as she snatched the phone from me and changed the message.

Only half the victory without you there to witness. C U in W tomoz? xxxxxx C

'Better,' Indie agreed, holding up the message for everyone else.

'But aren't you going to Windsor with Sarah?' Portia remarked, only she asked too late. Star, being Star, had already pressed 'Send.'

Freddie's reply came back at once.

C U tomoz. F xxx

'See!' Star trilled. 'You have to be more assertive with boys, darling. Look at Kevin, he's the perfect boyfriend. Well, just about perfect. I still have some work to do on him musically.'

Kevin was Billy's younger brother and quite possibly the sweetest boy we knew. He was putty in Star's hand and openly worshipped the ground she walked on. Even with Star's willful charm, I could *never* have that sort of relationship with Freddie. These heir-to-the-throne types like to keep a certain amount of power in their relationships. Kevin might enjoy Star's tantrums (well, we all did – she was hilariously outrageous in her treatment of boys) but Freds was not, and never would be, Kev. He was heir to the throne and would never settle for being number two in a relationship.

I took my mobile and stared at Fred's message. Even with three kisses, my fate was sealed – only not in a good way. Sarah was about to collide with the love of my life. A vision of her chasing Freddie through the streets of

Windsor with a question-and-answer form and a camera flashed through my mind.

As tired as I was, I knew I was not going to sleep well that night. In addition to the collision course with disaster, Honey's words continued to haunt me. I suppose during all my years of dreaming of making it to the Nationals, I hadn't really considered what that might mean to my grades. To girls like Honey and, well, all the other girls I knew, grades were not an issue. They could pursue their dreams with trust funds.

Honey might be a toxic toff but she still had a solid point. While I focused all my energy on fencing, it was inevitable that my grades would suffer. The GCSE exams were in six months, and my attention was spread very thin indeed, stretched as it was between Sarah and Bob's marital problems, my dream of being a sabreur par excellence, and snog-aging my way back into Fred's affections. I hadn't even factored in my GCSEs.

But Honey had. Bob was right when he said even idiots talk sense sometimes. The essay competition and its prize money was starting to seem like an increasingly attractive idea. After all, I had always wanted to be a writer. Maybe the essay competition wasn't such a bad idea. It might even be my big chance at having a proper career someday.

TEN

Royal Collision in Windsor

Sarah wore a Chanel suit to Mass the next morning. Not that there weren't other mothers in Chanel suits that morning. In fact it's a virtual mother's uniform at Saint Augustine's School for Young Ladies. What scared me was that Sarah does not wear Chanel suits, ever. I didn't even know she owned one. The only suits Sarah wears are track suits. I don't know how she used to dress when she grew up in England, but since living in LA she had definitely clung to the casual dress code – like latex shorts to an athlete.

Her hair, blonde like mine, was normally tied back in a ponytail, just in case she suddenly had an urge to jog somewhere. But now here she was in the chapel as we filed in, pink Chanel suit, matching pink Chanel shoes and bag and hair arranged artfully in a chignon. At six foot tall she looked like a pink stork.

As soon as my year began to file in, she began to jump

about and wave frantically. Presumably she was worried I might miss her loud cries of 'Calypso! Calypso! Darling! Boojems! Over here!'

Throughout Mass, she kept putting her arm around me as if I might escape (the thought did occur to me). She sang her hymns louder than anyone else, cuddled me like I was two and called out 'Ah-men,' twice during the sermon. Honey, who was sitting in the row in front, kept turning around and giving her little smiles and winks of encouragement.

I pinched Sarah on the arm over a dozen times to pull her into line. It was as if she had totally forgotten what a toxic witch Honey was. It was only about six months ago that Sarah and Bob flew over from LA to rescue me from one of Honey's poisonous pranks.

As if reading my mind, Honey cast me a look of smug, evil intent, which Sarah totally missed because she was singing reverently with her eyes tightly closed.

After Mass, Sarah swooped down on Sister Constance. 'Oh, Sister!' she cried ecstatically, grasping both Sister's hands and clasping them to her bosom. 'I just want to say how super it is to be back here. It is as if time has stood still. Frozen in that moment of pure joy that defined my years here at Saint Augustine's. It really is just like old times.' She spoke so loudly that Sister Constance could have heard her from a mile away. Everyone stared. Even the Year Sevens. I wanted to shrink up and die of embarrassment.

'Is your mother on medication, darling?' Honey asked in faux concern.

'Shouldn't you be running along, Honey?' Star said, giving her pinch and a shove. 'You wouldn't want to be late for your black mass now, would you!'

'Oh, Star,' Honey replied, still managing to ooze sarcasm while rubbing her pinched arm. 'Has your hilarity no end, darling?'

Star gave her a wrist burn, and Star is famous for the brutality of her burns. 'Guess not, *darling*,' she replied mildly, as Honey wrestled back her injured wrist.

'Ouch! Sister! Star just burned me –' Honey wailed, but Sister Constance didn't hear her cry for help because Sarah was moving into her conversational third gear.

'Sarah does seem on madly good form for a woman who's brokenhearted after running off on her husband,' Star whispered in my ear. '*Is* it possible that she is on medication, darling? My mother is, so I'm soooo not judging or anything.'

'I honestly don't know,' I whispered back. 'But she's been reverting since she got here and that's why I don't want to bump into Freddie while I'm with her,' I explained. 'If you see Kevin can you make up a lie about how I couldn't make it into Windsor because I had to, erm –'

'Darling, you shock me. Of course you can meet Freddie, and anyway, you can't ask someone to lie in the house of God!' Star teased as she put her arm around me supportively. 'Besides, Freddie's a big boy, he's going to be king one day, so I'm sure he'll be able to manage Sarah even if she is a bit more bonkers than usual.'

That's Star's philosophy with boys. She considers them charming fools, like circus tumblers placed on this earth for the amusement of girls. I wish I was more like Star, strong and unimpressed by the opposite sex. But I wasn't. Freds made my knees knock, my face redden and my hands shake. I didn't want to risk his feelings for me by exposing him to Sarah in the state she was in.

'Besides, Sarah's a laugh,' Star assured me, giving me another supportive hug. 'I bet he'd love to meet her.'

Sarah had hired a car, a horrible chav car, a true vehicle of shame. Not just because it was a chav-mobile but because after all her years in LA, Sarah had lost the art of using gears. As we crunched and bunny-hopped into Windsor, she cursed all the cars behind us leaning on their horns. She was just like a true American.

'Aw, shut up you Limey arseholes!' she bellowed out the window.

It was the first time I'd seen her criticise the English since she'd arrived. Suddenly things weren't so 'super.' I took a strange comfort in this and relaxed into my seat. Maybe she wasn't on medication, after all.

We decided to have lunch in the pizza place I'd first gone to with Freddie. I knew it was too early for Freddie to eat. In fact it was probably the safest place to hide from him in Windsor. I flashed back to the last time I'd been there with him, and remembered how he had kissed me under an awning as we took shelter from the rain. Today it was crisp and bright.

'What a super day. I love the sunlight of England, don't you?' Sarah asked passionately, looking up as a feeble ray of light broke through the sullen grey sky.

'Erm, well, it's a pretty rare occurrence, but yaah, I guess.'

She clutched my hand and looked into my eyes like a child that's had too many E-numbers. 'Let's both have a large-size, thick-crust pizza with lashings of cheese and pepperoni.'

'What about the carbs!' I cried out in shock. My parents view carbohydrates with the same suspicion other parents view drugs.

'Oh, don't be such a stick-in-the-mud, Boojie. How often do I get to have my baby all to myself, hey?' she asked as she reached out and pinched my cheek.

'Ow!' I rubbed my cheek. 'Look, Sarah could you *not* call me Boojie?' I insisted a little more brusquely than I meant to.

Sarah looked like she might cry.

I softened my tone. 'At least not in public. It's kind of babyish and, well, you haven't called me Boojie since I was a baby.' I have never felt soooo horrible. I could see she was about to tear up and, after all, this was a difficult time for her.

'I haven't done a lot of things since you were a little girl,

Calypso,' she almost sobbed. 'That's why I'm here. Your father has oppressed me for so long, and now I feel like I have a second chance. Bunny thinks this could be an opportunity to find the *real* me.'

'The *real* you?'

'Yes, the *real* Sarah!'

'I don't understand. If *you're* not the *real* Sarah . . .' I stopped myself before I said, 'you're barking.' 'And who on earth is Bunny and why would you listen to anything someone with a name like Bunny has told you?' I demanded crossly.

Sarah looked at me then like *I* was the mad one. 'Oh darling, try and understand please. I know it's hard on you, losing your father, but it's hard on me too.'

'Hang on, we haven't lost Bob. You've run off on him! Because of his Big One.' (I lowered my voice as I said the words). 'And what's this about him oppressing you? The only person in our family who's been oppressed is me, and you are just as much an oppressor as Bob. Remember the navel-piercing incident?'

'I was completely supportive of your navel piercing. It was Bob who made all the fuss.'

I opened and closed my mouth in shock. Parents are such liars. And the truth is I think Sarah actually believed that she *was* all chilled and up for navel piercing. But I was there the day she'd attacked the hapless navel piercer like a rottweiler. I remembered, all too clearly, her threat to have him incarcerated. Sure,

Bob had been there finishing off sentences for her, but she'd been part of the act.

'Have you even called Bob to tell him where you are and how you feel?' I asked. 'He told me he's almost finished the script. Maybe if you talked to him –'

'I don't wish to discuss that man. Let's just enjoy one another, darling. Let's have some real mother and daughter time.'

Her overuse of the word 'real' was really starting to bother me, almost as much as her use of my baby name.

'Well, he's still my father even if he is a slow writer.' I sulked. 'And what do you mean by *real*, Sarah? What other sort of time would we have?' I asked her even though it was all feeling a bit *surreal* to me.

'Well, you know, real as in, *real*.' She struggled a bit more to explain what 'real' actually meant, and then she went quiet and looked dazed, almost dopey, just like a woman on medication.

I had to ask. 'Look, Sarah, Mummy, can I ask you something? Something, well, personal?'

Sarah looked dementedly excited by this prospect. 'Oh, Calypso, ask me anything!' She gestured wildly, almost knocking a passing waiter off his feet. 'I don't want any secrets between us. I want us to have a really, really close mother-daughter bond. I don't want you to feel that you need to speak to a counselor when I'm here for you. Mummy's here for you now!' She held out her arms expansively. 'Ask me anything.'

The whole restaurant had gone silent and was waiting for me to speak. I bottled out and began fiddling with my napkin. 'It doesn't matter.'

'Have you got your period, darling?' she yelled – well, at least it seemed as if she yelled it, and people *were* looking.

'No!' I replied, horrified.

She patted my hand. 'Well, one day we'll have a special little mother-daughter talk about your pink cycle and how it will change your life forever and turn you into a *real* woman.'

'No, we won't. And anyway, I've been having my period for a year!'

Sarah grabbed my hands and squeezed them. 'Oh, Calypso, how wonderful. You're a real *woman* now!' She reached out and squeezed my hand. I thought she was about to break into song but instead she set her mouth in a bitter teenage grimace Honey would have been proud of.

'See, this is what Bob has done to us, don't you see?'

I shook my head, briefly wondering if it was even worth contradicting her. Okay, Bob might be a bit wrapped up in his script, but that didn't make him the root of all evil. Despite a sane little voice inside my head that said to let it go, I blurted, 'I don't think you can blame Bob for *that*, Sarah. Besides, I got my first period at school, so what was I supposed to do, send you an e-mail? "Dear Sarah and Bob, I am having my period today"?'

'Can't you see, you should have been able to share

something as momentous as that with your own mother? But no, Bob always *had* to be the centre of attention. Bob and his Big . . .' she paused, about to say 'One,' but after a short hesitation she said, 'Opus. Your father was like a vacuum of need, and I was always too focused on him when I should have been more focused on you, Calypso. That's what my therapist taught me.'

'Therapist? You're seeing a therapist?' I don't know why I said this when Sarah was giving every indication that she was going gah-gah and in need of professional help. I guess it was a shock, Sarah being so totally boring, grown-up and happy with Bob. Also, it's never easy to find out your own mother is in therapy. Your parents are meant to be rocks of solid purpose in a sea of turmoil.

'Of course I am. Everyone in LA is in therapy,' she declared.

'But you're not gah-gah!' I lied.

'Oh, don't be so English, darling. It was Bunny who suggested I leave Bob and come here to spend more time with you. I still talk to her every day on the phone. She's awfully good, Calypso. She's made me realise how I have always put Bob first and how I have allowed his needs to oppress me all these years.'

'Who is this Bunny woman and how would she know whether or not Bob's oppressed you, Sarah? This is mad. Bob couldn't oppress a fly. He's got his faults, I'll grant you what with his appalling dress sense and those horrible noises he makes when he eats, but that can't be classed as oppression, even by Hollywood standards.'

'Bunny is my therapist. She warned me that you might become hostile at the news of losing your father so suddenly.'

'I haven't *lost* him. I e-mailed him the other day. And he e-mailed me straight back. He's still my father even if he is annoying.'

She glared at me and I glared right back, and then I realised the waiter was standing there, and I went bright red.

Sarah took charge, slipping seamlessly from gah-gah loon to her mother superior bossy boots. 'We'll have two large thick-crust pizzas, thank you, double the cheese, double the pepperoni –'

'But I don't want pepperoni,' I interjected.

Sarah ignored me, waving my words away as if I were the mad one. 'Double everything in fact, and triple the carbs!' she insisted, glaring at me in a very oppressive way.

The waiter looked clearly unnerved and turned to me for support. I smiled reassuringly at the poor guy. He was only about nineteen and quite fit, I noticed. 'Two large. One Hawaiian, and one pepperoni and two Diet Cokes,' I told him sweetly. 'And make those *thin* crusts,' I added firmly as I gave Sarah a warning stare.

She didn't say another word until the pizzas arrived, and then she thanked the waiter effusively. We ate our meal in cold silence. I expect she had found this particular mother-daughter bonding session a bit of a letdown. I wondered how she'd describe it to her therapist, Bunny. But then after a while I began to feel bad because, whatever was going on with her and Bob, she was definitely going through a difficult time (although I was starting to think this Bunny might be more responsible than Bob for this whole drama). So as we were leaving the restaurant, I took my mad madre's hand in mine and thanked her for lunch. 'Would you like to have a look around the shops, Sarah?' I suggested brightly, hoping to coax her out of her mood.

She didn't need much encouragement. She wrapped her arm around my waist and gave me a squeeze. 'Sorry if I'm being a bit full on,' she explained. 'It's just that I'm still finding my feet as a single mom.'

I spoke to her gently. 'But Sarah, you're not really a single mom, are you?' I asked. Or was she a single mom? I wondered briefly, remembering the essay competition. 'Bob loves you. I know he can be annoying, especially when he slurps his cereal and plays the harmonica, but he does love us both and he does want you to go home. You two belong together. Who's going to finish off his sentences for him?' There, I'd said it. Bugger Bunny and her nutty therapy.

But Sarah was not so easily persuaded. 'I belong here,' she said, adding 'with you.' 'And you'll adore the house in Clapham, Boojie. It's right on the Common. I can't wait for you and your friends to have your sleepover party on the exeat weekend. I'll pick all of you up and we can go back on the train together. Won't that be super?'

Super. Public transport was not the standard form of conveyance for Saint Augustine girls, but I was certain my friends would be more than happy for the adventure. Apart from Honey, obviously. 'Yaah, that sounds great,' I agreed cheerfully.

'Super. We'll have a real girls' night in!'

'As opposed to one of those faux girls' nights in?' I teased, but my poor madre just looked at me as if I were speaking in tongues again, and then her eyes glazed over the way mad people's do.

'Sarah, you weren't serious about Bob not being part of your emotional thingamee were you?' I asked gently as the sun slipped behind a cloud for what I expected would be a very long visit.

'I don't want to talk about anything serious,' she said gaily. 'I just want to have fun with my Boojie.'

'Boojie?' A voice came from behind. It was Kevin, Star's boyfriend and Freddie's best mate.

'Hel-lo there!' my mother sang – yes *sang*.

'Erm, hello. Kevin Pyke, I'm a friend of Calypso's.' He extended his hand and gave me a look that said, 'I'm afraid. I want to run away.'

'My name's Sarah, Kevin. I'm Calypso's mummy.' With that, Sarah grabbed Kevin's hand, but not to shake it. Instead, she pulled him along with us down the cobbled lane, swinging his arm in one hand and mine in the other.

'Now, Kevin, I want to hear *all* about you. You and I are going to be super friends, I can just feel it.'

'Yes, Mrs Kelly,' Kevin agreed, but I could tell he was afraid. He kept trying to look me in the eye as a few drops of rain began to fall, but I couldn't face him.

'Isn't this simply super, kids? Don't you just love an English shower!'

Kevin laughed. 'Actually I think it's about to piss down, Mrs Kelly.'

'Sarah. You must call me Sarah. I don't want you to think of me as some old woman with no idea about current trends, Kevin. I'm a writer on one of your teen shows, *Gladesdale*. So, Kevin, tell me ALL about yourself. I want to know everything. I want to know what makes you tick. I want to know the *real* Kevin.'

'Right. Well there's not much to tell,' he told the mad madre. 'And see the thing is, love to chat and all, but have to run. Meeting the girlfriend, you see.'

Trust Star to be referred to with an article – I wondered if Freds referred to me as *the* girlfriend? I suspected not. I wondered if he even said 'my girlfriend,' but I doubted that as well.

'Ooooh, who's the lucky girl, Kevin?' Sarah pried embarrassingly.

'Sarah!' I scolded. 'Don't be such a busybody.'

'Star. She's, erm, a friend of Calypso's. Actually, Calypso will fill you in. I have to leg it or I'll be –'

'Oh, lovely. I know Star well. She came to stay with us

in LA when we were still a family . . .' She allowed her voice to trail off as if she couldn't go on, which was sooo not true. She was dying for Kevin to say something sympathetic so she could pour her heart out.

Poor Kevin looked like a fox caught in a trap. 'Okay. Well, sounds cool but Star will murder me if I'm late.' He pointed at me as he backed off. 'And Freddie is looking for you too, Calypso. Nice to meet you, Mrs Kelly, I mean Sarah,' he called out as he legged it down the lane.

With that, he was gone and so was my hope of finding a way of pretending to Freds that I hadn't actually made it into Windsor that day.

I was definitely going to have some material for my essay now. My life was looking increasingly tragic by the minute. And then it got really bad. 'Calypso!' Freddie called from the other end of the lane. He looked gorgeous; his dark hair that did funny sticky-out things without gel, still upright despite the increasing rain. I couldn't see his dazzling cornflower blue eyes yet, but I was drawn to him just like the moon is drawn to the earth, or is it the sun, or the other way around? The point it is, I longed to run towards him.

'Is that . . . is that . . . is that?' Sarah repeated, over and over again in a swoon.

My distressingly fit boyfriend began moving towards us. With each step he took, my mind threw up a thousand reasons why I should resist the overwhelming desperation within me to run for the hills.

My dread of being embarrassed by Sarah won. It took

me a split second to grab my mad madre's hand. 'Quick,' I hissed. 'We have to leg it. It's a game we play!' I explained.

'Oh, super,' Sarah squealed as we ran like a pair of bag snatchers down Bond Street. She was laughing and shrieking, probably exhilarated by how teenage and puerile it all was. Or perhaps this event would feature on an episode of *Gladesdale*. Or maybe it was just her medication. Either way, we arrived at her car in a state of soggy, giggly dishevelment.

My life was ruined. I had just run from my boyfriend, and however fit and wonderful Freds was, unlike Sarah, he was not going to see the fun in what I'd just done.

But I didn't have a chance to dwell on how gutted I was inside. I had to distract Sarah so she wouldn't want me to explain why I'd just dragged her away from Freds. It's times like this that blurting actually comes in quite handy. 'There's a competition,' I blagged. I know it was wicked to take advantage of my mother's madness, but I couldn't exactly tell her the truth, could I?

As it was, I didn't need to blag. Sarah was babbling away excitedly about how hilarious and outrageous we were, running off like that on Prince Frederick, as she insisted on calling him. 'Bob would die!' she said and tooted the horn with happiness.

'Definitely,' I lied. 'Now about this essay,' I continued.

'Wasn't it wonderful – the look on his face? I can't wait to tell Bunny. She's always urging me to be more playful.'

No doubt she would soon start wondering about when

she *would* meet Freds, so I was determined to distract her now with talk of the essay competition.

'Yes, so there's this essay-writing competition,' I insisted. 'An autobiographical sort of thing. You know, drawing on one's own life experience, that sort of thing.'

'Oh, Bunny is big on that. She has made me keep a Journal of Pain since I first started seeing her. I write down all the agonies I endure each day. That was how Bunny made me see the pattern of neglect I was suffering at the hands of your father. I'm soooo glad that you are finally able to see the value of committing your pain to paper, darling.'

'Yes,' I agreed uncertainly. 'It's not my usual field, but I think I'm going to have a shot at it. There's really big prize money if you win, and they're publishing the best five in the *Telegraph*, so there will be a lot of recognition.'

'Oh darling, a prize? Imagine if you win? Oh, this is exciting,' she exclaimed, finally tuning in.

'Yaah, well, I don't think my life's been nearly traumatic enough for me to win, but –'

'Boojems! Don't put yourself down. You're life has been full of pain. Shoved off to boarding school, tortured by that dreadful Honey girl, oppressed by an overbearing father and coming from a broken home –'

I cut her off before the violin chorus started up. 'Mmmm, but you see because it is about one's own life experience, it's bound to get, well, quite personal, you know what I mean.' I looked at Sarah for signs of how she might feel about this. Her gaze was fixed on the road. It was raining heavily now, and the wipers were making it difficult to see what was in front of us. Also, she was still having gear-stick problems. But I persisted. 'I thought I might write about us, you know, as in my family sort of thing. Like Gerald Durrel, you remember that book. *My Family and Other Animals*, Bob gave it to me when I was six.'

'Yes, darling, you're a very talented writer. You know I support all your creative endeavours.'

'So you don't mind?'

'Why would I mind?'

'No, no, there's no reason you would, but you know it might mean mentioning you and Bob? You are my family if you see what I am saying?'

'I still don't understand why you think I might mind. The truth will come out. We can't hide our pain under a bushel our entire lives, darling. That's what Bunny says. So you must write this essay. If Bob has a problem, he'll have to claim it as his own. I'm proud of you, Boojie,' she said. And I could tell she meant it. 'So, when do I get to meet this Frederick. We can't keep teasing him like this forever, Boojie.'

'No,' I agreed, my fingers firmly crossed behind my back. 'We can't.'

ELEVEN

The Risk of Taking Your Soft Toys Too Seriously

'You what?' demanded Star, for the thousandth time later that evening after Sarah had dropped me off at school.

'I told you what,' I replied through gritted teeth. 'Look, I'm not proud of it.'

'I think it's hilarious,' laughed Indie. She was funny when she laughed, mostly because of the way she put her hand over her mouth as if laughing at something truly shocking, which I suppose legging it from HRH was in a way.

'Sarah enjoyed it,' I added, as if giving my poor mad madre a good time made up for the mess I'd made of my relationship with Freds.

'Only she had no idea that the reason you were running away from the poor guy was because you're so embarrassed by *her*,' Star pointed out bluntly.

My face went bright red. 'That is soooo not true! I'm not embarrassed of Sarah. I love her.'

'Huh. So when you said you were too embarrassed to let Freddie and Sarah meet in Windsor, you were what? Deranged?' Star does a very good line in logic, which can be really annoying.

'If I was so embarrassed, I would have –'

'Legged it through Windsor? I'm really, really disappointed in you,' Star told me crossly, shaking her head so that her lovely red hair came out of its black leather star-studded hair strap. Every day she looked more and more the quintessential rock chick, which only added further kudos to her fearsome certainty about life and reminded me just how fearsomely uncertain I was about my own.

Indie had stopped laughing now too, which meant Star was even scaring her.

'You're *so* wrapped up in yourself, Calypso, you just don't even see how your actions impact on others! Poor Sarah, and I even feel sorry for his royal stuck-upness. He must of felt a right idiot, standing there in the rain while his girlfriend and her mother legged it down the lane, shrieking with laughter!' Star continued to scold.

'I tried to call Freddie to explain,' I told her, as if that should be an end to it. Not that I knew what I was going to say to him, but the word 'sorry' would definitely have featured. Each time I had dialled he had rejected my call, though. I could picture him, white with fury, pressing the 'Reject Call' button every time the name 'Calypso' came up on his mobile's screen. Maybe he'd even changed my name on his speed dial. I do that when I'm cross with people. Honey came up on my phone as EVIL ONE – not that she ever called me. Still, it gave me a cheap thrill.

I'd even tried txt-ing Freddie.

Plse stop rejecting my calls. I'm really, really sorry about this afternoon. Plse let me explain xxxxxxx C

But he remained unreachable.

Supper was fish nuggets, which I normally fall on like a famine victim, but I couldn't eat a morsel that night. Indie tried to get her security guys to hide the nuggets in their pockets, but they got caught by Sandra the dinner lady, and I was put on report for not eating my food.

Indie was really sympathetic, as was everyone apart from Star. I hate it when Star is angry with me, because firstly she's always right, and secondly the cold frost she exuded towards me that evening made me shiver.

After supper, Georgina, Clemmie, Arabella, Indie and Star hung out in my room. Everyone apart from Star was trying to come up with a way for me to win Freddie back. Honey was unusually quiet on the subject, and Honey being quiet on a topic that had everyone else gossiping was dangerous.

Eventually, Georgina joined Honey at the window sill to smoke and I tried to listen in to their low murmurings, but I caught only the occasional word like 'erm' and 'yaah' and 'darling.'

Arabella suggested a proper snail mail love letter on lovely embossed paper. 'It's got my family crest on it, but we can cross that out,' she added.

'Yes, what a brilliant idea. You could even be really Victorian and lacy and spray it with your scent, Calypso. I'm sure Freddie would swoon with love, unable to resist a letter explaining why his girlfriend is so embarrassed by the prospect of him and her mother meeting that she runs away at the very sight of him,' Star scoffed.

I felt really annoyed with her for being so bloody right.

Portia was reading a magazine on her bed. She'd given me a look of sympathy, but it wasn't her way to get overly involved in other people's petty problems.

'What about sending him a gorilla gram? Or his favourite pizza, with your name spelt out in sausage?' Clemmie suggested.

Even Star giggled at this.

I didn't giggle, though. I was truly ashamed of myself, and if my name spelt out in sausage would make things right with Freddie I was all up for trying it.

Georgina pulled her head in from the window. 'Why don't you go and see him face-to-face? You know, storm the ramparts of Eades?'

No one said anything at first. Eades was only a couple of miles away, but it meant climbing down the scaffolding, traversing Pullers' Wood, where attack dogs roamed looking for girls to eat, and slithering through the razor-wire fence that shielded our school from the outside world.

'But the attack dogs – you know I'm terrified of attack dogs,' I argued, even though I longed more than anything to confront Freddie face-to-face.

Honey pulled her head in from outside the window and picked up the Febreze. I imagined she was going to spray away the smell of smoke. I don't know how I survive being this naïve. I really don't.

'Which is why,' Honey said, holding the Febreze up and pointing it directly at me, 'you take my mace to defend yourself.' With that she squirted the Febreze right in my eyes, which made them sting and water like crazy.

'Honey!' Georgina scolded, snatching the spray from her friend.

'What? I was just showing her what she can do if the dogs pitch up and start tearing her apart,' Honey explained in a voice of child-like innocence as I rinsed my eyes out with water from the sink.

'Well, I think it's a perfect idea. Tobias suggested it earlier,' Georgina told us, holding her bear up. His wise face stared back at us solemnly. 'He's given it a lot of thought.'

I looked at Star, expecting her to roll her eyes, but instead she said. 'Right, so here's the plan. After lights out, we'll all convene here and help you escape. I'll txt Kevin to get directions to Freddie's room and find out the best access routes.'

'Billy mentioned there's wisteria running along the wall where Freddie's housed,' Portia added.

I looked at everyone's supportive faces.

'You can borrow my black trackie bums and black hoodie,' Clemmie offered.

All their faces were expectant. Honey was rustling about in the en suite. When she appeared, she pressed a small can of mace into my hand.

'Thank you,' I muttered, looking at the can. It had a cartoon picture of a girl spraying a man in the face.

'No trouble; Mummy bought it for me in Germany, you know, in case Miss Bibsmore gets too much for me. But don't accidentally squirt yourself in the dark, darling. It isn't Febreze, remember.' She laughed her crazed laugh at the memory.

'Right,' I agreed, still staring at the can because actually I am just the sort of girl who would squirt herself in the face with mace.

'Promise you'll only use it if the dog is *really* going to endanger your life?' Clemmie insisted sternly. She can't bear to think of any creature being hurt. She even hates it when we eat Jelly Babies, because she says they remind her of her little brother Sebastian.

'Of course I won't.' I sooo would, though, if the jaws of a dog were bearing down on me.

Star came over and gave me a hug. 'I'm really proud of you,' she said.

'You're doing the right thing,' Portia agreed.

'We'd better leg it back to our own rooms now, though,' Star said. 'We'll come back after Miss Bibsmore's done her rounds to help you get ready, okay?'

I nodded. I was mute with the enormity of the mission I was about to embark upon. A mission conceived by a soft toy. A mission which, if anything went wrong, could very easily end in my expulsion.

TWELVE

Scaling the Battlements of Eades

At eleven that night, Star and Portia climbed down the scaffolding with me, while Honey, Indie and Georgina watched from above, shining their torches on us.

Star and Portia said they'd come with me as far as the razor wire in case there were a serious emergency. Portia had drawn a map, which I tucked safely in my Snoopy bra – the closest thing I had to a sports bra. It was still raining, which Star pointed out was all the more incentive to run faster.

Things went well on the wet sprint through the school grounds, but no sooner were we in the woods than four attack dogs came bounding out at us like the hounds of hell. Star grabbed one by the collar and Portia grabbed another, but with my fear of dogs being what it is, all I could do was grab the trunk of a tree and start climbing. The two untethered dogs growled and snarled up at me.

'Climb down, you're setting them off,' Star called up to me.

'I'm setting *them* off?' I called down. They're the ones barking and baying for my blood.

'Only because they sense your fear.'

'Well I'm bloody afraid.'

'Here boy!' Star called to the dogs, and when they came to her, she fed them some sweets.

'Now, Calypso, now!' Portia urged. 'Sugared almonds won't hold them back forever.'

So I jumped down and legged it through the woods. My torch gave only enough light to keep me from running into trees, but hearing the footfalls of Portia and Star as they came up behind me made me feel braver. I was running so fast the effects of missing supper resulted in a stitch by the time we reached the razor wire, which looked as if it would tear us to ribbons.

'Okay, this is where we have to veer left,' Portia said, panting. Star continued to sprint purposefully ahead, running parallel to the wire.

'Or go back?' I suggested, only half joking as I held my side.

'According to Billy there's a green ribbon on the wire and after that a bush which conceals where the wire has a gap in it. That's where you'll slip through,' she added, ignoring my lame attempt at humour.

'Here it is,' called Star. When we caught up to her voice, it was coming from inside the bush. She looked so unlike a rock chick as her face peered out from the bush that I almost lost my fear.

'You'll be fine now. Kev and Billy are both expecting you. Billy's going to txt you if there's a problem,' Portia reminded me.

'So make sure your mobile's on vibrate. Kev will keep a lookout over the house. Remember it's the second house, second row on the right, after Chapel Row,' Star whispered.

'That's right, just keep your eye out for Poets Well,' Portia reminded me.

'Right, Poets Well. Eyes out,' I repeated.

'Because if you see that, you've gone too far,' she said.

I was already thinking I had gone too far.

'Good luck, and once you've sorted things out with Freddie, txt us and we'll be here to meet you, okay?'

I was drenched to the skin and hungry and my stitch was killing me as my friends disappeared through the woods. Worst of all I was alone in the dark.

After I struggled through the prickly bush, I looked out at the foreboding glow of spires and ancient gabled roofs of Eades all lit up by security lighting. A sense of hopelessness came over me, but there was no turning back now – well, not without a major confrontation with Star. So I moved through the pain the way I'd been taught to in fencing and sprinted towards the boardinghouses, clutching Honey's mace in one hand and my mobile in the other.

I repeated Star's directions in my head, second house,

second row, and right after the chapel. Whoops, was that turn right *at* the chapel, though, or right *after* the chapel? I decided the best course of action was to check my map, but in the heavy rain that was easier said than done.

I took shelter against a wall when I saw a security guard lighting up a cigarette farther down at one of the houses. That was when I noticed that the wall I was leaning against had wisteria growing over it. Portia had mentioned wisteria, so this must be it. I looked up, wondering if Freddie was up there. There were lights on and noises of boys talking or listening to televisions and music. At least up there I'd be out of the rain, which was really pissing down now, and surely some nice Eades boy would take me to my prince?

I grabbed a hold of a wisteria branch and tugged hard to check it could support my weight before slipping my foot into one of the branches and hoisting myself up. It was actually quite easy, and I was almost feeling a bit smug and action heroine-ish there for a moment as I scaled the wall of Eades. And then I reached the fist floor window, looked down and realised I was above Poets Well. 'Bugger,' I swore to myself. 'Calypso Kelly, you have gone too far.'

A window opened just above my head and a boy's face, a cigarette clenched between his lips, looked down on me.

'Hello there. What was that you were saying?'

'Oh, hi,' I said, smiling my most winning smile. 'I'm sort of looking for someone.'

'Not me, is it?' the face asked.

'No, someone else.'

'Jolly good, well, good luck. I hope you manage to track him down,' the boy said before pulling his head back in and slamming the window shut.

The wisteria wasn't feeling quite as stable as it had earlier. I think in my rain-drenched clothing I was probably twice as heavy as I normally was. I looked down on Poets Well and tried to find the bottle to climb back down and work out another way to Freddie's house. I sneezed really, really loudly. Not one of those public, polite sneezes either – you know the ones where people add 'God bless you' afterwards. No, this was a roaring loud sneeze that was probably heard back at Saint Augustine's. Normally I would only allow a sneeze like that to escape when I was certain I was all alone in a completely embarrassment-proof environment.

I heard the window opening above me again. 'God bless you,' the face from earlier reappeared. 'You sure you're not cold out there.'

I looked up, no longer capable of smiling, winningly or otherwise. 'Bloody freezing,' I admitted.

'Are you sure I won't do? As an interim measure, perhaps? At least it's warm in here, if you don't mind a bit of a mess.'

I was so relieved I almost let go my grip on the wisteria. 'Thank you,' I gushed as his hand reached down and my stranger pulled me up and helped me climb into his room.

THIRTEEN

You've Got to Know When to Neck It and Know When to Leg It

'My name's Malcolm, by the way. Feel free to use the bathroom to dry yourself off.' He was wearing boxer shorts with a rugby shirt over the top. With his thatch of red hair and green eyes, he reminded me of Star. He was definitely the best thing to happen to me in the last half hour, I decided.

'Thanks. I'm Calypso,' I said as my eyes travelled around the vast room. I knew that Eades boys all got their own rooms, but I had never been in one before. It was the size of most people's living rooms. He had a plasma screen television, DVD, laptop and of course the mess he had warned me of. Actually most of the mess seemed to consist of thousands of DVDs strewn all over the floor – and I mean *all* over the floor. Every square inch was covered in DVDs, including the square inches I was currently dripping on.

'Actually, I'll grab you a towel. I think we'd better contain you,' Malcolm said, treading his way carefully to the bathroom so as to avoid stepping on the DVDs. From the bathroom he chucked me a big black fluffy towel. I began to dab at my sodden clothing and hair in a hopeless attempt to dry myself off.

'Tell you what, Calypso,' Malcolm said, 'Chuck the towel down over the DVDs and once you get to the bathroom you can climb out of those wet clothes and put on my robe. It's virtually clean. If you like, you can spread your clothes over my radiators while we find your mystery man.'

'Thank you, that's really kind,' I said as I made my way towards the bathroom. I was feeling slightly uncomfortable about taking my clothes off in a boy's bathroom and changing into his robe, even if it was virtually clean. I mean, I didn't even know Malcolm. What if he were some sort of crazed rapist, or worse? As I opened the bathroom door I turned back, but he was crouched back on the floor with his back to me, totally absorbed in some sort of laborious DVD filing process. It was as if he'd forgotten all about my existence in his room.

The bathroom wasn't as luxurious as our bathroom back at Saint Augustine's. The tiling was a bit chipped and the mirror was so old it was all speckled. But it was such a relief to pull off my wet clothes that I decided I was mad to be so paranoid. Malcolm's robe was a green-and-maroon-striped Ralph Lauren affair and best of all, it was deliciously clean, fluffy and two sizes too big for me.

I gathered up my sodden clothes and walked back into the room as if everything were perfectly natural and normal.

'Drink?' Malcolm offered without looking up as I began to lay my clothes on his piping hot radiators.

'Yaah, a drink would be super,' I drawled, cringing at my ridiculous blurt. Super? Was I turning into my mother?

'Help yourself. The fridge is over there,' Malcolm told me as he gestured to the other side of the room. 'If everything doesn't fit on that radiator, there's another along the bed.

'Thanks,' I replied, cringing with embarrassment as I spread my wet Snoopy bra and knickers over the radiator behind his bed. I looked over at Malcolm, but as he wasn't showing anything more than a courteous disinterest in me, I figured it would be okay. I mean, they'd probably be dry in ten minutes and then I could get dressed and find Freds.

I placed my mobile and mace on the fridge.

'Sorry, excuse the poor selection. I'm not much of a drinker, I'm afraid,' Malcolm explained without looking up from his chore.

I opened the glass fridge door and suddenly it was like being back in Honey's limo again. It was full of miniature bottles of Veuve Clicquot. 'I could probably get one of the other guys to dig you up some vodka if you'd prefer?' he suggested, no doubt imagining that I was disappointed by his unvaried selection.

I didn't want to sound babyish and admit I actually thought he was offering me a Horlicks or something nice and sweet like that, so I said it was fine and took a bottle out.

'Should I, erm, open one for you?' I asked, uncertain of the etiquette rules of Eades boys and their fridges.

'Cheers,' he said, smiling at me as he ran his fingers through his hair in what looked like frustration. 'I shouldn't, but this is going to be a long night.'

I uncorked the two small bottles pretty skilfully, proving that even time spent in the company of someone as poisonous as Honey has its uses.

Malcolm placed his champagne beside him on the floor. He seemed too absorbed in his DVDs to care where I sat, so I perched on the edge of his bed. I still felt madly awkward, so I decided to spread out and look a bit more chilled as I took a gulp of the champagne. Instantly all the bubbles charged up my nose and I started choking and coughing.

'Unlike beer, it's better not to neck your champagne like that,' Malcolm suggested, suppressing a laugh. 'It's easier if you use the straw that's glued to the side,' he explained, pointing out the straw.

'Oh yaah, no, of course I know that. It's just, well, I prefer to knock it back, really,' I blurted in a blatantly ridiculous attempt at sounding sophisticated. And once I started I couldn't stop. 'Hic, hic, hic,' was my next sophisticated blurt. My plan to look all chilled and worldly was sinking fast.

'So who is it exactly that you are looking for?' Malcolm asked in the tone that suggested he was keen to be rid of the strange, wet girl hiccuping in his room.

'*Hic, hic, hic*,' I replied.

'Do you need something for your hiccups? A paper bag? A fright perhaps?' he asked, looking around his room for a solution.

He didn't have to look far, though. Before I could *hic* another word out, Portia's older brother, Tarquin, stormed into the room.

'Have you found that bloody DVD yet, McHamish?' Tarquin demanded crossly before he noticed me, stretched out across Malcolm's bed in a robe. He only gave me a cursory glance, but I clutched the robe to my neck as I imagined what he might be thinking.

'Still looking, man; the search goes on. I will be triumphant, though! I will be triumphant,' Malcolm declared, punching the air with his mini-bottle of Veuve.

By this point Tarquin had not only spotted me *hic, hic, hic*ing away on Malcolm' bed, but he'd also taken in my matching Snoopy bra and knickers (thank goodness I'd taken the precaution of wearing matching underwear, otherwise it could have been *really* embarrassing) flung over the radiator.

'Briggs, meet Calypso, she who would lure men from their whatsits.'

'Goals. Listen, I know you,' Tarquin said, pointing to me as if he wished he didn't. 'You're that friend of Portia's. Freddie's girlfriend.'

'*Hic*, yes, *hic*, yes. Nice to, *hic*, see, *hic*, you again, *hic*.' I replied giving him a little wave.

'She's been necking her champagne,' Malcolm explained, gesturing to me with his champagne. 'That's how she prefers to drink it apparently. I told her to use a straw, but girls, what can you do?' He shrugged.

I pulled Malcolm's robe even more tightly around me, suddenly acutely aware of how naked I was underneath.

The next minute, Billy burst in on my humiliation. 'Right McHamish, where's the bloody –.' He stopped short as he spotted me. He looked confused. 'Calypso? What's going on?'

'*Hic*, well, you, *hic*, I was . . .'

'Ah Pyke, my good man. Yes, your DVD is on the fridge.'

But Billy didn't seem to be interested in the whereabouts of his DVD. 'What are you doing *here*? In Malcolm's room?' he asked me irritably.

'Ah, the fair Calypso. Everyone seems to know this young wench. Found her hanging off my windowsill, wet as drowning rat. Said she could dry herself off before she continued her search for, what was his name again?'

'Freds!' I squeaked – yes, squeaked, like one of those soft

toys babies have. Because I wasn't answering Malcolm's question at all. Freds had just walked in and he did not look pleased to see me. Not a bit. If looks could burn, my matching Snoopy bra and knickers would have burst into flame, because his eyes were boring into them. I jumped up off the bed, desperate to explain the situation but all that came out was '*Hic.*'

Malcolm must have been the only one unaware of the dynamics of the drama being played out in his room. 'Now Freds, I've got your DVD, I think I put it –', Malcolm began, but Freds turned around and walked straight back out again, muttering something about how he couldn't believe this.

Well bugger that, the fighter in me said! I hadn't fought off attack dogs, wriggled through razor-wire fences, run through the rain and climbed wisteria bushes for nothing. No, I, Calypso Kelly, sabre champion of the Sheffield Open, was not giving up. I stuffed the mace and phone in one of the pockets of the robe, grabbed my Snoopy set and clothes and legged it after him.

That was when I ran into the Eades house matron, spilling my champagne all over her and me and, well, that was when things got really nasty.

Malcolm, Billy and Tarquin, who had also given chase, slammed into the matron and me.

'Aaah, good. I see you've met our matron, Kate. Kate, this is Calypso, she who distracts men from their –'

Kate just stared at him. 'Thank you, Mr McHamish, you can go back to your room.'

Billy and Tarquin followed him and that was that. I was alone with Kate, who in her twinset and pearls looked terrifyingly formidable.

FOURTEEN

Matron's Remedy for Hiccups

'There's a perfectly reasonable explanation for this,' I told Kate, trying to sound as authoritative as Honey and as aloof as Portia. But in addition to my lack of attire, I was also buckling under the additional hurt of Fred's storming off. Talk about taking the wind out of a girl's sails.

The matron gripped me by the robe and, well, robes being what they are, I didn't even try to argue or struggle, because, well, having a near-naked girl on her hands is at least a little better than an actual naked girl. Also, I still had the hiccups.

Malcolm's head popped out of his door, 'Any chance you can bring the robe back on your next visit, Calypso?' he asked.

Kate turned around to face him, and a horrible sense of doom came over me – not that I wasn't already feeling doom-ish enough about the evening's events, but I didn't want to land Malcolm in any sort of trouble when he'd been so hospitable.

'Where does this girl come from, Mr McHamish?' Kate enquired nicely, in the sort of voice one might ask the time.

'Good question, Kate. I have no idea of her origins. I did think I detected a slight transatlantic accent when I first came across her. She was hanging, wet as a stray cat, on the wisteria outside my window, looking for some chap. I invited her in to dry off before she continued her search.'

By the time he had finished his explanation, Billy, Tarquin and a few other boys had opened their doors to watch the scene.

'I see,' said Kate. 'Well, do any of you chaps know where she's from?' she put it to the ever-increasing number of boys coming out to have a look at me.

I felt myself shrinking inside the robe. 'My name's, *hic*, Calypso,' I told her quietly. '*Hic*, Calypso Kelly.'

'She's from Saint Augustine's,' Billy offered.

'A friend of my sister's,' Tarquin added darkly.

'Well, I'd better ring Sister Constance and inform her that I'm driving you back to school, Miss Kelly. It's a good thing our Head is in bed along with all the rest of the beaks.' Then she turned to the boys. 'Good night, gentlemen. And Mr McHamish, please don't smoke in the corridor; you know it's against fire regulations.'

'Right, yes, blast the bloody regulations. Such a lot of

rot.' He smiled at Kate, took a drag of his cigarette and stubbed it out on the floor and then took a sip of his champagne.

I was astonished that Kate didn't scold him, but clearly Eades boys had more power when it came to matrons than we did.

The boys all said good night to Kate as if she were an employee. Billy thanked her for looking after me, which made me feel like a stray dog. Then they all shut their doors, and I was alone with Kate.

As I looked at her and she looked at me, I began to fear repercussions. My brave adventure had come to a soggy and miserable failure of an end. Far from convincing Freds of my undying affection, I had totally alienated him.

Kate didn't say anything to me. She led me downstairs to her office, where she called Sister Constance. 'I have one of your girls here,' she explained. I couldn't hear what Sister said to Kate, but I imagined her attitude to the situation wouldn't be as casual as Kate's. 'No, no, that's fine, Sister. I'll drive her back,' Kate continued. 'Only three minutes away.'

Three minutes of terror away! Kate drove like a maniac. Her driving made Sister Regina's seem safe in comparison, and Sister Regina is too short to see over the wheel. I could see over the wheel, though, as we sped around hairpin bend after hairpin bend.

One good thing about her reckless driving was that it made speaking impossible and proved to be just the fright

I needed to rid myself of the wretched hiccups, which were really starting to hurt my tummy. Thankfully it was a short journey, but there is nothing edifying about being driven back to school after midnight in a boy's bathrobe by a matron who drives a smarter car than your own mother.

As we turned into my school's car park, I could see the silhouette of Sister Constance standing on the entrance porch, and I could tell from her expression that she was not her usual composed, meditative self. Shame over my behaviour gave way to fear of what my punishment would be.

Kate had to come around and virtually drag me out of the car, I was so frozen with fear.

'Thank you, Mrs Denning, I'll take the matter from here,' Sister Constance assured her. 'It was very good of you to bring her back.'

'Not at all, and please, Sister, call me Kate,' she replied sweetly as she walked back towards her car.

'I'm soooo sorry, Sister,' I began in my most remorseful voice.

'We'll discuss what's to be done about this matter when your mother arrives in the morning,' was Sister's curt reply.

'When my mother arrives? But she works.'

'I called her as soon as Mrs Denning called me. You are lucky that you were discovered by Mrs Denning, a most understanding young woman. I can't bear to think of the scandal should one of the masters have found you. Nonetheless, it was still my responsibility to call your mother. She will be here for a nine o'clock meeting.'

Gulp. 'What did she say?'

But Sister wasn't to be drawn, and merely escorted me to my dorm. Her silence was far worse than if she'd scolded me.

I crept into my room, planning to collect my pyjamas and change in the en suite, but I fell foul of Star, who was stretched out on my floor.

'What happened?' demanded Star excitedly, turning on her torch.

I wasn't in the mood to discuss my evening of disaster, even with my best friend, but Star isn't the sort of girl to let things drop. 'Let's see, I climbed up the wrong wall, where I was discovered by Malcolm clinging to the wisteria outside his room. He said I could dry my clothes in his room, so it was really lucky I wore my matching Snoopy –'

Star grabbed me round the shoulders. 'Wait? You don't mean Malcolm McHamish the filmmaker?'

'I don't know. He's an Eades boy in the Lower Sixth. Anyway so he offers me champagne. And then Portia's brother walks in, followed by Billy, followed by –'

'I sent Billy to look for you,' Portia whispered from her bed.

'Thanks, well, he found me and my Snoopy underwear drying on Malcolm's radiator and then –'

'Is Malcolm really, really fit with red hair?' Star probed.

'I think the two are mutually exclusive actually, darling,' Honey waded in.

'You're just jealous,' Star snapped back.

'You keep telling yourself that, Ginga features!' Honey replied nastily, referring to Star's own red hair.

I couldn't believe everyone kept interrupting me! How many of them had braved the wisteria of Eades in the pouring rain and ended up busted by a matron called Kate who drives like a lunatic? None, that's how many. Also, I could smell the delicious aroma of pizza. How could they have ordered pizza while I was drying my underwear in a strange boy's room? While I was virtually choking to death on champagne they should have been biting their nails with worry, not munching on a delicious illicit pizza.

'Look, doesn't anyone actually want to hear what happened?' I almost yelled. 'Otherwise I'm going to get into my pyjamas and go to bed,' I told them sulkily.

'Sorry, darling,' Star whispered. 'Keep going, I won't interrupt again, promise.'

'Right, so the matron caught me naked, well semi-naked. I was wearing Malcolm's robe – and yes he does have red hair – and then Freds walked in.'

'OMG! What did he say?' Star asked.

'*Shhhhh!*' Portia hushed. 'Let her finish.'

'Not much. Something like, "I don't believe this," and then he walked off in a strop.'

'Shit,' Star said simply.

'I know. Can you imagine? There I was, sitting on

Malcolm's bed, in Malcolm's robe, knocking back champagne. Anyway, I chased after him, which is when I ran into Kate.'

'Kate?'

'Oh yes, Kate's their matron, only she didn't look or act a bit matronly. I mean, Malcolm was standing right in front of her smoking and drinking, and she didn't do anything. Can you imagine!'

'All boys' schools are like that, darling. They treat them like grown men,' Portia explained. 'Whenever we go to Eades boating day, all the boys just wander around drinking and smoking, and when any of the beaks tell them to stop drinking they just say "Yes, sir" and carry on.'

Honey giggled. 'I think it's quite funny, actually.'

'What?'

'You being caught naked in another boy's room, darling,' she replied. 'I think it's hilarious, in fact. Freddie will never take you back now.'

'She's not a package,' Star snapped at her before turning to me. 'So anyway, what did this Kate woman say to you then?'

'Nothing. She grabbed me by the robe, took me down to her office, called Sister, drove me back here and that was it.'

'And what did Sister say?' asked Portia.

'She told me there will be a meeting with my mother tomorrow. I'm probably going to get expelled.'

'Why didn't you mace her?' Honey asked. 'Then you

could have run off back to school and no one would have been the wiser.'

'Oh yes, I should have maced her,' I agreed sarcastically.

Star sneered, 'And quite probably gone to jail. So anyway, what did Malcolm say?'

'Does it actually matter what Malcolm said or didn't say?' I replied hotly. I was getting quite cross now with the way Star was obsessing over this Malcolm. 'He didn't say much, and I can't be bothered remembering. In fact, I partly blame him for all this. If he hadn't invited me in, urged me to take off my clothes, dry them on his radiator and drink champagne, I wouldn't be in this mess! Look,' I added, pausing mid-rant. 'Sorry, but I'm tired, hungry and upset. I just want to go to bed. Not that I'll be able to sleep. Sarah will probably make me move to Clapham with her.'

'I'm sure Sister won't be *that* horrible,' Star assured me confidently.

'Just say you ran away because you were upset about Sarah leaving Bob and coming from a broken home, darling. Nuns hate broken homes,' Honey suggested. 'You could hint that they abuse you; that's bound to get you sympathy.'

Why did everyone keep saying I came from a broken home! 'I don't come from a broken home!' I snapped.

'Okay, okay, chill. God, I was only trying to be nice, darling,' Honey said crossly. 'It will tear at Sister's heart-strings, that's all. Think about it. She's let Georgina get away with loads since her father married Koo-Koo.'

'That's completely different,' I argued. 'Bob and Sarah will sort things out. I mean, they –'

'Hang on, Calypso,' Star interrupted just as I began to feel uncertain of my argument. 'As much as I hate to agree with Honey,' Star said, 'she has a point. Sarah and Bob are having problems, and I honestly don't think Sister will want to make things any tougher on Sarah or you. Just relax for now. You're upset and need some sleep. Things always seem better in the morning,' she assured me, giving me a hug.

I felt tears banking up behind my eyes as I hugged her back. 'Sorry if I was grumpy with you, and thanks for waiting up for me.'

'Don't be mad, we had fun. Just get some sleep. I'll see you at breakfast. Sweet dreams.'

'Night,' I replied.

'Night,' added Portia as Star left.

'At last,' groaned Honey, punching her pillow. 'Only children! They're always sooo selfish,' she sighed heavily.

If I wasn't so tired and emotional I would have laughed.

'Are you okay, Calypso?' Portia asked gently as I crept into the en suite to clean my teeth.

'Fine. I have to change,' I told her. I was too upset to talk.

'I ordered a pizza for you while you were out in case you were hungry when you got back. I noticed you didn't eat at supper. It's a small Hawaiian; the box is on your bed. It's probably cold now.'

I was soooo touched – and starving after my night of high drama – that I almost threw myself on her and cuddled her.

As it was, I changed into my Hello Kitty PJs and consumed the cold pizza in the solitude of the bathroom so I wouldn't disturb Honey. It was bliss.

FIFTEEN

The Quality of Mercy Is Not Strained – It's Drained

Ravaging the pizza pretty much sorted me out hunger-wise and even calmed me down enough to get to sleep. Waking up was another matter. I never thought I'd say it, but I actually missed Miss Cribb's little gong, which she used to bang millimetres from our ears until we woke up.

Miss Cribb's torture-by-gong seemed mild in comparison to Miss Bibsmore's stick. 'Oi, Miss Kelly. Time to git up,' she insisted, prodding at my ribs.

Even when I eventually darted out of bed, she managed a few more prods.

'All right!' I yelled. 'I'm up, I'm up!' I told her, dodging the stick as I struggled into my gown and slippers.

'Well, be that as it may, I'm in the rhythm now and prod

I will until you is in that bathroom making yerself presentable innit!'

'Fine!' I yelled back as I dived into the ensuite, locking the door behind me. My previous night's activities at Eades had left me looking like a drug-rehab patient. After a quick splash of water on my face, a flash brush of my teeth, I pulled my hairbrush through my hair and climbed into my uniform. By the time I ran past a mirror it was too late to do anything about my hideous frizzy acid rain hair. Apply the lip-gloss though I might, nothing was going to improve my confidence level that morning.

Everyone was really lovely to me in the ref at breakfast. Word was out that I had broken the fortress of Eades – even amongst the Year Sevens who worshipped anyone who had even pulled a boy – let alone entered the holy kingdom of fit boys.

Even Honey was sweet to me, offering me her croissant, which she'd dropped on the floor. She brushed it on my uniform before passing it to me faux kindly. 'Darling, you must be famished after last night's exertions,' she sympathised, rolling her eyes and flicking her beautiful hair – which only served to make me feel even more hideous. 'And I adore this American Tramp look you're going for this morning, it's soooo you.'

'Thanks,' I said, immune to anything Honey might care to throw at me. 'I look like a train wreck,' I told her, accepting the extra croissant even though I wasn't going to eat it. I wasn't that hungry thanks to Portia's thoughtfulness the night before.

Honey leaned in closer and whispered, 'Only, don't mention where you got that mace, darling, will you? If you do, you'll appreciate that I'll have to tell Daddy you lied, and I'd hate to give evidence against you in court. It would tear my heart in two.'

'What are you talking about?' I asked, having forgotten all about the mace, which was still in the pocket of Malcolm's robe in my room along with my phone.

'Well, sweetie darling, it would be libellous were you to mention my name to Sister Constance regarding the mace.' She pointed to her heart and looked at me with faux concern. 'I couldn't bear to visit you in Old Choky, darling.'

Indie gave her a poke in the ribs similar to the pokes Miss Bibsmore had rained down on me with her stick earlier.

'Ouch!' Honey screamed, but everyone ignored her, apart from Indie's security guys, who flinched as if desperate for the opportunity to shoot Honey.

'Libel is when you write it down, you illiterate chav,' Indie pointed out.

Star giggled and had to spit out her mouthful of hot chocolate before she snorted it up her nose. Then the bell rang and we all had to run off for room inspection, registration, chapel – and in my case the dreaded interview with Sister and Sarah.

'Is it true you were found naked in Prince Freddie's room?' A gaggle of tiny little Year Sevens asked – wide-eyed with awe as we made our way out towards registration later on.

'Yes,' Star told them, but all the good humour in the world couldn't stop the inevitable confrontation awaiting me in Sister's office.

Sarah was waiting on the wooden bench outside Sister's office dressed in the same pink Chanel suit she'd worn on Sunday. Her face was ashen, though, and her hair looked as dishevelled as my own.

'So, here we are, then, Calypso,' she said sternly. 'I really am at a loss as to what to say.'

'Yes, but I can explain, Sarah. Honestly, it isn't as bad as it seems.'

'I think you might find it's worse,' she told me ominously, looking miserably down at her hands. She had a quiver in her voice. 'Breaking into a boys' school. And naked? Oh, Calypso, what were you thinking?'

'I *wasn't* naked,' I told her outraged. 'At least not at first!' I blurted.

Unsurprisingly, this didn't mollify the madre. By the time Sister called 'Come!' Sarah looked on the verge of tears.

As usual, Sister was in silent meditation under a life-size statue of Christ that looked down on us from the crucifix above her chair. Her hands formed a steeple on the desk while her lips moved silently in prayer. Sarah and I waited for an invitation to be seated.

'Thank you for coming, Mrs Kelly. Please be seated,' Sister Constance said eventually, although her voice was laden with doom.

'Before you speak, Sister, I think there are mitigating circumstances in this case which you should know about,' Sarah began.

Sister shot her a warning look. 'Before *anyone* speaks, Mrs Kelly, I intend to pray for guidance from the Lord God, Our Father, in the handling of this matter, thank you.'

So, we all set off on a decade of the rosary, and I promise you I've never prayed so fervently in my life. When Sister spoke again it was to explain that she felt compelled to suspend me for the duration of term.

Sarah looked at her furiously. She rose out of her chair and loomed – yes loomed (which isn't as hard as you might think for an abnormally tall woman in heels) over Sister's ancient oak desk.

I shrank into my chair.

'Suspend?' Sarah spat out the word as if it were akin to 'murder.' 'After everything this poor child from a broken home has endured?' She pointed to me. I crumpled up into chair even further and began a slow slither to the floor.

Sister leant over her desk, presumably curious as to what I was up to.

Sarah was oblivious to all as she tore strips off our head nun. 'I am disappointed in you, Sister,' she railed. 'Disappointed with a capital "D"! With her father in Los

Angeles immersed in his own self-centred madness, her mother struggling to pay her fees while dealing with an emotionally trying time. Just imagine what it's done to this poor child? Have you no soul, Sister?' she demanded. 'Have you no mercy?'

Sister replied calmly and softly, 'We all have souls, Mrs Kelly. Even girls such as your daughter who run drunk and naked around Eades have souls.'

'I didn't run naked around Eades and I wasn't drunk. I just had the hiccups, that's all!' I cried out, but they both ignored me – partly because I was now crumpled on the floor.

'Well, then, Sister Constance. Where's your quality of mercy? Is it strained?' Sarah demanded to know. Sarah likes to paraphrase Shakespeare. It was usually a sign that she had dug herself into her argument and had no exit strategy in place. This was going to be a long and upsetting morning. The upside was I was missing Greek; the downside was, Sarah's speech would no doubt end in my expulsion.

Sister tried to interject at various points, but Sarah waved her away dismissively. 'It beggars the belief of any right-thinking moral person that you, a woman who has supposedly devoted yourself to the spiritual care of young ladies, can toss this poor child from a broken home onto the scrap heap of life to fend for herself while her mother is struggling to find her way in a new country and her father is on another continent, immersed in his bloody Big One!'

'Sit down, Mrs Kelly,' Sister commanded authoritatively.

Sarah obeyed, stunned I guess by Sister's transformation from earnest nun to terrifying draped woman. 'Now, get off the floor Miss Kelly. That is no place for a girl of Saint Augustine's to repose.'

'Yes, Sister,' Sarah and I chimed as I clambered back onto my chair.

'Now, as I said before your well-intentioned interruption, Mrs Kelly, my *inclination* is to suspend Calypso for the duration of the term. But one does not always give in to one's inclinations, does one?'

Sarah and I shook our heads fervently.

'So, as this is Calypso's GCSE year and her record, up until now, has been relatively blemish-free, I am prepared to be lenient. Taking in the circumstances of your parents' marital breakup and your mother's, erm, breakdown, Calypso, I am prepared to suspend your sentence and leave it as a weekend gating for now. However, and I mean this, so listen very carefully . . .'

Sarah and I both strained our ears to hear.

'Should you ever pull a stunt like this again, I warn you, I will not hesitate to give way to my inclinations and suspend you, GCSEs or not. Understood?'

'Oh, Sister. Thank you for showing such mercy,' Sarah grovelled shamelessly. 'Calypso learnt a very valuable lesson and I'm sure she's very sorry and grateful for your leniencey.'

I was not soooo grovelly or shameless, though. 'Hang on a minute, Sister. You haven't even asked me my side of the story. This is soooo unfair. I was only at Eades because Freds wouldn't take my calls and I had to say sorry about, well, never mind about what, but since when has saying sorry been a crime?' I blurted.

Sister looked down at her lap.

Sarah jabbed me in the ribs. 'Ouch!' I yelped. Was this Jab Calypso in the Ribs Day or something? 'I was only wearing Malcolm's robe because my own clothes were wet.'

'I think, Calypso, you have said and done quite enough.'

I scowled at her. Sarah patted my shoulder. 'There, there, Calypso, you've been under a lot of strain lately,' she soothed as if I were some sort of lunatic.

I shrugged her off. 'Besides, you can't gate me this weekend. I've got the tournament! Mr Wellend says people are watching me. Spies and BNFA-type people. He'll go bonkers.'

Sarah mouthed the word 'shut up' at me.

Sister looked up. 'The gating was not a suggestion, Miss Kelly. You are gated, young lady, tournament or no tournament,' Sister said in a tone of voice that brooked no further argument.

'But Bell End, he'll have my guts for garters,' I blurted.

'Have you heard the expression, "Skating on thin ice"?' Sister asked me.

I nodded.

'How about the expression "When you're in a hole, stop digging"?'

I nodded again.

'Well, Madam, you are skating on thin ice and digging one crater of a hole for yourself. As part of your gating you will also lose all mobile-phone privileges.'

'But you can't do that, it's against – something or other!' I shrieked. 'It's against European Law and violates my human rights under the, erm, Belgium Convention!' I hazarded.

Sister rose and glared. 'For the sake of your future here at Saint Augustine's School for Ladies, Calypso, I am terminating this meeting before you jeopardise the lenient punishment the Lord has guided me to grant you. Good morning, Mrs Kelly.'

And with that, Sister Constance swept out of her office, taking my future with her.

I looked up at our Lord on his cross. 'So that's what you call lenient, is it, oh Lord of Mercy?' I asked sarcastically.

'I've been fired,' Sarah said, quietly.

'Fired?'

'Yes, they're cutting back.'

I put my arm about her as if I were one of those rock-solid-type daughters as opposed to the dependent, emotionally needy daughter I really was. 'You're madly talented, Sarah, you'll be snapped up before you can say –'

'Snappy dialogue.'

'Exactly, snappy dialogue,' I agreed.

'No, that's why they fired me. They said I was too scripted, that my dialogue wasn't snappy enough.'

'Idiots,' I said.

We sat there for a bit. I stroked Sarah's back and she made a brave, resigned face. I didn't ask anything tricky about who'd pay my fees or how she'd afford the house or, well, anything that might yield an answer that might make me feel even worse.

But Sarah must have sensed the thoughts chasing through my mind because she said, 'I've got some savings; they will hold us for a few months, but after that –'

'And I might win the essay competition. You never know.'

Sarah smiled. 'You're everything to me, you know that, don't you, Calypso?'

I nodded as I squeezed her hand. 'I know. And, erm, sorry about the, you know, going to Eades thing.'

'Oh, darling Calypso, I don't mind about that, really. I did it myself more times than I care to remember. Do you really think I'd be cross with you about a streak through Eades?'

I didn't get a chance to tell her 'yes' because the bell for the next class rang, so I had to leg it to get my books for English.

SIXTEEN

The Extreme Trauma of Privilege

'Miss Kelly,' said Ms Topler as I wandered into class all of one minute late.

'Yes, Ms?'

'Come and see me after class, please.'

This was soooo typical. As if I didn't have enough on my plate, now Ms Topler wanted to give me a blue. I hated teachers.

I slumped into a chair next to Star. 'So what did Sister say?' she whispered.

'No mobile phone for a week and a gating.'

'That's not too bad.'

'Are you mad? How can I call Freddie to explain about being virtually naked in Malcolm's room? And I won't get to go to the fencing tournament with Portia and attract the attention of the spies and scouts.'

'What spies and scouts?' You're being paranoid. Bell End is clearly a loon. There *are* no spies and scouts,

Calypso, apart from in his deranged imagination,' Star assured me.

'I will not have chatting in my class, thank you, Star and Calypso,' Ms Topler called out.

'No, Ms Topler,' I answered. 'Star was just showing me what I missed.'

'You haven't missed anything, as Star well knows,' Ms Topler snapped. 'Now, open up your copies of *Sons and Lovers*. Miss Castle Orpington, could you please begin the fourth chapter for us.'

And so the lesson dragged and droned on. I almost fell asleep; in fact I did doze off a bit because the next thing I heard was the bell.

I grabbed my books and pencil case and started to make my way out in the shuffle of girls, but Ms Topler hadn't forgotten.

'Miss Kelly, I believe I asked you to stay back,' she called out to me.

'Oh, sorry, Ms Topler, my mind was on the incandescence of D.H. Lawrence.'

She rolled her eyes. 'Enough, Calypso. You are a talented pupil but a less talented fibber. Work on your strengths rather than your weaknesses.'

'Yes, Ms Topler.'

'Now take a seat while I get something that I hope might interest you.'

I sat down in a chair by the window and looked out over Pullers' Wood at the golden carpet of fallen leaves. The bare branches looked so forlorn – a bit like I felt. Ms Topler handed me a pamphlet. The same pamphlet Star had given me about the essay competition.

'I've given these entries out to the Year Tens and below, as the competition is limited to the Under Fifteens. You don't turn fifteen until after the end of this term, do you, though, Miss Kelly?'

'No,' I replied.

Ms Topler sat on the seat beside me, which meant I could smell her perfume, Red Door by Elizabeth Arden. I tried not to choke on the strong fumes and pretended to pay attention. 'I knew it. Don't you see what this all means?' she asked excitedly.

'That I don't get any proper birthday presents because my birthday is only days away from Christmas.'

'Don't be silly. It's just that people try to get you one big present,' she said, patting my arm.

'I think we both know that's a big lie,' I told her.

'Yes, perhaps it is. My birthday is on the twenty-fourth of December.'

'It sucks, doesn't it?' I blurted before I could help myself.

'Yes, it does rather,' agreed my teacher. 'But what doesn't suck is that your late birthday makes you eligible to enter the competition, and while I don't want to get your hopes up *too* high, I certainly think you have the ability to win this – if you put your heart and soul into it.'

I turned the pamphlet around in my hands and realised

that my gating might give me the opportunity to work on the essay. 'Thank you, Ms Topler, but do you really think my pathetic sufferings such as they are can compete with the other applicants?'

'Miss Kelly, you can't measure suffering. And besides, this is a writing competition. The judges will be judging you on how well you express your suffering, not on what your suffering has been.' She was looking into my eyes like a hypnotist.

'I guess,' I agreed as I began to realise that it was all about the writing, not the suffering. I'd been looking at it all the wrong way. Okay, so my life had been a bed of roses compared to some, but there is a universality about suffering, and Bob is always saying that being a successful writer is all about the ability to communicate the personal in the universal.

'Just consider this. Knowing all the other things you have on your plate, I wouldn't suggest this essay competition if I didn't think you had a real chance. You have a rare talent, Miss Kelly, and this could be your opportunity to show the country. At the very least to explore your potential.'

'Thank you, Ms Topler,' I said, smiling at her hopeful face.

'So you'll try it?'

'I'll give it my best shot.'

And then Ms Topler did something so unexpected it toppled me – quite literally to the ground. She slapped me really hard on the back and said, 'That's my girl!' And then she laughed and laughed and said. 'One big present indeed. You're absolutely right, Miss Kelly. It sucks.'

So now it was official. I was entering an autobiographical writing competition which would depict my suffering in all its middle-class glumness.

SEVENTEEN

Bell End's Sacred Sabre

I know my mobile had been confiscated, but there is e-mail, after all. Bob and Sarah were addicted to it. I wrote to Freddie trying to explain why I had tried to patch things up with him in a dressing gown in Malcolm's room, but he didn't reply.

Fine, *he* could sulk if he wanted to, but I was damned if I wasn't going to tell Bob what I thought of him.

Dear Bob,

I hope you are very pleased with yourself! Sarah has now lost her job thanks to you. I can't believe that a father of mine could be so cold and allow a woman to whom he once vowed to forsake above all others (including Big Ones) to end up on the scrap heap of life. You and your creative endeavours have been the downfall of this family. From this day forth I shall call you, well, I don't know what yet, but when I think of it, you can be certain it will make you sorry you were ever born. Also, now that poor Sarah has lost her job, how can she pay my fees and support herself? And her self-esteem is in ruins. And she's seeing a therapist called Bunny – well, phoning her, because this Bunny creature lives in LA. Anyway, it's all a Big Mess and it's all your fault. And I hate you. And I've just had a gating.

From your daughter Calypso.

PS: note the lack of xxx's and oooo's!!!

Talk about living at his laptop! His response came roaring back as defiant as a teenage girl's! And if, like me, you were expecting an e-mail of remorse, a few lines of his heartfelt shame or an explanation for driving Sarah to England – or a grovelling plea for me to forgive him – you'll be disappointed.

Dearest Daughter,

Sarah has spoken to me of your naked romp around the dormitory rooms of Eades! Please explain immediately.

Your loving father, Bob

NB:

xxxxxxxxxxxxxxxxxxxxxxxxxxxxxxxxxxxxxxxxxxxxxxxxxx

How dare he!

Dear 'Daddy,' [I wrote, righteous steam coming out of my ears]

Bugger off. I hate you and everything you stand for and

shan't write to you again. Consider yourself *personae non gratia.*

C.

PS: I soooo wasn't naked!

Since she moved to England, Sarah had been sending me little letters written on art gallery postcards, which I have lovingly pinned to my pin board.

'How could Bob let a woman like her slip through his fingers?' Star asked as postcard after postcard arrived. The rest of the time she went on and on about the competition. 'You are soooo winning that competition! I just know it.'

It was with some trepidation that I entered the salle, knowing I would have to tell Bell End that I wouldn't be attending the tournament on Saturday.

He bounded over like a spaniel in white breeches to greet me. 'Here she is!' he cried, clapping his hands with glee. Clearly no one had told him about my gating.

Portia joined him halfheartedly because word had spread through school already about my punishment. There was even a rather clever haiku in the downstairs loos about my Eades escapades, followed by another about my punishment.

'That's right, big round of applause, Portia. Crank it up there.'

It was soooo embarrassing. Seriously – he was standing on a block with his loud inhaler while the 'Ride of the Valkyries' played on a gramophone in the corner of the room.

'Take a bow, Kelly! You little champ.'

'Erm, Mr Wellend, I actually need to talk to you!'

'Plenty of time for talk after class, Kelly. Now how about you climb up on my shoulders for a victory run around the school, eh? Let's show them what we're made of, eh Kelly, eh!'

So that was that. What was I to say? He'd already bent down, so I climbed up onto his shoulders and we ran through the school, into classrooms and bedrooms, creating havoc and madness, especially in the convent. Sister Regina, who was soooo obviously expecting us, had a big spread of Battenberg cakes and tea set out for Portia, Bell End and myself. The nuns were only allowed to eat the cucumber sandwiches, and a very sulky atmosphere prevailed.

'We're all very proud of you Calypso,' they told me at one time or another, usually when I passed them a piece of illicit Battenberg cake.

When we arrived back in the salle, I couldn't put my moment of truth off any longer, though.

'Mr Wellend, I have to tell you something.'

He ruffled my hair affectionately.

'You can tell me anything, Kelly, anything. As long as you distinguish yourself at the Brighton Open on Saturday that is, ha-ha-ha.'

'Oh! Well, that's it, you see. I've been g-g-g-g-gated.'

Bell End thwacked me on the back – and really hard too. 'What was that? A piece of cake going down the wrong way? Oh yes, mark my words, Kelly, Brighton will be where we really stick it to them. The scouts all gathered. The scene all set. It's going to be a bloodbath, my girl. And I, for one, can't wait. So without further ado, I hereby present you with this blade of death that I distinguished myself with all those years ago at the Olympics.'

That was when he passed me a sabre, which I accepted. Well, better in my hands than his, was my reasoning. At least I'd be armed if he went crazy upon hearing the news that I really wasn't going to Brighton on Saturday. I studied the weapon, which was slightly rusty, and noted with some amusement that it had the words 'KILL, SLAY, MAIM' scratched childishly into the guard.

'That's really kind, Mr Wellend. I'll treasure it.'

'Steady up there, Kelly. You can't keep it, you idiot. I won silver with that.' He snatched it back crossly. I was just showing you, yer brainless girl. What kind of fool would give a weapon like this away to an untried schoolgirl. I barely know you, child.'

'Oh, sorry, my mistake, Mr Wellend, but it does bring me to the thing I had to tell you actually, about my, erm, gating on Saturday, see.'

Bell End's face started to go a nasty shade of purple. 'Gated? What do you mean gated? Sister can't gate you on Saturday. We've got the tournament!'

I was really regretting giving him his sabre back so quickly. 'Yes, that's what I said when Sister Constance gated me, funnily enough.' I laughed as best I could.

'And she took my mobile privileges off me, which I think is madly unfair and draconian. Okay, so I ran half-naked around Eades and drank a bit of champagne, but honestly –'

'What would you want to be drinking champagne and running around naked for when you've got the Nationals coming up?' Bell End demanded hotly. 'You should be practising your footwork, Kelly.'

'I wasn't properly naked, Mr Wellend. I mean, I was wearing a robe.'

'I'm not interested in your nudity, but what's robes got to do with it? You're not Harry bloody Potter, girl. Robes? What were you wearing robes for? What's a sabreur want with robes?' Bell End demanded hotly.

Portia, who had been standing nearby waiting for the fireworks, gave him a pat on the back. 'She'll still be at the regionals sir, and *I'll* be coming on Saturday.'

'You're a good little fencer, Briggs,' Bell End turned to her seemingly composed momentarily. 'But the scouts! The BNFA spies? What am I to tell them? I've set my trap, Briggs! Planned every intricate move to lure them into my web. Kelly! What have you done to me?' he cried out like a man in true pain.

'Well, see, sir, the thing is, I was I looking for my boyfriend to say sorry because –'

'I don't care if you were looking for the Holy Grail, you stupid girl. They don't put you on the National Team because you've chased down a spineless boyfriend in a robe.

What kind of nancy boy has you playing hide-and-seek with him, anyway?'

'Erm, Prince Freddie, sir.'

Bell End shook his head. 'I blame those romantic novels they feed you. Prince bloody Freddie, indeed! I bet it was that Eades fencing master set the whole thing up. Entrapment, that's what it is. I'll be complaining to the BNFA, I will. Entrapment.'

'But can't Calypso meet the scouts and, erm, spies at the regionals?' Portia suggested gently.

Bell End bent his sword into the piste in fury. 'No, she bloody can't! These men don't have memories. Here today, gone tomorrow. No!' With that he threw his prized sabre down the piste.

'Get out of my sight, Kelly. You've let me down. You've let everyone down. My plan to make you an Olympian, blown away like a house of straw. Spineless, big girl's blouse, that's all you are. Robes! Git out of my sight. Out, I say!'

I began to run out of the salle, tears streaming down my face.

Then Bell End shouted, 'Where do you think you're going, Kelly?'

I turned. 'Out of your sight, Bell End, I mean Mr Wellend,' I whimpered.

He slapped his forehead like a truly frustrated man. 'I don't believe this, lily-livered girls. Git back in here.' He pointed to the floor. 'Drop and give me twenty, now.'

I looked at Portia. Portia shrugged.

'Are you deaf as well as stupid, Kelly? Drop, both of you. Yes, you too, Briggs. I daresay they'd have you in a robe as well if you'd won the tournament. Give me twenty.'

So drop we did and gave him twenty press-ups.

That was how my week of fencing continued. Bell End ranting about his scout ruse being ruined followed by punishing exercises and rants about 'bloody robes.' I don't think Portia was too impressed with me for bringing the wrath of Bell End down on us, either.

EIGHTEEN

The Return of Octavia

Bell End's mood towards me didn't improve over the rest of the week. His sacred sabre didn't appear again, which I took as significant. Nor did the rain let up. Freddie continued to reject all my calls, which I now had to make from a call box that was a half-mile trek in the rain from the dorm. He also ignored all my e-mails. On the up side I really did try and pull my tights up when it came to my studies and handed in an outstanding Greek translation, which I was pretty sure would garner me an A, or a B, at least. Definitely a C anyway.

Sarah e-mailed me every day, but her attempt at sounding upbeat and her overuse of the word 'super' didn't fool me. She was going on loads of interviews and her agent was 'confident.' I wished I were as confident as this agent.

Portia had already left for the tournament by the time I woke up on Saturday. It was pissing down with rain still, and breakfast was only stale cereal and powdered milk due to some transport strike. Star and Indie decided to hang with me rather than go into Windsor with everyone else, which was really sweet of them, especially because I knew how much Star wanted to see Kev.

The truth was, as kind as it was of Star to stay with me, I would have rather been on my own and worked on my essay. Having overcome my earlier reservations, I was now keen to get cracking on the essay competition.

After breakfast, I lay in my bed and thought about what I would write. Three thousand words of personal life-changing trauma seemed a lot for an almost-fifteen-year old. It's funny, but the more I thought about my life, the more sorrow I saw.

Being an American in an English girls' boarding school.

The misery that Bob's need to pursue his own creative endeavours had wrought on our family.

My concern for Sarah's loneliness and the sense of failure she felt.

How I felt about her leaving Bob to have her regressionary breakdown in London.

And then there was Freds, who wouldn't talk to me.

Oh, and let's not forget the toxic Honey, using me as her torture toy at every opportunity these past four years.

Slowly I began to see that there really was some class-A trauma going on in my life. In fact, would three thousand words be enough?

Honey, Clemmie and Arabella headed off to Windsor after lessons at one o'clock but Star and Indie charged into my room just as I was making some really serious breakthroughs. I told them I was busy, but Star gave me a speech about solidarity and standing shoulder to shoulder with the suffering of the sisterhood or something Star-ish like that. So I put my essay aside and gave in.

'I just know you'll win this writing competition, Calypso,' Indie said, displaying a confidence in me she really had no reason to have, given she'd only known me half a term.

'I told her what a genius you are with words,' Star explained.

'And I seriously love *The Nun*,' Indie added, referring to the magazine I'd set up in Year Ten. 'I'd love to hear what you've written so far,' she pleaded.

So I read them out what I'd written, giving a little cough to set the mood. 'Talk about random. This was the worst-case scenario in my long history of worst-case scenarios. But then, my entire life is a random series of worst-case scenarios. At fourteen you start to realise these things.' I looked around my audience and smiled hopefully.

'Go on,' Star urged, her eyes bright with anticipation.

'Erm, that's as far as I've got, actually,' I explained.

'Oh,' she said, *très* unimpressed Then she rolled her eyes at me so I rolled mine back at her, then Indie rolled hers at both of us. I suspect we could have gone on like this until we had a fit or dislocated an eye, but we were interrupted by a tapping sound at the window.

'It's Kev!' cried Star, rushing over to open the window for her very wet boyfriend.

'And Malcolm,' I added, recognising that red thatch of hair even though it was plastered to his head.

'And Freds!' Indie yelped as the shamefaced grin of my one and only true love lit up our dark little room. I didn't care how wet he was as he pulled me into his arms and snog-aged me into a state of bliss. When we drew breath he asked if I could ever forgive him for being such a paranoid idiot.

Malcolm tussled Fred's hair and grinned at me. 'The appropriate answer would be no, Calypso,' he advised. 'Oh, by the way, I brought you this,' he added passing me a miniature bottle of Veuve. 'And don't worry, I took the precaution of removing the straw for you already,' he teased.

I know I should have just been happy that Freds had forgiven me, but I couldn't help wondering what had changed his mind. I hoped it was sleepless night upon sleepless night remembering our kisses that had made him realise he couldn't live without me. But I suspected Malcolm might have had something to do with it.

Speaking of Malcolm, I couldn't help notice the way Indie was staring at him, like a huntress eyeing up her prey. Freddie had his arms around me still, and I nuzzled his neck the way Kev was nuzzling Star's.

Star pulled away, though. 'I'm a huge fan of your work, Malcolm,' she gushed.

'Cheers, and you are?'

'Sorry, I said. 'This is Star and this is Indie and –' but Indie took it from there.

'Star's told me *all* about your films, especially *Trousers in Cannes*. I can't wait to see it,' she practically gushed. 'I love experimental silent film. Voices are soooo overrated.'

'You haven't been advertising again, have you McHamish?' Freddie teased, giving Malcolm a friendly shove (right in the direction of Indie, I noted).

'How did you know we'd be here?' I asked Freds. 'I was meant to be in Brighton today.'

'Yaah, but you're not. Thanks to me,' Freddie explained, looking shamefaced. 'Kev told me. I'm really sorry about how I reacted last week. I guess I was just so shocked, seeing you there on McHamish's bed.'

'He was particularly pissed off about your rather fetching Snoopy bra and knickers on my radiator,' Malcolm ribbed.

Freddie went red.

'Oh, I know. It must of looked terrible, what with my trackie bums and –'

Star slashed her hand across her neck, indicating now would be a perfect opportunity for me to shut up.

'I wasn't aware they did matching Snoopy lingerie,' Malcolm added unhelpfully. 'Cute little ensemble, Pyke,' he explained to Kev. 'You see, they had little Woodstocks on them and everything. Very arty. I'm not normally a lingerie man myself, but personally I've always felt that Woodstock was way underrated. He carried that cartoon strip as far as I can tell.'

I glared at him.

'Oh, by the way, Calypso,' he continued unabashed. 'Could I grab my robe back?'

'Sure, it's hanging on the back of the en suite door there,' I told him before turning back to Freds. 'But I only came to Eades to see you Freds. I didn't even know Malcolm then and I was just soooo wet and lost and well –'

Freddie put his hands up in resignation. 'I know, mea culpa, mea culpa, McHamish told all. The vine, the rain, the cold, but Calypso we need to get something straight.'

'Yes?'

'I get pissed off when you do these totally random unexpected inexplicable, illogical things. It's just confusing and makes me feel, well, insecure, I suppose.'

'How can you be insecure, Freds, when you've got a girl who's prepared to brave that wisteria bush in the rain. Tomkins broke his collarbone trying that stunt, remember,' Malcolm pointed out.

I was almost swooning, though, at the idea that I had the capacity to make an HRH *insecure*. Sorry, but how hot is that?

Star, who'd been towelling off Kev's hair, waded in to my defence. She's never had much time for Freds and wasn't going to let him off his sulk that easily. 'She was only looking for you! It's a wonder she didn't catch pneumonia and die. If it weren't for Malcolm helping her out, we might all be at her funeral now, not listening to you whine about how insecure you are.' She may as well have added 'You stuck up royal high horse,' given the tone she used.

Freds responded by going red and wiping his hand through his own dripping wet hair. 'I've been a bit of a shit, haven't I?'

I can't tell you how adorable he looked. I wanted to give him a towel and dry him off like Star had Kev, but I got the feeling Star would flip out if I did.

'Yes, you are a shit,' Star told him crossly. 'A royal bloody shit, now get down on your knees and apologise to all of us. To Calypso, for believing the worst of her. Then you can apologise to Malcolm for not being more grateful to him for helping your girlfriend out. And last but not least you can say sorry to Indie and me for having to put up with Calypso being so bloody miserable all week when she's got enough on her plate with her parents splitting up. Oh, and to Kev for being your mate and having to put up with your misplaced sense of grandeur twenty-four-seven. Insecure my arse.'

Indie giggled, and I noticed Malcolm looking at her like a lovesick puppy.

Freddie wiped some raindrops off his face. God, he was fit. I really wished Star could see how lovely he was, which I bet she would if she got to know him properly. 'Erm, can we go somewhere on our own for a chat?' he asked me quietly.

After checking whether Star had heard, I nodded, too happy to trust myself to speak. Star was busily dabbing Kev's nose with the towel.

'Calypso and I are just going to nip into the bathroom for a chat,' he said looking straight at Star. 'Before I go I'd just like to say, to all of you, especially Calypso, obviously, who's the best girlfriend a boy could wish for.' Then, and this is true, I swear, he got down on his knees and arms outstretched said, 'Forgive me, ladies and McHamish and Kev, for I have done yea wrong.'

Malcolm gave him a gentle kick. 'Piss off, you idiot, you were always crap at drama.' And then everyone laughed – even Star (well, she rolled her eyes and smiled) – and Freds and I went into the en suite for a quiet chat.

So there we were, his insecure Royal Highness and me. He sat on the loo and I sat on his lap, and after a nice bit of pulling, he took my chin in his hands and turned my head to his own. I was forced to look into his eyes, which always gives me this melted-chocolate feeling. 'I am sorry, Calypso.'

I nodded mutely, staring into the gorgeousity of his face.

'Oh shit, what kind of king will I make? I always seem to get the wrong end of the stick. And I didn't even think about what you must be going through with your parents separating. God, are you okay?'

I nodded. 'You know 'rents.'

'Yes, my parents are the ones responsible for the security dopes I'm always trying to shake.

I giggled. 'I think you should count yourself lucky. Mine are just plain nuts.'

'Well so are mine, but at least I let you meet mine. You, on the other hand, didn't want to subject your mother to the horror of me! How do you think I felt when you legged it down the lane? I presume you've told her all sorts of horrible lies about me.'

I went so red I thought my eyes would start bleeding. 'No, it wasn't you, it was her. Sarah's gone completely mad since she left Bob. She's started reverting. I couldn't subject you to that.'

'Reverting?'

'Regressing, you know, talking to me like I'm three, and, well, you don't want to hear about my problems.'

'See. This is what I'm talking about. You are maddening, Calypso. Of course I want to talk about your reverting mother. I want to talk about everything with you. But you're always sending me these mixed signals.'

'Me?'

'Yes, you. You're never doing what you're meant to be doing, never where you're meant to be, and you never even say what I think you're going to say. And after all that phone confusion rubbish before half term, it's like mixed signal after mixed signal. I feel like I can never relax. I know loads of our problems were down to Honey, and we're over that, but despite Star's opinion of me I actually do get insecure where you're concerned because you won't let me get to know you properly. You really are like Cinderella, disappearing every time I feel like we're getting close, and all I'm left with is a glass slipper that doesn't fit anyone else.'

Then he kissed me for a very, very, very long lime. When we stopped I wiped a wet tentacle of hair from his forehead.

'You're not like any other girl I've ever met, Calypso. Apart from being madly stunning and adorable, you are the singularly most infuriatingly difficult girlfriend a boy ever had.'

I was about to kiss him again, but he pushed me away.

'No, I will not be distracted from my prepared speech,' he teased, laughingly. 'I've thought about this a lot while I've been sulking, and the truth is (he did a nervous throat-clearing thing) I love you, Calypso, and everything you do drives me crazy.'

Shocked didn't even come close to how I was feeling at that moment, but before I could form an articulate sentence, we all heard the *tap, tap, tap* of Miss Bibsmore's stick coming down the corridor towards us. The duct tape must have fallen off her carpet-square silencer.

I grabbed Freds and dived out of the en suite. Star looked at me. Kev looked at Freds. Indie looked at Malcolm.

'She's going to come in here,' Star hissed, looking around at all of us, her eyes large saucers of terror.

I looked outside, where it had started to hail.

'They haven't got time to make it out,' I said, as Miss Bibsmore's stick could be heard outside our door.

'Here,' Star told the boys, chucking clothes from

Honey's drawer at them in bundles and shoving them into the en suite.

She had no sooner slammed the door on them when Miss Bibsmore entered our room in her awkward little shuffle. 'I've brought you some sweets, Miss Kelly,' she said as she passed a bag of jelly beans over to me. 'I know this gating is difficult for you an' all, what with the fencing competition, but discipline is discipline.'

I heard noises coming from the en suite, and so I shook the packet of jelly beans loudly in the pathetic hope of drowning out the boy's racket and cried, 'Thank you, Miss Bibsmore, you're soooo sweet.'

Why were boys so loud, even when they are supposed to quiet? I had to keep rattling on. 'Yes, Miss Bibsmore. Thank you, Miss Bibsmore. That is sooo, kind, Miss Bibsmore,' I said, as loudly as I could without shouting.

Star and Indie joined in with 'Aren't you a duck, Miss Bibsmore! You are the best house mother ever! So kind. Poor Calypso. She just loves jelly beans.'

'All right, all right! I might be crippled, but I is not deaf! Leastways not last time I heard,' Miss Bibsmore cried, holding her hands over her ears.

The boys in the en suite began to giggle.

'What was that?' asked our house spinster. 'Have you got company?'

Indie dived to the rescue. 'Just a few chums from an upper year. They came down to, erm, help us with erm –'

'Some hard sums,' added Star. Talk about a lame excuse,

normally Star is razor sharp when it comes to quick-thinking excuses.

'Their bathroom was blocked, so I said they could use mine,' I explained.

'Oh yes, well, very generous of you, Miss Kelly, I'm sure.' But she didn't look totally convinced.

Then the boys giggled even louder. Thanks, guys.

Placing one of her arthritic hands on the doorknob of the en suite, Miss Bibsmore demanded that the 'girls' show themselves. Please, please, please I thought, you *have* locked the door!

But they hadn't locked the door. Of course they hadn't done anything as sensible as that. What was I thinking? They were boys.

'Out you git,' Miss Bibsmore clucked, poking her stick into the en suite to hustle the boys out.

Malcolm, Freds, and Kevin wriggled out, deftly dodging the blows of Miss Bibsmore's stick. Each had a towel wrapped around his head as a turban, each with a face smeared with makeup a three-year-old child would be proud of. Malcolm was wearing his robe, while Freds and Kevin were each dressed in Honey's trackie bums and hoodies. They looked like transvestites who hadn't quite found their way around the makeup counter yet. Malcolm had daubed body glitter all over his face.

'What are your names, girls?' Miss Bibsmore asked suspiciously, eyeing up my boyfriend and his friends.

'My name's Octavia,' Freds replied in a falsetto voice that could break glass.

'Oh, my darling girl,' Miss Bibsmore cried out, almost weeping with joy as she tossed her stick to the floor and threw her arms around my boyfriend (who loved me) with an abandon I'd never seen. 'You've come back, Octavia. I knew you would. The others said you'd gone and got yourself preggers. Oh, you dear, dear, dear girl.'

After that she began to cry. 'This little poppet here was like a daughter to me an' all.' She gave Fred's cheek a big pinch. 'Then one day some horrible boy from Eades pitched up here on a motorbike, mind, and took 'er off. Never saw her again.'

'Heavens,' said Indie, still transfixed by Malcolm, *avec* makeup and all. It was obvious she fancied him like mad.

'But I'm back now, Miss,' Freds squeaked. 'I've only dropped in for the day, though – the little tot needs me now.'

'Oh, so the rumours were true,' Miss Bibsmore grumbled. 'But maybe that's for the best. A baby has clearly helped you to grow into a fine young woman, dear,' Miss Bibsmore said. 'Mind you, a girl with your looks and figure doesn't need all that muck on her face, in my opinion.' She patted Freds on the cheek.

'Seems like just yesterday, Miss,' Freds agreed, grinning stupidly.

'I could sit here and chat all day,' Miss Bibsmore said wistfully.

'Oh, please stay,' Malcolm begged in the most ridiculous attempt at sounding like a girl I'd ever heard. It took a lot of discipline not to grab Miss Bibsmore's stick and whack him with it, I can tell you. I don't know what he could have been thinking. Indie on the other hand seemed deeply impressed, as if Malcolm was some sort of really talented god-like boy and not the fool he clearly was.

'No, girls, I just dropped in to see how poor Calypso was getting on, but I can see she's not short of a friend or two, and for that I'm pleased.' She beamed at the boys as well as at Star and Indie as she said this. 'No, unfortunately, I've promised the nuns a game of poker and I can't let *them* down now, can I?'

'Octavia' and friends shook their heads as if saddened to miss out on the company of our house mistress.

Miss Bibsmore opened her arms expansively. 'Well, then, give your Bibby a big hug, eh Octavia? And next time I see you, I don't want to see all that muck on your face, innit.'

With that, our house mistress wrapped 'Octavia' in a big cuddle, said a tearful farewell and waved as she waddled off.

As the sound of her stick disappeared down the corridor, we all used pillows to smother our giggles.

'He's always popular with the old girls, is our Freds,' Malcolm teased.

Freds hit him with the pillow he'd been suffocating his laughter with and after that a pillow-and-duvet-and-anything-soft-we-could-lay-our-hands-on fight ensued.

Afterwards we kissed some more, but eventually the boys had to leave. Indie gave Malcolm a kiss, on the lips, when they were leaving, which of course meant a massive grilling from Star and me afterwards.

When Honey returned from Windsor later, she asked, 'Why is there makeup all over my pillow and duvet?'

But all we could do was laugh.

Nothing could spoil my high. Freds loved me!

NINETEEN

It's Your Love Life or Your Life!

It's funny, but these last couple of terms – since meeting Freds – I never imagined it could be possible to survive life without a mobile phone. Who would have thought that there were ways of struggling through? Fred's visit helped because now I was no longer plagued by guilt that I was an inconsiderate, mean and selfish girlfriend. Also, Portia was letting me use her phone, so that was a lot easier than trekking to the public phone box, but it still wasn't the same without txt messages to read and reread under the covers after lights out.

The real reason for my joie de vivre, though, was that Freds loved me.

Just to remind myself of this sublime fact I wrote it on my pencil case during double maths. When Star saw it, she thumped me with it over the head.

'Don't be such a lovesick puppy. You should be focusing on the essay competition,' she scolded.

'*Ow*,' I said, rubbing my head. 'I'm not going to have the brains left to focus on anything at this rate if you keep thumping me.'

Actually, I had thrown myself into the task of writing my essay. It started off quite well too, with all that pathos about being an American and coming from Hollywood and being packed off to boarding school, where I was tortured by Honey – all the obviously tragic things like that. I changed Honey's name to Sweetie, but otherwise it was all true, just as the competition rules dictated.

But then, when I started on the part about my parents and their breakup, I began to feel that I might be showing Bob and Sarah in a rather poor light. Bob was coming across in the essay as this self-obsessed brute who put his stupid old opus over and above his family, when clearly as a father and husband he should be loving and earning money to support us. But what could I do with only 3,000 words with which to depict my agony?

Sarah wasn't coming over too well in the essay, either. What with her regression issues, she was coming across as a bit of a spoilt child. I blamed the 3,000-word limit, which didn't allow me to explain how genuinely kind and generous she was. I began to ramble on about how in sickness and in health she always put me first, but that had made the essay too long, so I had to cut it out.

Eventually I showed what I'd written to Ms Topler.

Ms Topler and I have had our issues over the years. She thinks literature is Charlotte Brontë and other odd bores, whereas I think literature is Nancy Mitford. Come to think of it Nancy's best-selling book was a thinly veiled essay on her family. Then again, some of her relatives never spoke to her again after it was published.

The next day, Ms Topler collared me in the corridor on my way to chapel. She was rapturous in her praise. 'This is magnificent writing, Calypso. So real. So straight from the heart. So eloquent! Meaningful and simply dripping with pain.'

'So you don't think it might upset my parents . . . you know, all that talk of Bob's Big One and Sarah's self-interest?'

She laughed. 'Dear Miss Kelly, you are such a button. No, I don't think it reads as anything other than truly truthful and beautiful.'

'I mean, they are really kind people in their own mad way. But all parents are mad, aren't they?'

Ms Topler looked at me pityingly. 'Naturally you must cling to that delusion if it helps,' she replied, patting me on the head, but I heard her mutter, 'Poor dear Calypso.'

'What's that supposed to mean?' I asked hotly.

'Nothing, dear, and you're right. I'm sure they do love you. In their own selfish way,' she added sotto voce.

'And Sarah is a darling, really.'

'As I said Calypso, it is a real tribute to you that you always seek out the good in others. That is the nature of the creative soul.'

Portia had distinguished herself at the tournament in Brighton on Saturday, which meant Bell End softened his position towards me a little bit. When I say softened, he was still coming at me with two sabres and yelling things to me along the lines of, 'It's your love life or your life, Kelly! Your choice, my privilege! Hah, hah, hah!' My torso and arms now had a sort of blue mottled appearance – a look more fetching on a marble statue than a real, live girl, I suspect. I gathered from Portia that the scouts were still hot on the scent of Bell End's talent (me), and he was gearing up for the regionals in a big way.

After our practise session on Monday, Portia and I agreed that our training had taken on a sinister military aspect we weren't entirely comfortable with. And I don't just mean physically. I suppose this wasn't helped by Bell End referring to us as Sergeant Briggs and Private Kelly.

'Why can't I be a sergeant?' I asked, because, well, Private Kelly sounded a bit pervy to me.

'You'll get your stripes when you've earned them, Private. When you've shown your general that it's sabreur first, second and third for you. No boys, no life, git it?'

'Oh yes, I "git" it, Sir,' I replied petulantly.

'That's General to you, Private.'

'I suppose I always knew he was insane, but this is too much,' I said to Portia as we changed after practice.

'I love him. I think he's really determined to help us through the regionals, you know. Seriously, it's as if it's personal for him. How's your mother, by the way?' she asked, peeling off her breeches.

'Better,' I replied. 'I mean, she's found a job which she's really excited about. Only it's not writing. She's on the *Ricky and Trudie* show doing the "What's Happening in Hollywood" slot.'

Portia grimaced. 'Be careful, darling. If Honey gets wind that your mother's on a daytime television program, she'll torture you mercilessly. You know what a venomous snob she is about television. As far as she's concerned, it's right up there with High Street labels.'

'Or even as bad as people who don't have their own personal stylists?' I joked.

'Darling, I'm serious. She'll go for the jugular.'

After we showered, I headed off to the pet shed to give little Dorothy a run. Georgina was already there. 'Calypso, I heard about your mother. I'm really sorry.'

I looked at her dumbfounded. 'What's happened?' I asked, terrified she'd finally been carted off in a pram.

'Honey told me she's on some chavie television program. I stood up for you, of course. As if Sarah would do something as lame as that,' she told me. 'But she's telling everyone, darling. Here, hold Dorothy. She's been telling me about how much she misses you, haven't you bunnikins?'

I took my darling rabbit and stroked her softer-than-soft ears. She wriggled her nose and gave me a little nip. 'I think she wants a run,' I suggested. 'Have you fed her?'

'Yes, but only a bit. I hoped you'd come so you could

feed her the other half. But, darling, what are we going to do about Honey and these hideous rumours?'

'The thing is,' I began as Dorothy hopped happily about the pet run. 'It's true. Sarah *is* doing the "What's Happening in Hollywood" slot on *Ricky and Trudie*.'

Georgina laughed. 'Brilliant. I love that slot. I bet Honey's seethingly jealous that she's not on a show with "What's Happening" in the title. Let's all make a point of asking Miss Bibsmore to record it for us so we can watch it after prep. That way we can get one over on Honey and say how marvellous we think Sarah is. I bet Portia will be up for it.'

'Well, Clemmie will cheer for anything,' I agreed.

'This is going to be soooo cool!' Georgina laughed.

Sure enough, as soon as we saw Honey at supper she began going on about my plebbie mother and her chavie job. 'It's poor tragic Calypso we must rally around,' she opined to all the girls at our table, as if she really, really cared about me.

Everyone, apart from Clems, pretended to be as shocked as Honey was. Clemmie had to be led away by Arabella though, because she'd snorted her soup out her nostrils with uncontrollable laughter.

Miss Bibsmore had been only too delighted to oblige us with recording Sarah's slot. After prep, when she invited us to the television room to see Sarah's debut, Honey was caught on the back foot.

Sarah was wearing a bright red suit with enormous

shoulder pads, which must have excavated from the eighties. She'd also done something worryingly weird with her hair.

'Oh, poor Calypso,' Honey bleated. 'She looks like a tragic attempt at Jackie Collins.'

'I think she looks utterly Hollywood, darling,' Georgina insisted loyally.

'Quite,' Honey agreed as if she and Georgina were of the same mind.

Actually, it turned out Sarah wasn't as embarrassing as I feared she'd be. In fact, she seemed to have her Hollywood banter down pat as she spoke easily about Brad this and Tom that and Madonna the other. 'Of course Jude is lovely in person, but well, so many Hollywood men seem to think marriage and children are just another role they're playing,' she said at one point. I couldn't help thinking that this remark was meant more for Bob than poor Jude.

'Never mind, darling,' Honey soothed, when Sarah's slot ended. 'Your mother has to do what she has to do to make ends meet. We all know of your sad upbringing, and we forgive you. I'm sure no one of our world need ever know how low Sarah has stooped this time.' Then she gave me a cuddle.

I just kept chanting away to myself: Freds loves me, Freds loves me, Freds loves me. Then later on, I added a vicious and cutting diatribe about the cruelty of 'Sweetie' in my competition essay.

This essay was proving to be truly cathartic.

TWENTY

Saint Augustine's Fencing Army Engages the Enemy

Two marvellous things happened on Saturday. Firstly, my mobile phone privileges were reinstated. Secondly, Sarah (dressed as an American cheerleader, pom-poms and all), Sister Regina (who had made a sweet little knitted flag with 'Go Calypso and Port' embroidered across it – I guess she ran out of room for the 'I' and the 'A'), Bell End, Portia (Sergeant Briggs) and myself (Private Kelly) set off to Eades in the school mini-bus for the regionals. In other words, I was about to see Freds.

Freds, who loved me.

'So what's the deal with Freds, darling? Are we to run away or attack him this time?' asked Sarah conspiratorially.

Bell End blasted us before I could answer. 'Attack, of course. Always attack, attack, attack! None of my troops will be running away. Never heard such rot.'

'Actually, I really want you to meet him properly this time,' I told Sarah, who clapped her hands with glee. I hoped I was making the right decision.

'Right, Private,' said Bell End, 'You and the sergeant collect your kit. I'll head in and start the reconnaissance. In the event of any questions, Private, refer to your superior officer, in this case Sergeant Briggs.'

I rolled my eyes. Not just because of the madness he was spouting but because he was wearing a red beret and had some kind of riding crop made of plastic tucked under his arm like a real general's cane.

'I'm still the captain of this team,' I reminded him.

'This is a new game plan, Private. All carefully crafted while you were running around drunk as a skunk in robes with Eades boys. I won't brook any argument when it comes to strategy, understood?' He was glaring at me so hard I backed down. 'Sister and Sarah, you come in with me to act as cover,' he barked. 'And none of that banner business this time. We'll be presenting a professional dignified front in this battle.'

'Ooooh yes, Mr Wellend,' clucked Sister Regina, hiding her knitted flag behind her back. She was obviously madly impressed by General Bell End's new persona. Nuns are soooo guileless.

Registration passed without incident, and as soon as Portia – sorry, Sergeant Briggs – and I were kitted out we looked about for our boyfriends. There were probably about a hundred fencers in the hall. Between them, the presidents armed with clipboards, the gaggles of fan clubs and not to forget, Bell End's scouts and spies lurking ominously in the shadows (well, according to Bell End anyway) we couldn't see Freds or Billy before the pools were called.

Portia and I began our stretches while the names were read out. Bell End, Sarah and Sister stood by as unobtrusively as a short man in a red beret, a nun with knitted flag and a middle-aged woman in a teen cheerleader's outfit can. Portia and I both got a really high seeding, so that by the time the direct eliminations began the wind was truly in our sails. Because this was Eades and not Sheffield, I felt I had more of a reputation at stake. Jam-smeared banners were fine in a county I was unlikely to return to, but this was my manor – well, the manor I pulled fit boys from.

I won my first direct elimination bout, effortlessly dispatching seed number sixty-five at fifteen-one. And I only allowed her that one hit because I thought she was about to cry.

Portia won hers too, and Sarah and Sister began jumping with glee.

'Good show, Sergeant Briggs, Private Kelly. But don't let your guard down. Constant vigilance, as you never know what your enemy has planned. They set traps, these scum,' he warned, looking around at the friendly faces of the girls milling about the hall. 'Oh yes, I've been eavesdropping on some of the conversations, and they're a bloody nasty lot, these girls. As nasty a lot as you'll ever see.'

That was when a girl from Saint Leonard's came skipping over to say hi to Portia. 'Darling, I just got through by the skin of my teeth. How's Tarkie, I haven't heard from him for a –'

Bell End dived over, wedging himself between the two girls. 'Sergeant Briggs, go and join Majors Sarah and Regina. I won't have my troops subverted by the likes of you,' he growled at Portia's friend.

'Don't worry about him,' I told the poor girl as I led her away. 'He goes a bit mad during these competitions.'

'Bloody nutter. You should report him. And what's with that beret and the plastic magician's stick?' she asked.

'Yes, the beret is a new touch. It, erm, goes with the pom-poms on the cheerleader, though,' I told her, pointing out my mad madre's attire.

My next bout was with a much hardier opponent. I'd fenced her before in Sheffield and she knew my form as well as I knew hers. She was slighter and shorter than I and devilishly swift to boot. I had to stretch myself to the limit for every one of the hits I made. Eventually I clenched the victory at fifteen-thirteen, but I was bruised and tired at the end.

I went over to the refreshment table for a juice. Freddie was already there, looking pretty glum until he saw me with my sweaty hair plastered to my head.

'How's it going?' I asked, trying not to be shallow and

obsess on my sweaty, dishevelled appearance. I suspected it wasn't going well for Freds despite the fact that he looked as fit as ever and his hair was still doing that lovely sticky-up thing that always made my tummy flip.

'I'm already out, rinsed by a snotty little Harrovian.'

'At least it wasn't a Wimbledonian,' I offered, which made him laugh.

'I've got a break before the semi-finals,' I told him.

'Well, then, my champion, would you like to take a short perambulation around the back of the scoreboards. I hear that's where they fix the scores.'

'And hide from the scouts and spies,' I joked. I'd told Freddie all about my mad fencing master's paranoid delusions.

'Well, then, it's a duty more than a pleasure, really, when we think of it like that. Can't let these horrid spies go unchecked.'

So we snuck around the back of the hall, avoiding Bell End and company until we reached the large blackboard. It was only used for recording the scores of school matches, as it wasn't that big, but it provided the perfect hiding spot for a pulling session.

'I forgot how lovely you smell,' Freds told me as he drew me into his stinky neck – only it smelt lovely to me. I seriously doubted my smell was lovely, though. But the fact that he said it made me swoon with love for him even more, so I blurted, 'I love you!'

Freds pulled away from me, and for a horrifying moment I thought he was going to do a runner, he looked so baffled.

But he didn't run off, he just smiled and then wrapped his arms around me so hard that he lifted me off the ground. 'So does that mean I get a formal introduction to your mother?'

'How do you know she's here?'

'Something about the pom-pom-laden cheerleader dress.' He shrugged. 'She has that Kelly look about her.'

I don't know why this pleased me so much. I guess it was relief or something that I didn't have to hide such an important part of my life (Freds) from one of the most important people in my life. So I kissed him some more.

TWENTY-ONE

Pulling Princes

As our lips roamed over one another, I was vaguely aware of announcements being made, but I remained otherwise oblivious to everything apart from Freds. That is, right up until the point at which his lips were cruelly wrenched from mine by Bell End, who thwacked HRH with his stupid faux riding crop.

I mean, seriously, that had to be illegal for a start! Striking a royal presence?

I didn't need to seek confirmation on this. Freddie's security dived on my general and began beating him to a pulp. It was soooo unfair because Bell End didn't stand a chance. He was so small you couldn't even see him under Freddie's men. Not that a pileup of chino-wearing thugs with earpieces were going to shut our doughty general up.

He kept yelling, 'Subversion! Foul Play! Bad Form! Alert the BFA!' as he valiantly flailed about with his broken plastic riding crop. Eventually the stun guns and batons defeated him, though, and nothing more than the odd squeak could be heard.

'Freds! You've got to call them off,' I begged, clutching Freddie's arm. 'That's my general!'

Freds looked at me like I was insane. 'Your what?'

'My fencing master. Bell End.'

'Oh, right. Shit! Okay, chaps, that's enough,' he yelled, kicking the brutes on top.

'I'm really sorry, Calypso,' he said kissing my forehead as he kicked his thugs, 'but they have authority to act in what they consider my best interest in matters of security. It would seem they've assessed your general as a class-A threat. All we can do really is wait it out, and obviously I'll cover any, erm, medical requirements.' He gave his men a few more kicks with his foot, though.

The real salvation came in the form of Majors Sister and Sarah, who launched themselves on Fred's thugs with a professional level of violence that was really quite shocking. Within thirty seconds, Sister Regina had one of the guys in a headlock while Sarah began stuffing her pom-poms in his mouth.

By the time Sister and Sarah had called it a day, most of Fred's security guys had pom-poms up their noses and another was entwined in Sister's knitted flag. Another was nursing a bitten ear, although I think that might have been the work of Bell End.

The whole hall was gathered around our group by this stage.

Some idiot with a clipboard made a daft remark about Bell End and his friends bringing the sport into disrepute with their brawling, which only set Bell End (his beret now askew) off again.

'Freddie, this is my mother, Sarah,' I said (with a fair amount of pride, I might add) as I pushed her forward in her little mini-skirt.

Freddie took her hand, and Sarah simpered away as he kissed it. 'What a long awaited pleasure, Mrs Kelly.'

'Oh, call me Sarah, Your Royal Highness,' giggled my mad madre, giving Freds her best approximation of a curtsey while all around us fencers and their fans were dashing from piste to piste for matches and names that were being announced over the loudspeaker.

'Don't be so daft, Sarah,' Sister Regina told her gruffly, pulling her away. 'He's just like anybody else. He's not a saint, woman. Where's your Catholic pride?' Sister demanded. None of the nuns are particularly keen on boys or royalty, so Freds was not a hit with my little nun.

As I watched the two of them hitting it off, I couldn't for the life of me believe I was ever terrified of Sarah and Freds meeting. I guess knowing he loved me had made me more secure. They were flirting so ferociously I almost got jealous before I remembered that it was *me* he was pulling, not Sarah. I didn't get to witness their meeting for long, though, as my name was called and I had to weave my way through the crowds to the other end of the hall.

My opponent, her fan club lined up behind her, was already doing a few low lunges on the piste when I pitched up. As we sized up for the first play, I was still distracted by recent events. Then Freddie and Sarah turned up, and Freddie cupped his hands and called out, quite loudly so everyone could hear, 'Give me a C! Give me an A! Give me an L! Give me a Y! Give me a P! Give me an S! Give me an O! Goooooo Calypso!' And a few of my opponent's fans wolf-whistled at Sarah, who was doing her cheerleader stuff beside him.

At that point things became clear. I might not have a fan club the size of my opponent, but I had something better. I had a prince who loved me.

I shook hands with my opponent, unable to hold back my happiness. I was grinning from ear to ear as I told her I hoped she'd do brilliantly. This love business had somehow taken the killer instinct out of me. My opponent wasn't brimming with the same good will towards me, though. She squeezed my hand so hard it really hurt. 'Good luck, *bitch*, you're going to need it,' she warned me sweetly. There was something about her sickly faux sweetness which reminded me of Honey.

'Thanks for the warning, daaarling,' I replied sarcastically, dragging out 'darling' with as much contempt as I could. I wasn't going to be beaten by a toxic Honey-clone in front of Freds.

Fifteen points later, she was resplendent in her humiliation. And I told her so. 'Loosing becomes you, daaarling,' I whispered as we shook hands – right after she had said 'You were lucky, that's all!'

Lucky? Me? Hello, which one of us was writing an essay

on the great tragedies of her life? Me, that's who. Freddie swung me around and snog-aged. Then he held my sweaty face in his hands and said, 'Did I tell you I love you even more when you win?'

'Unhand that sergeant!' Bell End yelled. Only neither of us took any notice. I was only a private, after all. It was only when he began slapping us with his beret did we realise our mistake. Making it to the finals had apparently earned me a promotion. I was now a sergeant too.

We all repaired to the refreshment table, where Portia ran up to me and said, 'Guess what! I've made it through to the finals, darling! Can you believe it?'

'OMG! Me too!'

'Aaaah!' squealed Portia with an uncharacteristic loss of her aristocratic demeanour as we kept hugging one another and jumping up and down on the spot.

'This is huge!' I said. 'We're against each other!'

'I know, let's go to the loo,' she suggested.

We didn't stop to share our news but dashed and darted through the crowds and into the loos, where we splashed ourselves with water and gave one another blow-by-blow accounts of our triumphs. It was as if we were just about to play a practice bout or something. There wasn't a bit of competitive tension between us. Maybe because we'd got all that out of our system before half term?

'You do realise that this poses a rather nasty conundrum for our fans, though, Calypso.'

I put my hand over my mouth in horror. 'How's Bell

End going to abuse us? He just made me a sergeant, you know.'

Back at the refreshment table, Sister and Sarah were stuffing themselves with Battenberg cakes and tea, chatting to Freds ten to the dozen, crumbs flying everywhere.

'I watch your mother's television slot,' Freds told me.

'He thinks I'm really fit, which mean "hot,"' she explained, a blush spreading across her face. 'Apparently all the boys at Eades do – think I'm fit,' Sarah boasted, giggling like the teenager she so seriously wasn't.

'Well, you are a damn fine-looking woman, Major. Don't need a bunch of wet-behind-the-ears schoolboys telling yer that, do you?' Bell End remarked. He was wearing his beret again and had his silver Olympic medal out, but his little plastic stick was now in two parts, broken by the royal thugs. Even so, he looked very impressive.

'You're a handsome little chap yourself, Mr Wellend,' Sister Regina told him sweetly.

'We've been working on our battle chants,' Sarah whispered conspiratorialy to me. 'We don't want to favour either of you. I hope you don't mind, darling, but the general says that even though I'm your mother, I'm not to show favouritism.'

'No, of course,' I agreed happily.

'You do understand,' she added. 'Portia needs our support too.

'Fine,' I breezed, blissfully ignorant of what awaited us.

'Your fabulous legs run in the family, then,' Freds remarked sexily in my ear.

'Don't be so pervy. How dare you look at my mother's legs!' I teased.

'Well, there's not a lot else to look at, is there? I mean, to look at her, she's all legs.'

I looked over at my mother. He had a point.

When our names were called to the piste, Portia and I made our way there arm in arm. A phalanx of the fittest boys England has to offer had assembled in great numbers all around the piste, presumably with the intention of watching the final. I recognised Billy, Kev, Malcolm and a few others, but the mass was just soooo daunting.

Portia and I knew each other's form so well we could impersonate one another. As we pulled our masks down before the president had even called play, I knew that thought must be on Portia's mind too. We had the same master, we were one another's practise partners. We could match each other skill for skill. Portia's technique was flawless, and I knew that I would have to raise my thinking level beyond textbook tactics if that buzzer was to blare for me fifteen times.

There were no cheers or cries of abuse as we advanced. I emptied my mind and entered a state of pure focus in which all that existed was my blade and her blade. Portia knew only too well my preference for attack. I loved the aggression of sabre, whereas Portia had spent three years as an épéeist and loved a genius riposte. Her defence was flawless, and I knew she was relying on me to attack. So fighting aggressively against my friend in this bout would be playing to her strengths.

I had to draw her out with a bluff.

I straightened my arm to threaten her target area, but I didn't advance, goading her to attempt to clear my blade. As Portia stepped forward to beat my blade, I surprised her with a disengagement and landed a viper-quick strike to her wrist. The buzzer was the only applause required.

It was a tiring, strategic battle, fought almost as much in our minds as on the piste. It really was as Professor Sullivan, our old master, had always warned: a physical game of chess.

By the time the president called 'Fourteen, fourteen, bout point!' we were both drained physically and mentally. Everything hinged on the next three seconds, and yet behind my mask I was smiling. I was proud not just of myself but because whatever happened in the next few moments we were both going to the Nationals.

Portia's poise betrayed none of her strategic intent. But I knew that aloof demeanour now. I knew what she was about to do – or so I thought. I planned to draw her out again – after all, I was the aggressive fencer – but Portia surprised me. No sooner had the President called play than Portia leapt forward, delivering a terrifying volley of attacks, and though I parried successfully there was no way I could have landed a riposte. She was like a lunatic Samurai. Bollocks to her aloof demeanour, this was war.

With a flash of insight, I trapped her blade in an

envelopment, giving me that micro-second to plan my next move. Portia disengaged, readying herself for her next assault, but she'd betrayed herself, and it was too late. My blade flicked across her stomach in a deft attack she could never have anticipated. The buzzer trumpeted my victory, and the crowd erupted into tumultuous applause.

The president formalised my win. 'Fifteen-fourteen, victory Kelly.'

I tore off my mask, spraying my adoring crowd with a deluge of sweat as I saluted Portia with an old-world flourish, and then the president with the standard casual flick. Portia, her hair as disgusting as mine, ran forward, and dispensing with the formal handshake, swept me up in a toast cuddle. A cuddle that soon turned into a group hippie hug when Bell End, Sarah, Sister, Freddie and Billy joined us.

It was all so mad after that. The long prophesised scout materialised in the form of a be-suited BFA representative inviting Portia and me to try out for the British national team. Even Malcolm whisked me into a whirl. 'Miss Kelly, what a killer you turned out to be!'

'Thanks, Malcolm, that's really sweet.'

'So, thing is, can you give this DVD to that scrumptious friend of yours, Indie?'

'Yaah, sure,' I said, slightly dazed.

'Cool. See you round, then.' He waved as he turned to leave, and I watched his distinctive head of red hair disappear into the crowd.

It was all a whirl of congratulations, adulations and cup presentations after that. I had to stand on a stage for the ceremony as all the boys clapped for me. Freds was at the front with Portia and Billy, clapping and whistling madly. Bell End was sobbing uncontrollably with pride, although my mother and Sister Regina tried to console him. My only regret was how sweaty I was.

TWENTY-TWO

Sarah's Car of Shame

After the match, I wondered if I would ever get over such a high. Freds loved me. I loved Freds. I was going on to the Nationals and best of all, so was Portia. It was a fairy tale come true. Even Portia chucked her aloof demeanour that night back in the dorm for a celebratory party in Georgina, Star and Indie's room.

It was Tobias's idea. These things usually are.

'But I thought he'd given up drinking?' I remarked, referring to his recent bout in detox.

'He's fallen off the wagon, darlings,' Georgina explained, covering Tobias's ears. Her lower lip wobbled with the faux sorrow of it all. 'I think the best cure might be for him to let off a bit of steam, don't you?'

We most certainly did. Piling our tuck and Body Shop Specials in the middle of the room, Indie offered to do the DJ-ing, which essentially meant sticking CDs in her laptop. Soon everyone, including Portia, was dancing on the beds wildly. Honey took her usual dancing spot by the mirror so she could see herself better. Or as Star whispered in my ear, 'She's checking that she still has a reflection.'

Nothing could spoil our high that night. Even Miss Bibsmore was late doing her rounds. When she did pop her head in, all she did was tell us that while we deserved a 'bit of a party,' we should try and keep the noise down.

I had to concede that Honey said nothing bitchy to me all evening. Well, nothing at first. Even when I tried on Indie's cool mini-skirt and it was too tight around the hips. She even asked if she could cadge a ride from me to Windsor the next day. Sarah was picking me up to take me to lunch with Freds. That's why I was trying on Indie's clothes, to find something truly stupendous to wear.

'I want something that says I'm stunning and wonderful and lovable,' I explained to my friends.

'And I have a wonderful house in Clapham, darling. You must come and stay, Your Royal Highness. We'll get out our best serviettes and you can sit on the lounge and watch some chav telly,' Honey added in a common accent.

I knew I'd been naive to think she could resist taking the piss forever.

'You do such a great chav accent, darling,' Star marvelled. 'Scarily good in fact. Are you sure you don't have a little chav blood in your gene pool?'

Honey looked like she wanted to mace Star, but instead all she did was laugh as if she thought Star were really funny. Then she turned to me and said, 'So, you and the adorable Sarah are lunching with Freds tomorrow, are you?'

'We're meeting up for a pizza, if that's what you mean by "lunching,"' I said.

'Poor Sarah.' Honey sighed, pausing presumably to think up what her next spiteful remark could be.

'I love Sarah,' Georgina interrupted as she danced around the room with Tobias, who was already pretty tipsy by the look of him. 'She's cool. Tobias adores her too,' she added as she did a dance spin with Tobias and fell dizzily onto the floor. 'He's a marvellous dancer, but I think he's had too much to drink,' Georgina continued, which I think was her way of changing the subject. Georgina is about the only person Honey is scared of. Georgina said that's because she knows where the bodies are buried. Star used to say that's because Georgina helped her bury them. But that was before Star decided that Georgina was cool, after all.

We finally went to bed around midnight, but Portia and I were still too high to go to sleep, so we went over and over our triumphs of that day, speculating on what the Nationals would be like and trying not to get too over-excited in case we didn't do well.

On Sunday we had a full fry-up for breakfast. Portia and I were eating loads more than we were used to, but all I seemed to do was get skinnier and taller.

After Mass finished at one, Sarah arrived in the car of shame to pick up me, Portia and Honey. Portia was lovely and gracious, of course, but Honey was sooo Honey, I could have thumped her.

Actually I could have thumped Sarah too, when I saw what she wearing.

Okay, I love her. She's the best, but a powder blue floral skirt and matching jacket with a powder blue handbag and pillbox hat?

'Have you been to Oxfam, Sarah?' I asked crossly.

'What are you talking about, Calypso?' Sarah replied, patting the monstrosity on top of her head. But as she looked around the faces of everyone milling around us, the gravity of her mad outfit began to sink in. 'Honey called me last night and told me that it was royal protocol to, erm, dress like the queen when meeting royals.'

Honey giggled.

Portia said nothing.

'Royal protocol?'

We were standing beside the car of shame in the car park where taxis were pulling in to pick girls up for trips into Windsor. Honey wasn't the only person laughing.

Actually the only people *not* laughing were Portia, Sarah and myself. Even the taxi drivers gathered in the forecourt were having a good chuckle.

Sarah was clearly flustered, and with everyone pointing and giggling she began to cry.

I turned on Honey. 'You are such a bitch,' I told her. 'How dare you torture my mother, you sick psycho toff.'

Honey began filing her nails. 'Don't you hate cuticles, darling? I mean, what do they even do?' she asked.

Portia spoke up before I could grapple the file off Honey

and stab her with it. 'Sorry, Sarah, sorry, Calypso, but I forgot something. I'll be back in one minute. Don't leave without me,' she said before dashing back into the dorm.

'Don't worry,' I said, between clenched teeth, 'The only person we'll be leaving without is *you*,' I told Honey.

Honey rolled her eyes. 'God, I was only joking. Who would have thought anyone could be soooo stupid as to believe that you have to dress like the queen to eat pizza with the prince?'

Poor Sarah. 'Look Mummy, you get in the car while we decide what to do. Honey, you bugger off.'

'Don't be insane, I'm coming into Windsor with you. You've offered me a lift, and if I don't go with you, I'll have no one to go with.'

'Good,' I told her as I climbed into the car and slammed the door, locking her out.

Honey was banging on the car doors when Portia returned. I let her in on the other side and she chucked a pair of jeans and a hoodie over to Sarah. 'You can wriggle into these in the car. You can pull over at Windsor Great Park – you know, where they play polo before we turn off into Windsor. I've brought some trainers too. My feet are enormous so anyone can fit into them, more or less.'

'Oh, thank you Portia, dear. You really are a super girl. I won't forget this.'

'Just drive, Mummy,' I told her.

Honey was still banging on the window of the car of shame as we drove out of the car park. It was with some satisfaction that I watched her run into a puddle as she was chasing us down the gravel drive.

Lunch was perfect. Freds found everything about Sarah hilarious – in a good way. Even when she started explaining to him about leaving Bob, he was really sweet and sympathetic. I was ashamed that I had been embarrassed of my mother. He even asked Sarah for a signed photograph of herself to pin on his board. 'You're quite the star at Eades at the moment. Malcolm records your Hollywood slot, and we all watch it. Your interview with Tom Hanks was hilarious, especially when you kept asking him about his interest in Scientology.'

'I get my Toms confused.'

'Easily done,' Freds agreed.

After pizza, Sarah was so cool she even went off to look at the shops so that Freds and I could spend some 'quality time' together. I still couldn't believe I had been such a paranoid bitch, not wanting her to meet my boyfriend. I have the best mother in the world, even if she does drive the car of shame.

TWENTY-THREE

The Clapham Commoners

Unfortunately the car of shame wasn't big enough to squeeze in Star, Indie, Georgina, Tobias, Portia, Clemmie, Arabella, Honey, all the pets and me on our journey to London on the exeat weekend. So Sarah picked us all up in a fleet of taxis, and we rode to Clapham on the train.

Sarah chatted away happily about what she'd done to the house. 'You're going to love it, Boojie,' she enthused. 'It's right on the Common,' she added.

I was stroking Dorothy, so I missed the look on Honey's face as she giggled.

'How perfect that a commoner like you should live on the Common.'

'Yes, isn't it? Those houses are as rare as hens' teeth,' Sarah explained, missing the jibe.

Honey couldn't stop giggling, so Star draped Brian over her, which calmed her right down. 'I think he likes you,'

Star said as she menaced Honey's nose with Brian. Honey's sharp intake of breath was hilarious. It wasn't often we got a treat like this.

We got off the train at Waterloo and took two black cabs to Clapham. As we wound our way into the area, I noticed a strong police presence and notices asking for information on murders and rapes. Honey opened the window and waved to the bobbies on their beat.

'Darling,' she said to me, 'what a lovely area, and imagine, you even have your own police force in bullet-proof armour.'

I ignored her and pretended I was txt-ing Freds, which I wasn't, because I'd already sent him a txt he hadn't replied to yet, and I didn't want to appear tragic.

As we pulled up in front of the largest house on the Common, I was struck by how lovely it looked. Honey was delighted too as she moaned. 'Oh dear, Victorian architecture. How pokey. I can't bear modern architecture. Anything post-Georgian makes me cringe,' she groaned, visibly shivering.

'Wow,' Georgina gasped as she climbed out of the cab with Tobias. 'It's really big.'

Tobias looked impressed too.

Sarah was excited as she opened the door and ushered us all in. 'Isn't this super, our first official house party!' She giggled like a small girl.

'I'd hardly call it a house party,' Honey sneered as she

cast her gaze around the lack of marble floors and wall-to-wall antiques.

'I've tried to make it comfy,' Sarah explained.

'I can tell,' replied Honey, picking up a Galle replica lamp and grimacing.

'Oh cool, a plasma television and DVD,' Indie said, rushing over and looking through the collection of DVDs. 'Sarah, is this the show you worked on in the States?'

'Yes, it was nothing wonderful, I assure you, Indie, but it paid the fees.'

Honey enveloped Sarah in a hug. 'Poverty must be so harsh, Sarah. I can tell that just by looking at the enormous pores on your skin. I can't imagine the envy that must wrack your every waking moment. Always knowing that you will never amount to anything, no matter how hard you try. Mediocrity is the death of creativity, Mummy says.'

'Oh, so that's how your soul died, is it, darling?' Star asked. 'Actually, Honey,' she added looking at her watch, 'isn't it time for your formaldehyde injection?'

Honey was as ever a little slow with her comeback, and Star was pulling off her Doc Martens boots and flopping on the big, squishy white sofa by the time Honey made her sneering retort.

Everyone ignored her. Indie was busy loading one of Sarah's DVDs into the player, and everyone else was snuggling up on the sofa to watch. Eventually Honey announced: 'I could murder a G & T. Do you have staff,

Sarah, or will you have to prepare it for me yourself?' I almost giggled at her attempt at a sympathetic pout.

Sarah wasn't taking any more nonsense from Honey, though. 'I'll need to see your ID before I can do that, Honey. I don't support underage drinking, and while you're in my home you'll live by my rules.'

'Fine,' Honey snapped. 'You tragic Americans. I don't know how you put up with yourselves. Have you never heard of the word "hospitality"?'

Sarah ignored her.

'Oh, all right I'll get it myself! Where's the kitchen?' she demanded, flouncing out of the room.

I made a sign to Sarah to ignore her. I couldn't bear the thought of putting up with Honey and my poor madre at loggerheads all weekend. If a drink would slow down Honey's brain, a drink she must have.

Sarah was catching on. 'Oh, I am sorry, Honey,' she called out. 'But without the staff to show me around, I haven't managed to find the kitchen yet.'

Everyone (apart from Honey) laughed at this, especially me. The weekend was getting off to a rather good start.

Later, Georgina insisted we all check out the house. 'Come on, Sarah, show us around,' she begged, pulling Sarah up off the sofa. 'Tobias is a real sticky beak, so you'll have to lock up anything you don't want him to poke about in.'

'And can we let Dorothy, Brian and Hilda wander around, Sarah?' Star enquired.

'Hilda is the, erm, rat, isn't she?' Sarah asked lightly, but I could tell she was slightly anxious.

'Well, theoretically. She's madly bright, though. You should see her on her little wheel,' Star told her as she pulled Hilda from her pocket.

I could tell Sarah wanted to scream, but instead she reached out bravely and gave Hilda a little stroke on the head and even managed to limit herself to a little yelp when Hilda bit her.

'See, she adores you,' Star said, and as Hilda was already scuttling around the sofa, there wasn't much Sarah could do or say. 'And Brian will just follow us about,' Star added. 'He's desperately dependent and clingy, you see.'

'Clingy!' Sarah shrieked. 'Is that safe?'

Star smiled her most adorable rock chick smile – the one that showed her tongue piercing. 'Oh, Sarah, you are soooo funny. Brian's the cuddliest snake you could hope to meet.' The next minute Brian was draped around Sarah's shoulders like a feather boa, and Sarah didn't seem to mind. Instead she said brightly, 'Let's have that tour.'

The house turned out to be enormous. Not all the rooms were furnished, which suited us fine as we decided to use the biggest one as our sleepover room. Indie suggested we just lay down duvets and pillows. Sarah was delighted at Indie's suggestion and offered to add an Arabic theme with rugs and bowls of Lebanese sweets.

We'd arranged to meet up with Billy, Kev, Freds and Malcolm on the KR. Given my poverty, I suggested we take the bus, as if that might actually be fun, cramming in with a lot of strangers on a freezing bus in our skimpy mini-skirts and heels.

Sarah gave us directions, but our lack of street-smart savvy landed us miles away. Honey was whining, of course, but so was Tobias, who can't bear being lost. Even Indie lost her temper, and told off her security guys for being incompetent. Our mood wasn't helped by the drug-warning boxes perched on lampposts which blared out threatening messages about the dangers of finding ourselves in prison should we wish to purchase drugs.

'I'd like to purchase some drugs,' Honey declared. 'I wonder if that nice man over there in the baggy trousers and balaclava on his head could help us? As he's your neighbour, Calypso, perhaps you should ask?'

I didn't deign to reply, but I had to admit the area *was* pretty dodgy in parts. Smart, gentrified houses and chichi boutiques were cheek to jowl with council estates and crack dens and not a black cab in sight. Eventually we climbed on a bus, but we were half an hour late for the boys, who had already finished off their lattes by the time we caught up with them in one of the seventy-two Starbucks on the KR.

After the compulsory air kissing we headed off down the KR, Freddie and Indie had their security guys stay a decent distance away from us, but they seemed incapable of blending in and kept bumping into us and stumbling over one another.

After a while they began to get on Indie's nerves. 'You look like something out of *Reservoir Dogs*. Can't you at least try and blend in a bit?' Indie demanded crossly.

Even though I was getting used to being trailed by security guards, I didn't think I'd like having to live with them, especially during breaks, when a girl needed to pull a boy. And Indie was definitely determined to pull Malcolm.

Between all of us we knew every second person we passed. My lips got quite numb with all the *mwah-mwah-mwah*-ing we did. We went into the Cadogan Arms so that Honey could satisfy her craving for a drink, and then we went to Partridges to find some more trendy outfits that we could share.

The boys were coming back to Clapham with us, and Freds had the bright idea that it might be fun to try public transport. Malcolm came up with the bright idea of disguising themselves and their security guys with lipstick and eye shadow. I suppose it *was* quite funny. Also it reminded me of the day Malcolm, Kev and Freds had scaled the scaffolding of our dorm house and disguised themselves as girls to fool Miss Bibsmore.

I don't know whose bright idea it was to get off at the wrong stop, but suddenly we were on Landor Road. Problem was, we'd left the security guys on the bus!

'We should wait for them, I guess,' Freds groaned, kicking listlessly at a used syringe on the street.

'They're big boys. They can take care of themselves.

Besides, they've been really irritating me today,' Indie insisted, looking at Malcolm as she spoke.

Malcolm was looking at her as he had been all day. 'We'll take care of you,' he said, putting a protective arm around her. Only clearly he meant *he* planned to take care of her. She fluttered her eyelashes at him.

Freds noticed the chemistry between them too and gave my hand a squeeze. We wandered off in the direction in which the bus had vanished. At the corner, under a lamp that had had its light smashed out, we were offered drugs by a large guy with gold teeth and a hoodie pulled up over his head, Gandalf-style.

The drug-warning box we walked past was still operational and cheerfully chiming, 'You can be imprisoned for both possession and intent to supply illegal substances. Please report any drug activity to the police.'

'Skunk weed, crack?' offered Gandalf.

Malcolm turned around pleasantly and asked, 'What is skunk weed exactly?' Gandalf looked him up and down as if Malcolm were a bone he might want to chew. I began to feel scared. 'Only is it weed or is it a specific type of weed?' he probed.

'Are you shitting me, bro?' Gandalf asked, coming toward our little group with menace. He stuck his face right up against Malcolm's. 'Because I is warning you now, sunshine. I don't like to be shit.'

'No, well, I imagine you wouldn't,' agreed Malcolm in a friendly enough way. 'But I assure you that shitting you was never my intention,' he added, all easy charm. He was clearly oblivious to any sense of danger.

Freds and Billy tried to pull Malcolm away.

Star, Georgina and the rest of us – apart from Honey – lurked in the background nervously. Well, I was nervous. Star looked quite relaxed with Brian slung around her neck like a feather boa. I suppose this was all perfectly normal for the daughter of Tiger from Dirge. In fact I think one of his big hits was titled "Scoring Skunk."

'Come on, man,' Billy urged, tugging on the hood of Malcolm's Ralphie.

'Poncy little shit,' snarled Gandalf, grabbing the front of Malcolm's Ralphie. That was when I realised that there were a few other Gandalf clones lurking around other lampposts nearby. Then Gandalf pulled his other hand out of his pocket and I saw the gold of the knuckle duster glint as he pulled his fist back to smash Malcolm's face.

I was about to scream when Honey suddenly came forward and maced Gandalf – scoring a direct hit. But all the mace did for Gandalf was what the Febreze had done for me. It teared him up a bit, but didn't completely incapacitate him. He was still holding Malcolm and now calling loudly for his brethren. So Honey maced him again, only this time she was inches away and taking a bit of a risk if you ask me. But she was as relaxed as could be as she emptied the contents of the mace can into Gandalf's face.

Howling in pain, the guy eventually let go of Malcolm

and we all legged it down the road – the brethren and their injured brother in hot pursuit. For such big guys they could run pretty fast, too. One of them collared Kev and was about to launch his fist in his face when Honey smashed one of her Jimmy Choos on his head over and over again. Another of them got hold of Malcolm, but Indie jumped on his back, giving Malcolm the chance to smash his forehead into the guy's nose.

The security men eventually arrived in time to use their stun guns on the dozens of Gandalf brethren flooding out of a nearby council estate armed to the teeth with knives and God knows what else. 'Get out of here, will you!' one of the security guys yelled at us.

So we legged it, closely followed by a number of Gandalfs, but all those cross-country runs we'd been tortured with over years were starting to make sense now. I guess drugs had depleted the Gandalfs' level of physical fitness because they were slobs compared to the girls of Saint Augustine's and the boys of Eades. Even the security guards had more breath in them than the Gandalfs – one of whom even resorted to using a Ventolin spray, he was wheezing so badly.

We finally lost them after about a hundred yards. The security guys were not impressed with us, but they were sensible enough to take us into a café and get some sweet tea into us.

We all piled into the loo at the café to clean ourselves up and fix our hair. As we were coming out we bumped into the boys, who'd all been preening themselves as well. Poor Malcolm had a torn shirt. 'Don't worry about it. I've got dozens,' he replied when Indie began to fuss.

'There is no way we can let Sarah know about what just happened, guys, okay?' I insisted.

'Why not?' Honey asked. 'She does live here. They may well be her friends,' Honey suggested.

And just when I was starting to like her for saving us from Gandalf.

'Don't be more of an idiot than you already are, Honey,' Freddie told her firmly, and she relented sulkily, even going so far as to admit she was only joking.

Sarah threw open the door to us and sang, 'Hel-lo! I was just about to call out a search party,' she joked in blissful ignorance. 'How was your day?'

We all answered, 'Super!'

Malcolm elaborated with fanciful tales of ambassadors and caviar, which made Indie giggle. But I could tell by the looks passing between the security guys that they wanted to throttle Malcolm and Honey and quite possibly the rest of us.

As I sat there watching Honey going along with our ruse to keep the fight from Sarah, I was impressed. Could this be a new side of Honey?

'So you caught up with lots of friends, then?' Sarah enquired directly of Honey.

'Oh yes, Sarah,' Honey agreed gleefully. 'And some of your neighbours,' she added.

Everyone glared at her, imagining she was about to blow our cover.

'Air kisses all round,' Honey simpered. 'In fact, Glasgow kisses for some, wasn't it, Malcolm?' she added just to make us squirm, I think.

'Oh, Malcolm, what are you like?' Sarah teased, completely oblivious to the undertones of the conversation and probably ignorant of what a Glasgow kiss even was.

'Been to Glasgow, then, have you, Honey?' Malcolm asked – obviously joking.

'Darling? *Moi* go north of the M25?' Then she did that horrible laugh she does where her collagen lips bubble up. And like everyone, I breathed a sigh of relief. Honey had definitely saved our butts on the street and she was even playing along to protect Sarah from the truth. Yet deep down she was still the Honey we knew and love/hated and, funnily enough, I took an odd sort of comfort in that.

I could tell Star was thinking the same thing because she winked, first at me and then at Georgina, Portia and even Tobias while Sarah explained the games she'd set up all over the floor: Twister, Cluedo, Hungry Hungry Hippos – a whole variety of babyish games. Bless, I thought, determined not to be embarrassed.

'I thought we might all play some games?' she suggested excitedly.

'Cool,' agreed Malcolm. 'I love Hungry Hungry Hippos.'

And it *was* cool. I don't think I've ever laughed so hard

as when Freds' and Indie's security guys fell into a tangled Twister heap.

The only downside of the whole weekend was that I didn't get to kiss Freds – well, not nearly enough.

TWENTY-FOUR

Bob's Big Bombshell

After such a wonderful weekend with Sarah, I felt the need to write to Bob. Sarah had gone from a reverting infant to a brilliantly independent woman (with a bit of help from Bunny, whom I heard her speaking to on the phone). Despite all her reverting and madness, I was really proud of my mother for managing to set up a house, land a job in a country where she had no professional history, get fired and land another job which had transformed her into a minor celebrity. And all the way through she'd been there for me, taking me to lunch, supporting my fencing and impressing my friends and boyfriend.

And where was Bob during this transformation? Swanning around like an eighteenth-century dandy, draped over his wretched script, all thoughts of family responsibility forgotten. Even Freds hinted that he thought Bob was a loser.

And I couldn't have that.

Either Bob was going to have to sort himself out, or I was

going to give Sarah my full support. Which meant giving Bob the boot. I think writing my essay had helped to stimulate my sense of injustice. Every night at prep after I'd done my course work, I tackled the edits Ms Topler had suggested for my essay. I think it was when I was writing about Bob humiliating me at the navel-piercing shop in Beverly Hills that I realised I had to confront him properly. Face-to-face, even. The arrogance of the man knew no bounds, and he needed to be brought down a peg or two.

Dear Father,
Enough is enough. The only good thing you had going for you (Sarah) has set up a lovely home in a rapidly gentrifying area of London and is presenting a really cool show and is admired by teenage boys everywhere as the hottest woman on television. I plan to advise Sarah to divorce you because you suck and Sarah rocks. Put that in your script!
Yours sincerely,
Calypso

PS: Not that you'd care, but I won the regionals and this Saturday I intend to win the Nationals at the Crystal Palace Sports Centre, which happens to be where the British Olympic team trains and Sarah will be there supporting me. She has been cheering me on at every match since she moved over here while you've been self-absorbed and unfeeling.

I studied my expertly crafted email for some time, making a few minor adjustments. Bob had an eagle eye when it came to lapses in grammar. He could bang on for hours about the imperfect past participle as used in England. He should have married Ms Topler – she would have given him a run for his money. When I was sure it was just right, I pressed 'Send,' revelling in the note of defiance as the mouse clicked.

I was about to go back to my essay about the great tragedy that was my life when I got a response from Bob.

> Congratulations darling,
> [Darling indeed, if he thought he could sweeten me up with darlings he had a huh and a half coming his way!]
> I am thrilled that both you and Sarah are flourishing in England. I am so thrilled in fact that I have just decided to come to the tournament on Saturday to see my little girl trounce the competition.
> Your loving father,
> XXX Bob

Oh bugger. How dare he abuse my stern, reprimanding e-mail, which was meant to make him *très* remorseful and depressed, and use it as an excuse to inflict himself on poor Sarah and stress her out just as she was starting to enjoy herself again. Bob's presence at the Nationals could be catastrophic. Stupid, stupid Calypso, for even mentioning the tournament, I scolded myself. If Bob did carry out his threat and come to the tournament and distress Sarah, it would be all my fault. I had to do something! I had to stop this.

But first I had to write a lot of really mean things about him in my essay. My fingers moved like a righteous gale over the keyboard as day after day I poured my feelings into the essay. When it was finished, I was quite proud. Any guilt I may once have harboured over my exposing my family as dysfunctional had dissolved. Just like my enthusiasm for the Nationals, I realised. After all, how could I face the Nationals with Bob there upsetting Sarah?

If Bob turned up, I was going to have to keep him away from Sarah at all costs. I decided to enlist the General to fight the good fight. Bell End was a man who didn't flinch in battle and, more importantly, he loved a paranoid delusion like no one else.

That night, while Honey was visiting her horrid sister, Poppy, I shared my fear with Portia about Bob coming to the Nationals.

Portia was more circumspect than I about the Bob thing. 'If he's so broke, how can he afford to fly out here? And where would he stay? I doubt Sarah is going to take him back. She strikes me as being an extremely determined woman.'

'But how can I risk it? I can't focus on my fencing knowing my father and mother are involved in their own field of combat across the arena somewhere. And Sister Regina is too tiny to help.'

'Darling, you're being silly. Don't you recall what Sister did to Fred's security guards? One of them was still wearing a plaster on his nose last weekend.'

I giggled at the memory. 'This isn't funny,' I told her.

She giggled too. 'It is, really.'

'I'm thinking of telling Bell End tomorrow.'

'I don't think that's a good idea,' she advised as Honey returned to our room.

I knew I was right to tell Bell End, though.

'It's the bloody BFA!' he hissed. 'They've put him up to it, I'll be damned. They've been trying to bring me down since I won this silver,' he snarled, brandishing his medal at me.

'No, actually I don't think you understand what I'm trying to explain, sir. I mean General. Bob, that's my father, and Major Sarah, well, we can't let them meet at the Nationals! It will traumatise not just Sarah but, well, everyone actually.' *Me especially*, I wanted to say.

'Bloody fine little woman, your mother. No, you leave it to me, Kelly. This goes deeper than some petty marital dispute. I've seen this sort of thing before, girl. Subversion on an impressive scale. You're still a neophyte to the ways of the BFA.'

'A what?'

'A kindergartener.'

He was insane.

Portia was right. I shouldn't have told him about Bob.

He patted me on my head – no mean feat, as I towered a

good six inches above him. 'You let me look after little Sarah. I'll keep this bastard Bob at bay.'

Portia came into the salle then, so our conversation was cut short, but I don't think prolonging it would have made me feel more confident.

'Right, get changed and we'll begin the drill. I can feel the spirit of Jerzy Pawlowski in the salle today, girlies.'

As we dashed towards the changing rooms, Portia joked, 'How many ways of moving forward do you have?'

But I couldn't even pretend to joke that day. The usual good humour a girl feels during the last week of Christmas term was noticeably absent for me. Not even the ebullient mood of Ms Topler as I handed in my completed essay on the last day of term had lightened my mood.

Apart from the overseas students, all the other girls had already left for the Christmas break – Portia and I had been given special permission to stay over Friday night due to the Nationals. The school felt eerily empty by Friday evening as Portia and I helped Bell End load the mini-bus, so we all jumped when Ms Topler came running out side.

'Dear child, dear, dear Miss Kelly! I wept.'

'Oh, I'm sorry,' I told her, wondering what I'd done to upset her.

'No no no, I wept tears of sorrow!' She insisted, as if this were a good thing. 'I wept tears of helplessness. I wept tears of horror.'

I knew she was referring to the essay now, but horror?

Maybe I had over-egged the pudding of my tragic life a little too much.

'Yes, and finally I wept tears of pride at the tribute to literature that you placed in my hands this morning,' Ms Topler praised.

'Stand away from the bus!' Bell End yelled as he manoeuvred our fencing kits in. Then he muttered something about saboteurs being everywhere. 'Only authorised fencers, Ms Topler.'

'Oh, I see. Well I'll bid you good night, then,' she replied awkwardly. 'But thank you, Calypso. I just wanted to praise your work and to assure you that I know brilliance when I read it, and what's more, I know you're going to win this competition.'

'Of course she's going to win. Haven't bin training her up to lose, yer silly woman!' Bell End yelled at my poor English literature teacher.

'Thank you, Ms Topler,' I called out as she ran towards the safety of the school.

TWENTY-FIVE

Bob at Bay

Sister Regina sat up front with Bell End on the short drive to Crystal Palace sport's centre in London. Sarah was going to meet us there, as it wasn't that far, coming from Clapham. I wished now that I hadn't been so specific about where the Nationals were being held.

As we drove past the long rows of suburban houses under Heathrow's busy flight path, I wondered if Bob had already flown in. Maybe he was already here, lurking in London somewhere?

'So, have you got a photograph of this father of yours, Kelly?' asked Bell End.

'Yes,' I admitted, passing a snap taken last summer, when all had been rosy and cosy at chez Kelly.

'Are you certain you want to light the fuse on this?' Portia asked me quietly as Bell End grabbed my photograph and stuck it on the rearview mirror.

'See this man here, Sister?' He jabbed at my father's smiling face.

Sister perched her pince-nez on her nose and peered at

the friendly face of Bob. He was wearing shorts and t-shirt at the beach, his arm around Sarah and me.

Sister Regina studied the photograph for some time before exclaiming. 'Oh, that's our lovely Sarah. Doesn't she look tanned? And soooo slim too. What a wonderful figure she has for a woman her age, don't you think, Mr Bell End?' Poor Sister was starting to pick up on our nickname for our master.

'I'm not interested in the blasted woman's legs, Sister,' he snapped gruffly. 'It's the man beside her.' He jabbed at my father's face again. 'Kelly's father. He intends to disrupt the finals, Sister. Sabotage us. Ruin everything. We've got to stop this man.'

Sister turned around. Her elderly face creased with years of fervent prayer and kindness.

'Is this true, Calypso? Does your father wish us ill?'

'Well, you know how my mother's left him?'

Sister nodded. 'A very sad business, although talking to Sarah I feel a great sense of love for your father inside her. And regardless of Sarah's sadness over Bob's Big One, why would your own father want you to do badly, dear?'

I blushed, worried now that I'd started Bell End off – and he was not a man to be held back. 'That's not really the point, Sister. It's just that I know it will upset Sarah seeing him at this stage, and oh, I don't know. She's had such a tough time settling back in England, Sister. And now she's finally on her feet, I don't want him bullying her.'

Sister peered more closely at the photograph. 'But he looks like such a kind man, Calypso.'

'Kind, my foot,' said Bell End gruffly. 'Man's out to sabotage us, Sister. You have to leave sentiment out of the bloody thing. Do you want our girl to fail? Do you want Major Sarah upset?'

'Oh! No, General. Dear Calypso, no. We can't have that,' Sister agreed. 'I was just saying he looks like such a nice man. But of course if he intends to muck our Sarah about or interfere with Calypso's sporting achievements, he'll meet with fierce resistance from me, General.'

'I wouldn't be surprised to learn he's been despatched by one of the competitors in a dirty-tricks campaign,' Bell End muttered.

'Isn't that a bit elaborate, Mr Wellend?' Portia asked reasonably.

'You don't know what elaborate means, Briggs. They'll stoop to anything. This is the Nationals. If you girls get through, you'll be invited to try out for the National Team. We're talking big money, not just prestige. There will be sponsorship deals; Adidas, Leon Paul, everyone will be after you. The world will be your oyster. There's a lot of money and status involved here. And people are more than happy to get their hands dirty for the sake of that as I know only too well.'

'Yes, but Mr Wellend, we're talking about Calypso's father, Bob,' Portia reminded him reasonably. 'Not a BFA saboteur!' Under her breath, she added, 'If they even exist.'

'Look,' I said, trying to steer things round to the real

issue. 'I just don't want Sarah upset today, okay? Despite her own problems, she's backed me all the way this term. She's really excited about today, and I don't want Bob upsetting her.'

'Good woman is Sarah, solid gold. All right, Kelly, leave it to Sister and me. We won't let this Bob geezer get a look in, will we, Sister?'

'No, Mr Wellend. We don't want our dear Sarah upset. I'm knitting her a lovely little mauve collar.' With that she held up her knitting, and sure enough the beginnings of something mauve and ghastly were already emerging. Knowing Sarah, she'd wear it too. Bless.

'So, you just focus on your form, Kelly. Leave the externals to us. Now, how many ways of moving forward have you got, girls?'

Portia and I replied, 'As many as we need,' and were rewarded with a rare laugh from our fencing master.

Freds had sent me a txt that morning wishing me luck, but I hadn't expected to see him at the event. But there he was, waiting patiently for us, along with Billy and Malcolm under the arch. I could make out his gorgeousness as we made our way on the long walk down towards the arch of the sports centre.

Despite its name, Crystal Palace wasn't really a palace, nor was it made of crystal. But it was a massive complex and Freds looked dwarfed as he leaned against the arch with his friends. As he was about to give me a hug, Bell End dropped our kit and grabbed Freds by the collar of his

Ralphie. 'I've got other business today, Sonny, but I've got your face etched in my mind, filed under 'enemy,' so don't think I'm off my guard.'

'Right, sir, I'll keep that in mind,' Freddie replied, calmly rearranging his collar.

Malcolm, who had been smoking a cigarette, flicked it on the ground and put it out with his foot. He extended his hand to Bell End. 'McHamish,' he said warmly.

'Just watch your step, mister. I've got your number so I don't need your name, git it?'

Billy didn't say anything.

Sister gave Malcolm a shy little wave. 'Aren't you a good-looking bunch of chaps? Would you like a biscuit?' She produced a tin of biscuits from under her voluminous habit. 'Sister Michael made them, so I don't recommend you try too many. The last batch she made tasted like worms. She always overdoes the coconut. Hangover from the war.'

The boys turned down her offer politely and smiled at Portia and me. Then our uneasy little party wandered through to reception, where the noise of the crowds milling round and running about was deafening. The arched ceilings made everything echo ominously. I felt like a tiny ant as I joined the queue with Portia to have our names ticked off.

After registration, I took Freds aside for a word about Bob. He was really sweet and assured me not to worry. Billy was still going through registration, so Freds called Malcolm over and the mug shot of my father was passed around once more. I suddenly felt like I was presenting my father as some kind of target to a group of hit men.

'Don't worry yourself, young Calypso, my little champagne-quaffing chum,' Malcolm assured me. 'He won't know what's hit him if he comes within a hundred yards of you. You saw what I did to that Gandalf chap. I'll plant a Glasgow kiss on him if he starts mucking the glorious Sarah about while I'm around.'

'He's not dangerous,' I shrieked. 'He's my father. I don't want him hurt or anything!' I was beginning to feel that I had ignited a fire that could never be extinguished. This is what I always do. It's what I've done all my life. 'I just don't want him upsetting Sarah,' I tried to explain as the boys were jostled away by a fencing team coming through.

Freds and Malcolm told me they were off to see if they could find Billy before saying their laters and leaving me alone. Well, not alone. I had my posse, but I still felt like a little ant in a giant hive. I didn't know my way around.

Having only come an hour away from school, Portia and I were already in our kit, but after registration we went to the loo to confab. That was where we found Sarah applying makeup – odd in itself, as she was a great believer in 'natural beauty.'

'Hello, darlings, isn't this super? You must be excited. I know I'm exhilarated by all this bustle.'

'You won't be for long,' I almost blurted. And then it turned out I'd actually said it. Typical. Stupid, stupid, stupid Calypso.

'Whatever do you mean, Calypso? Is something wrong?'

'Just nerves,' Portia assured her, giving me a warning look.

'Yes, well the adrenaline is bound to be coursing through you, Boojie, but you have to learn to centre yourself. Find your chi.'

'My chi? And where on earth might I find my chi?' I asked, my nerves jangling around my body.

Sarah looked lost. 'Erm, well, you can find your chi anywhere. It can just sneak up on you, really. The point is, nothing exists beyond the now. Remember what Bob always says?'

'Oh, I remember what Bob always says,' Portia said brightly. 'Swell.'

Sarah laughed. 'Oh dear, I do miss the old boy. I'm really quite giddy at the thought that he might turn up today to support you.'

'No, you're not,' I told my mother. 'He oppresses you. You don't want him to see you, he'll ruin your equilibrium. And how do you even know he's going to turn up?'

Sarah wrapped her arms around me and rocked me gently. 'Oh, Boojie, you rock my world.'

'My world is rocking, that's for sure,' I told her. 'But that doesn't answer my question.'

'Well, enough navel gazing,' Sarah insisted briskly as she grabbed Portia and me by the hands and led us out into the swarming humanity of the hall.

TWENTY-SIX

And Just as They Were Bringing in My Crown!

Portia and I passed Billy and the others en route to our pools, which were to be held in the basketball courts. It was so packed in the hall now with fencers, BFA representatives, parents, fans and Bell End's saboteurs, that no one even noticed Billy and Freds giving Portia and me a pre-match snog-age session.

Sarah spotted Sister at the cafeteria on the first floor and said she'd watch us from up there, where there was a glass front and comfy seats. Also, the scoreboards were in there, she explained. 'I saw it on the map.'

Bell End was nowhere to be seen.

I felt a tug on my arm as I was walking on the walkway towards the basketball courts. A Year Seven girl from Saint Leonard's offered me her fencing kit bag and a pen. 'Could you sign my bag please, Miss Kelly?' she asked sweetly.

'Erm, why?' I asked, confused.

'I saw your picture in *The Sword* when you won the South East Cup.'

'Oh, sure,' I agreed, signing my name, feeling like a total fraud.

After the girl left, Portia took the piss, 'When I grow up, I want to be just like you, Miss Kelly.'

I was about to laugh when I spotted him, my father, Bob, standing down in the pit, an arena where the boy's pools were taking place. He was on his own, but Freds and Malcolm were only yards away from him. I felt this terrible, almost painful, pang of affection for my poor father in that moment. He looked so small and lost down in the pit and I was hit with memories of all the times he'd been there for me, cheering me on, applauding all my efforts. However hopeless I was at something, Bob had always said, 'You did swell, Princess, just swell.' I remembered how Bob had built the little stage in the living room so I could act and do my tragic little song-and-dance routines. My rendition of 'How Much Is That Doggy in the Window?' used to have him in tears.

'Oh shit,' I said to Portia, pointing. 'There he is.'

'Bell End?'

'No, Bob. Look down in the arena.'

Portia took me by the shoulders. 'Honestly, Calypso, now is not the time to obsess about him. Sarah is fine. She's with Sister upstairs in the cafeteria.'

'But she'll see him.'

'I don't get the impression she minds. She sounded like she was looking forward to seeing him.'

I was confused but just then I could hear my name being called, so I charged off to my designated piste.

The next time I saw Bob was in the arena during my second direct elimination bout. The boys' matches were going on down one end and the girls' were at the other. Sister and Sarah were still upstairs with their tea. Their enthusiasm for fencing must have dwindled somewhat from those heady days in Sheffield because now they were content to watch us from afar, waving vaguely as they chatted and dunked their biscuits in their tea. After all their mad enthusiasm, a part of me now felt neglected.

But I had other things on my mind. Bob knew where I was now because the announcers had insensitively called my bout over the intercom.

Bell End was furious. 'I asked them to use your code name too.'

'I don't have a code name, sir,' I reminded him.

'You do now, girl. I told them your name was Princess Jelly Bean.'

'Princess Jelly Bean? What? Couldn't you do better than that?'

'Well, I didn't want to get you mixed up with any other princesses that might be here. Figured Jelly Bean was safe.'

'It's also insane.'

'Still, the point is, that they didn't use it. Saboteurs, *see*! I warned you. I'm going up there now to sort this out.

They've put you in jeopardy. This Bob will sniff you out now, no trouble.'

That reminded me. I sniffed my pits – just at the point that Freds came over with Malcolm to wish me luck.

'How's Billy doing?' I asked, wind-milling my arm as if I were merely exercising rather than pit sniffing.

'He's still in. The last bout was close, though.'

'Got a cigarette, Calypso?' Malcolm asked.

'Are you mad?' I asked him. I was, after all, wearing a skintight white fencing outfit electrically wired and sans pockets. Quite apart from the fact that I wasn't a smoker, the only thing I could keep on my person was sweat.

'No? Oh well, Portia? Got any fags?'

Portia continued with her low lunges, not even deigning to answer his absurd request with a look.

'Bit whiffy in here,' Malcolm remarked, and then wandered off.

After trouncing my next opponent, I went up to the cafeteria with Portia, as we both had a break. Bob hadn't approached me so far, but I could feel him watching me, so I took a circuitous route with Portia up the stairs. Sister and Sarah had clearly OD-ed on tea and biscuits and were bouncing about the cafeteria like Ping-Pong balls.

Sarah was wearing the mauve collar that Sister must have finished. 'Look, look what Sister made me!' Sarah squealed, dancing about with glee.

The collar was too tragic for words, but I wasn't going to be the one to pop her bubble. The poor old madre may as well squeeze in what fun she could before Bob turned up to break her heart.

'It's very, erm, fetching,' I told her, trying to get her to sit and calm down.

'Oh, darling, I'm glad you like it. Today is such an exciting day, isn't it?' she asked with an intensity I put down to the caffeine.

'Yes, Sarah, it is an exciting day.'

'I have a special surprise for you too, later,' she said, bopping about like a wind-up toy.

Oh dear, I thought, fearing she'd commissioned Sister to knit me a collar too. 'Fabulous,' I said with as much enthusiasm as I could muster. 'I'm really looking forward to it.'

Portia came back with juices, and we sat down and stretched our aching muscles before our names were called again.

Bell End must have worked his magic because when the final bout was called, my name was announced as Princess Jelly Bean.

As I forced my way through the crowd onto the piste, I was aware of Sarah, Sister, Bell End, Malcolm and Freds all together. I shrugged off my concern that Bob may have already seen them, because while people weren't exactly jeering me, there was the odd bit of tittering and a few snide cries of, 'Go, Princess Jelly Bean!'

Portia had been knocked out in the semi-finals so she was there to wire me up and give me a few words of encouragement. 'Darling, don't think of anything else. This bout is all that matters to you now. Everything else can wait.'

My opponent was my old foe from the finals in Sheffield, Jenny. I feared for poor Jenny and her fans, with Bell End being as wound up as he was, but I smiled at her kindly, figuring she probably still hadn't recovered from his horrible abuse at our last match.

But I was wrong. Oh, so wrong. When we tapped one another's equipment to make sure the electrics were working, she 'tapped' my blade clean out of my hand.

I watched as it bounced across the floor beyond the piste. Okay. We were playing nasty.

'Slay the foul little bitch,' came Bell End's echoing roar, audible to everyone in the enormous arena. Sister Regina added, 'Yes, you go on and slay her, Calypso! Nasty girl, nasty girl.'

Jenny punched the air with her fist. 'You're dead meat, Jelly Bean!' she yelled to the mighty cheer of her fans.

What did she think this was, *Gladiator II*?

I put my hand out to shake hers. She twisted it behind my back and was about to threaten me, but the president stepped in and handed her a red card, meaning she had already lost herself a valuable point.

Her emotional decrepitude could only work to my advantage, I decided. Even so, there was every chance that the two of us would be asked to join the National Team regardless of who won. Actually, that would make her my fencing buddy – but I could deal with that. After all, my roommate this term had been Honey, and I'd survived her.

Just the same, my first advance was poor. The spirit of Jerzy Pawlowski seemed to have abandoned me just when I needed him most. For all Portia's encouragement, my mind wasn't focused on the game. It was on Bob and Sarah, so I couldn't believe it when I began to strip points from Jenny. Jenny's blade was a secondary consideration as I took my eyes off Jenny to search the crowd for my father. I just couldn't force myself to concentrate the way I knew I should. My brain kept telling me 'Focus!' but my heart kept telling me 'Your family needs you.'

I heard Freds yell my name, and as I turned to look, I inadvertently clipped my blade on Jenny's glove, earning me yet another undeserved point. Just as the fight was meeting its climax of thirteen, nine in my favour, I spotted Bob making his way towards Sarah.

In my horror, I stumbled backwards, clearing myself of Jenny's attack and my guard connected with the pit of her stomach. Another point to me. It was ridiculous. I was playing like a random bluffer in a poker game, and yet it was my lack of strategy which seemed to be throwing Jenny off. Then I realised what was really happening. Jenny thought she was in combat with the girl she'd fought in Sheffield and was trying to outwit me by referring to my previous form. But the Calypso Kelly she'd fought in Sheffield was not the Princess Jelly Bean she was up against now.

And then it happened – Bob tapped Sarah on the shoulder, she spun around, he took hold of her shoulders and kissed her.

The president called play again, but I couldn't drag my eyes away from Bell End, who wasted no time in launching his body into Bob's, rugby tackling him to the ground. At that moment, Jenny launched into a lethal lunge. I flailed about with my blade impotently, causing her blade to run harmlessly up my left sleeve. Yet even in my emotional turmoil, I was winning. The president was about to call halt for the sake of my arm's safety, but I brought my blade down on Jenny's shoulder before he had the chance. The victory was mine.

I tore off my mask as the buzzer blared and the crowd roared its support. Jenny threw her blade across the piste in a fit of fury as I went to shake her hand.

Okay. Fine.

So to Bell End and Bob I flew. The scene that awaited me was not dignified. Bell End was rolling and flailing about the floor on top of Bob with Sarah on top of him, begging him to 'leave my man alone.'

Sister was getting in the odd kick at Bob's head, but mostly she was running around the heap, entangling their bodies with her yarn.

Neither my parents nor Sister Regina were the best of fighters, and Bell End was more of a mouthpiece for violence than a physical threat, so no *real* damage was being done. Still, it wasn't quite the dignified end to my winning the Nationals that I had envisioned.

Freds and Portia helped me pull them all apart.

'Miss Kelly,' a be-suited man said as he extended a hand to me. 'I represent the British National Fencing Team and I wondered –'

'Is this the blighter?' yelled Malcolm, suddenly appearing on the scene, fag in mouth.

The BFA rep took a step back, but Malcolm was pointing at Bob, who was now being dusted down lovingly by Sarah. What on earth was she thinking? If I didn't know better, I'd say she was thrilled to see him. Freds was occupied keeping Bell End in a headlock. Sister was happily rewinding her yarn into a neat ball.

'Yes, that's the subversive bastard, git him!' Bell End yelled to Malcolm, who happily obliged by removing his fag and head-butting my poor father with an effortlessness only a true Scot can carry off.

I was still holding the BFA representative's hand. 'Hello, I'm Calypso Kelly. These people have nothing to do with me.'

'No, I would hope not. Could we go somewhere quiet to speak,' he suggested.

So I went off with Jim, the BFA representative, and he asked me if I'd join the National Team. It should have been the happiest news of my life, but I couldn't shake off the image of Bob kissing Sarah, which diluted my joy considerably.

Of course I said how excited I was to be invited onto the National Team, but after we'd gone over the formalities and I'd given him my details, I immediately rushed back to the aid of my parents. I had half an hour at most to sort their marital problems out before I would have to go on the stage to collect my cup.

Sarah grabbed me in cuddle. 'Oh, Boojems, we're soooo proud of our baby, aren't we, darling?'

Darling?

'Bob has sold his Big One for two million pounds – that's sterling, not dollars – isn't that marvellous, Calypso?' Sarah cooed like a dove. 'We reconciled last night. It was heaven.'

Sister Regina agreed it was a lot of money but I silenced her with a glare.

Two million pounds was a lot of money (well, to me it was – even if it would seemed chump change to girls like Star and my other friends), but that wasn't the point. There were principles at stake and I was nothing if not a girl jam-packed with principles.

'You don't just reconcile with someone because they sell a script for a lot of money, Sarah,' I lectured. 'And you well know it! After everything that's happened, I think you might have consulted me or at least Bunny. I'm sure she won't be too thrilled to learn that you are back with your oppressor merely because he's come into some loot,' I scolded.

'Nice to see you too, Princess Jelly Bean,' my father said.

Naturally I ignored him and turned to my boyfriend for backup. 'Don't you agree, Freddie?'

'Sorry, what was that, Calypso?' he asked, his eyes darting about the room as he took a step backwards. 'I might just go and see what Billy's up to. Coming McHamish?' he asked, pulling on his friend's shirt.

'No, this is interesting. Might come in handy with my ethics paper. Go on, Bob, go on, Sarah and Calypso,' urged Malcolm eagerly.

'Yes,' agreed Bell End, who looked like he wanted another go at Bob. 'Go on, *Bob*.' He spat my father's name out as if it were a gob of mucus.

All Sarah and Bob did was laugh. Yes, laugh. And what was more sickening is that they looked into one another's eyes as they laughed. After all I'd been through, trying to support Sarah, make my father see sense and deal personally with their breakup, their laughter felt like a betrayal.

'I don't see what's so funny,' I told them imperiously, standing upright in my sweaty white fencing outfit, my mask under one arm, leaning on my sabre to add a bit of authority, if not menace, to my speech.

'Oh, darling, we're not laughing at you, it's just the situation. We're happy. Truly happy. And it's not the money. Well, we're very pleased with that aspect, obviously.' Sarah giggled like a teenager.

'I really think you should consult with Bunny,' I hissed to her.

'We both spoke to Bunny after you came to stay with me in Clapham with your friends. In fact it was Bunny who felt that it was time for Bob and me to talk.' See what I mean about parents being drama queens and hypocrites? I should have listened to Star all along.

'What do you mean, Bunny thought it was time? Time to throw your principles over and return to an oppressive man who can't pour his own granola, just because he's sold his horrible old stupid script?'

'No, we spoke because Honey had a bit too much to drink that weekend, and while you were all asleep she let slip about the fight with the drug dealers.'

'I knew Honey was behind this,' I shrieked, turning to Portia. 'I knew she'd try something like this! I knew it,' I railed.

'Knew what?' Portia asked, looking at me like I was crazed. 'That she'd be instrumental in getting your parents back together?'

Sarah said, 'Darling, she wasn't being mean. She'd had a bit to drink and started opening up to me about her own parents' split. She told me how it had destroyed her life. She can be a really lovely girl when she's –'

'Drunk,' I spat.

'Please don't be bitter. It's a long story, but basically Bob and I are going to marriage guidance. We even talked about him going back to work –'

'I offered,' Bob added in his defence.

'Good man,' interjected Malcolm.

'Shut up, Malcolm,' I told him before turning to Bob. 'Oh, I bet you offered,' I said sarcastically. 'Offered in an emotionally blackmailing sort of way.'

'This is fantastic, the intrigue and dynamics behind a typical middle-class American family,' Malcolm glowed. 'Are Americans always so against their parents' reconciling?'

'Shut up, Malcolm,' Sarah said. 'He did offer to get a job, Calypso, and quite genuinely, but I couldn't let him. Not after all the time I'd put into supporting him to pursue his dream. Marriage is all about supporting one another through thick and thin, good times and bad. Bob had a dream and I wanted to support him in his creative endeavours,' Sarah explained as I stood there pressing my sabre deeper and deeper into the ground with all the force of my fury. The blade was bent to snapping point as I glared at my parents in teenage defiance.

'You've changed your tune,' I muttered.

'I knew he needed to finish it. I was just sick and tired of being neglected. It was complicated. I was conflicted. We both were, but relationships are full of misunderstandings. Bunny is a brilliant marriage therapist,' Sarah enthused.

'Bunny is a marriage therapist!' I cried in anguish.

'Who's Bunny?' asked Malcolm. 'She sounds fun.' But everyone ignored him.

'I know I vented some of my anger with Bob on you, darling,' Sarah admitted, patting my fencing mask, which was still tucked under my arm. 'It was wrong of me, but I was so angry about the sacrifices I'd made even though they were sacrifices I chose to make. I was conflicted.'

'So basically you used me? I was your emotional dart-board?'

'Oh no, I love your father, really. I never stopped loving him. You must know that. We made love all night last night, Calypso. It was just like the first time,' Sarah elaborated for me and anyone else in earshot.

Freds looked as horrified as Malcolm looked intrigued. Portia distracted Sister by launching into an animated discussion with her about her knitting. Bell End went puce in the face. Thank God that was when I was called to accept my cup.

Later, Adidas and Leon Paul marketing reps came to offer me sponsorship deals for the new kit I'd need to fence internationally and to cover my transport costs. Then Bell End started yakking on proudly and loudly about how I was a real GBR now and not a Great Badger Rapist. But even then all I could think of was Bob and Sarah, having sex.

'Thanks for sharing your sex forensics, Mom,' I said later when the reps had left. I was hoping to put her in her proper parental place. Why do 'rents always have to make everything about them? Why do they always have to spoil their children's triumphs? This should have been *my* day, but now it was poisoned by an image that would be tattooed on my brain for the rest of my life. Okay, so I was a bit pleased that they were sorting things out together, but I wished I hadn't already submitted that essay. Imagining my parents doing it, now that was *real* trauma.

Things got even worse after all the fanfare quieted down and we were leaving the building. Bob tweaked my cheek in front of everyone. 'See, my little Queen of the Doomsday Prophesies, didn't I tell you it would all work out?'

'Ah, let me think. No! You let me deal with Sarah's breakdown all on my own while you selfishly pursued your Big One. Then you swan in here, ruin my day and expect me to cheer because you've finally sold your script and can pay attention to your wife again.'

Bob ruffled my hair the way he knows I hate. 'Hey, don't underestimate Sarah. That slot she's been doing over here interviewing celebrities has been picked up at home by NBC. Besides, maybe one day when you ask me for a car you'll think differently,' he joked.

'I am not that materialistic,' I told him sharply, while secretly wondering what sort of car he'd let me have.

'Hey, give your old man a break. I knew I was almost done when Sarah said she'd had enough. I was working on the last scene. And she'd made sacrifices for the script as well. I couldn't let her down. And don't forget, love is all about supporting one another's creative endeavours, Calypso.'

I shrugged him off as he tried to cuddle me, but he pulled me under his arm. 'I do give Sarah credit. In fact the script is called *To Sarah, with Love*.'

'They'll never let you keep that,' I told him, trying to suppress a smile. I could feel myself beginning to soften.

'It's written in the contract, Boojie.' Oh this was great, now they were both reverting and referring to me in baby names.

Maybe Sister, Billy, Portia and Freds were right. Maybe one day I would forgive them. One thing was for sure, Bell End never would. Freds and Malcolm both tried to convince me that Sarah and Bob looked sweet together, but I know that was just because Bob had worked his charm on Freds by slapping him on the back and calling him 'buddy.' Buddy? Talk about sickening, but Freds seemed delighted with the term.

The worst of it came when they enveloped me in one of those gross family hugs Bob and Sarah have always insisted on.

'Isn't it marvellous,' Sister twittered. 'Marriage is a holy sacrament, after all. And two lovely people like you with a sweet little girl like Calypso for a daughter. Why, you're the perfect family.'

And that's when it hit me. I had just written an essay about my suffering at the hands of this perfect family. An essay that had made Ms Topler weep with horror and wail with sorrow at the pain, pathos, torment and misery I had endured as an American girl packed off to a boarding school in England by the cruel Bob and self-involved Sarah. An essay, more importantly, that Ms Topler was convinced would win the competition and be plastered all over the pages of Britain's best-selling newspaper.

An essay that Bob and Sarah must absolutely never, ever

read, because if they did, they would disown me and my happy family would be shot to smithereens. Passages I had written, which had seemed so poetic, inspired and heartfelt at the time I had written them, now seemed vitriolic and self-serving. Thank goodness Ms Topler was such a lousy English teacher and wouldn't know literature if it came and bit her on the nose. There was no way my miserable essay of personal suffering would have any chance of winning. Would it? Besides, I had other far more pleasant things to dwell on.

'Freds loves me, Freds loves me,' I chanted to myself. And as if on cue, he put his arms around me. 'So, Princess Jelly Bean,' he whispered in my ear. 'I noticed there's nothing much going on behind the scoreboard . . . care to investigate?'

Acknowledgements

I am always fully aware how fortunate I am to have such a sensational and perspicacious agent as Laura Dail and an editor of the calibre and genius of Melanie Cecka. My only regret is that you are both on the other side of the Atlantic – although that provides me with the perfect excuse to visit New York more often.

When I first conjured up the fictional world of Saint Augustine's, I was inspired by my school experiences and those of my children, especially Cordelia and her friends. Then Eric Hewitson drew me a map, to make sure my characters and I wouldn't get lost in this imaginary world. But if I did lose my way around the school grounds of Saint Augustine's, I'd definitely want to be with girls like the gang at Bloomsbury USA – Melanie Cecka, Victoria Arms, Deb Shapiro, Rachel Wasdyke, Kate Kubert, Heather Scott, Stacy Cantor and my agent, Laura Dail – because it would be such a laugh.

Thanks again to Mike Storrings for his cover design. And as ever, thank you, thank you, thank you to my extended family (including your increasing assortment of odd pets, SP).

Last but never least, coronets and shout-outs to all Calypso's readers!

Dumping Princes

• • •

Not every frog who wears a crown turns out to be a prince . . .

ONE

Sound the Alert! Americans Are Storming the Castle!

According to my darling 'rentals, I lack a sense of proportion. Oh, and I thrive on melodrama.

They base this on something that happened in the Beverly Centre shopping mall when I was three years old, which was henceforth referred to as 'The Incident.'

Whenever the 'rents want to back up their claims of my lack of proportion and need for drama, they mention The Incident. Allegedly, it involved a Christmas tree, a pair of black lace knickers and a police report.

The padre usually adds something daft like, 'One day you'll go too far, Calypso Kelly.' To which my madre will nod sagely and say, 'All right, well, I think we've made our point. Let's not go *there* again.'

The mad 'rents, who insist I call them Sarah and Bob, are not going to win any prizes for their own sense of proportion or lack of drama. And as for going *too far*, well, they crossed that line years ago when they named me Calypso and packed me off to boarding school in England so I wouldn't become 'too Hollywood' – whatever that means.

No, Sarah and Bob are the very apex of dramarama. They tell lies. Yes, whopping great porkies – and I'm not just talking about the alleged Incident in the mall or the Tooth Fairy. They also told me I was the cleverest, prettiest, most talented girl in all the world. That's what I mean. They're sweet, but daft as socks.

Anyway, on this particular day, I was over the moon-arama for an indisputably good reason! I was off to stay with Their Royal Majesties. But every silver lining has a cloud: my parents were driving me and staying for luncheon.

Absolutely nothing was going to spoil my excitement over going to visit my fit prince in his Scottish castle, that enormous grey stony one with the fairy-tale turrets, where kilt-ish carryons such as reeling, haggis eating, grouse shooting and jigs like the Gay Gordons are *de rigueur*. They often show the royal family standing outside their castle on television and in magazines. It is très, très divine.

All I had to say to anyone who doubted our love would last was, eat your knickers. I was still – pinch yourselves – pulling Prince Freddie, as regularly as I reasonably could. I mean, heirs to the throne do spend a lot of time in training to be king, which was tedious. But I never complained.

No, I was determined not to be a tragic, clingy-type girlfriend. My wildly independent American streak still thrived!

You'd think any normal parents might be proud that their daughter was dating the heir to the crown, but no, no, no, no, no. That would be too sensible for Bob and Sarah. 'You don't think you're being a bit melodramatic about this relationship with Freddie, do you, Calypso?' Bob suggested as we hit the M1 motorway. 'I mean, you've only just turned fifteen last week and you're acting like you're going to marry the boy.'

I turned up the volume on my iPod and started humming loudly to a particularly tuneless and depressing song which my best friend, Star, wrote. It's called 'The Only Guarantee in Life Is School Sucks.'

I think she got the idea for the song from our three-thousand-year-old religious studies teacher, Sister Bethlehem. She's always banging on about how there are no guarantees in life, which is a blatant lie, because you can always guarantee that Sister Bethlehem will fall asleep in class. Mind you, there are certain Old Testament books that send me off into a good snooze. Like Leviticus.

Even so, I am feverishly fond of old Sister Bethlehem. She is always teaching us useful life skills, like how to win money by betting on things – such as who cut off Samson's hair in the Bible.

'Yes, girls, you can win quite a tidy sum of money on that one,' she told us once. 'A lot of people will tell you it was Delilah, but if they bothered to read the Good Book more closely, they'd realise she actually called for a servant to lop off his locks. Mark my words, if you're ever short of a pound, that one will come in very handy. I won a fiver off Father Conway two years on the trot with that one.'

But back to guarantees. I could guarantee I would never, never, never tire of Freddie's lips. So don't start running a book on that because you will lose. The 'rentals call it puppy love, but then again, they *are* absurdly old and quite, quite foolish.

Freds didn't seem keen for me to visit him in his palatial grandeur initially. I can't think why, after I exposed him to the lunacy of Sarah and Bob. But eventually, after aggressive hinting on my part (what is it with boys that they can't take hints?), he caved and invited me to stay the weekend at Harthnoon Castle. I guess he finally realised that if he kept me and his Kiltland retreat apart for much longer, I would start growing paws from all my shameless begging.

It was all quite surreal being invited to stay with the Royal Family. Like the rest of the world, I'd seen Freds and his family in their mad kilts doing photo calls outside Harthnoon Castle. But like every other girl who has drooled over this fit prince, I never imagined in my maddest of mad dreams that I'd ever actually be invited to stay with him there. Okay, so maybe in my maddest dreams . . . but then, what girl my age hasn't? Freds was the object of desire for teenage girls worldwide.

Apart from my best friend, Star, that is.

Star thought he was 'an arrogant, boring, unworthy drip with bad taste in clothes.' Oh, and did I mention, seriously unworthy of *moi*? Then again, Star didn't think any boy was good enough for any girl. Not because she's from the Isle of Lesbos or anything, it's just that she had a much higher opinion of girls than of boys. But then if you met her father, Tiger, from the legendary rock band Dirge, you'd understand why. It's a wonder she isn't deeply unhinged.

Love her though I do, her snide comments about how "stuck up" Freds was were becoming très, très, très annoying. He couldn't be that stuck up if he loved an American Freak like me, could he? Well, that's what my psycho toff anti-girlfriend Honey said, anyway. It's hardly ideal when I have to cite something the poisonous Honey has said to defend something as fundamental as my love for Freddie.

Star had been ultra horrible about Freds, especially after she dumped his best friend, Kev. Oh yes, that's my latest news flash. Hold onto your knickers – my best friend had gone over to the mad side. After she dumped Kev, she started on this loony mission to get *me* to dump *Freds*, which was as maddening as a drawer of tangled tights.

My fainting attacks began when she dumped Kev. 'You what?' I asked as she brought me around, using the age-old tickling method. Kev was Fred's best friend, and the symmetry of *my* best friend hanging out with *his* best friend was a vital element in the joy of loving Freds. She couldn't dump Kev! She couldn't. 'You can't dump Kev,' I told her.

'Well, I did,' said Star. 'I told you I wanted to start the year with a clean slate, darling,' she reminded me, referring to the New Year resolutions we'd made together in her bedroom wing while her parents and their celebrity friends rock-and-rolled the night away.

My resolutions were the normal unrealistic goals of a teenage girl; stop picking at my spots and develop more savoir-faire and va-va-va-voom. To that end, I was going to start littering my sentences with loads of foreign words and *bon mots*. I was also harbouring deep hopes of doing well in my GCSE exams and wowing them with my fencing prowess in Italy, where I would be participating in my first international tournament. I'd had a letter about the Italian trip over the break, but with Christmas, my birthday and my parents' constant canoodling, I hadn't had a chance to get properly excited about it. Especially as Freds wasn't on the national team, which meant even more time I wouldn't get to spend with him.

'I thought you meant stuff like, erm, taking those blue extensions out of your hair and perfecting your French accent,' I told her. 'Not dumping perfectly good boy-friends!'

Star scoffed. 'Calypso, don't you ever wonder if there's more to life than boys?'

'No!' I blurted. 'I mean, of course I wonder that all the time.'

'We're still young, darling. Don't you think we should be focusing on our dreams rather than spotty boys?'

I decided not to say anything lame about how Freds *was* my dream – well, my dream boyfriend anyway. But he is. And he is not in the least bit spotty!

And then in the car driving up to Kiltland, the padre said much the same thing. 'I know you want to impress Freds and his folks, but don't you think taking a trunk of outfits for a weekend stay is a bit over the top?'

'You really have no idea, Bob,' I told him, and then I brooded about whether he was right. I mean, I didn't want Freds or the king and queen to think I was desperate to impress. Even if I was.

TWO

The Collision of Parental Culture Shock

As the 'rents drove our car of shame up to the castle, we had to pass a large crowd of royal watchers. I call it the car of shame not *just* because it's not a chauffeur-driven Rolls Royce like all my other friends' cars. No, it has a bumper sticker that reads – this is true, by the way – HONK IF YOU'RE IN LURVE!

Très, très mortifying.

The fans were keeping vigil in the rain in the hope of spotting their beloved royals. Quite a few of them were holding placards with WE LOVE YOU PRINCE FREDDIE! printed on them. I had to give quite a few death stares to the more brazen girls whose signs promised all sorts of indecent pleasures to my lovely Freds.

Bob and Sarah, on the other hand, felt compelled to give the hussies a little wave as security ushered us through. My 'rentals are soooo delusional. It was as if they thought *they* were royalty or something.

I would have ducked down on the floor of the car of shame if I wasn't so afraid of ruining my outfit, which was too feverishly stunning for words. Unfortunately, Freds had seen it before, because my cruel padre had refused to hand over his precious plastic. 'You don't ever give a boy the idea you care too much' was his excuse.

To ensure I'd fit in amongst the royals at Harthnoon Castle, I'd been practising my regal walk over Christmas. I wished I wasn't so freakishly tall, though. I know I prayed for a growth spurt a few years back, but honestly, it was getting ridiculous. I was seriously worried my long blond-ish locks would get caught up in low-hanging chandeliers.

Freds told me that he loves everything about me, but I'm sure I've grown ten feet since he last saw me two weeks ago. It would be a great test of his love if he could still care for me once I started swinging from his family's chandelier by my hair during afternoon tea.

As someone wonderfully good and great in the Bible, or another heavy book, once remarked, 'so many problems, so few solutions.' Or maybe that was, 'so many people, so few fish'? I was cramming so much knowledge into my brain for my GCSEs at the moment, my head was about to explode. That would teach the examination board a lesson or two.

Everyone knows how divinely fit and marvellous my prince is, so I won't bang on too much about His Royal Handsomeness. I'll just mention that in the beginning, I had to pinch myself that I, Calypso Kelly, onetime Queen of the School Losers Association at the toffer-than-thou English girls' boarding school I attend, was pulling a prince. All the other girls at Saint Augustine's live in a world of total freedom, Daddy's plastic, mummy's contacts, personal manservants, chauffer-driven Rolls Royces, bodyguards, society pages and titles that go back hundreds of years. Whereas I have a family that can trace itself back to Kentucky, Sarah and Bob, a car of shame, curfew rules and a fixed allowance.

Then again, I was the one going out with the prince.

Sometimes I even pinched myself when I was kissing him and screamed out: 'Ouch!' Freds found that a trifle weird. Mind you, he found a lot of things about me peculiar. But he was perfection itself, and I honestly couldn't imagine ever breaking up with him.

Okay, so there *was* one teensy weensy fly in the ointment of our perfect love, and when I say teensy weensy, I mean smaller than an iota, so strictly speaking it's not even visible under a microscope. The scoop is . . . he's pretty, erm, normal, really.

Yes, normal, as in just like a regular non-royal-type person. Not a bit mad or even mildly eccentric in the least. But that's a good thing, right?

Well, you try telling Star that!

I know what you're thinking, he's a prince, he can't be boring. But it's true, the most shocking secret about the royals is just how boringly, boringly ordinary they are. And I say that with the utmost love and respect. Seriously, not only do they wander about the palace without their crowns and magisterial robes on, they do things like eat toast for breakfast! Ordinary old toast! Can you believe it? I couldn't.

When Freds first told me this shocking news regarding his family's penchant for toast, I had to grip onto him to stop fainting. I imagined they'd eat special royal-type food specially developed by royal scientists and organic health experts. But no, they ate normal food, chatted away about the weather and watched television like everyone else. And, oh my giddy aunt . . . they don't even have cable!

I would die without cable.

The one *slight* worry I had on receiving my invite to Harthnoon was how to get out of shooting things. Freds and his family love nothing better than a good shoot at the expense of some poor creature. I'm not a big fan of shooting things, as Freds knows perfectly well. But I figured I was on display, so I had to devise a cunning plan to escape the shoot without upsetting the symmetry of this longed-for weekend.

Star warned me that if I told his family I didn't like killing things, they would think me freakish. I feared they thought me freakish anyway after my 'rentals, Sarah and Bob, tongue-kissed one another when they dropped me off in Scotland around noon. What if the king and queen were soooo normal they did things like peer out the curtains? I thought. *Quelle horreur!*

Am I wrong to wish that Bob and Sarah wouldn't

tongue-kiss in public? They thought I should be pleased that they were back together after their six-week separation last term. I *was* pleased. Of course I was pleased. They were hopeless without one another. All I was asking was that they stop slobbering over each other all the time.

Of course that's exactly what they did on our arrival – kiss. What if the tabloids got a shot of my parents kissing like teenagers at the castle?

'Stop that, you two,' I scolded. 'What will the royal family think of you?'

'Chill out, Calypso, they're just people like us,' Bob said.

'Just people!' I squawked like a madder-than-mad thing. 'Like us?'

Even the liveried footman, who was getting my trunk out of the boot, looked shocked. I was close to certain that the king and queen *don't* pull in public – if they even pull at all.

'Heck, do we tip this guy or what?' asked Bob, pulling out his wallet. He actually talks like that too. Words like 'gee,' 'swell' and 'hip' litter his every sentence. When I was younger and more vulnerable, I used to walk on the other side of the street from him or sit in a different booth in diners. I'm a lot stronger now.

'Erm, no,' I told him with the authority of a person who gets her information on the royal family from Google. 'Just give me some cash,' I said firmly, wrestling with his wallet. 'You're meant to leave your tip *after* your stay.' Well, that is the deal for country house stays – according to www.englisheysnobs.com – and this was sort of like a country house, just a really, really big one with turrets and a moat.

'But *we're* not staying,' Sarah pointed out reasonably enough. 'We're heading off for our romantic weekend after luncheon.'

I wished they'd stop banging on about their 'romantic' weekend. I really didn't want to imagine what they planned to get up to.

'No, but I'm staying,' I hissed, not wanting the lurking footman to hear. 'So give it to me.' I tugged the wallet out of Bob's hand, deftly relieving it of a bunch of readies.

Bob gave me one of his "one day you'll go too far, Calypso Kelly" looks, but Freds had come out by that point, so Bob didn't say anything. I know this sounds shallow and culturally small-minded, but I was quite pleased that Freds wasn't wearing a kilt. Not that I don't love a kilt on a boy, it's just, well, it makes me feel like grabbing his arm and doing the Gay Gordons or some other loony reel.

But Freds was sans kilt and his black hair was doing that wildly wonderful sticky-outy thing I loved so much. His eyes looked bluer than blue too in the Scottish air. It was a crisp, bright day, and he looked soooo fit in his regulation navy blue Ralph Lauren thin knit jumper over pale blue Ralph Lauren shirt, neutral-coloured trousers and some sort of hiking-type boot, which my mother pointed out. Trust Sarah. The boy is a god and all she could say was, 'See how sensible his shoes are, Calypso?'

Seeing Freds resplendent in all his worshipful beauty, I was glad I'd pulled out all the stops on my own outfit. I was wearing no makeup (apart from six inches of lip-gloss and lashings of mascara), because boys really go for the natural look. I had also splurged on a new brown corduroy mini-skirt from Top Shop, and the green cashmere jumper Star had given me for Christmas matched my green sequined slippers perfectly. To think that Sarah had actually tried to make me change into Wellington boots before we left! Yes, Wellington boots.

'Believe me, his parents will respect you for it,' she'd said as I was dressing to leave. 'Scotland can be very wet and boggy.'

I didn't even know what boggy was, but I'm sure the royals don't muck about in it. So hoping to silence Sarah with my royal knowledge, I asked, 'Who thinks Wellington boots are suitable footwear for lunch with the royal family?' I asked, and then I said, 'Mr and Mrs No One. That's who.'

You'd think that would have silenced the mad madre, but no, she went on and on for another ten million years about the virtues of Wellington boots over sequined slippers. I have no idea how she ever pulled Bob if her idea of seductive footwear is a pair of rubber boots.

To tell the truth, I don't want to know.

I pretended to faint just to shut her up, only coming to when it was time to get in the car. My new swooning/fainting strategy had proved an invaluable weapon in this war against parental insanity.

My parents had been invited to "take luncheon with Their Majesties," which sounds madly grand, but as it turned out, luncheon consisted only of nasty cold meats, a selection of peculiar cheeses that smelt like a hiker's sweaty socks and some horrible old red wine.

Bob and Sarah seemed totally at home with Queen Adelaide and King Alfred. And being Bob and Sarah, they were calling them Addie and Al by the time they left. I was mouthing 'don't' and waving my hands to stop them all through lunch, but they refused to acknowledge me. Apart from Bob, who mouthed 'paranoid' back at me.

As I stood beside Freds to wave them good-bye, they kissed one another *again*. I decided that was soooo going to be the last time I took them to meet a boyfriend's parents. Not that I planned on having another boyfriend or anything. No, Freds was the perfect boyfriend for me. Although I wouldn't mind if he grew a few more inches.

THREE

The Most Spectacular Fib

Actually, Freds' parents had taken a shine to Bob and Sarah. Me, on the other hand? Well, apparently they thought I was 'sickly and sniffly.' Okay, so I had forced Freds to tell me what they thought of me. I just think he could have put it a tad more kindly.

'I think it was the runny nose,' Freds added, by means of explanation.

Oh yes, my cold. My genius excuse for not going on the shoot the following day. It was really a most spectacularly elaborate fib. I'd even gone to the trouble of cunningly rubbing a handkerchief with chili oil to produce the glassy-eyed, runny nose effect. It was a tip I'd picked up at Saint Augustine's to get out of a class.

So, while the royals were off killing things, I sat in the library (just like at Saint Augustine's only sans computers). Freds' twinkly-eyed gran sat with me. She was quite sweet and very merry, knocking back sherry after sherry and prank calling the staff. We got on quite well in a drunken old duck/sober teenager sort of way. Unfortunately her two old Labradors kept nipping me. 'That's their way of saying hello, don't you know,' Gran had explained as they gnawed my legs off.

Sarah's parents had died in a car accident when I was small, and Bob's parents lived in Kentucky, so I barely ever saw them. When I did, they obsessed about my milk intake, like I was some sort of calf or something. Freds' gran, on the other hand, made me try a glass of sherry, which tastes like cough mixture. I think I may have got a bit tipsy, because I started calling her Bea instead of Ma'am. Also, I let Bea use my mobile to call the butler, who was refusing to answer her calls on the house phones after numerous pranks informing him of all sorts of scandalous untruths about what he got up to in his free time. Honestly, she was soooo funny I chortled my knickers off.

I was still chortling away like the Laughing Cavalier in that famous painting that hangs in the Wallace Collection when Freds and his 'rents came back from killing innocent creatures. The Laughing Cavalier in the painting doesn't look like he's laughing – he looks like he's grinning in a knowing, pervy way if you ask me.

So I suppose that didn't look too good.

Freds gave me a disappointed look as we all gathered in the drawing room, which looked out onto a lovely loch. I was peering out in the hope of seeing a monster or something fascinating like that when the queen asked, 'How's your cold, Calypso?'

'My what?' I replied, having completely forgotten my elaborate ruse.

'Your cold?' Freddie reminded me – a bit sternly.

'Oh, that.' I produced my handkerchief and took a deep sniff, which set me off coughing, which in turn set the Labradors off on another nipping attack on my legs. 'A little better, I think.'

'Oh marvellous,' the king replied, slapping the arms of his chair with delight. 'We wouldn't want you to miss your mother's marvellous show because of illness.' Honestly, Freds' 'rents were as bonkeresque as mine. First toast and now this!

I'd love to have missed Sarah's 'marvellous' show. I think Freds knew that, because he gave me one of his cautioning looks, which were becoming far too regular for my liking.

'No, no, I can't get enough of *Harley Village*,' I told them with a great deal of feeling. I was getting scarily good at this lying thing.

Harley Village is *the* most agonisingly dreary dramarama about a village in Yorkshire where a missing pig is front-page news. It had been Britain's highest-rated series for fifty years or something, and Sarah was sadly proud to have this new gig. I don't know why she couldn't have kept up her morning celebrity slot. The boys at Eades adored the madre's morning show – which of course meant kudos for me.

Sarah could talk about how atmospheric *Harley Village*

is until the cows came home, but as far as I was concerned, it was a show about miserable wet people arguing over whose umbrella was whose.

'Splendid,' said the king.

'Excellent,' agreed the queen.

'Bollocks,' blurted Bea. For a micro-moment, I actually thought the exclamation had come from me. Then Bea winked at me, and I had to snort so deeply into my handkerchief to smother my laughter, I almost passed out.

That was the worst thing about the weekend: my fake cold. Once I'd faked the cold to avoid the shoot, I couldn't exactly make a miraculous recovery without everyone becoming suspicious. It was merde! I had to sniffle and cough all weekend. And as it turned out, my cold was totally pointless.

As I was having my good-bye kiss alone with Freds in one of the turreted towers that smelt of moss, I naively confided in him about how and why I'd lied about having a cold. He knew how much I hated shooting animals, so I thought he'd understand. Actually, I had hoped he'd laugh like a mad thing and spin me around in his arms, but all he did was give me another one of his disappointed looks. I hated his disappointed looks. Every time he gave me one, I felt myself becoming dimmer in his eyes. Then he said, 'It was a *clay* pigeon shoot, Calypso. I am perfectly aware how *anti* you are.'

I don't know how he does it, but he manages to make my dislike of murdering animals sound like treason.

Is it my fault no one ever tells me anything? Buggery boyfriends and their stupid expectations and disappointed looks. It wasn't easy sniffing on that chili-soaked handkerchief all weekend. But did he give me any thanks, or any respect, or encouragement? No.

Now his parents thought I was sickly and sniffly and they would probably banish me from all their castles forever, and Freds and I would be confined to cafés and pizza shops like ordinary girls and boys. Merde, merde and double algebra merde.

Basically, the weekend was not the triumph I had hoped it would be, and I returned to London in a major sulk. The icing on the cake was that my green bejewelled slippers got all soggy when Freds took me walking in some bogs. 'You should have worn Wellingtons,' he told me.

And then just when I thought life couldn't get any worse, I ended up with a really nasty cold.

FOUR

Witness to Madness

I left the castle feeling less than magical.

When I arrived back at the house my parents were renting in Clapham, London – The Clap House, as my evil anti-girlfriend Honey O'Hare had named it – my life took another nosedive.

Sarah and Bob pitched up to my bedroom, swung open the door (without so much as a courteous knock) and declared in one voice, 'We have decided to get married, Calypso.'

All I said was, 'Fine,' because, well, the 'rents are always lobbing up and saying the most random things.

I was listening to my favourite song on the really cool green iPod they'd given me for my combined birthday/ Christmas present. Oh, and txting Freds at the same time because some ancient Greek chap in a toga (or was it a bath?) once said, 'Life is too short to limit oneself to one activity at a time.' Then again, I might have read that it in a fortune cookie.

However, my parents' announcement slowly began to

seep into my consciousness, and I pressed Send before I'd even added any x's. I turned around to face them, ripped my earphones out of my ears and stated the blindingly obvious. 'But you *are* married!'

They giggled like loons.

And then a horrible idea occurred to me. 'You've not been buying things off hooded men on the Landor Road?' I asked sternly, because the last thing I needed was my mad parents to start smoking weed and end up like Star's father, Tiger. Yes, he was probably in a semi-vegetative state on his kitchen floor even at that moment. Star claimed the reason he called everyone 'man' was because he had no memory cells left. It must be très, très mortifying having a father like Tiger.

Bob and Sarah have never shown an interest in exploring drug culture, but they are extremely gullible, especially Bob. Honestly, since coming to London in December he's been mugged like nine times. That's more than once a week. No matter how many times I tell him not to pull his entire wallet out when he wants to give a pound to a beggar at a crowded tube station, he persists in doing it. Proving that parents need round-the-clock supervision. I really don't know how they'll cope once I grow up.

Bob and Sarah looked into one another's eyes and laughed. They had been doing that a lot since they got back together, which is why I'd been forced into this unwanted role as a sensible parent-type person rather than the irresponsible adolescent I *should* have been.

'No, Calypso, we're not smoking weeeeed,' they reassured me. 'It's just that we've never been married in England,' Sarah explained.

'You haven't been married in Mississippi either, Sarah; that's not the point,' I told the mad madre calmly. 'You can't just go round the world marrying one another. It's probably not even legal.'

'Why not?' Bob asked, giving my mother's bottom a playful pinch, which made her squeal.

'It's called bigamy, Bob,' I told him, even though I don't know if marrying the same person over and over *is* called bigamy. But I do know it is madness. They didn't listen, though. I watched my giggling 'rents for a bit longer as they tickled and kissed in my doorway.

In the face of such parental madness, I put my earphones back in and said, 'Fine,' with the dismissive tone that any teenager whose parents have just fallen back in love will be only too familiar with.

There was no talking them out of it, either. During the last week of the Christmas holidays, Bob and Sarah had had a marriage blessing in Windsor Chapel. And that's another thing. Of all the picturesque places to wed, they chose the one a few steps from one of Freddie's family castles. When I begged them to choose another lovely church, they rolled their eyes and said I was being 'paranoid.' They've been saying that a lot lately. Luckily Freds and his 'rents were still up in their Kiltland castle.

Bob's parents, affectionately known as The Gams, came

out for the blessing and gave me twenty dollars worth of book vouchers from their local bookstore in Kentucky.

I've never even been to Kentucky, so I don't know what they could have been thinking.

After the 'wedding,' which was really only a blessing, Bob and Sarah threw a big party back at the Clap House. It's actually a really lovely house, and Sarah and Bob invited all my friends to the reception and said they could sleep over, which made me feel more supportive of their madness. But then Sarah and Bob spoilt everything by a very public, very passionate kiss as they cut the cake. It lasted – this is true, by the way – forty-nine painfully embarrassing seconds. I timed it on my mobile while all my friends took photos of them with their camera phones.

I was witnessing insanity in its truest form.

'They're soooo cute,' Star squealed as she took photo after photo of the cute couple snog-aging.

FIVE

H to the O to the N to the E to the Y

The kissing didn't stop after the wedding/blessing affair, either. They were still doing it when they took me back for my first day of term. I had been really looking forward to being dropped off at school by my parents too. This was the first time in years that I didn't have to make my own way to Saint Augustine's from the airport after the LAX-to-Heathrow hell flight.

It was a festival of luxury being driven back to school by the 'rents, even if it was in a car of shame which neither of them could drive properly. The biggest advantage to having Sarah and Bob drive me to school was they could help carry my madly heavy trunk and fencing kit up the stairs to the dorms just like all the other girls' parents and valets. Hoorah! Well . . . that was the plan I'd hatched in Calypso's Very Own Fantasyland at least.

My school is an odd little world within an odd little world. For an American, it's sort of like a culture shock within a culture shock. Sarah sent me to this school because she was born in England and she went here – and loved it. I never thought I would love it, but after four years of being the school misfit, I had actually started to get into the swing of it. But maybe that's because I'm more or less into the swing of being a misfit too.

As we drove down the fern-lined track to the entrance of Saint Augustine's, we passed small groups of tiny little nuns wandering along holding hands. They all waved at us, and Bob tooted the horn. The nuns are soooo sweet. They never punish us or roll their eyes at us like other grown-ups. Also, they sneak us into their convent sometimes for little tea parties and ply us with sweets and Battenberg cake.

As we parked the car of shame alongside the Bentleys, Range Rovers and Rolls Royces, Bob and Sarah declared they'd better not carry more than the trunk.

'We wouldn't want to put our backs out,' Bob said.

'Never mind that my vertebrae have been cracking under the strain for years!' I muttered.

It was agreed that I would lug the shoulder-cutting fencing kit, my hand luggage and my rabbit, Dorothy Parker. Not that I'm *totally* complaining. I love carrying Dorothy (especially in her new lime green leather carrier). I don't trust anyone with my fencing kit, and I definitely didn't want Sarah and Bob near my hand luggage, as it contained my Body Shop Specials – aka vodka. Also, the trunk weighed like five thousand pounds!

The problems only arose when, halfway up, they attempted another kiss. Obviously they'd never studied basic physics, because by taking their hands off the trunk it went belting down the narrow winding stairs, knocking a gaggle of parents, valets and other girls flying in the process.

I was struggling with my own load some way behind them when one of the girls they'd knocked fell back into me, and I was sent sprawling in a heap on the stone floor at the foot of the stairs. Neither Bob nor Sarah bothered to see if I was okay. I don't think they'd even registered the disaster their snog-aging had caused.

I was just checking Dorothy when the Not So Honourable Honey O'Hare and her horrible manservant, Oopa, followed by some random guy in orange Buddhist robes, stepped over me as if I were roadkill.

Honey addressed me in that special psycho-toff sneering way she has perfected over a zillion put-downs. 'Oh, the American refugee has returned. I thought the new immigration regulations would have seen you off.' Then she pursed her collagen-enhanced lips and laughed hyena-like at her own wit. Between her Botox and her collagen implants, her face was pulled in all directions. It was not a pretty sight.

Oopa just stood wheezing evilly by her side. His spine was probably breaking under the weight of Honey's LVT steamer trunk and custom-made LVT luggage, but I was soooo over feeling sorry for Oopa after the way he had reacted the last time I offered to help him. The Buddhist monk guy was looking peacefully into the middle distance.

I didn't respond to Honey's attack. It's a survival skill I picked up over my four years at Saint Augustine's. I had faced my fear-of-fears last term when I shared a room with her, but I wasn't sharing a bedroom with her this term, so our *froidure* was back on. My *modus operandi* was to have as little to do with her as possible.

Honey wasn't finished with *me* though. She opened her mouth as if about to launch into one of her 'H to the O to the N to the E to the Y' rants. Then she looked up and stopped.

I followed her gaze and saw what had captured her attention. Bob and Sarah were standing under the stained glass window of Mary and the infant Jesus, wearing the same look of rapt adoration for one another they'd been sporting all holiday – and giggling.

'That,' Honey sneered, pointing at Bob and Sarah with one of her evil talons, 'is the most revolting sight I have ever endured.' Then she did her signature shiver of disgust before taking a deep breath and setting off up the stairs followed by her manservant and the Buddhist monk–type chap.

If she hadn't been Honey, I would have agreed with her. Instead I silently gathered my rabbit and kit together and followed her as imperiously as I could. Like most of the girls and parents, she was tanned from her New Year ski trip to Val d'Isere. But unlike them, she was wearing the most revealing yellow sundress and gold Jimmy Choo strappy sandals. Of course, she was also wearing those other two never-be-seen-without Sloane accessories: the implausibly small bejewelled phone (permanently glued to ear) and a five-hundred-dollar pash wrapped around her neck like an African tribal choker.

Halfway up, Honey turned and ran her eyes up and down me like an evil prison guard's searchlight. Under her scrutiny, I looked down at my unremarkable outfit to see what the problem was. I even checked the soles of my dilapidated green bejewelled slippers as I waited for her attack.

Eventually she said, 'Well?'

So I said, 'Well what?'

'Your chavscum parents are blocking the stairwell, you American Freak.'

I craned my neck and saw she was right. Oh my giddy aunt, it was unbelievable. They were *still* canoodling, completely oblivious to all the people who were struggling to squeeze past them. I called out sharply, 'Sarah and Bob! Stop that at once!'

You can see how badly this role reversal was affecting me.

SIX

Bohemian Rhapsody in the Dorm

This term I was rooming with two of my first choices: boy-crazed, adorably sentimental Clementine and a princess from Nigeria, Indiamacca – known as Clems and Indie, respectively. Both girls were already in the room chatting on their tiny phones – Indie's phone is soooo feverishly cool. It is purple enamel and has her name picked out in *real* diamonds.

Clems' parents and my parents were chatting together as they unpacked our clothes. Clems' little brother Sebastian was opening and shutting the wardrobe door, pretending to be a savage animal and biting the clothes as they were being placed inside by the grown-ups. He was three now and looking less and less like a Jelly Baby and more and more like a bad elf.

Indie's valet was unpacking for his mistress, while her security guards were decorating the room in her trademark purple.

I was so used to the madness of my school life in England now that I barely gave a second glance to the two burly suits in buzz cuts balanced on dainty floral stools as they hung the purple curtains.

I hadn't seen Indie or Clemmie since last term, so I was far more desperate to hear their goss. But before the hugs and air-kisses were over, I overheard Sarah say to Clemmie's parents (and anyone else with hearing in the building), 'Yes, we got married at Christmas. It was soooo romantic.'

Seriously, this was atrocious. I was sure Indie's valet and security men couldn't care less about Bob and Sarah's marital unions. But Clemmie's parents were another matter. Clems' 'rents were not bohemian rhapsodies like Star's or mine. No, they were your normal, madly conservative, Tory-voting 'rentals.

This was an emergency. Acting on instinct, I dove over Indie's valet, who was carefully placing designer casuals in the drawer under her bed, clamped my hand over Sarah's mouth, and cried out, 'Stop saying that!' Turning to Clems' 'rents, I explained, 'Honestly, they were married years before I was born! It was just a repeat performance. I don't want any trouble.'

Mr and Mrs Fraser Marks looked at me as if I were a mad adolescent on hormonal meltdown. Then Clems' madre spoke directly to Sarah. 'Yes, Clementine told us about the blessing. Congratulations to you both.'

I removed my hand from Sarah's mouth and pretended

that I had merely been brushing her face for crumbs. Sarah shook her head and frowned, so I planted a dutiful-daughter kiss on her nose.

Bob gave me one of his "you're so paranoid, Calypso" glares. I slunk back over to Indie and Clemmie. Stupid, stupid, stupid Calypso – I wish I'd fainted instead.

Sebastian pointed at me and said, 'Bad fox.'

'He's a cute little fellow,' Bob said, and laughed when Sebastian sunk his teeth in my hand and said, 'Bad fox, bad fox, bad fox.'

No one so much as scolded him. Star is right. It's unbelievable what boys get away with.

Clems' father said, 'Clemmie was most upset she was unable to attend, but we were skiing.'

'Star sent me photos, though,' Clemmie piped up as she ran her Mason Pearson through her long straight blonde hair, which now hung below her waist.

'Yes, we, erm, thought the cake looked very lovely,' her parents agreed uncomfortably. Obviously they'd seen the tongue swallowing shot as txted by Star.

'Swell,' said Bob. Yes, he actually said 'swell.'

'You two make such a cute couple,' Indie told my parents.

Why does everyone keep saying my 'rents are cute? If I said 'swell,' the whole of England would take the piss for the next ten zillion years. Yet for some reason everything Bob and Sarah say or do is met with cries of, 'They're soooo cute.'

Hello Kitty toasters that toast Hello Kitty faces onto your bread are cute. Bob and Sarah are vaudevillian paragons if anything. Why can't they keep a pleasing balloon's distance between them at all times, like normal parents?

'Let's take Dorothy down to the pet shed,' I suggested to Clemmie, who had already taken my rabbit out of her carrier for a hop.

'Good idea,' she agreed as Dorothy gave her a punishing nip. Dorothy became quite the prima donna when left in her carrier for too long.

'I'll join you,' Indie added, checking her modelesque figure in the mirror as she rearranged her purple pash around her neck. 'Edwards, can you supervise the rest of the decorations?' she asked her valet. He gave her a little bow.

'We're going to take Dorothy down to the pet shed,' I told the loony madre and padre. They were still busy extolling the revolutionary effects of their remarriage to Clems' parents. Would you believe my father was talking about writing a script based on their rapprochement? That's what he was going to call his screenplay, *The Rapprochement*!

'Okay, bye, Calypso. Call us tomorrow and let us know how you're settling in,' Bob told me as he planted a kiss on my head.

Sarah, barely able to pull herself away from the conversation, just gave me the American hand sign for okay, which made my friends tear up with laughter. When I first pitched up in this land of rain and drizzle, I soon learned that it is not de rigueur to make hand gestures to people who are actually close enough to hear you speak. I suppose I should be glad she didn't try and high-five me. She does that too.

Sure enough, all the way down to the pet shed, Clemmie and Indie started dementedly hand-signing to one another. This is what the English do; take the piss (or as we say at school, extract the urine). It's a national pastime. Even the nuns and staff do it.

SEVEN

Operation Dumping Boys

Star was already standing in the snow-frosted pet run with her pet rat and snake. She was wearing her regulation Doc Martens (pink today), tartan mini-skirt and a ripped designer cashmere jumper. Her reticulated python, Brian, was slung around her neck like a pash, while Hilda the rat was peeping out her jumper, completing her rock royalty look. Even with punk accoutrements, Star still looked like a naughty cherub with her long strawberry-blonde hair, big green eyes and milky white skin.

I spotted Honey and Georgina sharing a fag in the trees of Pullers' Wood. From a distance they looked like sisters with their willowy figures and long blonde hair. Like Honey, Georgina's legs were completely exposed, but at least Georgina was wearing a black cashmere jumper and a baby blue pash around her neck as a nod to the weather. She was also hugging her teddy bear, Tobias, who is a full fee-paying student at Saint Augustine's.

After an excited session of air-kissing, Star pointed into the trees and smirked. 'Have you seen Honey's new bodyguard?'

I spotted the orange-robed Buddhist lurking in the woods nearby, seemingly in some deep meditation-type activity.

'Yaah, I saw him earlier. What's that about?' I asked.

'Honey's afraid there may be a plot to kidnap her now that her latest stepfather is in the House of Lords.'

'But, erm, aren't Buddhists meant to be all meditative and peaceful?' I asked.

'Yaah totally. But nonviolent security is really big at the moment. *Tatler* did some big spread on nonviolent security firms in Knightsbridge,' Clems explained.

I felt like fainting with the madness of it all, but then Georgina spotted us and came running over.

After another air-kiss-a-thon, I passed Dorothy to Georgina, who co-owns her with me. 'Dorothy! You've turned into a chubba lub!' she told our plump little rabbit through chattering teeth. 'You'll never be model-spotted now, darling.' She kissed Dorothy on the nose.

'Blame Sarah,' I told her, giving Dorothy's ears a little scratch. 'She wouldn't stop feeding her scraps even though I kept telling her, she's a sentient being and not a recycling bin!'

'Hilda's put on weight too,' Star said, referring to her pet rat. 'I've had to put her on the GI diet for rats. Mummy had a specialist flown out from New York to council her.'

The rest of us nodded gravely, as if having dietary specialists flown in to keep a rat's figure trim was a perfectly reasonable thing to do. When I first arrived at Saint Augustine's, I found everything about these spoilt, confident, sophisticated girls peculiar. I guess after you've lived with people long enough, though, you get used to their odd little ways.

When I was certain Honey couldn't hear us, I asked Georgina, 'Who's Honey rooming with?'

'Fenella and Perdita at Polo Central,' replied Georgina, referring to the polo twins.

Fenella and Perdita were not only identical twins but mad keen polo players. Their ponies were stabled nearby, and they were wildly popular with the polo boys at Eades who only spoke in polo-speak.

'It is seriously funny,' Georgina continued. 'Honey came to find me for a whinge. Apparently, every spare inch of wall space was already plastered with pictures of polo ponies and fit players by the time she arrived. She was absolutely livid, and Siddhartha, her security guard, kept telling her to breathe. Tobias laughed so hard he practically fell apart at the seams.'

We all knew how Tobias felt, because the first thing Honey did once her manservant had unpacked was to cover her pin board and wall space with paparazzi shots of herself. Honey adores society shots of herself chatting to other society clones. I could well imagine that she may have met her It Girl match with Fen and Perdita, who didn't rate anything outside the world of polo. They'd have absolutely no patience with Honey's bitchy humour, which meant Honey would have to hang out in someone else's room in order to get her bitch fix.

Oh no! Honey Hell, here I come.

Don't be so paranoid, I told myself. Honey would probably go to Georgina's room. After all, they went to nursery school together, and their bio fathers hunt together. 'What about you, Georgina, who are you rooming with?' I inquired idly, hoping it would be someone Honey-friendly.

'Beatrice and Izzie,' Georgina replied, failing to suppress her laughter. Izzie was quite scary, only in a less confrontational way than Honey.

I had heard on the txt-vine that Honey had pulled Izzie's boyfriend at some New Year's party in Val d'Isere. 'Is it true that Honey had a lip-fest with Izzie's boyfriend?' I asked now as my panic began to set in.

Star and Georgina looked at one another and burst out laughing. 'It was hilarious. When Izzie walked in and saw Honey in our room, she spat the dummy, darling. She gave Honey the most ferocious look, it almost melted Honey's collagen!'

'What did Honey do?' Clemmie asked, her Tiffany-box blue eyes wide with curiosity.

Georgina shrugged. 'You know Honey, she would have got on her high horse, but Izzie looked like she might slap her, so she brazened it out and denied everything. Put it this way; I don't think Honey will be visiting my room very much this term.'

I wasn't being paranoid. 'So hang on. If her room's out because of Fen and Perdita, and your room's out because of Izzie, where will Honey hang out?' I asked, trying to keep the desperation out of my voice.

'I'm rooming with Portia and Arabella,' Star said. 'So she won't *dare* come near us.'

'Don't worry, darling,' Indie said, reading my mind and throwing a comforting arm around me. 'She hates me too.'

This was true, but while Indie would give as good as she got where Honey was concerned, her presence alone might not be enough to keep Honey away. The fly in the ointment was Clemmie, who was soooo nice to everyone, including Honey. I had been Honey's torture toy from the day I arrived at Saint Augustine's. With my American accent, lack of grand ancestors or old money, I was a red flag to a mad bull. It was as inevitable as brown slops on a Sunday. Our room would become Honey's new torture parlour.

As if summoned by satanic forces, Honey tottered over to join us. Her orange-robed bodyguard followed at a serene distance. 'Laters, peasants. I'm going back up to the institution,' she groaned, flicking her butt at my feet as she sprayed herself with Febreze to get rid of the smoke smell. Then, confirming my worst fears, she added to Clemmie, 'I'll see you à la mo, Clems. I'll be hanging out in your room this term. Fen and Perdita are too polo for words, and I've soooo much to tell you, darling.'

'Laters,' Clemmie said, smiling sweetly at Honey.

'Laters,' we all added to Honey's blue-with-cold back. But for me, the word 'laters' held more than a touch of menace.

'I know she'll haunt our room,' I blurted after her entourage was out of earshot.

'So did you dump Freds?' Star asked, changing the subject in her usual radical way.

'Why on earth would I dump Freds?'

'Erm . . . because he makes you fall asleep and snore?'

'He soooo does not.'

'Well, he finds you disappointing.'

'Don't be mad. He does not find me disappointing.'

'Well, why did you say he did?'

'I didn't.'

'Yes, you did. And that's another thing. All you do is go on and on *ad infinitum* about Freds.'

I briefly toyed with the idea of fainting to avoid this tedious conversational cul-de-sac, but then Georgina agreed with Star. 'We *do* spend far too much time obsessing over boys.'

I looked from girl to girl. I was suddenly surrounded by an anti-boy cult. 'Boys are a vital part of existence!' I reminded them.

'I quite like boys. Well, pulling boys anyway,' Clemmie added. She was looking practically as horrified as me.

Indie didn't look too keen on the boy-dumping idea either. She hadn't said anything, but I was almost certain-ish she'd been fantasising about Malcolm all through the holidays.

Star looked directly at her as she said, 'I'm going to be more like Indie and focus on my music.'

Indie nodded expressionlessly, blinded by the brightness of Star's million-watt personality. There was also the small detail that Indie hadn't actually pulled Malcolm yet.

'What about Malcolm?' I tested Indie.

'Who's Malcolm?' she asked, blinking her chocolaty eyes with confusion – as if she wasn't sick with love for him at all.

I looked around at my friends. They were all in this Dumping Freddie scheme together. It was a cabal of evil.

So I fainted.

EIGHT

In Defence of the Realm

'I'm not dumping Freds,' I told Star firmly after she'd put Brian on top of me to bring me round. She had even made him give me a little kiss with his flicky-out tongue. 'It's taken me all my life to pull a prince and I'm not about to throw him back now, just as things are going well.' I passed Brian back.

'We can still pull boys, though, can't we?' pleaded Clemmie again. Pulling boys was, after all, her favourite sport. The thing about Clemmie was, once she'd pulled them, she tossed them right back. And she never thought about them again.

Star ignored her. Placing her hands on my shoulders, she looked straight into my eyes. 'You'll be too busy for Freds, darling. Apart from your fencing and your GCSEs, you promised to help Indie and me with our lyrics, remember.'

Whoops. I had almost forgotten about agreeing to write lyrics for Star and Indie's band. Their main interest was writing miserable minor chord compositions about the horrors of being rock royalty – or in Indie's case, real royalty – and going to the most exclusive boarding school in England. Love them though I do, their songs made me feel like attending my own funeral. Star knows that lyrics aren't her strong point, so when Indie came to the school with her guitar last term, Star started harbouring a dream that the three of us would combine our talents for the greater good of music. She'd sing and play bass, Indie would play lead guitar – or 'the six strings of the devil,' as Father Conway calls it – and I'd write the words.

'But I haven't written anything yet,' I admitted. 'I mean, with Bob and Sarah here and –'

'I know, that's exactly what I'm talking about. We've all got soooo much going on. Boys will just be in the way. Besides, Freds is too freakishly normal for you.'

I wished she'd stop saying that.

'Star's right,' Georgina said as she placed Dorothy on the snow-frosted grass for a hop.

'Et tu, Georgina?' I cried, shoving an imagined dagger into my heart.

She nudged me affectionately. 'Pulling boys is fun, but the whole boyfriend saga has become très, très, très boring, darling. No offence, Calypso.'

'But what about love?' I asked, deeply offended.

'Now *I* feel like fainting,' Star groaned. 'I dumped Kev, and he was low maintenance, darling.' What she really meant was, he did anything she said. 'Freddie is *far* too high maintenance.'

'He's not a GI diet,' I said crossly. 'He's my boyfriend.

Whatever happened to "for better or worse"? It's not as if we're together twenty-four-seven or anything sad like that. I'm here at school all the time. Well, apart from exeats and weekends after Saturday classes.'

'How many times a day do you txt him?' Georgina asked me as she plaited her long, blonde, obedient hair.

'I don't know. A few.' I shrugged, running a hand through my own rebellious blonde locks that never obeyed a single command.

'Over twenty?' Star asked, folding her arms and contorting her gorgeous features, taking on the expression of a menopausal matron.

I shrugged again. 'Maybe. I don't exactly chalk them up.' I tried to flick my hair in a careless gesture of defiance, but it got stuck to my lip-gloss and I spent the next few minutes wiping it off. I picked up Dorothy, partly because I thought her little paws might be frozen but mostly for emotional comfort. She was all wiggly and eager to be put back down.

'Okay, so, let's say you txt him twenty times a day,' Georgina suggested. 'Then, for argument's sake, let's say he txts you back twenty times. That's forty txts you're reading and rereading.'

'You're scarily good at hard sums, darling,' I told her sarcastically. Then to be horrible, I teased, 'Maybe you should marry Mr Templeton?' Mr Templeton was our horrible little maths teacher who would have put even dear old Einstein off his hard sums.

But all Georgina did was roll her eyes.

'Plus, you agonise for ages and ages over your txts. And then you analyse whatever he txts you,' Star added.

'That is soooo untrue,' I lied.

Star and the others all giggled. I suppose I have forwarded a lot of my txts to Star before sending them to Freds. But still, she shouldn't have put the Doc Marten in like that.

'I've had soooo many conversations with you, Calypso, agonising over the number of kisses you should send Freddie and analysing the significance of how many he sends to you. And then there are all those txts you forward me.'

Talk about betrayal. 'Hah!' was all I could say to my traitor of a friend. I looked to Clemmie and Indie for support, but their eyes remained fixed on Star. Star can be très, très persuasive.

'I just think we should get the whole boy thing into perspective, Calypso.'

'What does "into perspective" mean?' I asked, rolling my eyes like a loon.

'Spending less time focusing on boyfriends and more time focusing on the things we really want to do, like music and writing.'

'I just like pulling boys, really,' Clemmie piped up.

I loved Clemmie.

Star looked at our boy-mad friend and smiled. 'Pulling them is fine, I'm not talking about that. It's just once you start hanging out too much with one boy and daydreaming about him, it becomes a pain.'

I didn't find daydreaming about Freds the least bit painful. But I didn't say anything. He was the perfect boyfriend. He had the most lovely sticky-outy black hair and kissable lips and he always made me feel wonderful, apart from when he gave me disappointed looks. But that hadn't happened for, well, since the other day. Which proved he must be getting used to my odd ways. Which meant now was not the time to dump him.

Star clicked her fingers in front of my face. 'See! Look at yourself, Calypso. You're drifting off into Freddieland right now. I can see it in your eyes. They've gone all moon-shaped.'

And so another circus of laughter ensued.

A snowflake landed on my nose. As more flakes followed, I put my hands out to catch them. I usually loved it when it snows, but all I felt then was a horrible sense of doom. My mother calls me the Queen of Doomsday Prophesies. But then again she also thinks boys will respect me more if I wear Wellies.

'How did Kev take the dump?' I asked Star, hoping to divert attention away from Freds and me.

'Oh, he cried,' Star replied. If it wasn't Star, I would have sworn I detected a wobble in her voice. 'And then I cried,' she added. 'It was quite the cry-fest, actually.'

'That's really sad,' I told her, but all she did was shrug as we both watched the white snowflakes falling on her pink Doc Martens.

'Yaah, but then I told myself: Indie, Calypso and I are

going to be flat out with Sloaney Trash, and I did a cartwheel.'

'What's Sloaney Trash?' asked Clemmie.

'That's what we're calling the band,' Indie told her. 'We only decided last night.'

'Nice of you to tell *me*.' I sulked.

'We did phone,' Indie said. 'And we can still change it. It's just an idea, but we thought you'd like the ironic angle.'

'We didn't just call once either,' Star added. 'We called and called and called. Your mobile was engaged.'

Whoops-a-daisy. I was on the phone with Freds all night. They'd only left one voice mail and by the time I got it, it was really late.

'I'm tucking Dorothy up in the pet shed before she freezes,' Georgina said as she dashed off.

'Indie's got some fab ideas for lyrics,' Star said as she scraped her foot through the thin veil of snow. 'The music wing's finished now and we've got the use of the studio. You've always wanted to be a proper writer. Aren't you excited, Calypso?'

'Yaah, of course,' I replied hesitantly.

I should have known better. Star was always trying to push me towards my dreams. Last term, she had persuaded me to enter a national newspaper's essay competition. The winner hadn't been announced yet. Not that I would win or anything. At least I hoped not. The rules were to give an autobiographical account of suffering or trauma in a teen-ager's life. I'd opted to write about the pain of my own parents' madder-than-mad, short-lived split, only I had to use a little artistic licence to spice it up.

I know it was *meant* to be autobiographical, but who wants to read about a boring old couple having a midlife crisis? No one, that's who. And anyway, how was I to know that no sooner had I handed it in, than they'd go and reunite like love's young dream? I would die a thousand deaths if I did actually win, because then it would be published in the national press, and Bob and Sarah would read it and kill me.

Star nudged me. 'Are you okay, Calypso?' she asked.

'Yaah, I was just thinking about the essay. They're judging it soon.'

'Oh my God,' she squealed, clamping her hand over her mouth.

'Imagine if you win?' Clemmie said.

Then Star said something truly horrifying 'Think of it, the whole country reading your essay.'

'Sarah and Bob are back together now and totally in love. They'd die if they read what I wrote – after they kill me first,' I said.

'I'm sure you're just being paranoid,' Star insisted, trying to wrap Brian around my neck again. It is a major strugglerama, trying to pretend I like Brian all the time. 'You worry too much, darling. You overanalyse everything.'

'I do not!' I protested, even though it was true.

'You always have. And since you've added a boy like Freds to your list of things to fret about, you've turned into a lovesick puppy who can't think of anything but him.' Star grabbed me by the shoulders again and looked into my eyes as if about to hypnotise me. 'You're fifteen, Calypso. Life's just beginning. You need to live a little! I mean, it's not as if you're going to marry him, is it?'

Isn't it? Okay, so it probably isn't, but I still couldn't believe she was saying all this. Well, I could. She's never been a Freddie fan, but more worrisome than that, she was also stubborn, and in all the time I'd known her, I'd never known her to let something drop. Take the essay thing. There was no way I would have written that essay if Star hadn't made me.

'Come on, my legs are blue,' Georgina urged, having returned from putting Dorothy in the luxurious heated pet shed. 'Quick, peasants, let's leg it before we turn to snow statues.'

Back at the dorm, all had been transformed. The 'rents had gone home, and Indie's people had turned our bedroom into an interior design magazine spread. There were purple velvet cushions embroidered with gold crests strewn across the room, and our beds were draped in purple velvet splendour. The old oil paintings of saints and the bright red panic buttons by the beds were all that remained to remind us we were at school. The panic buttons had been installed recently, and as far as I knew, they'd never been used. But as I flopped on my bed, I had an overwhelming urge to press mine.

NINE

Enterprising Initiatives

We were all sprawled on our beds, listening to our iPods, scrolling through txt messages and listlessly flicking through magazines, when Miss Bibsmore hobbled into our room. She'd gone back to wrapping carpet and duct tape around her walking stick, so we hadn't heard her approach.

''Ello, girls,' she screeched.

I think I speak for all when I say her appearance came as a shock. I mean, Miss Bibsmore's no runway model at the best of times, but that evening she was crumpled over her stick even farther than usual. More freakish than that, she was wearing a massive pair of fluffy dog slippers with big floppy ears and plastic stick-on eyes. Animal slippers are de rigueur for house spinsters, so it was really the tatty old dressing gown over the floral flannel nightie that cracked me up.

'Are you alright, Miss Bibsmore?' I asked, slightly concerned by her appearance.

'Don't you worry about me, luvvie. I'm just feeling a bit

orf – it's the menopause, you see. My womb hurts something chronic and my back's playing up. It's a cruel god that cursed us with these 'ormones, dearie, I'll tell you that for free,' she said.

As if anyone would pay for that gem of philosophy! None of us really knew how to respond, so we just nodded.

'All unpacked I see,' Miss Bibsmore remarked with approval. 'Not like some I could mention.' She was looking at the door as she spoke, and I turned to see Honey.

'What will you be after then, Madam?' Miss Bibsmore asked my anti-friend. 'This isn't your room last time I looked.'

Honey's always doing battle with house spinsters, or anyone else she sees as inferior, which is basically anyone who doesn't want to take her photograph and place it in *Tatler*. The exception was Miss Bibsmore, who wasn't in the least bit rattled by Honey's poisonous put-downs. Which was probably why all Honey said was, 'Oh, shut up, you insane old woman,' before walking off in a huff. Mild by Honey's standards.

'How was your Christmas, Miss Bibsmore?' Indie, Clemmie and I asked as we each took one of our two earphones out.

'Oh, it was triffic, luvvies, simply triffic.' Her eyes travelled about the room, which was clean, thankfully. 'Lovely job you've done on the room, girls,' she remarked, hobbling across the room to feel the fabric of the curtains. 'That'd be silk an' all. Real class, that's what that is and it'll be all your work, I'll hazard, Your Highness,' she said to Indie.

'I really wish you'd call me Indie, Miss Bibsmore,' Indie told her, while continuing to rock her head in time to the music.

'Oh, I couldn't do that, Your Highness,' Miss Bibsmore said, horrified by the thought. 'It wouldn't be right, not with you being proper royal an' all,' she insisted.

The truth was, there were a number of royals at my school, including a few princesses, loads of countesses and ladies and the odd duchess. But none of them got royal highness-ed like Indie. Using your title at school was considered *de trop*. Freds is next in line to the throne but even he never uses his title. The plain truth was, Indie had charmed her way into Miss Bibsmore's heart.

'Well I'll be off then. Me rheumatism is playing up something rotten,' she moaned. 'Mind you, don't get muck on the princess's spreads with those shoes of yours, Miss Fraser Marks,' she warned Clemmie.

'Deffo,' replied Clemmie, scrutinising her *Tatler*.

'And 'ow's your poor mother, Miss Kelly? Staying on a bit in England by all reports now yer father is up and joined 'er.'

'Yes, Miss Bibsmore.'

'That must be nice for you, luvvie. I 'eard as much. It's the nuns, yer see. They like a good natter. Not that I'm one for gossip nor nothing.'

'No, Miss Bibsmore,' we all agreed in the Saint Augustine's tone of perceived obedience and respect.

'Well, I'll be gittin back on my rounds, then. Cheerio, girls. Good-bye, Your Highness.'

'Bye, Miss Bibsmore,' we called after her, as if her visit had been the highlight of our day.

'What do you think of Star's idea about our dumping our boyfriends?' I asked casually, as if I wasn't at all desperate for support from my roommates.

'I don't have a boyfriend,' Indie replied as she lazily scrolled through her txts on her little bejewelled purple phone.

'What about Malcolm?' I asked, hoping to rattle her.

Indie was saved from responding by Clemmie, who blurted, 'She didn't say we couldn't *pull* boys, just that we shouldn't get all clingy about any one boy in particular.'

I looked over at Indie, but she was still scrolling away, seemingly unbothered by Star's Operation Dumping Boys.

I decided to visit Lady Portia Herrington Briggs. She was on the national sabre team with me and had been my fencing partner since Star had chucked sabre to focus on her minor chord compositions. Given that Star and Portia were sharing this term, I wondered if Star would start giving Portia grief about her boyfriend, who happened to be Kev's older brother, Billy. The dating habits of English public schools are très, très incestuous.

Portia is blessed with one of those cool aristocratic demeanours. She's aloof without being in the least bit arrogant. I've never seen her ruffled or rattled or acting loopy like other teenagers. Even when we fence, her luxuriously thick, long raven mane remains hair-commercial perfect. If she wasn't so lovely and sweet, her perfection could easily mark her out for secret hatred. As it is, no one has a bad word to say about her, not that she's a pushover. Even Honey tempers her psycho-toff rants when Portia's around.

When I walked in, Star, Portia and Arabella had a Lower Sixth girl in their room selling ghastly handmade jewelry as part of the school's Enterprise Awareness scheme. The scheme claimed to provide girls with the skills needed to be entrepreneurial businesswomen. I think that was stretching it. The fact of the matter was the students only bought whatever the Lower Sixth came up with because the proceeds went towards the Sunday Supper, which was a treat our year was now privileged to enjoy.

I picked up one of the gaudy plastic beads on coloured string and asked how much it was.

'A tenner. We're doing a really cool music night and getting in the caterers from Eades to do a proper Burns Night feast,' the older girl explained. 'Sans haggis, naturally.'

'What will you pipe in then?' I asked, relieved as I relived the memory of last year's horrible haggis. Burns Night is one of those mad Scottish traditions like caber tossing, reeling and kilt wearing. The Scots really are exquisitely bonkers. Take Clems and Malcolm for example. Burns Night is a cool idea though as it's the celebration of their national poet – and there isn't enough celebrating of national poets, if you ask me.

'A giant pizza,' the Sixth girl replied.

'Cool.'

'The real news is that we're performing,' Star added, holding out an arm covered in coloured bead bracelets. 'So buy up big darling.' Even though most of the Enterprise Initiative products are often revolting bits of jewelry or hoodies with mad slogans emblazoned across them, we all buy and wear them. It's sort of a cult thing. Occasionally they even turn up on eBay, where they are snatched up for exorbitant sums of money by girls who missed out. The trouble is that these cult items bring new depth to the saying "so last term." No girl would be seen dead in last term's Enterprise Initiative.

'Wow, that's really cool about you and Indie playing. Does Indie know?' I asked.

'No, but I've told you,' Star insisted, 'because I want you to write something for it. It will be our first big gig, and if it goes well, we can lay down the tracks on CD,' she explained. 'You did say you wanted to write some songs for us.' Her green eyes were sparkling with infectious enthusiasm, and in that moment I decided she was probably right. Not about the boy thing, but about focusing on our dreams. It wouldn't do me any harm to try my hand at writing lyrics.

'I'm on the case,' I assured her as I studied the bracelet horrors I was about to blow my term allowance on. 'I'm just waiting for the, erm . . . inspiration.'

Star rolled her eyes and shook her head at my dismal lie. The best and worst thing about best friends is they know you so well.

I purchased a bundle of plastic bead horrors, and when groups of girls started piling into the room, I snuck off down to the pet shed and rang Freddie.

'Hey,' he answered. 'What's up?'

'Just wanted to hear your voice,' I told him as I watched Hilda running herself ragged on her little rat wheel. 'And to make sure we're still on for Saturday afternoon,' I added casually, in case, like Star, he thought I was a lovesick puppy.

'Definitely,' he agreed, before ruining my life by adding, 'unless something comes up.'

TEN

Peace, Love and Buddhist Security

The next day, Clemmie, Indie and I slept through the 6:45 a.m. bell. Miss Bibsmore had to come and poke us in the ribs with her stick after the third bell. By then it was 7:10, giving us twenty minutes to clean our teeth, get dressed into our vile uniforms and leg it to the ref and devour what food we could before chapel. I couldn't find any of my horrible maroon pleated skirts.

Clems offered me one of hers, which was indecently short on me. I'd definitely get a blue if not an ASBO for lewdity.

Fortunately, after four years, we were all experts in the art of flying down the narrow stone steps. In the ref, we grabbed a couple of croissants (one for each pocket) and gulped a hot chocolate each.

Mass had already started by the time we crept into the chapel. Father Conway was banging on about how our mortal bodies belong to Our Lady and that we shouldn't allow anyone to defile them. I hoped the nurse from the infirmary was listening. She was always defiling our bodies with violent needle jabs.

As if reading my mind, Indie whispered, 'We'd best remind Sister in the infirmary about that next time she gives us our flu jabs,' which sent me off giggling.

We always had a full Latin mass on the first day back. After that it was just a twenty-minute prayer and hymn service, unless it was a feast day. I heard my tummy rumbling and was madly tempted to sneak-eat my pocket croissants, but not even Honey would be that sacrilegious. Eventually Father Conway wrapped up his sermon with a fervent wish that this would be another successful academic term, and being a new year, an *annus mirabilis.*

After mass we had to race back upstairs for room inspection. I had another look for my buggery skirts, but they had obviously done a runner. Probably too embarrassed to be seen on my freakishly long stick-like legs.

I was so self-conscious of how high Clem's skirt was riding up that I developed a special bent-knee run, pulling the skirt down as I scuttled about the corridors, which was how I happened to bump into Honey's new security guy. I'd like to see the kidnapper brave enough to take on Honey. Not that this man in orange robes looked particularly hard. Maybe he would meditate the kidnappers into surrender?

'Sorry, miss,' he said as my head hit his orange-robed knees.

Sister Constance wasn't too keen on personal security guards. At Eades they were part of the furniture. They even had their own housing block, which had resulted in all sorts of tragic nobodies hiring security just to show off.

'That's okay,' I told him. 'It was totally my fault.' Then I waddled off, still tugging my skirt down while Honey screamed about how she would sue the knickers off me if I damaged her bodyguard.

'What's wrong?' Portia asked after she'd watched me waddle into class and take my seat beside her in Latin. Only four of us were doing Latin for our GCSEs. For some unfathomable reason, parents find small classes a good thing. But then they're not the ones having to defend themselves against the madness of Miss Mills and her ilk without backup.

'My skirts have done a runner,' I explained. 'Clems leant me one of hers, but it's too short.

Portia smiled. 'You can borrow mine, darling. At least we're closer in height. Listen, I didn't get to finish the translations we were meant to do over the break. Do you think Miss Mills will believe me if I say, *Canis meus id comedit*?'

I laughed, remembering the translations we'd amused ourselves with during dull Latin lectures last term. 'Your dog ate it?'

'Too obvious, you think?'

'Here,' I said, passing my book over. 'You'd better copy mine.' Some loopy Lower Sixth girls had told me that dead languages were easy A grades. I thought that meant I could snooze and gossip my way through class, but Miss Mills ruined that little illusion quick smart. As she entered the room that morning, she rambled off the old *In nomine patras, et filie et spirtitus sancti*, then started gabbing away *ad absurdum* about how much work we were expected to put in this term.

What did she think Latin was, exactly? A living language? Honestly, teachers are a breed apart. This was proved beyond doubt when she passed us a booklet titled – and I'm not making this up – *How to Pass Your Exams (And Enjoy Yourself)*.

Honestly, I don't know why I bother attending classes at all sometimes. The picture on the front of the booklet depicted a skateboarder. Now what, I ask you, has skateboarding got to do with passing your Latin GCSE? Nothing, that's what. For a start, skateboards and the clothes that go with them are banned at our school.

Things didn't get better when Miss Mills urged us to open our booklet, where saying after pithy saying urged us to do unnatural things like, 'Convert linear notes to MIND MAPS.'

I turned to a page decorated in wizards, fat television show hosts and musical scores urging us to learn, 'VISUALLY, ORALLY, AURALLY and KINAESTHETICALLY.' Portia and I looked at each other and shook our heads.

I passed Portia a note.

I just bumped into Honey's security guy in the corridor.

She passed one back.

He seems weirdly nice for a Honey person?

I wrote back:

Who'd want to steal Honey, though?

Portia wrote:

Maybe someone out there's got a hit on her?

I responded:

No one asked me to chip in.

And then we started laughing like that Laughing Cavalier chap that hangs in the Wallace Collection in London. We went there on an art excursion in Year Eight although Star and I nicked off to Selfridges and tried on wigs. It was still très, très culturally enhancing, I assure you.

We were laughing so feverishly that I actually fell off my chair. Even Portia, with her aloof demeanour and centuries of breeding, only barely managed to keep her balance.

Miss Mills loomed over me as I lay sprawled on the floor. But instead of saying something charitable and nice like 'Are you all right, dear?' she snatched up our notes and read them.

I'm sure that reading the personal correspondence of other people can't be legal. Still, I thought hopefully, even horrible old Miss Mills must see the joke? But no, instead of joining in our circus of hilarity, she made us stay back and translate our notes into Latin after class. Honestly, some teachers really should be sectioned under the Lack of Humour Act.

Her stupid punishment made us late for our lunchtime fencing practice. We ran like mad things down the corridors. Well, I ran like a mad thing because I had to do a sort of running waddle so I could keep my knickers covered with Clem's tiny skirt. As we took a short pause while passing a nun, I asked Portia about Billy, hoping to garner support against Star's Dumping Boys crusade.

'I've dumped him,' she said.

I fainted.

Okay, I didn't actually faint, because then Portia nudged me and said, 'Just joking, darling.'

But then she added, 'We *are* on a break, though. At least until after the GCSEs. We agreed it would be too stressful, especially now we're both on the national team. I'm really excited about going to Italy, aren't you, darling? I hear the Italian fencing standard is the best in the world after the Hungarians. Basically Billy and I agreed to prioritise fencing and exams.'

Then I actually did faint.

Honey's Buddhist guard helped me up – and saw my knickers, which was mortifying because they were a pair that had once been white but had turned grey in the wash.

Honey had a total Honey Fit. 'What the bloody hell do you think you're doing using my security? And as for you, Siddhartha, you are supposed to have your eyes on your principle at all times. Someone could have kidnapped *me* while you were touching her.'

Siddhartha looked ashamed. 'Sorry, Miss,' he said to his principle.

'My father's paying you to guard *me*, not *her*,' she shrieked, pointing one of her long talons at me. 'Why would anybody want to steal *her*?'

ELEVEN

Not Fair Was Made to Fare

Portia and I had to run off because we were having another laughing fit and didn't want to get a stitch before fencing. Now that we had been selected for the national team and were heading off to Italy for our first international tournament, we had pledged to devote as much time as we could to extra practice. The Italian fencing team was one of the best in the world, which was a bit daunting.

Our South African fencing master, Bell End, was as mad as a drawer of old ladies' knickers. He was sitting on the floor, reading *Sword* magazine. He didn't look up when we came in so we sailed past him, through the armoury and into the changing rooms. We were both feverish with excitement, as this would be the first time we would be fencing with our GBR international kit.

The outfits fit so perfectly, we did some Milanese modelling struts and said 'Mama mia' and 'Ooh la la.'

It was one of those blissfully va-va-va-voom moments that I will never forget. Actually, I could quite fancy myself in my new gear. I couldn't wait to show it off to Freds. It was all so feverishly exciting.

When we came out, Bell End was still on the floor reading his magazine, only now he was lying facedown, his head propped on his hands. I looked at Portia and she looked at me in that way you do when wondering if a teacher has reached the straightjacket stage.

I did my 'this is awkward' cough.

Portia slapped me on the back and asked, 'Is this an inconvenient time, sir?' with all the serenity you'd expect of true nobility.

Bell End looked up at us as if we were strangers. 'I'm not in the mood for fencing,' he replied gruffly.

'Shall we come back later perhaps, Mr Wellend?' she inquired, remembering to use his real name.

'If you like,' he muttered like a sullen child.

Talk about exasperating. 'But sir, we've got our first international tournament in Italy to prepare for,' I protested, ignoring Portia's warning look. Honestly, if I had had a Bibsmore stick, I would have poked him with it.

Bell End looked up at me and smiled. 'There's the spirit, Kelly! Don't take no for an answer.' Then he jumped up with the agility you expect from an Olympic Silver medal winner and slapped me on the back so hard I'm pretty certain he dislodged a few vital organs. For a short little stout South African, he's fiercely muscular.

'Right! Let's be having you first, Kelly. Briggsie, wire her up.'

Portia wired me up.

Bell End grabbed a sabre and mask from the salle d'armes and wired himself to the electrical device that would record our points. He saluted me with his embarrassing signature salute. Oh my God, it was soooo tragic. His blade made a threatening swishing sound as he carved the letter *W* in the air.

He called 'play' and began an aggressive shuffle towards me using the funny little steps you spend most of your fencing career practicing.

'I'm Italian, an arrogant, unpredictable nasty bit of work,' he told me in his thick South African accent as he made a swiping lunge.

What was it with teachers and role-playing? Was there something in their curriculum that recommended it? If so, the suits who come up with these things should be lined up against a wall and pelted with water balloons, I thought, only to realise too late that Bell End had pulled back his sabre and punched the blade into my chest.

'Ow, that hurt,' I gasped over the buzz of the electrical point recorder.

You're not really meant to hit your opponent overly hard, but Bell End knew, as I did, that while you could be carded for overly aggressive play, you could usually get away with a lot before that red card came your way.

Bell End chuckled mercilessly at my agony as I limped back to the *en guard* line clutching my ribs.

Teachers are soooo hilarious.

He called 'play' again.

We advanced down the piste. I was sore but determined to avenge myself. Bell End was still pressing on with his role-play. 'Yes, my father's father was killed in a duel. I myself am prepared to play dirty.' Seriously, his fake Italian accent was a shocker.

The man was a clinical case study in lunacy. I'm sure the school could make a fortune selling his mind to science and build all the new science wings they want, I was thinking as Bell End gained priority once again and stole the point. All these intellectual musings on the fencing piste were costing me dearly. I know it will be a huge loss to the world, but I think I shall have to abandon philosophy as a calling if I plan to distinguish myself as a sabreur.

'I am a molto-talented player,' my master taunted dementedly from the en garde line before calling 'play' again. 'I took my first baby step in the salle, and I know all the tricks,' he ranted away as we advanced towards one another purposefully. 'I know that for every red card I get, I'll still get away with a few illegal manoeuvres.' He laughed like a crazy man.

I lunged.

'I'm smart enough to stop short of eviction, though,' he warned as he deftly slipped his blade under mine and executed a cut to my arm, knocking my sabre clean out of my hand. And then, to add insult to injury, he thwacked me across the legs as I was grappling impotently with the sword dangling pathetically from its wires.

'That is soooo not legal!' I shouted through the plastic guard of my mask. 'The legs aren't even a target!'

'Quite right, Kelly.' He snickered. 'The naughty Italian girl will be issued with a warning, but not a red card yet, I hazard. She likes seeing her opponents unnerved,' Bell End said nastily. 'Are you unnerved, Kelly? Are you frightened? Is your belly filled with butterflies and your mind trembling with terror?'

'Yes, of course I'm bloody unnerved. My fencing master is the apex of loondom. What pupil in her right mind wouldn't be unnerved?' I yelled back at him.

He continued to play with a reckless disregard for the rules of engagement. Every time I pointed out a breech of rules or etiquette to him he'd either say, 'Ah, but the president didn't see that' or 'Quite right, Kelly. Another yellow card to the naughty Italian.'

When I realised the victory was about to be stolen from me by a cheating nutcase with schizophrenic disorders, it all got too much for me. After another illegal point was awarded to the 'nasty Italian girl,' I completely flipped.

I tore off my mask so I could fight my corner properly. Turning to my friend, I said, 'That point was illegal. Portia, you saw that!'

Portia went to open her mouth, but Bell End put his hand up before she could get a word out. 'That's a red card to you, Kelly, for removing your mask during play. Your opponent couldn't be happier. Your mistake has put her only one point away from victory. If this is how you intend to play in Italy in two weeks, you may as well buy yourself a clown suit now!'

'Daft fool,' I muttered as I angrily shoved my mask back on. I bet none of the other members of the national team had to suffer the indignity of a fencing master like Bell End. I bet they all had nice, reasonable, polished masters with poise and decorum and a sense of fair play.

But in the words of someone who had time for idle thoughts, 'ours is not to reason why, ours is but to do or die.' And to that end, if we were playing dirty I would play dirtier. The next point would be mine. I would make bloody sure of it. No nutty South African with a bad Italian accent was going to cheat me out of victory.

I executed a flawless lunge and hit Bell End slap bang in the middle of his chest. Hah!

I paused, the way you do awaiting for the victorious buzz of the recorder, but no pleasing sound came. Nothing. In my pause, Bell End cut his sabre down on mine, releasing a deafening buzz that declared the victory his.

I tore off my mask. My eyes were flashing with fury. 'But I hit *you*!' I insisted. 'Portia saw it. You must have felt it, sir!' I was furious now. There was no way I was conceding that point. No buggery way. 'There must be something wrong with your lamé!' I insisted, chucking my sabre down the piste.

'Well spotted, naive little American girl. You will do

well next time to be sure all electrics are working *before* the game has started instead of waiting until after your opponent's victory. If you call foul after the match like that in Italy, it will look tacky and mean-spirited, Kelly.'

I couldn't believe it. This was wrong for soooo many reasons. 'But I tested my sabre on your lamé before play and it was working!' I told him.

'Ah yes, so you did, Miss Kelly. So tell me, how did the naughty Italian girl cheat you of your victory?'

I wasn't going to be drawn. 'Fine,' I said churlishly. 'The naughty Italian won,' I agreed, turning to leave. I didn't think fainting would be an effective weapon in my fight against Bell End. He'd probably run me through with his sabre while I was lying in a helpless heap.

'Don't give in to defeat so easily, Kelly. Look here.'

'What?' I said, turning back to face him.

'This little switch here,' he said, removing his sabre from the electrical wire and pointing inside the guard. 'It allows me to switch my electrics on or off as suits me.' He passed his sabre over to me to examine.

'Oh, my giddy aunt!' I gasped as I saw the small switch concealed inside the guard. 'Check this out, Portia.'

Bell End looked delighted as we examined his tricked-out sabre. 'Didn't you watch the Olympic DVDs?' he asked.

I vaguely remembered an incident where a fencer was disqualified for having just such a switch inside his guard. 'But that guy was disqualified,' I said now.

'Only because they found him out, Kelly. The fool triggered the switch when his opponent was nowhere near the combat area. Your opponents in Italy may not be so stupid. The lesson for today, girls, is don't trust anyone.'

Bell End then went on to fence Portia in a completely clean and reasonable way. She totally rinsed him.

Life is soooo unfair. I probably would have gone into a deep sulk if Bell End hadn't handed us our tickets to Florence. 'Your first international tournament is in two weeks' time. Tickets and accommodations all courtesy of your sponsors. Make sure you distinguish yourselves, and maybe next time they'll send you business class. More to the point, I don't want my name dragged through the dirt by a couple of big girls' blouses.'

'No, Mr Wellend,' we replied, clutching our tickets to our chests and bouncing up and down.

I'd never been to Italy. 'I wonder how Italians kiss,' I mused as Portia and I were changing. 'Not that I intend on trying them out or anything, but one does wonder.'

'Does *one*?' Portia asked, raising one eyebrow in that special aristocratic way she has.

'I was born with a naturally inquisitive nature, Portia, that's all. Of course I'm completely happy with Freds, who happens to be the best kisser in the world. No Italian Lothario holds the slightest attraction for moi, darling.'

She slapped me across the legs with her smelly vest, and I slapped her with mine. Italy was going to be très, très cool with bells on!

TWELVE

Buddhist Security Alert

That night we had an illegal post-lights-out party in our room. After four years we were accomplished at post-lights-out parties, which Star thinks should be encouraged rather than banned.

I agree. I mean, they force us to do all sorts of other mad things, like three-legged-racing and javelin throwing. But if we were to go about chucking javelins and tearing through Windsor with our legs tied together, the school would have a lot to answer for. And anyway, what reasonable adult actually expects girls our age to go to bed before midnight? None, that's how many.

Indie pulled the bin away from the door so Miss Bibsmore couldn't hear our whispers. Then Honey lit up a fag and suggested we play one of her psycho-toff games called 'If you were a piece of fruit, what would you be?' 'For example, people would think of me as a star fruit because I'm exotic, expensive and sweet,' she explained, her implausibly long lashes flapping about her face like blinds.

'Shall we not play that game?' Portia sighed. She was knitting – or trying to knit – a scarf for her father. It was looking more like a swizzle stick, but I could tell she had big hopes for it, so I didn't say anything.

But Honey pressed on. 'And Calypso would probably be, say, an apple. Cheap and common. Now what would Star be?' she asked, struggling to wrinkle her Botox-bulging brow in thought.

'A fruit fly,' Star snapped, squirting Honey with Febreze. 'Blow your smoke out the window and let the rest of us talk about something *real* now, please?'

Honey waved the smoke away from her own face. Because she knows smoking causes wrinkles, she has developed this mad way of smoking where she holds her cigarette at arm's length, brings it in for a quick puff and extends her arm again. Then she blows the smoke in another direction, usually at my face. 'Fine, we can talk about what I got up to on my hols, darlings,' she conceded. 'I was soooo wildly popular in Val d'Isere this year. It must be my new breast implants. I had *every* designer begging me to wear their clothes at this season's shows. Every club owner was grovelling for me to make an *entrance* at their club. I had to keep telling them, "darlings, I'm just one gorgeous It Girl, and as generous as I am, I can't be everywhere at once, can I?" ' Then she did her little honky toff laugh and went on with other tales of how she'd impressed, adored and papped.

It was like a psychotic bedtime story.

I began to nod off at the start of a story of how some alcohol brand had asked her to be their new face. 'They said they wanted something young, fresh and exotic.'

'So basically they could simply use a star fruit and save on costs?' Star asked faux-innocently.

I swear, if there had been a bomb in the room you could have heard it tick. The silence was broken by Georgina, who asked about my weekend with the royal family.

'Oh, my giddy aunt! I forgot to tell you, they don't even have cable.'

The whole room gasped.

'Tell her about the disappointed looks Freds kept giving you,' Star urged.

'Disappointed looks?' Georgina repeated, looking confused.

Star shook her head in disgust.

I glared at her, furious at her betrayal. 'Erm, well, Star's exaggerating really.'

Then Star started up about how Freds was a boring idiot unworthy of her best friend, so I interrupted with the story of how I'd faked a cold to avoid going on the shoot.

'Did you use the chili oil on—,' Georgina asked.

'It was a clay pigeon shoot,' Star explained, delving into the marshmallow bag on the floor.

'Well, I didn't know it was a clay pigeon shoot at the time, did I? I thought they were off to murder lovely living birds, like grouse or pheasants or something.'

Honey looked so shocked, I thought her face had

moved. 'Only chavs, foreigners and peasants of the lowest order shoot birds in January,' she spat at me. 'They're too fat and slow at this time of year. It's bad sportsmanship. Besides, it's not even grouse season.'

'Whatever! How was I meant to know when you shoot grouse? I'm not sure I've *seen* a grouse, and even if I have, I definitely wouldn't shoot it. And it's not because I'm a foreigner. I'm just quite firm on not shooting things,' I explained. 'Not even clay pigeons. So there.'

Tobias diffused the situation, announcing – through Georgina – that he couldn't bear lies.

'One wonders if boys are worth the trouble, darlings,' added Indie as she stretched out like a black cat on her bed and put her feet on the wall.

'This one doesn't wonder. I *know* they're not worth the trouble,' Star said as she braided her hair in front of the mirror.

'Oh, shut up, Star, you boring little child of a drugged-out has-been. You're just jealous of Calypso because she's got Freddie and you're too much of a freak to have a decent boyfriend.' Honey sneered from the windowsill where she was blowing out smoke.

What new hyper-reality was this? I couldn't believe that Honey of all people had come to *my* defence. Especially when I didn't even need rescuing. Besides, Star could have any boy she wanted.

Not that Star was bothered by Honey's slur on her pulling prowess. She merely picked up the Febreze and sprayed Honey's bum. 'Unlike you, when it comes to boys, I *choose* to refuse à la mo. Remind me, have you ever even had a proper boyfriend?'

Honey turned around to face us. I could physically feel her face throbbing with the indignity of the slight.

'Of course I have,' Honey insisted. 'Boys go mad for me.'

'Yes, yes, yes, darling, we know you're a slapper. You pull anyone in the least bit titled, regardless of whether they're even fit. But have you ever had an *actual* boyfriend?'

I could be wrong, but I was almost certain Honey hesitated before she said, 'Loads.'

'Oh really? Name them,' Indie said, a wide grin on her face.

'More like shame them,' Star added, laughing. 'Who'd go out with *you*?'

Suddenly the florescent lights went on. 'What's this?' Miss Bibsmore hissed from the doorway. 'You move that bin, Miss O'Hare, and git back to yer own room.'

'That is soooo unfair,' Honey fumed. I spotted Siddhartha peeking in the room and waved at him to bugger off.

'Unfair was made to fare,' replied Miss Bibsmore with a cackle. Then she turned to see what I was waving at and came face-to-face with Honey's Buddhist.

'What's this, then?' she asked, poking her stick at Siddhartha.

'My security guard,' Honey responded irritably.

Miss Bibsmore looked well cross. 'Your flaming what?' she railed. Even her fluffy dog slippers looked cross.

'Daddy thinks someone might be trying to kidnap me,' Honey replied casually.

'And what's that got to do with this fellow in a sari, then?' Miss Bibsmore wanted to know.

'He's a Buddhist monk, you ignoramus!' Honey said through clenched teeth.

'Ignorant, am I? Well leastways, no one's trying to kidnap me.'

'As if,' Honey muttered. Then she turned to us. 'Laters, peasants, I'm off to bed!' But as she went to squeeze past Miss Bibsmore, she was blocked by our house spinster's stick.

'Not so fast, Miss O'Hare. Rules is rules. No gentleman callers in the dorm.'

'Move aside, you mad old loon, or I'll have Siddhartha meditate you out of existence.'

Miss Bibsmore's stick continued to block Honey's exit. I know it's hard to imagine that a woman in a flannelette nightie and fluffy dog slippers can look fearsome, but Miss Bibsmore pulled it off. I was genuinely scared.

Honey sighed heavily. 'Listen, you bog ignorant chav, he's *not* a gentleman caller, he's a nonviolent licensed Buddhist security person.'

'I don't care if he's a reincarnated canary, Madam High and Mighty. He's got no business in a girls' dormitory innit. It's not proper, specially with a princess present an' all. I'm going to have to report this to Sister Constance, I am!'

Honey looked down on our dumpy little hunched house spinster in her grubby robe and dog slippers. 'Sister Constance has been fully informed about the threats made against my person. Now stand aside or I shall have Siddhartha deal with you.'

I don't suppose I was the only one wondering how a nonviolent Buddhist would deal with a fierce house spinster with a stick. Meditating her out of existence seemed a bit unlikely.

'Sort her out, Siddhartha,' Honey ordered, and next thing, Siddhartha produced a bronze cylinder on a stick from his robes and starting spinning it and chanting.

'Oh my God, he's got a gun!' Indie shrieked.

We all hit the floor, apart from Honey, Siddhartha and Miss Bibsmore, who brought her stick down on Siddhartha's prayer wheel. Honey screamed. I think I might have too, and then Indie pushed the panic button.

'Oh, lovely,' Star joked above the wail of the sirens. 'We've just summoned the police.'

Miss Bibsmore wasn't finished with Honey's Buddhist, though. She's quite the master of the ancient art of stickery, so I don't think anyone was surprised to see her whack Siddhartha over the head. Siddhartha lifted up his robes and legged it down the corridor to Miss Bibsmore's cries of, 'That's right, you big chicken in yer girlie frock. Cluck, cluck, cluck.'

It was all very undignified, and I suspect a severe blow to the credibility of Buddhist security guards everywhere.

The panic alarm was still blaring and Honey was still screaming when the police finally arrived.

'Alright, Sarge, it's just the O'Hare girl again,' one of the bobsters said into his walkie-talkie thingamee. 'We got a bloke outside in an orange sari an' all. Says he's from some Buddhist defence team sent to guard her from kidnappers, over.'

We heard a great deal of chuckling from the other end.

I know how the sarge felt. We all had to stuff our mouths with our duvets to stop chortling. The alarm was finally turned off, and Miss Bibsmore led the officers of the law to Sister's office, dragging Honey with her by the ear.

'Aren't you glad you came to England to go to school?' Star asked as she dove under the covers with me.

THIRTEEN

The Sword of Damocles

Even though we were up most of the night chatting about Honey's Latest Prank, we all woke up at the first bell. After breakfast, chapel and room inspection, we loped off to English with Ms Topler. English being a core subject of the curriculum, we all had to do it. Which meant Star and I got to sit together. On top of each desk was a copy of *How to Pass Your Exams (And Enjoy Yourself)*.

I sat next to Star, who was decorating her booklet with some sort of musical score. I tried to read the booklet, which recommended taking breaks from study to walk the dog. What dog? I didn't even have a dog. I shut the book and set about a more disciplined and constructive activity: seeing how long I could go without writing *I love Freds* on my pencil case.

Star must have sensed my love battle because she looked up from her musical score and drew a heart on my hand in permanent marker. Then she added an *L* in the middle. Presumably it was intended to signify Loser rather than Love.

I snatched the marker off her and was about to draw a heart with an arrow through it on Star's hand when Ms Topler walked in. She was wearing an appallingly creepy pink floral dress with a pink cable-knit cardigan. Even her shoes were pink. They were those horrendous plastic ones that make a nauseating squelchy sound as you walk. Poor old dear, no wonder she's never found love and has to look to tragic cases like Thomas Hardy for comfort.

'Good morning, girls,' she trilled.

We all stood. 'Good Morning, Miss Topler, and may God bless you,' we chanted in the tone of worshipful respect which Saint Augustine's girls are famous for.

After a perfunctory '*In nomine patras, et filie et spiritus sancti,*' Miss Topler began jumping up and down as if she needed to do a wee. Then she clapped her hands together. 'Before we get under way on our term's work, I have a very exciting announcement to make.'

I thought she was going to say something mind-numbing, like how much fun she'd had with the metaphysical poets over the break. She always goes on about metaphysical poets when we all know they took vast amounts of narcotic drugs and hardly ever finished their poems. Whenever you point out blindingly obvious facts like this to Ms Topler, though, she showers you in blues.

But as it turned out, the metaphysical poets couldn't have been further from her mind. No, her announcement was worse than the worst metaphysical poem.

She clapped her hands, and like a guillotine falling on

my neck, she said, 'Calypso Kelly's essay, "My Family and Utter Madness," has been short-listed for the National Under Sixteens Essay Competition.'

Then she started the class off on a round of applause.

'Breathe,' Star told me as I swooned – and it wasn't even a fake swoon. In fact, it was very nearly a real faint!

'Breathe,' Star repeated. You know things are bad when you have to be reminded to do basic things like breathe.

'In, out, breathe, breathe!' Star urged as my head hit the desk with a thud.

'Is something the matter with our little heroine?' Ms Topler asked excitedly. I lifted my head as she strode towards me like a tall pink meringue. 'Oh, my giddy aunt,' I muttered. 'My life is over. If you have any *amore* for me whatsoever you'll kill me now, Star. Use a compass, a pencil, just shove it in my aura or aorta or whatever it is that makes you bleed to death. Please, Star, I beg of you.'

Ms Topler looked concerned.

'She's just overcome,' Star said. 'She often becomes a danger to herself when she's excited. I might take her out for a bit of air, if that's okay?'

Ms Topler concurred, harbouring the insane illusion that a bit of air was going to make things okay.

After Star had led me down the corridor, she gave me a hug. 'Don't worry. I'm sure you won't *win*.'

'But you told me last term that you were sure I *would* win.'

'I just said that so you'd enter,' she told me, grinning

broadly. 'It's an essay competition for people who've experienced great tragedy in their lives. *Great* tragedy! That's hardly *you*, Calypso.'

'But you told me last term that it *was*!' I said hotly. 'You said that Bob and Sarah's split was traumatic and tragic.'

'No, I didn't!' she argued. 'You've got a life of bliss and wonderfulness. You get to go back to LA and drive around in golf carts, and your parents aren't drug-addled rockers who can't remember your name.'

I glared at her. 'I assure you that you most certainly did urge me to enter. In fact I don't think saying you used strong-armed emotional force would be too far off the mark.'

'Well, maybe I did. But darling, I only did it for your own good.'

'It's not good to be murdered by your parents!'

'You're overreacting,' Star insisted.

'No, I am not. My essay will be published and Bob and Sarah will read about how totally insane they are!'

'What do you mean?'

Sometimes Star can be remarkably stupid and forgetful. I was starting to feel I'd get a more reasoned conversation from Tobias. 'You told me to write about the effect their breakup had on me!'

'So?'

'Well, one naturally uses a bit of artistic license to bring out the, you know, tragedy and pathos of one's situation.'

'Oh, does one?' she mocked.

'I just wrote about how crazy Bob and Sarah are – you know the regressing thing with Sarah; Bob's self-obsession with his Big One; and then I sort of inflated the whole drama for artistic effect.'

Star looked horrified. 'But they're so in love.'

'They weren't so in love then. They were separated, Star. Sarah was calling me Boojie and Bob was being distant and arrogant.'

'Bugger,' my friend exclaimed. 'Let's pray they don't buy the paper that day.' By the way she looked at me, I knew she had realised the full horror of my predicament.

When we went back to class, Ms Topler informed me of my reprieve. None of the essays would be published until after the judging, which was after half term. Phew, phew and double algebra phew.

My next class was double Greek, and we were subjected to a lecture on Damocles – who demonstrated the precariousness of happiness by making the chief sandal wearer of Ancient Greece sit under a sword dangling from a single hair. I don't know if that was ironic, but it was unnerving hearing about Damocles and his sword when I had one of my own hanging above me.

FOURTEEN

When Good Fantasies Go Bad

Damocles and his sword fear was long forgotten by Saturday afternoon, after classes ended. I was off to see Freds in Windsor! Despite his worrying txt the previous Sunday, nothing had 'come up,' and our rendezvous was going ahead as planned. I even attempted a celebratory cartwheel in our room, but my freakishly long legs got tangled in the curtains and the whole shooting match came tumbling down.

Luckily all Indie did was tickle me until I almost peed my pants and had a couple of her security guys re-hang the curtains.

Freds had been relatively quiet during the week. I'd tortured myself over Freds' lack of txts privately, but I didn't dare say anything in case it set Star off on her rant about boys taking up valuable creative brain space. Also, I'd been sufficiently distracted writing lyrics for Star and

Indie, which meant coming up with loads of words that rhymed with 'angst' and 'anger.'

I'd taken a taxi into Windsor with Arabella and Clemmie, who, judging by their outfits, were out on the pull big-time. They waited with me outside the taxi drop-off place where I was rendezvousing with Freds.

'I hope he brings some fit friends,' Clemmie said as we huddled under the awning.

'I told him I was coming in with you, so I'm sure he'll bring someone,' I told her as we watched our bare legs go blue with cold. I wish tights weren't so uncool. I know I could have worn jeans, but I'd worn jeans last time I saw Freds. Oh the sheer merde-arama of true love.

I'd actually asked Freds to bring a couple of mates along to amuse Clems and Bells so I could be alone with him. I hadn't seen him since the Scottish Fiasco as Star was now referring to my trip to wildest Kiltland. She kept giving me her impersonation of his disappointed looks, which had everyone apart from me lying on the floor and kicking their legs in the air with mirth. Now, 'mirth' is a good word. Loads of words rhyme with 'mirth.'

Freddie arrived bang on time looking gorgeous. Hah! And true to his word, he'd brought Malcolm and another boy.

'This is Orlando,' he said, introducing a fit guy I'd heard of but never met. He was semi-famous in a school chat room sort of way for being the 18th Lord of Hunte, a famous DJ on the public school circuit, and for running a Web site about Sloanes. It was meant to be a piss-take of

Sloaney values and dress, but loads of people (like Honey) took it tragically seriously. Orlando was wearing a really un-Sloaney Saville Row suit with a rugby jersey underneath and frayed white tennis shoes.

'You're looking blindingly beautiful today, Calypso,' Malcolm remarked, which made everyone muffle chortles. Apart from Freds, who stood by sullenly. Freds has been suspicious of Malcolm and me since last term, when I'd got stuck in the rain trying to climb the wall at Eades in the middle of the night. I was trying to get to Freds, but everything got muddled when I was caught in Malcolm's room in his robe while my clothes dried. Anyway, I think it's feverishly touching that Fred is so jealous, even though of course he doesn't need to be. As fit as Malcolm is, he's blatantly keen on Indie.

'So everything's cool with your parents now, then?' Malcolm asked.

'I told you about their marriage blessing, McHamish,' Freddie chided, nudging Malcolm, who nudged him back. Then that turned into a nudge-fest as Malcolm replied, 'Yaah, but I thought you were lying, didn't I?'

Freds and I both rolled our eyes, and Freds squeezed me into his chest and kissed the top of my head. Then he suggested we go for pizza. I nodded, and Freds told the others we'd catch them later as he put his arm around my shoulders and pulled me down the lane.

'That's okay, we'll join you,' Malcolm said, trailing after us with the others in tow.

Even though I was looking forward to time alone with Freds, neither of us could really say anything without appearing rude. Just the same, I thought to myself, Freds could have at least given me a significant look – a look that said 'oh how I wish it were just you and me, Calypso, darling.'

But he didn't.

All six of us set off down the cobbled lanes, slipping in the sludgy snow and catching one another. I slipped a few more times than necessary so Freds could catch me. Oh winter love, I love it.

At our pizza haunt we all sat at a big table in the corner. Freds pulled a seat out for me and sat next to me. He has so much savoir-faire.

Arabella was blatantly flirting with Malcolm, which was pointless given the fatal attraction Indie held for him. Meanwhile, Clems was fluttering her eyelashes in Orlando's direction. I asked Freds how Kev was.

'Brilliant,' Freds said tonelessly as he scanned the menu.

'Oh!' I remarked, moving closer to him and pretending to scan the menu – as if my pizza choice seriously mattered. I always have Hawaiian and Freds always has pepperoni – it's our thing.

'Why, what's up?' he asked, finally sensing that all was not well in Calypso's Very Own Fantasyland.

'Nothing,' I fibbed because I was hoping to hear tales of Kev's broken heart. In Calypso's Very Own Fantasyland, I had imagined Freds pleading for my intervention for the sake of his best friend's health. Nothing would give me more joy than to reunite Kev and Star so we could be the perfect foursome we once were.

Even though Star hadn't actually mentioned him since she announced dumping him, I felt sure she must still *like* him. I mean, seriously. He did *everything* she said. And he was fit and he could fence like a demon. All her talk about boys being a pain was just that, talk. That's what I'd talked myself into believing anyway. 'Just, well, Star told me they broke up, and I thought Kev might have said something.'

'Yaah, probably for the best. Things had run their course there, I gather,' Freds answered.

'Run their *what*?' I blurted.

'Their course,' he repeated, looking at me like I was a right bonkermaniac.

If I could have done that thing the girl did in *The Exorcist* and swivelled my head around and around and around, that's what I would have done. Instead, my eyes popped out of my head and fell on the floor – well virtually.

'Star has GCSEs to focus on,' he added. And then he looked at me as if he were noticing me for the very first time and said, 'You've got your GCSEs too, haven't you?'

'So?' I asked, wondering what on earth he was on about. Who wants to talk about feverishly dreary GCSEs when there are lips to be kissed and lovely sticky-outy hair to be stroked?

'Well, I'm just saying, you probably have a lot of, erm, time constraints.'

I had no idea where his head was. I know boys are from a different planet, but this was *different* different. There was no room to faint in the crowded restaurant, so I slumped on the table and snored. That at least made him touch my hair, although it was more of a ruffle – sort of like you might give a dog.

Having ruined my lovely hairstyle, he looked at the others and asked, 'Shall we just order three large mixed and split them?'

'Not for me,' Malcolm said, looking at me as he pushed his chair back. 'I might get going, actually. Good to see you girls,' he said vaguely, and then he just walked out of the café.

It was peculiar the way he backed out of the café, still looking at me as if trying to convey something. I presumed he wanted news of Indie or something, but he only had to ask.

Orlando told Freds to go ahead and order three large mixed anyway. Then the two of them started chatting about Eades stuff, and I was left to join in a conversation with Clemmie and Bells about our rabbits. I know they're my friends, and rabbits are adorable, but Clems and Arabella and me – well, we see each other every day. Actually, I share a room with Clemmie every night. Love rabbits though I do, I didn't need to come all the way into Windsor to chat about them. I came to pull Freds!

FIFTEEN

Pi-Squared Shockarama

It wasn't until after the pizzas were finished that we finally got a chance to be alone. Freds took control, saying to Orlando, 'We're off now, Hunte, see you back at school.'

I loved hearing him say *we*. It made me feel warm and wanted. It was a shame Hunte was too busy being love-bombed by Arabella and Clems to notice.

I snuggled under Freds' arm as he chucked some money down and we set off into the snow. Outside I pulled his arm around me even more tightly. 'I'm freezing,' I told him, fluttering my lashes seductively. At least, it would have been seductive if they hadn't been glued together from all the mascara I was wearing. As it was I had to pretend I had something in my eye, and Freds dabbed at me with his handkerchief.

'Do you want my jacket?' he asked, pulling away and removing his cashmere coat. 'No, you flaming idiot! I want your arms around me,' I screamed inside.

Then he looked down at my legs and said, 'You're blue. Why aren't you wearing tights, Calypso?'

What was he, my grandmother? 'Oh, I don't feel the cold,' I lied.

'I thought you Californians were all sun-worshipping surf queens,' he teased.

'We *do* get snow in California you know,' I told him. 'It's only an hour's drive from LA.'

He laughed. And then, just as I started to feel perfect and blissful, he shoved his hands in the pockets of his chinos and said, 'So, you've got a lot on, what with your GCSEs and your tournament in Italy.'

'I wish you were coming to Italy,' I told him. 'Is there anyway you could tag along?'

He laughed as if I'd only been joking, which I found très vexing. He was a prince after all, and he wasn't doing GCSEs. Why couldn't he come to Italy?

Then he looked all serious again. 'I know Billy's training *really* hard.'

'So are Portia and I,' I told him. 'Every lunch hour we're en guarding our heads off in the salle.'

'That's what I thought. I really support you, which is why I want you to know I'd completely understand if you wanted a break.'

I felt cold now. Ice cold. 'A break from what?' I asked, as if I didn't know what the word 'break' meant.

He looked at his shoes. Why do boys do that when they're going to say something awful? To change the mood

I added, 'I wouldn't mind a break from this weather. Snuggle up to me,' I said, not wanting the conversation to continue any further.

Freds ignored me. 'Well, us. I mean you and me. I just don't want you to feel, you know . . .'

His voice trailed off as he looked me in the eye.

'No, I don't,' I told him. 'I don't know what you're banging on about, actually.'

'I just don't want you to feel like you have to hang out with me when you need to focus on other things like fencing. I know how hard you worked to get onto the international team, and I don't want you to think of us as an obligation.'

I breathed out. Phew. He didn't want to break up at all, he was just feeling insecure and I was just being paranoid. 'You're not an obligation,' I reassured him. Then I gave him a playful nudge, hoping to nudge him into taking his hands out of his pockets and putting them around me again where they belonged. 'You're a pleasure.'

'You know what I mean, Calypso. Portia and Billy are taking time out, and Kev and Star and . . .'

'We're not musketeers, Freddie,' I said. 'We don't have to follow our mates as if they were a conga line.'

He didn't even smile. Actually he didn't even look at me. He went back to fixating on his shoes, which as far as I could tell looked perfectly unremarkable. 'I'm just saying I know you have a lot on, so if you, well, you know, want to have a break or something, I'd understand.'

I bent down and looked up into his face so I could look him in the eye. 'Are you trying to tell me something, Freddie?' My heart was pounding. He looked more awkward than I'd ever seen him. The next seconds of silence were painful. I closed my eyes, terrified that he was about to dump me. But he ended my agony by putting his arms around me. He kissed me gently on the lips. I felt so warm and perfect inside again. Everything was fine! Well, I did a pretty good job of convincing myself that everything would be all right anyway. I pretended the awful bit where he'd mentioned a break was down to insecurity and his honourable intentions to give me more time for my endeavours.

When we stopped kissing and looked into each other's eyes, Freds was smiling. So I smiled too. 'Let's put you in a taxi,' he said, kissing my frozen nose.

I was still floating on a turbulent sea of confusion ten minutes later as I turned into the lane that led to Saint Augustine's. Now I knew what it felt like to float above your pain. Everything was okay, I told myself. Freds was just having an insecurity complex. But as I watched the deodorising cardboard tree hanging from the rear-view mirror, nothing really felt okay. The deodorising tree wasn't deodorising the taxi, and I wasn't doing a good job of feeling on top of the world.

It wasn't until I entered the main building that I realised I had left Clems and Arabella in Windsor, breaking the school rule of go in threes, stay in threes, come back in threes. I was about to call them and apologise, but when I checked my phone, I noticed the time. Curfew was still two hours away. And I didn't need Mr Templeton to do that sum for me! I could have stayed two hours longer with Freds.

I called Clemmie and Arabella and apologised for leaving them. They said they were about to go to the cinema with Orlando and another friend of his, Yo. I couldn't help feeling that Freds should have taken *me* to the cinema. Talk about hitting the ground with a thud. It was pointless fainting, as there was no one around to notice.

As much as I kept telling myself that Freds' suggestion that I might want to take a break was motivated by honourable intentions, I couldn't shake the horrible gnawing in my stomach. I headed to the music wing in search of Indie and Star. Maybe writing some disaffected teen lyrics would make me feel better.

The music wing wasn't officially opened yet. That treat would come in two weeks when the plaque was finished. Star was privileged to have early access because her father had paid for it. It looked more like Abbey Road Recording Studios than a school music wing, probably because Star's father's platinum albums lined the walls of the lobby-ish area. As I wandered through the entrance corridor, I kept expecting a beautiful receptionist to dive out and offer me Evian. Even a few stoned roadies would not have seemed out of place. The only jarring note was an oil painting of Our Lady with a set of rosary beads.

I expected to find Star and Indie, but Malcolm was there as well. I don't know why I was so surprised to see him, given he'd snuck into Saint Augustine's last term.

'Ah, Calypso! At last. Champagne?' he asked, pulling a mini bottle of Veuve Clicquot out of the six-pack by his feet.

Drinking champagne and having a boy on the premises could lead to a suspension, but Malcolm looked so at home with Star's bass guitar around his neck that I forgot the risk we were all taking. I nodded my acceptance to the offer of champagne, even though I don't really like the stuff. I was in shock, really. A shock which was about to intensify by pi square when Malcolm uttered the impossible words, 'I daresay you need a drink after being dumped.'

SIXTEEN

Bonkeratus, Bonkeratum, Bonkerama

As it was, I did an actual faint and crumpled up at Malcolm's feet. I felt quite the Georgian lady – you know those 'gels' Miss Austen wrote about in such yawn-making detail. They do one of those swooney wooneys and the next minute, Darcy or some other git goes into feverish overdrive to bring the corseted lass around.

Back in the twenty-first century, I came to, looked up and saw Malcolm looking mildly curious rather than alarmed. He was preoccupied with easing the cork off the miniature champagne bottle.

Star and Indie helped me up, and Star gave me a cuddle. 'How dare he dump *you*!' she declared hotly.

'He didn't dump me,' I insisted. 'He hasn't dumped me!' I pointed at Malcolm. 'He's just being Scottish!'

All eyes turned to Malcolm, who had successfully removed the cork and was now giving it a sniff and wrinkling his nose. He turned to me and winced before saying, 'Sorry, I appear to have set the veritable cat out amongst the veritable whatsits.'

Malcolm stuck the straw in the miniature bottle and held it to my lips. Why was this mad loon of a boy always trying to shove alcohol down my neck?

'Drink deeply from the well of fizz, Calypso. In the words of Madame Bollinger, "I drink it when I am happy, I drink it when I am sad." Besides, you don't want to take anything I say seriously. I've probably got it all wrong. He was no doubt off to dump some other hapless girl and not your good self after all. Forget everything I said.'

I pushed the champagne away and roughly wiped a tear from my cheek. Malcolm hadn't got it wrong. Deep down I knew that. All that guff Freds had been burbling in Windsor about how he'd understand if I wanted to take a break. He had wanted to dump me all along. He'd just bottled out because he didn't want me to cry, or make a scene, or do something disappointing.

'If you ask me, he was a bit wet for you anyway,' Malcolm remarked, sipping the champagne himself.

'I agree,' said Star. 'Wet as soggy gym socks. You're much better off without him.'

Star would say that. Operation Dumping Boys was going splendidly – well, in a reverse sort of way anyway.

'Better off without whom?' my *bête noire*, Honey, asked

as she wandered into the studio wearing yet another slinky sundress. Her bony arms were covered in nicotine patches but she was still smoking a fag.

'Freds dumped Calypso,' Malcolm said, offering her a miniature.

'Poor lamb,' Honey said, taking the bottle. 'Here, have a nicotine patch, darling, they really give you a lift,' she offered, peeling one off her arm and slapping it on my forehead. Then she plonked herself down on the floor beside me and put her arm around my shoulder as if she really, really cared.

I didn't know what was worse. My despair that Freds didn't love me anymore or having Honey pretend to pity me. She blew a plume of smoke in my face, which made me cough, so she sprayed the air around me with Febreze, which made my eyes tear up. 'Poor, sad little tragic Calypso. You must feel like utter dirt. You must feel as though your life's not worth living. You must feel like slashing your wrists or diving from the bell tower to your macabre and bloody death – or at least a coma. I know I would if I were you.'

'She's far better off without him,' Malcolm said stoutly, roughly snatching back the bottle of champagne he'd given Honey.

'I'm not better off without him, though,' I insisted. 'He's not a drip and he didn't actually dump me!' I carried on, my voice rising into a hysterical screech. Très unattractive, I know, but I was like one of those crazed women in films who have just had a horrible shock and need a good slap.

Honey slapped me hard across the face.

Then Star slapped Honey back even harder.

Malcolm must have wondered what kind of slappity-slap circus he'd entered, but he didn't show it. Not that I was thinking about Malcolm's feelings at the time. I was remembering Freds' good-bye kiss and how lovely and real it had felt. Oh God, it was all so confusing. Please God, let Malcolm be wrong. Freds loves me. He told me so.

Besides, Malcolm wasn't even one of Freds' mates. Malcolm was in the year above and made weird art movie thingies that Freds wasn't keen on. 'Malcolm's got it all wrong. It must have been a mistake,' I told everyone. 'Freds loves me.'

Honey snickered.

No one else looked convinced either.

'He's still wet,' Malcolm muttered as he swizzled the straw of his champagne.

Star agreed enthusiastically.

Sucking hard on her cigarette, Honey nodded. Blowing a series of artful smoke rings in my eyes, she said, 'Soz, darling' and sprayed me with Febreze.

I didn't rise to their bait, though. *They* hadn't been there in Windsor in the snow when Freds kissed me good-bye. *They* couldn't grasp the true depth of his *je ne sais quoi* or his savoir-faire. Okay, so he wasn't exactly the life of the party, but he made me feel special, and without wanting to sound shallow, he was heir to the throne. Every girl in the world worshipped him – apart from Star.

'And what's with his hair?' Malcolm asked, shaking his head. 'You should see the pots of gel in his room. Has it delivered by the lorry load every Monday, the vain git.'

'Freds doesn't use gel,' I blurted, because everyone knows that boys who use gel are très, très tragic.

Malcolm shook his head. 'You never did find your way into his room, did you, Calypso? For if you had, well. Gel Central, I'm afraid.'

Star giggled. 'I know, he looks like such a chav.'

Indie giggled. 'Gel is soooo sad. You'd think one of his lackeys would tell him.'

Even Honey laughed – well, as best she could.

I looked around at the faces of my friends and Honey. I wanted to be alone with Star and tell her how terrible I felt, but I knew she'd just say stuff like how I was better off without him. This scenario was, after all, just what she wanted. But then she surprised me by announcing, 'Listen, though, seriously, we can't allow this to happen. Freddie can't be allowed to dump Calypso.'

I could have kissed her! No wonder I loved Star so much. To quote from some addled Latin text we were translating, she is most definitely the *ne plus ultra* of girlfriends, the alpha and omega of friends.

When she came over and hugged me, I hugged her back so hard she made a squeaking sound. Everything would be okay now.

'No Saint Augustine's girl has ever been dumped. We're the ones who do the dumping,' she told me.

'But he didn't actually *dump* me,' I reminded her.

'Okay, so he chickened out, but according to Malcolm, that was his plan.'

I looked over at Malcolm, who shrugged and nodded in the affirmative.

'It's an immutable fact, my darling bestest friend in the world,' Star said to me. 'No boy, not even a prince, has ever dumped a Saint Augustine's girl. Ever.'

Just then Georgina walked in with Tobias. What was this, Humiliation Central? 'Apparently there was some incident of a Stowe boy dumping some girl in the sixties,' she said, clearly already *au fait* with my shame. Maybe Freds had pasted posters declaring his dumping intentions over Windsor.

'Typical,' Malcolm sneered. 'What do you expect from Stowe?'

'Sister Constance will flip when she hears one of her girls has been dumped,' Honey said gleefully.

Star gave her a warning look. 'Do you want a wrist burn, Honey?'

Honey grabbed her thin little wrists in fear.

'No one is telling Sister. Freds hasn't *officially* dumped Calypso *yet*,' Star said, the word 'yet' going through my heart like a dagger. 'There's still time to save the situation if we act quickly.'

Georgina gave me Tobias to hug. He was wearing a fetching little black Prada jumper and some vintage Vivienne Westwood bondage trousers, teemed with workman's earmuffs - presumably to protect his ears from the noise of Star and Indie's music. 'Tobias said you're not to worry, darling, we'll sort it out.'

Just then I heard my txt alert going off.

Honey grabbed my bag off the chair and pulled out my phone. '"Soz and all that, but I think we should take a break! I'll call later, F,"' she read. Then she made a really sad, pitying face that made her pumped-up collagen-enhanced lips loll around her chin.

Star snatched my mobile from her and scanned the message. 'Bugger. What an absolute jerk,' she said, chucking the phone to me in disgust.

'The txt dump is a low blow,' Malcolm said. 'Even for a wet prince lathered in chav gel.'

I read the txt myself, wanting it say something other than what Honey and Star had read. But it didn't.

Soz and all that, but I think we should take a break! I'll call later, F

It was true. I had been dumped by the heir to the throne. What's more, I had been dumped by txt, an instrument designed for flirting and sending lovely messages to friends! All the confusion I had felt earlier drained out of me as I read and reread the stark cruelty of the words.

All I felt now was outrage and anger. I looked up at the concerned faces of the others and stood up in fury. 'Right. He's toast.'

Malcolm raised his bottle in the air. 'Here's to toasting the little wet!' I know that it wasn't the time to be thinking such things, but hearing him call Freds 'the little wet' suddenly made me realise that Malcolm was actually quite fit.

Georgina, Honey, Indie and Star all grabbed a bottle each and clunked them against Malcolm's.

'Toast!' everyone declared.

Then Indie turned to me and said, 'You could always perform The Counter Dump. A girl at Cheltenham Ladies had to do The Counter Dump once – the guy was destroyed! He never pulled again.'

SEVENTEEN

The Mechanics of The Counter Dump

How many teenagers can you fit in a dorm room built to accommodate three girls? Forty-two, that's how many – the entire Year Eleven. There were girls on ledges, girls on cupboards, even girls in the bath in the en suite – all of them wearing the hideous plastic bead bracelets of Enterprise Initiative.

By that evening, I had become a cause celeb, only not in a good way like Nelson Mandela or that woman who is trying to bring down the cruel regime in Burma. No, my name had become associated with shame. The word was out. Girls, teachers, nuns and house spinsters were all aghast that one of their own, a Saint Augustine's girl, had been so brutally dumped.

Walking down corridors, you could hear snatches of conversation like, 'I just don't understand how it could have happened,' and 'I heard he uses *gel*.'

I was as much at a loss to understand my dumping as

they were. I had no answers, only questions. But all I really wanted was a solution, and that's what Indie promised she had.

'Right. The main thing is to restore honour to our school, right?' she asked.

'And to Calypso,' Star added.

'*Especially* to Calypso,' Indie agreed, smiling sweetly at me. 'The skillful execution of The Counter Dump is based on Calypso getting Freds in a lather over her again and then just as he realises that life without her isn't worth living, she dumps him.'

'Here, here!' the room cheered.

'Believe me, I've witnessed a Counter Dump firsthand. It will make Freds feel like a pig's dinner for the rest of his life. He will never pull another girl again.'

Everyone seemed thrilled by this outcome. I mean, I know he dumped me, but a pig's dinner? I don't know that I'd wish that on anyone – not that I have the slightest clue what pig's dinners consist of.

'Seriously, he will never pull again,' Indie repeated for dramatic effect.

An image of Freds as a Lady Haversham character flashed through my mind and I giggled, which set everyone else off. As I looked around at the faces of the girls perched and squeezed into our tiny room, I couldn't help but be touched. It was a coming together of the school such as I'd never witnessed. Even Honey – who was perched companionably with Polo Central on the wardrobe – thought The Counter Dump was the only way for me to regain my dignity. I was shocked that Honey felt I had any dignity in need of restoration, given she'd spent the last four years trying to strip me of it.

'Calypso?' Indie asked.

Portia nudged me from my musings and I realised a speech was required, so I blurted, 'I want to see Freds grovel.'

The girls started clapping and banging their legs on whatever they could. Spurred by this show of *belle esprit*, I continued, 'I want to rinse him good and proper. Horrible boy, hiding his nasty cruel streak under such lovely sticky-outy hair and kissable lips.'

More cheers went up and my emotions were swept along with the fervour of the crowd. Maybe Freds *should* feel like a pig's dinner, at least for a bit. I certainly hoped he'd never pull again. That would teach him.

'Speech! Speech!' everyone cried.

Feeling rather like Cicero on a good day, I began, 'Boys and their enormous egos. Who does he think he is? Apart from the prince of the United Bollocky Pollicky Kingdom, I mean. If we let him get away with dumping me, well, it will be open season on all of us!'

The roar of the crowd rivalled any Roman mob. It was a wonder we weren't being plagued by house spinsters left, right and centre.

Star clapped her hands flamenco-style to call the meeting to order. 'Right, so basically the honour not just of Calypso, but of the entire school is at stake! Agreed?

There was more banging of feet on the floor, the sides of wardrobes, cupboards, walls or baths as everyone showed their support. Then Star said, 'Indie has suggested that Calypso bring Freds to his knees by performing The Counter Dump, a manoeuvre guaranteed to knock the stuffing out of the most egotistical of boys.'

Georgina covered poor Tobias's ears – as a soft toy, he doesn't like talk about knocking the stuffing out of things.

'How dare he dump me by txt,' I said – for like the thousandth millionth time since receiving his horrible txt.

'At least now you can see him for the enormous idiot he is,' Star pointed out. 'I told you that you should dump him after that fiasco with the fake cold in Scotland,' Star told me.

'And I told you that I hate being told "I told you so,"' I replied.

Star blushed. 'Sorry, darling. Think of it as fodder for your lyrics,' she advised more gently, chucking me her lip-gloss. 'We'll all help you avenge your honour.'

'Don't be so culturally insensitive,' Honey argued hotly. 'Think of Calypso, poor love; she's American, and everyone knows they don't know what honour is.'

Star took off her shoe and threw it at Honey. But our *bête noire* caught it adroitly, looked at the label, screwed up her nose job and chucked it right back.

I know I should have felt insulted by what Honey said, but the horror of it all was, I was worried she might be right! I really wasn't in the least bit worried about my bloody honour, or the school's honour for that matter. I wanted to sob uncontrollably into my pillow and then pretend it was Freds and thump it.

'Indie's right, though. The only thing to do is seduce him all over again, and then when he's down on his knees with love for you, txt him a dump message,' Fenella said, without looking up from the copy of *Horse and Hound* she was flicking through.

'I didn't seduce him in the first place, though – I trounced him at sabre,' I explained.

'What's sabre?' Perdita asked.

'It's like something you do with swords, only not on horseback, darling,' Georgina explained.

'Huh,' Perdita nodded. 'Like water polo, you mean?'

'Exactly,' Star agreed, rolling her eyes at me.

'So this seduction business, how do we go about it, precisely?' Portia asked. 'No offence, but Calypso is no Mata Hari.'

'I think we'll need a decoy,' Honey suggested. 'Perhaps I could pull Freds to distract him and . . .'

'He said he'd call,' Portia reminded her calmly with the sort of poise only a girl who can trace her title back generations can possess. Like Star, most of the rest of the world just wants to throw shoes at Honey. 'Let's presume he'll be true to his word and call Calypso.'

I grabbed my mobile and checked it was on. 'But what should I say when he does call?' I asked. 'If he actually does call, I mean,' I added, as doubts engulfed me.

'Whatever you do, you must not answer it,' Indie advised sternly.

'I can't do that,' I told her. It was true, I'm not one of those people that can call-screen. I go doo-lally with curiosity.

Star took the phone from me and started pressing buttons. 'I've put it on mute and on mute it will stay,' she told me firmly, tossing it back to me.

'Do you think he will leave a message, though?' I asked.

'No,' Perdita said knowledgably. 'Boys don't ever leave unpleasant messages. He might just say he'll call back, or see you at the next polo match or ask you to call him.'

'On Saturday,' said Star. 'When Calypso and posse head into Windsor, we should arrange to meet Malcolm and get him to bring his entourage. That way, when Freds sees you, you'll be surrounded by friends and fit boys.'

It did sound like a cool plan, but was Malcolm the ideal decoy? 'What if he doesn't care that I'm with Malcolm's entourage and a posse of girls?' I asked, because really, and I know this is sinfully self-centred, I wanted him to care so much that he'd sob at the sight of me and beg me to take him back. Of course I would spurn him, but still I wanted to know he cared first.

Star chortled, 'Oh darling, I do love you for being so naive when it comes to boys. Freds may not be deep, but his ego is enormous. He'll notice you with Malcolm. Remember how jealous he was when you accidentally climbed into Malcolm's room at Eades that night in the rain?'

'But he knows Malcolm and Indie are practically an item. He'll just presume I'm a cling-on.'

Indie looked shocked. 'Since when have Malcolm and moi been an item?'

I blinked so hard with confusion I began to get a migraine. 'Erm, forever?'

'Are you mad?' she replied – though clearly the question was meant to be rhetorical. 'Malcolm's cool but . . .' She shook her braids and said, 'Portia, you explain.'

EIGHTEEN

It Was All Très, Très, Très Befuddling

All forty-two girls were silent as Portia rolled her eyes and said, 'Indie's pulled Tarquin.'

Georgina threw Tobias at her. 'Tobias can't bear secrets. Why didn't you tell us?' she asked furiously.

The rest of the room muttered their displeasure. Indie kissed Tobias on the nose and threw him back to Georgina. 'Because you and Star were banging on about how we should stop being so boy-obsessed.'

'Has no one in this school heard of the word *proportion*?' Star groaned.

'I thought you and Malcolm were an item, too,' Perdita added.

'Buggery slops,' Star cursed. 'Anyway, everyone, let's stay on message. *When* Freds approaches you, seething with jealousy, you have to be really carefree and breezy. Charming but distant, you know, sort of look at him and smile as if you can't quite remember who he is.'

'Don't be *too* obvious, though,' Georgina warned as she brushed Tobias's fur. 'I mean, boys aren't that clever, but they usually know when they are being played.'

'That's true. Be a bit flirty without actually flirting, if you know what I mean,' Arabella suggested. 'You know, twirl your hair, pout your lips and titter gaily.'

'What? Freds will think I'm mad if I start tittering gaily, or tittering in any way for that matter. And as for pouting and twirling my hair, well . . . he'll think my madness is out of hand and call for the asylum lorry to take me to an island of loons.'

'She's right,' agreed Honey. Then she looked at me with big blue sad-eyed pity. 'Poor, poor tragically butch Calypso. I'll help you learn the art of seduction, darling,' she advised in a mildly threatening sort of way. 'Seduction is my middle name.'

The awful thing was, Seduction probably *was* Honey's middle name. After all, her sister Poppy's middle name was Minxy-Darling. I swear, Minxy-Darling. No wonder they're the twisted sisters.

'The thing is,' advised Indie seriously, 'is that you have to get him to want you back really, really badly.'

'Desperately badly,' Bells added.

'And then when he thinks he's won you back, you have to dump him from a great height,' Indie explained.

'And destroy his hopes and dreams of ever being loved again,' Honey concluded as she admired her reflection in her Chanel compact.

'Can any of the rest of us pull him, I mean once The Counter Dump is over?' Clems piped up.

We were all laughing loudly when Miss Bibsmore entered, her dressing gown billowing. She was in a furious mood. 'I've been listening to yous girls from behind the door an' all. No one's pulling that little sod again, do you hear?' she railed, waving her stick around the room, almost knocking girls' heads off. 'Treating a lovely girl like Miss Kelly worse than you'd treat a mongrel dog. All the teachers and nuns are behind you on this an' all. You mark my words. You girls have got to teach this cheeky pup that a Saint Augustine's girl 'as pride innit. Boys like His Nibs aren't for the likes of ladies like yourselves. He'll be blacklisted by this school and no bones about it neither. I've got a good mind to recommend to Sister that we start a hate club like what we did for . . . well, never you mind about that.'

'A hate club.' Honey said the words like they were a dream come true. 'That would be soooo cool. We could have badges and a Web site and plan attacks.'

'Yes, well, that sort of thing,' Miss Bibsmore conceded, clearly perturbed to be on the same team as Honey.

The bearded Miss Cribbe, our house spinster from last year, poked her head around the door. ''Ello, dearies, now don't be a stranger where I is concerned neither. If there's anything I can do to put His Nibs in his place, you just let me know.'

All the girls cheered and then the nuns appeared.

'And don't forget us old things up at the convent,' piped up little Sister Regina, her face crinkled with years of prayer and concern. 'We may not have had a great deal of experience with boys, but we're all behind you on this. Sister Constance has told us to lend you every support. Though I must say, Freddie seemed like such a lovely young man when we met him at the Nationals. A real gentleman he was.'

I was quite moved. It was all very touching if a little daunting, the realisation that everyone was being so supportive. I know I felt enraged with Freds, but was I really up to performing The Counter Dump?

'I blame the parents, I do,' Miss Bibsmore told Sister stoutly. 'Spoilt and pampered he is, like a prize bull.'

That set all of us off on a chortle jag again, which sent girls tumbling off wardrobes and chests of drawers.

Miss Bibsmore waved her stick at us. 'Now there's nothing to giggle at here, girls. The school's honour is at stake.'

Laughter aside, the bitter sadness of my situation came home after everyone had gone back to their own rooms. I finally found the bottle to answer Sarah and Bob's txt from yesterday asking about me, my school work and that cur of curs, Freddie.

School is totally pants but I'm bearing up. xxx C.
PS: Fred's fab and sends love.

I mean, I couldn't exactly tell them that Freds had dumped me by txt, could I? Knowing Sarah and Bob, I bet they would have set off in the car of shame, dragged him from the comfort of his bed at Eades and given him one of their really, really long lectures.

Just the same, writing that lie of lies about Freds sending love made me cry myself to sleep.

NINETEEN

Snoozely Woozely Does It

I solved the mystery of my missing skirts Monday morning when Indie found them wedged behind the completely useless non-heat-radiating radiator in our room.

'Sebastian probably hid them there.' Clems giggled. But I couldn't feel cross about Sebastian as all my cross feelings were focused on Freds.

Down in the chaos of clashing dishes and chatter in the ref, Star waved us over to her table, where she'd saved us a bench. 'I called Malcolm this morning and he's totally on for Operation Counter Dump,' she told us as we sat down. 'We're all convening in Windsor on Saturday at two.'

'He's going to get a posse together of fit boys from his film club too,' Portia added. 'Tarkie told me.'

I imagined a hellish troop of pimpled film buffs in tight black clothes banging on about Federico Fellini and almost died with the dreariness of it all, but Indie was wriggling excitedly in her seat, so I didn't verbalise my doubts. Tarquin was fit enough, though – and a member of Malcolm's film club – so Indie was no doubt over the moonarama at the prospect of seeing him.

But my enthusiasm was somewhat diluted. First, I wasn't convinced that Freds would even show on Saturday. And second, even if he did show, I wasn't sure he'd be that devastated to see me with my posse chatting to Malcolm and his nerdy film club in their stupid tight black clothes.

But Star was on a mission. 'See, everything's going according to plan,' she told me, shoving a piece of croissant in my mouth so I couldn't argue.

After chapel and room inspection we made our way to maths, where Mr Templeton was eager to arouse our young minds with hard sums and amusing theorems. He actually talked like that.

'I've got something really exciting to stimulate those little grey cells of yours today, girls,' he told us as he rubbed his hands together like some Machiavellian priest of evil.

We tried to look spellbound and interested – or at least not about to expire from boredom - but it was très, très challenging.

'Yes, girls! It's my favourite subject, and I sincerely hope it will soon be yours. It's called trigonometry, or as our ancient Latin friends called it, *trigonometria*.'

I don't think I was the only girl in the class wondering what ancient Latin friends he or any of the rest of us had. I doubt he has any friends frankly, not with his tragic capacity for delusion.

Most of the class were either pocket-eating their breakfast, checking txts under their desks or writing whimsical things about boys on their stationery.

But Mr Templeton was undeterred. He banged on relentlessly, making up even more ridiculous words like 'sine,' 'cos' and some other thingameepiglets. I put my head on the desk for a nice little snoozy woozy. I hadn't slept well the night before because of all the Counter Dump issues.

The next thing I knew, a piece of chalk hit me on the head. I swear it practically decapitated me. If that's not against European Human Rights legislation, I don't know what is.

'Miss Kelly, were you asleep?' Mr Templeton asked.

Seriously, the man was the apex of all that is sadly mad about grown-ups. 'Of course I was asleep!' I blurted as I rubbed my sore little head.

How could anyone keep their eyes open with someone banging on about the measurement of triangles? I don't even like triangles. They're unnatural. Then again so is Mr Templeton.

Still it was my duty as a well-brought-up student to humour the horrible little man. So I said – ultra, ultra sweetly – 'Sorry, Mr Templeton. I was just having a nice little dream about sine, cos and the, erm, that other lovely trigonomonstic thingamee you were telling us about.'

Mr Templeton was not even mildly mollified by my excuse. 'Fine, then you'll have no trouble giving me three blues on the fascinating tables I was just explaining to everyone, will you?'

Seriously, those heady days when Pythagoras could hold a crowd spellbound with theorems and tricky sums were long gone, with no small thanks to teachers like Mr Templeton.

All in all it was a pretty blue week for me. Every time I tried to have a bit of a snooze in class, some sadistic teacher would slap a pile of blues on me.

I suppose it did distract me from thinking about Freds, who called me once a night. It took more willpower than I ever knew I had not to answer my phone. As predicted by the wise girls of Polo Central, though, he left no message. If I hadn't been so tired from practising for our trip to Florence with the national fencing team, I would have agonised over why he only bothered to call once a night. Did that mean he only thought of my poor broken heart once? Or was he being all dignified and decent and trying not to stalk me?

I would have liked him to call a hundred desperate times a day. I would have liked to hear him sobbing away disgracefully on my answer service. At least then I would know that my charms were powerful enough to bring a boy to tears. As it was, I just felt annoyed. Which is why I started writing songs.

I know it was just a first draft of my first song ever, but

by Friday I thought it was going quite magnifique, I really, really did. I was so tremulous with pride, I rushed to the music wing to share my opus with Indie and Star, whom I hoped would give my self-esteem that much-needed lift.

They took the pages from me, and Star read the lyrics out but without injecting any feeling into them whatsoever.

He stole my heart with his sticky-outy hair
and then he broke it in two, oooh, oooh.
My heart is soooo broken and my mind's so confused,
and I don't know what to dooo, oooh, ooh.
If I wasn't afraid of getting more blues,
I'd take my sabre and cut him in two,
yes, that's exactly what I'd do! Oooh! Oooh!
That's exactly what I'd do, oooooooooooooh yaaaaaah.

Star and Indie said it was a good first effort, which was a bit underwhelming. Still, they had a go at writing the melody for it – if you can call the noise their band makes melodious.

Indie did a great job singing the lyrics though, which in my humble opinion sounded brilliant and feverishly meaningful. But Star said it wasn't long enough, and Indie suggested I might want to 'rework it a bit.'

'Or maybe even a lot,' added Star.

Like most rock royalty, Star's honesty could occasionally do with a little reining in. On the piste I could usually get the better of her, but in the music room she was madder than Bell End during the Nationals.

I left them to belt out some minor chords on their own while I sought solace in the pet shed, where Dorothy gave me some much-needed love and affection. I swear rabbits are ultra-sentient as far as creatures go, with little on their minds other than lettuce and carrots.

TWENTY

My Style Statement Depended on the Whims of a Psycho Toff

Sister Constance let Year Eleven off Saturday lessons so we could 'beautify ourselves for Operation Counter Dump,' which I must say was very Christian of her. She also let us order in pizza! The entire school almost fell over in shock. I know we do it all the time, but we do it secretly and smuggle in the delivery guy using the stealth and cunning that boarding school nurtures in teen minds.

Seriously though, getting dressed that day was more nerve-racking than getting dressed for my first social or VIP ball. My outfit had to be *ultra de rigueur*. When I say the pressure was on, I'm speaking euphemistically, you understand – or is that eurithmically? Either way, it was very stressful.

My outfit was largely inspired and owned by Honey.

For all her flaws, she does have her good points. Like Siddhartha, for example. We were all growing awfully fond of her orange-robed pacifist. Even Miss Bibsmore was developing a soft spot for him. Also, Honey did have an unreasonable number of designer outfits and shoes.

'Darling, you simply can't wear your own tragic clothes if you're serious about seducing poor Freddie,' my evil anti-girlfriend told me. 'I mean, they're probably the reason he dumped you, sweetie.' She was filing her talons as she explained this fact, adding, 'Besides, he has his pick of the crop, and well . . .' She let her sentence trail off, let the nail file fall to the floor and wiped an imagined tear from her eye. She always managed to make me feel that my life was too, too sad for mere words to express – and so she said it all with gestures. She's a perfectionist at miming my inadequacy.

Star et al agreed with her choice of coffee-coloured suede micro-mini. 'Oh yes, legs are always very now,' Georgina advised. The micro-mini was teamed with butter-coloured suede Jimmy Choos, which I feared would end in disaster. 'But what if I get them wet or dirty?' I asked fearfully. The last thing I wanted was to be hunted down by Honey and murdered for ruining her boots.

'Oh darling, they are soooo last term. It was you or the bin for them, to be perfectly honest.'

'Freds won't know that they're last season. Boys are hopeless on clothes,' Portia said kindly. 'Tarkie's got absolutely no idea about fashion, and Daddy's man sees to all his clothes.'

'I always think Tarquin looks really cool,' Indie said, which made us all tease her mercilessly about how feverishly infatuated she was with the ever-so-serious Lord Tarquin.

Star insisted I wear her ripped cashmere jumper. She said it would give me "attitude."

'The attitude of a girl with no boyfriend,' Honey remarked tartly. 'Well, if that's the look you're after, peasants, be my guest.' She sneered, lighting up a fag. Which provoked Star to pull out the Febreze and spray it all over my clothes and hair, making me choke. Seriously, my nerves were shredded by the time I'd been turned into boy bait.

Even though it was below zero, I wasn't allowed to wear tights 'because no one wants to pull a girl in granny tights,' as Georgina pointed out. 'Even Tobias can't bear them.' She grimaced as if the very thought of me in tights might be giving her a migraine.

Miss Bibsmore popped her head around the corner. 'She's right, duckie, you don't want to look like an old granny.'

'Oh well, you'd know, you horrible old hag,' Honey sniped.

Miss Bibsmore didn't rise to the bait. She merely shuffled off in her giant dog slippers. I think she knew that my style statement that day was in the hands of a psycho toff – and the last thing anyone wanted to do that day was set Honey off.

Georgina insisted on lending me one of her priceless pashes, which I'd been coveting since I first saw her wear it at the start of term. It was soooo gloriously soft and adorable, it reminded me of Dorothy until Honey wrapped it tightly around my neck like a hangman's noose.

Portia leant me her really beautiful diamond chandelier earrings, and Clems and Indie did my hair, which took an age because we wanted it to look wild and windswept and yet stay perfectly still. Indie had all sorts of lacquers and potions for that. Clems had a professional turbo hair dryer, which I was fairly certain started life as an aircraft engine.

I didn't wear any makeup whatsoever, apart from six inches of lip-gloss and three tubes of mascara, because everyone knows boys prefer the natural look.

My entire year was decked out in similar finery. Even the Polo twins looked like a Saint Tropez fantasy in tiny pleated skirts and gold strappy sandals. But it wasn't just them, everyone looked fantastic. Looking around at my beautiful posse as we began climbing into our taxis, I was struck by an overwhelming sense of pride. Bob's always banging on about the bonds of true friendship, but then he also bangs on about scrubbing vegetables, so I don't listen to him if I can help it. But for once, I really felt I understood what he meant – not about the veggie scrubbing, but about friendship and sisterhood. All these people were coming out for me, well, me and the school honour. I barely knew some of the girls, but they were there for me.

Braving the cold with their bare legs, all for the sake of my honour. It was a humbling experience.

Sister Constance and the rest of the nuns and all of the house spinsters were assembled in a long line on the gravel driveway to wave us off. Sister Regina and Sister Bethlehem had stitched a banner saying COUNTER DUMP YOUR SOCKS OFF GIRLS! which was très, très sweet and would have made me weep if my eyes weren't so weighed down with mascara. Miss Bibsmore saluted us with her stick. It almost brought a tear to my eye. Almost, because then I suddenly started to buckle under the monumental pressure of what I was about to do.

Fortunately, my *bête noir* took that moment to pinch me really hard on the arm and said, 'You look virtually pullable, darling.'

Actually we all looked ultra splendid. Everyone's heard that rumour about how Saint Augustine's girls have to take a test proving their beauty and a good figure rather than their intelligence to gain entry. I don't know if the rumours are true, but we really were stunning. And I say that with true humility and grace.

TWENTY-ONE

Lights-Camera-Action, Your Majesty

I had to hand it to Malcolm. He had pulled out all the stops for Operation Counter Dump. The film club, which I had imagined to be a small group of nerdy pale-skinned Goths, turned out to be gods freshly arrived from the heights of Mount Olympus.

I wasn't the only one gaping that day either. Over sixty wildly fit boys dressed in cool, ultra-anti-Sloane gear had assembled on the bridge in front of the castle town of Windsor. They looked, like, well, they looked like extras for a really well-lit independent film, actually. And they attracted a great deal of attention from locals and tourists alike.

Indie, Star, Georgina, Clems, Portia, Honey, Arabella, Fen, Perdita and – well, I won't go on listing them. But just picture forty-two Year Elevens, done up like catwalk models, climbing out of a fleet of taxis and minivans. And then picture those same girls coming face-to-face with the fittest boys Eades had to offer.

There was quite a kafuffle, I can tell you.

It was like a social without teachers. A capital VIP ball without bouncers – although personal security guards were everywhere, obviously. Siddhartha, in his flowing orange robes and revolving prayer wheel, stood apart from the other buzz cuts in their sharp suits and earpieces. I don't think the other security guys fully accepted him as one of their own. You could sort of sense their collective scorn for his monkish robes and peaceful demeanour.

As the boys came towards us like a tray of delicious walking sweets, tongues were lolling. That paragon of fitness, Lord Orlando Hunte, whom I'd met last Saturday, was using a video camera to film the two groups as they approached one another. We must have looked magnificently arty. It was one of those lights-camera-action moments that only comes around once in a lifetime – unless you're an It Girl or a Hollywood Star.

Malcolm was holding a megaphone, but sadly he didn't use it when he said, 'May I say, you look absolutely stunning this afternoon, Calypso?'

I didn't blush, but that was only because it was so cold and I couldn't feel my face. My heart did a little summersault, though. I was really touched, not just by his compliment, but by what he'd done for me. I mean, this whole dazzling show was all for me. And now that I knew he wasn't seeing Indie . . .

'Yes, Malcolm, you may tell me I look absolutely stunning this afternoon as long as I can thank you for, well, arranging all this,' I told him as I gestured at his posse.

'Desperate times call for desperate measures and all that,' he said grimly.

I wasn't quite sure what he meant by that, but I didn't get a chance to ask because he put the megaphone to his lips and shouted, 'I want to say on behalf of the Eades Film Society gathered here today that we are honoured to act as your decoys. Be assured, stunning creatures of Saint Augustine's, most of these gentlemen have dramatic experience of some sort, and everyone assembled here is one hundred percent on board with your, erm, Counter Dump situation. Isn't that right, gentlemen?' he asked his entourage.

I have to admit, I was finding him quite masterful and impressive. It didn't matter to me that most of the boys had ignored Malcolm's speech and continued chatting amongst themselves (apart from a few like Tarquin and Billy, who had wandered into the Saint Augustine's crowd to chat with girls they knew). On the other hand, the tourists and general public on the other hand, were openly gawking at this magnifique gathering.

Malcolm acted as if they'd all cheered him like the Romans cheered Mark Antony when he came to bury Caesar, not to praise him. I quite admired him for that.

'Right,' he said to the preoccupied crowd. 'So the plan is for Pyke elder to call Pyke younger and give him the signal to lead our quarry into the trap.'

I didn't like to interrupt his speech, but I tapped him on the shoulder. 'What quarry might that be?'

Malcolm looked confused. Then again, Malcolm always looked a little baffled. I think it's because his mind's always on a trillion things at once.

'Freddie,' Billy – otherwise known as Pyke elder – explained.

'Oh right, of course,' I said.

'You've got it.' I think Billy was finding the whole situation the apex of madness. 'So all set for Florence tomorrow?'

All this dumping and counter dumping had rather distracted me from my Big Dream, but I could hardly admit that to Billy, so I just nodded. Which is mad, because long before Freddie came into my life, all I thought about was being an international sabre champion. And now that the chance to make my mark was in my grasp, I was boy obsessing just as Star had warned.

Malcolm passed the megaphone to one of his entourage and asked Billy to make the call to Kev. He began to look around vaguely. Maybe he was searching for his director's chair.

Billy went over to the bridge so he could make the call to his brother in semi-privacy. When he came back, he gave Malcolm the nod. It was all very conspiratorial and exciting. I began to feel quite giddy.

Malcolm grabbed the megaphone back and told his film society, 'Right, gentlemen, this is it. You're having a jolly good time with this collection of stunningly fit girls. Just remember your roles. You're happy. You're relaxed. These are your salad days, chaps. Into character, move into the set, flirt with feeling and, action!'

With that, something miraculous happened. Suddenly, every boy was in animated conversation with the girls. I don't just mean the obvious suspects like Billy chatting to Portia, or Tarquin to Indie, but everyone seemed paired up even though there were about twenty more boys than girls. Though if you ask me, three to one is the perfect boy-girl ratio for any social situation. I even spotted Star flirting outrageously with Orlando. She was using that très obvious touching-the-buttons-of-his-shirt-as-she-spoke trick. Orlando looked bedazzled.

Next, Malcolm threw the full strength of his personality at me. He told me he'd fancied me from the moment he'd discovered me clinging to the wisteria vine outside his room like a wet rat. He told me that ever since that night he'd been distracted by thoughts of me. 'You see, the reason I kept on filing my DVDs and pretended not to take the least bit of notice of you was because I was terrified that I'd expose myself as an infatuated idiot. And that you'd despise me and think me pathetic.'

My jaw dropped for a bit as I tried to fathom whether he meant any of this stuff or was just acting 'in character.' All I could think of to say was, 'Oh fiddlesticks!' Honestly, I don't know where these hopeless blurtings come from.

'The plain truth of the matter, Calypso,' he said as he

brushed his hand across my jaw line and down my neck, which made me feel all wobbly and faint, 'is that I've never actually met anyone as funny or as diverse as you.'

'Gosh,' I blurted, staring up into his eyes. It was quite a change flirting with a boy who was miles taller than me. It does become quite tiresome flirting with the top of a boy's head – even if it does have really cool sticky-outy hair on it.

'You never cease to surprise me, Calypso. Sometimes after I've seen you or spoken to you, I have to hide in a cupboard and chortle myself sick.'

'Gosh!' I repeated. I can't remember all the things he said, but then I'm not such a loon that I actually believed him. I knew he was just trying to create the right dramatic effect. He was a director after all, and his role was to flirt. So in response to his speech to me, I rewarded him with one of my own flirtastic speeches.

'Oh Malcolm, I was mesmerised by you the moment I saw your head poke out of the window,' I told him as I twirled a tentacle of hair between my fingers. 'And I thought you were wildly sophisticated when you told me I could dry my wet clothes on your radiator. Actually, I was feverishly impressed that your radiator was warm; ours are only really there to give the idea of warmth. Oh, and also when you came to stay at the Clap House, I was ultra, ultra, ultra impressed by the way you dealt with those Gandalfs on the Landor Road. What was it, a Glasgow . . . ?'

'Kiss,' he said. It was probably my imagination, but he

seemed so close at that moment I thought I could feel his breath on my lips.

'That's it, *kiss*,' I agreed. 'Glasgow kiss.' And then for some unfathomable reason I did a Honey and batted my eyelashes and touched a button on his shirt. I suppose saying the word 'kiss' repeatedly to an older fit boy is enough to make any girl blush.

I was so giddy with my faux flirtarama, that I didn't notice Kev and Freds approach.

TWENTY-TWO

When Good Plans Go Bad

Freds was right by my shoulder when I finally felt his presence. I turned around and there he was. God he was soooo gorgeous. Soooo maddeningly fit, and he was standing so close I could smell that lovely lemony smell that was Freds. It was all I could do not to dribble.

'So what's all this, McHamish?' Freds asked cheerfully. He waved his arm at the gathered crew without even looking at me.

He was bloody smiling, in fact. He didn't look in the least bit heartbroken to see me – even in my stunning outfit! So I stared right into the centre of his soul. At least this forced him to notice me, but all he said was, 'How's it going, Calypso?'

I think 'flabbergasted' is the word – or is it 'flabberdashery'? Anyway, I was totally flabberdasheried, so I blurted, 'Fine, thank you very muchly,' in the most blankety blank way I could. I was still boring my eyes into his soul, but then he went and looked over my shoulder – quite a feat in itself given my height – and addressed Malcolm. It was as if I didn't even exist. 'Another film, McHamish, is it?' he asked.

Oh, this was brilliant. After all the effort my friends and I had put into my outfit. After all my careful non-application of makeup and Star's elaborate plans for The Counter Dump, not to mention her success at getting all these gods, I mean boys, together, this was how it was going to end. Freds was meant to realise what a fool he'd been to dump me, fall on his knees and beg me to take him back so I could dump him.

Instead, he appeared to be more interested in what a pack of boys he saw every day of the week was up to. I looked around at everyone. Couldn't he see they were all there for *moi*? For the sake of my dignity, in fact. But there was Freds, totally oblivious to all the organisation that had gone into creating the perfect circumstances for a Counter Dump.

It was a Waterloo if ever there was one. After all our careful strategising, Freds and Malcolm were going to have a nice little chat about the film society and my dignity would be forgotten. Talk about double Latin with knobs on.

That was when Malcolm kissed me. Not an air-kiss, or a peck on the cheek like your beardy aunt might give you after a few too many sherries. No, a proper snog-age. A proper grown-up, swoony woony, wobbly-kneed snog-age.

Ooh-la-la and va-va-va-voom! Malcolm knew a thing or two (or three, or four, or five) about this kissing business. He could run one of those kissing booths at county fairs when he grew up and positively rake in the cash. Though I don't suppose parents send their sons to the most prestigious boarding school in the world to have them setting up kissing booths.

It was such a mind-blowing kiss that even my brain stopped working. All I could do was feel and smell, and Malcolm felt and smelt lovely. Not like Freds, who always smelt of lemons. No, Malcolm smelt of boy, only in a nice way. If you could bottle Malcolm's smell you'd make trillions, I promise you.

I had the most alarming wobbly feeling in my tummy and disorientation of my little grey cells. I even started raising my left foot off the ground without any sort of cognitive instruction whatsoever.

And then he dipped me.

Yes, I swear, he dipped me! All I could think was ooh-la-la, this is just like in the movies. And then I remembered. This was a movie – well, sort of like a movie. Malcolm was playing the part of the gallant selfless hero making the idiot ex-boyfriend jealous.

Malcolm lifted me from the dip and I opened my eyes, which I hadn't even realised were closed. I knew boys liked you to close your eyes when they kissed you, but, well, I usually couldn't help looking at their scrunched-up little faces. Star says it's one of the few moments in life you get to see a boy vulnerable.

So anyway, I came to from my ooh-la-la moment and looked at Malcolm and realised for the first time how green his eyes were. Obviously, I already knew he had green eyes. A lot of these strawberry-blonde types with ivory skin are prone to green eyes. Malcolm's eyes were the colour of grass after the rain when all the positive (or is it negative?) ions are running rampant.

Then I looked around me like a blinking rabbit and saw everyone was staring at us. Everyone but Freds that is. He wasn't behind me anymore. Typical, I thought. I get dipped by an older fit boy, right under his stuck-up nose, and he wanders off. We couldn't afford to lose the evil prince at this delicate stage of The Counter Dump. So I asked the crowd at large, 'Where's Freds gone?'

Malcolm was still looking at me. He touched my chin and kissed me lightly on the lips.

'Where's who gone?' he asked.

'Freds!' I repeated. 'He's legged it.'

Malcolm looked around then as if coming to from a dream, but by that stage I'd already spotted Freds. He was only a few yards away, but there were lots of boys and girls between him and me, all flirting outrageously with one another, so he was sort of hidden from view. As I got a glimpse of his face, though, he looked distressed rather than bored. Also, he was sort of wobbling near the edge of the bridge.

For a moment it crossed my mind that maybe he *had* witnessed our snog-age after all and really was jealous and upset! And that made me feel even more confused.

Malcolm looked rather magnificent and powerful and superhero-ish as he moved towards Freds, especially when he shoved a few of the film society guys aside. I followed in his slipstream.

Malcolm cried out, 'He's not falling off the bridge, is he?'

The next thing I saw was my prince disappearing.

Then we all heard an almighty splash as he hit the Thames.

TWENTY-THREE

The Drowning Dreams of a Teenage Egoist

Malcolm yelled into his megaphone, 'Boy down!' and panic ensued as the security guys went loopity loopy loo. It was like a game of skittles gone wrong, the way they were all bumping into one another. Because a grave and terrible accident had befallen the heir to the throne, no one was laughing at their mad rush to get down the tiny cobbled steps with their enormous fat feet. But there was something vaudevillian about it all.

By the time they had descended one set of stairs, Freds had been washed to the other side of the bridge, so they had to rush in the other direction to mount their chaotic rescue mission.

It wasn't just Freddie's security on the case either. All of the other buzz cuts were falling over one another in their eagerness to rescue the drowning prince. You could hear their brains thinking, I swear! They were saying, 'Oh let me be the one to save His Majesty, please, Lord, let it be *me*!'

I say drowning because I'm prone to exaggeration, but actually, it must have been freezing in the Thames. The swans looked pretty chilly, and even outside the water, my legs were blue. I know people swim the Channel, but then they rub themselves with goose fat first, don't they? I was fairly sure Freds hadn't taken any such precaution.

The Eades Film Society and my own friends were all hanging off the bridge, yelling out, 'Freddie! Are you okay?'

As if anyone flailing about in a Thames swill in January could possibly be okay.

Just the same I joined them, dashing from one side of the bridge railings to the other as we watched our liege being helplessly washed downstream. Tourists were taking pictures of him. It was très, très tasteless and made me feel sick to the core. Sometimes I really have to question the morals of my fellow humans.

Eventually, I pushed my way through to the front of the crowd, spotted Freds and yelled out something not very useful to him like 'hang on!'

I don't think he heard me, though. He was focusing on trying to swim in subzero temperatures, against the current.

There was a woman on the bridge calling out to a gaggle – or is that a signature? – of swans. She's a bit of a Windsor fixture, actually. Mad as a pack of socks. She was wearing a big old grubby mac and bobble hat with earflaps, and as usual she was chucking chunks of bread to the swans.

So while the heir to the throne was drowning and the security guys were being pointless, the mad old woman continued to lob lumps of bread at her swans until one of the wretched bits hit poor Freds on the head.

Within a microsecond he was being mobbed by hundreds of frenzied swans. It was a horrifying sight! I'm normally quite fond of swans. I've spent many a happy moment watching the Windsor swans glide serenely down the Thames. But there was nothing serene about the way they were mobbing Freds. Seriously, they were all over him, wings and beaks lashing out in all directions in their feverish attempt to retrieve the lump of bread, which must have become wedged under Fred's collar.

He was utterly helpless to escape the ferocious force of flapping, hissing swans dragging their prince down into the depths of the current. I'm sure the irony wasn't lost on him either. It was just so wrong to see the monarch's own birds – which no one else is allowed to touch or eat apart from some odd college up at Oxford or something – attacking the future king.

'Leave him alone!' I screamed at the swans.

But would they listen? No. Daft birds. And the mad old woman was egging them on. 'Git him, my dearies! You git him! Trying to steal thee bread. You git him my dearies!'

Thee bread? Who talks like that? Proper loons, that's who.

The whole situation was just too dreadful. What if the tabloids got a shot of the swans trying to drown the prince? Everyone would say I was responsible. And they'd be right. If I hadn't attempted the stupid Counter Dump, Malcolm wouldn't have pulled me, and Freds wouldn't have fallen in the Thames and been flapped to death by ducks.

The prince's death would be on my hands.

I wouldn't be surprised if I was banished from England forever after this. Poor Bob and Sarah, imagining their beloved daughter happily floating on a blissful cloud of royal love, when actually I was a horrible prince killer.

Then I saw a flash of orange. It was Siddhartha diving into the Thames – and a truly magnificent sight it was. Seriously, he was like some wonderful orange-robed Olympian swimmer. What's more, he succeeded where the scrambling, bumbling, buzz cuts with their guns and wide boy attitudes had failed. He reached Freddie and bravely fought the swans off with his prayer wheel. He didn't hit them or anything unpeaceful like that, just sort of spun it around so it made a noise.

Anyway, taking the heir to the throne in one of his fin-like arms, he swam powerfully to the banks where the other security guys were eagerly waiting to take the glory. Oh yes, they threw their jackets over Freds and led him off to a fleet of waiting ambulances as if they'd been the heroes of the hour. The tabloid press was out in force by now, but I was too worried about Freds to bother death staring them. I tried to get through the crowd to the ambulance, but I was too late. Malcolm wrapped his own jacket around Siddhartha and led him off.

I just stood there alone, useless and embarrassed. 'Darling, are you all right?' Honey asked. 'Thank goodness my man had the presence of mind to rescue Freds or he might have died and you would have gone down for manslaughter, darling. You must feel terribly grateful and guilty.'

As numb as I was, I actually did feel grateful, and guilty. Honey was right. It was my fault.

'Darling, I couldn't bear to think of you languishing away in cold Old Chokey. Of course I'd send you care packages, although in my position you must realise our friendship could never continue. A girl of my social standing couldn't be seen associating with a con.'

'No, of course not,' I said, not really listening. Now was not the time to listen to psychobabble.

Star threw her arms around me and gave Honey a poke. 'Leg it, Honey, before I push *you* off the bridge,' she warned. 'Calypso didn't push Freddie in; he fell.'

Honey tried to raise her eyebrows but the Botox had paralyzed her brow so it just looked like her eyes were popping out of their sockets. 'Fine, I was just trying to be supportive.'

'Siddhartha was brilliant, though,' Star conceded. 'Malcolm's taken him back to Eades for a hot shower and a change of clothes.'

Honey went off on one. 'Well that's highly illegal. A security guard should never leave his or her principle.

Malcolm should have asked me before taking my man away.'

'The guy had just been dragged out of a freezing river, Honey,' Star pointed out. 'I think you should be grateful that someone had the semblance of mind to treat the hero of the hour.'

I could see it killed Honey to agree with Star, but after a short battle with herself she replied, 'Of course, I suppose under the circumstances I'll let it pass. He'd better dress him in orange, though. I don't want people mistaking him for a common security guard,' Honey warned. 'It's all been most distressing for me. Tell Siddhartha he can collect me at the pub. I'm going for a nice relaxing vod and ton. I'll see you back at the asylum, peasants,' she said, and flounced off.

Star put her arm around me. 'By the way, that was some kiss you had with Malcolm, darling!'

I knew she was just trying to lighten the mood and take my mind off Freds, but it only made me feel worse. And more confused, because it had been *some* kiss, even if it was just acting.

TWENTY-FOUR

A Severe Attack of the Mea Culpas

There were no girls lining the driveway to Saint Augustine's on our return. No banner-waving nuns skipping about triumphantly. No cheering house spinsters. Not even Misty – Miss Cribbe's incontinent spaniel – was there to lift a leg in salute. No, the drive was as empty as a desert. Bad news travels quickly in the royal county of Berkshire, I can tell you that much.

Operation Counter Dump had been a spectacular failure, and Saint Augustine's is feverishly keen to hush up spectacular failures. Instead of supportive, hopeful looks, *everyone* was giving me disappointed looks.

But other people's opinion wasn't my major concern. Freds was. I had to make sure he was okay. I needed to talk to him, to explain. But Eades had closed ranks like a rugby scrum or Fort Knox, or is that the CIA? The point is, they weren't leaking any news about the prince. Notice my use of the article, 'the' prince, not 'my' prince. He wasn't my prince anymore, and even though he was a wicked girl-dumping boy, I still cared for him. You don't just switch your feelings off for someone because they've dumped you by txt.

I spent the first part of the evening ringing/txting/e-mailing him to make sure he was okay. Then Star pointed out that his phone probably wasn't working if it was wet. I would have sent a carrier pigeon if I could have laid my hands on one. I even considered sending Dorothy. I mean, surely it would have melted the coldest heart to see little Dorothy hoppity hopping along with one of those little scrolls attached to her collar. Unfortunately, she has as much sense of direction (and intelligence) as a fig. Even amongst her fellow rabbits, she's known as the Queen of Daftness.

After all my energetic attempts at contacting Freds, I felt overcome by exhaustion and threw myself on my bed like Ophelia in that painting by Millais. Okay, so Ophelia threw herself in some reeds, but where was I supposed to find reeds at that time of night? I couldn't even bring myself to go down to supper to face the buggery grey slops even if it did mean being marked down as a suspected anorexic. Nothing seemed to matter now. I was in the grip of a powerful bout of ennui.

Star tried to drag me out of my ennui (also known as my pillow), but I shunned her.

'Come on, darling, you have to eat,' she pleaded, pulling at my limp body. You're flying to Florence tomorrow, and you'll need the energy to rinse the Italians.'

'Bring back something in your pocket for me,' I told her, punching my pillow in a vain attempt to make it more comfortable. Sarah hasn't bought me a new pillow since Year Seven, which means it is now as hard and thin as cardboard. 'Anyway, I don't want to go to Florence.'

'Don't be daft, all this will be forgotten once you get to Italy, and I can't bring back mash and chops in my pocket. Besides, I'm so ravenous I'll probably woof down everything I can get my lips around.'

'Oh well, if you can eat with a half-drowned boy on your conscience, don't let me stop you,' I told her.

'Darling, I am sure he's fine. If you're really worried, ring Malcolm and find out what's going on.'

'Ring Malcolm?' I shrieked, pulling my face out of my pillow. 'Are you mad? I can't ring Malcolm after our circus of snog-age! Can't you see, my nutty little friend, I'm the reason Freds fell in the Thames and almost drowned.'

'No, you're not. It was a loose cobble, that's all. Could have happened to anyone.'

'A loose cobble?' I repeated, remembering how careful you have to be, especially at the end of the bridge heading to Windsor Castle. There was a large gap in the railing at the end where people tether their bikes and the cobbles slip down into the Thames.

'Yes, a loose cobble. I told you it wasn't your fault. Now stop being morbid and come down to supper.'

I was in a dense and confusing soup of emotions. I mean, of course I didn't like feeling guilty, but at least guilt made me feel central to the tragedy. 'So, he *wasn't* overcome by jealousy?'

Star shrugged.

I sighed. 'Well, cobble or no cobble, he still fell in the Thames because of our stupid attempt at honour saving. Admit it, the entire Counter Dump plan was an exercise in madness from start to finish.'

Star tutted.

'It's true. I mean Freds has practically grown up in Windsor Castle and he's never fallen in the Thames before, has he?' With that, I pressed my face into my cardboard pillow again, striking a moving pose of *mea culpa* if ever there was one. Although I wasn't certain how long I could keep it up. It's not easy to breathe through cardboard.

'Well, I hate to say I told you so, but I did tell you to dump Freds at the start of term. If only you'd listened to me, none of this would have happened.' Before I could reply Star flounced out of my room. Only then she came back and asked, 'So, what was it like? Kissing Malcolm, I mean.'

I threw a purple cushion at her.

There was no way I was calling Malcolm. I was never going to think of him or speak to him again. In fact, I would never so much as look at him. If I passed him on the streets of Windsor, I resolved to avert my eyes and pretend to be absorbed in something else.

Unfortunately, my subconscious refused to cooperate.

Once Star was off to feed from the refractory slops trough, I fell asleep and dreamed of kissing Malcolm again. It was très, très distressing, especially when I woke up and discovered I had two missed calls from him – but he hadn't left a message. Typical boys.

When the others came back from supper, they were really sweet. Indie, Clems, Arabella, Portia, Star and even Honey had all smuggled something back for me. Unfortunately, it was covered in pocket lint, so it wasn't all that appetising, but I was grateful for the thought.

Everyone tried to chivvy me out of my attack of the *mea culpaisms*, apart from Honey, who kept shaking her head and saying things like, 'You must feel awfully responsible, darling.'

But everyone ignored Honey.

Portia reminded me that we were flying to Italy the next day for our first outing with the national team. Poor naive child, she probably thought that a trip to Italy was all it would take to lift my spirits.

'I won't be able to go now,' I told her sorrowfully.

'Darling, I know you feel bad about the way things worked out today, but you have to put it from your mind now. Apart from anything else, you have an obligation to the team.'

I lifted my face millimetres from the pillow and inhaled some air. Then I said, 'I honestly can't see how I'll be much use to the team when I'm paralysed with shame and misery.' Then I pushed my face back into my pillow of shame to demonstrate my point.

Georgina held the face of Tobias up to me so that his nose was rubbing against my cheek. 'Darling, please pull yourself together. You know Tobias can't bear defeatist attitudes, and no one will remember the failed Counter Dump if you come back with a cup.'

'And Bell End will run you through with his sabre if you don't regain your focus,' Portia pointed out. 'And there's the rest of the team to consider, not to mention your nemesis, Jenny Frogmorten. What will toilet-mouth Jenny say? She'll say you're a chicken and make mad clucking sounds. You can't give her the satisfaction. Come on, darling, let's pack.'

The thought of Jenny galvanised me into immediate action. Portia was right, *mea culpa* or no *mea culpa*, I wasn't going to have Jenny Frogmorten make clucking noises about me.

After we packed, we unpacked.

And then we packed and unpacked and packed some more because The Rules dictated that we were only allowed one piece of hand luggage for our three-night stay in the Style Central Paradise of Italy. Oh, the bally merdeness of it all.

'How can a girl be expected to squeeze hair dryers, straightening tongs, makeup bag and a don't-I-look-effortlessly-fabulous wardrobe into one piece of hand luggage? It defies the laws of physics and nature!' I said.

Portia was as frantic and frustrated as me. We were putting things in and taking them out all night long. Now I knew how Sisyphus felt, rolling his wretched stone up and down the hill night and day.

Still, at least it took my mind off my shame . . . and kissing Malcolm. I checked my mobile one more time before entrusting it to Indie. It was a wrench being parted from my mobile, I can tell you. But as it didn't have roaming, I wouldn't have a signal in Italy anyway.

TWENTY-FIVE

Sic Transit Gloria Mundi

By all accounts, the battle in the convent over who would act as our chaperones was bitterly fought. Sister Regina and Sister Bethlehem were the elected winners. The rancour amongst the other nuns was palpable when we knocked on the door the next morning. I suspected Sister Regina of rigging the Hail Mary competition, or whatever other mad nun method they used to decide the vote.

Heaven knows how Sister Bethlehem landed herself a trip to Italy, though. I mean, I don't want to be disrespectful about old nuns or anything, but she is over one hundred years old and rapidly slipping into her peaceful end via sleep. If she'd been awake for more than an hour in any one day in the past decade, I'd eat my knickers.

Bell End had to carry her to the van.

And he dropped her.

But not even that woke her up.

The other chaperone was Sister Regina, who had done us proud at the Nationals. I was quite pleased to see her little four-foot frame sitting proudly alongside Bell End on her cushion in the van. She tooted the horn she was so excited, which woke up Sister Bethlehem, who rambled off a decade of the rosary before falling back into a deep sleep. How these two nuns were going to protect us from bottom-pinching Italians was anyone's guess.

As we drove towards Gatwick, I couldn't help reflecting on last term's trips to tournaments when Sarah had accompanied us. Now all I warranted was a last-minute phone call. I suppose she was too busy snog-aging Bob these days to bother with my fencing competitions. Actually, on second thought, it was better they didn't come to Italy. Those two certainly didn't need to fan the flames of their romance in Florence, one of the world's most romantic cities.

The plan was that Portia, Bell End, the nuns and I would meet the rest of the national team at Gatwick, three hours before the flight. Yes, you heard correctly, three hours!

'Why three hours?' I asked, because to be honest, I could have used the extra sleep. Clems' snoring was not improving despite the rather stylish nose clip Indie and I had manufactured for her out of duct tape and hair clips.

'To avoid delays, Kelly. Put your brain into gear, girl,' Bell End turned around and yelled at me. Seriously, he was so wound up, the veins in his neck were throbbing. He was stressed enough at the national tournaments last term, and I began to fear what was he going to be like at our first international tournament.

At the airport, people were yelling, children were weeping and one horrible man in flip-flops – yes flip-flops – told our little Sister Regina to 'bugger off' when she asked for directions to the check-in counter.

Sister Regina was ever so sweet about it too. All she said was, 'God bless you, my son.'

I felt like slapping him about the face with one of his snotty little flip-flops, but Sister Bethlehem stomped on his foot with her wooden clogs. For a woman who passed her first century last year, she has a lot of fight left in her – when she's not asleep, that is.

Bell End had been off at the loo during our encounter with flip-flop man, but when I told him about the incident, he became enraged. 'I'd have run the blighter through with my sword, had I been here.' Then he looked at me as if I should have meted out a similar punishment. 'Well, Sisters, I shan't leave your side again. While blaggards like that crawl the earth, decent men must be on their guard.'

Portia and I were quite pleased when Billy found us. After we'd dispensed with the requisite air-kisses, it didn't escape my eagle eye that a certain longing look passed between Billy and Portia. Even in this barren hall of airline chaos, love would have its way.

'How's Freds?' I asked him after their longing gaze had become très embarrassing.

'Not too well,' he told me, turning his deep blue eyes onto me. 'He spent the night in the infirmary, apparently.'

'I feel really bad,' I told him, hoping that he'd say something reassuring like, 'Don't blame yourself, Calypso. Why, chaps like Freds fall in the Thames all the time.' But all he did was nod and go back to gazing longingly at Portia.

A bit later, we spotted Jenny and a few other members of the national team lurking outside a bookstore. Jenny gave me a death glare. After everything that had happened at the Nationals, I was resigned to having Jenny as my anti-girlfriend. I was far from scared, however. Mostly because I doubted her ability to out-psycho Honey. Not to boast, but years of being blanked by girls at Saint Augustine's had given me a profound ability to out–death stare the best of them.

Bell End dived on a tall gentlemen in a cravat. The guy looked like he'd just swallowed his own bottom when he clapped eyes on our mad master.

'Ah, Commodore!' Bell End cried, shaking the man's hand vigorously. 'How the devil are you, mate?' Then he slapped the poor fellow hard across the arse. I think Bell End was aiming for the guy's back but missed. The Commodore was very tall compared to Bell End.

But Bell End laughed like there was no tomorrow.

'Girls, meet The Commodore, the head of the GBR national team. He and I were warriors once. *Mano a mano* and all that.' He then gave a little bow and – I am not lying

– clicked his heals together. It was all rather tragic and tear jerking. I know it's disloyal, but sometimes I wish Bell End had a bit more élan like our last fencing master, Professor Sullivan.

The Commodore didn't look pleased to see his old comrade. 'Yes, well, that was all a very long time ago.'

Bell End winked at Portia and me. It was très, très mortifying. 'Many a time I gave The Commodore here a good thrashing, eh?'

Comparing the implausibly tall form of The Commodore and the short, stocky build of our master, I somehow doubted it.

I think Bell End sensed a collective dubiousness amongst the crowd because he continued. 'Bigger the target, the more you've got to work with, see.' Then, he started leaping and darting about The Commodore, using his finger as an imaginary sabre to jab him.

It was beyond mortifying.

'I'm sure you distinguished yourself admirably, Mr Wellend,' Sister Regina said, her little arms folded neatly inside the sleeves of her habit.

I could tell Sister Regina wasn't impressed by The Commodore. Years of convent living had bred in her an innate distrust of men. Bell End was one thing – apart from anything else he was very kind and gallant with her. But I could tell she definitely considered this chap in the cravat a stuck-up fool of the highest order.

I was inclined to agree with her on the basis that the guy

was wearing trousers that barely reached his ankles, and don't even get me started on the cravat. I gave him a little bow just the same, which sent Portia off into a fit of chortles. Sister Bethlehem had fallen asleep on my hand luggage by this stage, so we agreed to leave her there until the rest of the team arrived.

Portia and I sat on her hand luggage and practiced the élan, panache, vitesse, finesse and va-va-voom we'd need if we were to cope with the sophisticated rigours of Italy. Come to think of it, all those qualities were French, though I'm sure the Italians have the same qualities and more. It's no secret that the Italians rule the world in matters of *amore* and *la dolce vita*, which I think means beautiful life, or nice biscuits – one or the other. Also, Italy gave us Michelangelo's *David,* the fittest statue ever chiselled. I think His Marbleness might even be in Florence, actually.

'We must visit *David* while we're in Florence,' I remarked to Portia, as she sat glamorously on her hand luggage, flicking through *Italian Vogue.* How anyone could look glamorous on the floor of an airport, I'll never know. I suppose the *Italian Vogue* helped. The centuries of breeding didn't hurt either.

'Yaah, deffo,' she agreed, turning another page. 'And lots of lovely leather shops,' she added. 'The moment we arrive we shall hit the Ponte Vecchio. *Pronte!*'

That was another thing; Portia spoke Italian. Not surprising really, given she did and knew everything that is deemed to be sophisticated. No wonder Freds had dumped me. I was about as sophisticated as Disneyland. 'I think the only word I know in Italian is *amore*,' I told Portia dismally. 'And the only boy I've ever *amore*-ed, dumped me.'

'*Pazzo*,' Portia said.

I wasn't sure *pazzo* sounded very *simpatico*, so I added, 'Oh, and I know *simpatico*, *molto*, *grazie*, *prego*, *bella*, *avanti* and *mal*.'

'So practically fluent,' Portia remarked.

'*Molto fluento*,' I agreed as I fanned myself with my ticket at the shock of discovering I knew an entire language I'd never even studied. 'Sister Constance is right. The teenage brain truly is remarkably absorbent.'

'Still, you'd best absorb *pazzo* while you're at it darling,' Portia insisted.

'*Pazzo*?'

'It means "bonkers,"' she explained.

I wasn't quite sure what she meant by that remark, but I didn't want to go there. 'Do you think we should start smoking?' I asked. 'I mean, all Italians smoke, don't they? We don't want to appear feverishly unworldly in front of all those fit Italian fencing boys.'

Portia shook her head. 'I'm not smoking. We're not going to choke our lungs when we're going to Italy to represent our country in a sporting event.'

I almost fainted when she said that – the representing 'our' country bit, I mean.

As I looked around at our entourage, it started to really

sink in. We were going to Florence to represent *our* country. I know I'm American. I mean, I was born there. I grew up on cheeseburgers and Cokes just like millions of other American teens with *pazzo* 'rentals. But as I was going to school in England, I could hardly be much use to the American fencing team, could I? But maybe, just maybe, if I did really, really feverishly well, one day I *would* fence for my real country. My secret dream – the dream of me fencing for the US in the Olympics – suddenly seemed closer.

I was distracted in my wild imaginings by Jenny, who had embarked on a pathetic attempt at chatting up Billy. I wondered briefly if Portia was jealous, but I suppose she noticed, as I did, that he didn't take his adoring gaze off Portia for a moment.

The rest of the team arrived in dribs and drabs. There were eighteen fencers on the team altogether; three girls and three boys on the foil, épée and sabre teams, respectively. It didn't escape Jenny's notice that Portia and I were the only team members with an entourage.

'God, you're such babies, needing a teacher and nuns to look after you,' she scorned. 'My parents let me do everything on my own,' she boasted.

I was rather disappointed in her standard of poisonous put-downs. Jenny had a long way to go before she could challenge Honey for the crown of Torture Queen.

The schools and families of the other team members clearly trusted their charges to The Commodore, which struck me as *molto* irresponsible. In addition to Bell End and the nuns, we also had a physiotherapist – a man of rather extraordinary physical proportions. Mind you, he'd be more likely to trip over a muscle than be of any use in a skirmish.

Bell End had introduced him earlier as Dr Draculochovichidoo or some mad name like that and then went on to explain that Dr Draculochovichidoo was there to tend to muscular aches and injuries.

'To keep your body oiled and fully operational' was how he actually put it.

Utterly *pazzo*.

Gatwick was experiencing delays that day. Big surprise there. We finally boarded the flight nine hours later. Yes, nine. I counted off the passing of each torturously boring hour out loud, hoping to teach Bell End a lesson about arriving too early for flights. But he pretended to ignore me.

Portia was seated between Billy and another really fit boy on the sabre team who had every jaw on the Alitalia plane scraping the floor in awe. Some heiresses get all the luck.

Bell End sat beside The Commodore. The physio guy was in front with a couple of pimply foilists. His name being unpronounceable, we decided to call him Fizz Whiz. When I say *we*, I mean Sister Regina and Sister Bethlehem, who were seated on either side of me. Sister Bethlehem was out like a light before they started showing us how to put our seat belts on and jump off the inflatable shoots. Sister Regina proved a chatty and lively companion, especially after the drinks trolley had been around a few times.

'Sister, you can't keep stealing all those brandies,' I scolded my little bearded nun as she pocketed another handful when the flight attendant wasn't looking.

'They're for Sister Bethlehem,' she explained sweetly when the flight attendant turned around and caught her red-handed. The flight attendant must have fallen for her charms because she said '*va bene*,' handed Sister another bundle of brandies and winked.

By the time we disembarked at Pisa airport, Sister had pocketed about five dozen brandy miniatures. Mind you, I think Bell End had drunk about the same amount on the flight. He wove around customs like a shopping trolley with a dodgy wheel, boasting about his Olympic medal, flashing it to the customs officials and anyone else we passed. The Italians showed a congenial aloofness, which I admired.

Because there were so many of us, we needed a coach to take us all to our pensione in Florence. I was too tired to take much in, but from the little I saw from the coach window, Florence was the very apex of *bellissima*. Everything looked so postcard historic, and as for the Italians, well, they were everywhere; smoking their heads off and sipping espresso just as I had always imagined.

'I think you might be wrong about the smoking thing,' I told Portia. 'They're all at it.'

But she assured me she was right. 'I bet they're tourists anyway,' she told me with enormous authority. 'Probably French. Then she curled her upper lip in distain.

The Pensione Bella was down a cobbled lane that was far too narrow for the coach, so we had to lug our kit for something like, oh, five thousand yards. I finally saw the sense in the hand luggage rule.

Pensione Bella was lovely. It was *bella*, in fact. It was run by a little old lady about the same height as Sister Regina who refused to speak to anyone other than our little nun. And it wasn't because no one else spoke Italian either. She snubbed Portia like she was of lowly peasant stock and sneered at my feverishly convincing Italian-accented English. Also, she kept using words that began with 'mal,' which I know from my Latin classes means 'evil.'

Bell End and the Signora had a bit of a battle over the luggage-carrying business, but Signora Santospirito physically beat him off. Hitting him over the head, she shouted, *'Tchuk! Tchuk! Malfagio, tchuk!'* Which I can only imagine was très, très unkind. Poor Bell End.

He valiantly attempted to regain his gallantry by carrying Sister Bethlehem in a fireman's lift up the stairs. But as she slept through the entire exhausting haul, it was a thankless task. Jenny made a sneering remark about him, which made me feel even more protective of our mad old master.

We'd agreed to convene in the courtyard in half an hour, or as The Commodore put it – twenty-three-hundred hours sharp, whatever that meant. Despite how exhausted and grotty we all felt, and the lateness of the hour, The Commodore was most insistent that we go over our strategies for the fencing pools tomorrow. The sensible suggestion offered up by Billy that we chat about it over breakfast the next day was spurned. Apparently, The Commodore liked *total* silence at breakfast.

When the Signora finally deigned to hand over the key to our funny little attic room, Portia and I were left with Jenny as our roommate. A feverish *dêja vu* feeling of sharing with Honey last term washed over me.

Our scheduled meeting only gave Portia, Jenny and me ten minutes in which to fight over who could use the bathroom. Portia and I decided with a shared look to let Jenny win. At Saint Augustine's we knew the importance of avoiding the small battles and saving your muscle for the big ones. I think Jenny was peeved that we'd caved so easily.

To freshen up, Portia and I squirted one another with Evian. Then we changed into something more stylishly *belle*. Also, while Jenny was taking a bath, we enjoyed our view of the sepia-and-burnt-umber-tinted city with its narrow lanes, arched bridges and domed roofs. Portia tried to teach me a bit more vital Italian, but I assured her that I'd get by with my gift for accents.

From where we stood on the funny old metal beds with their lovely white damask spreads, we could see the Ponte Vecchio arched over the Arno River. It looked most *tranquillo,* which according to Portia means . . . tranquil.

A last look in our aged-speckled mirror revealed that while Portia oozed style from every aristocratic pore of her being, Jenny and I would have to make do with lashings of lip-gloss and mascara. I thought I sensed a slight thawing in Jenny as I offered her my lip-gloss. Everyone knows lip-gloss is the international symbol of friendship for girls everywhere. But then she dashed my hopes by saying, 'You'd better not have herpes, Kelly.'

She still used it, though.

Then I began to worry that *she* might have herpes, but I didn't say anything. I had to save my energy for the big battles.

TWENTY-SIX

The Insubordination of The Commodore

The meeting was held in the lovely downstairs courtyard. It was a large open tiled area lit by tea-lights. In the centre, there was a marble fountain with a cherub peeing in its own little puddle. The atmosphere was most un-*tranquillo*, though.

I had imagined we were convening to get to know one another. We'd all been introduced at the airport, but I had forgotten almost everyone's names because we'd peeled off into our own little groups pretty much straightaway.

Eventually, The Commodore stood up, which was daunting in itself given his height, and then he coughed. I moved my chair away a bit in case he had a germ – I mean, I didn't want to be sick for my first international tournament.

'Right, well, everyone seems to be present and correct,' he began – whatever that meant. 'Welcome to, erm, Florence. I hope you have all settled in. The tournament will kick off with the pools at eleven hundred hours tomorrow. I propose we go on patrol at o-six hundred hours.'

'What do you mean by "on patrol," exactly?' I asked anxiously. I am not a girl born to patrol at o-six hundred hours or any other hour for that matter.

'I agree,' Billy added. 'If we're not going to the salle until eleven, why do we have to go on patrol at six?'

The Commodore pointed at Billy, which according to Sister Constance is the vilest thing you can do to another human being. Then again, Sister Constance has led a very sheltered life in the convent and doesn't watch cable television. 'I'll warn you now, Pyke, I won't tolerate insubordination in my ranks.'

'Oh, sod off then,' Sister Regina told him, which turned the courtyard into a gigglerama that even had Signora Santospirito joining in. That was how The Commodore's authority began its downward slide. I sensed it would be a festival of insubordination from that point on.

I also confirmed that Sister Regina had already been tucking into her brandy stash when she brazenly pulled a few miniature bottles from her sleeve and poured them into glasses, which were miraculously produced by the Signora. She passed the miniatures to Sister Bethlehem, Bell End, Fizz Whizz and the Signora – significantly, there was no glass set down for The Commodore. I noticed a vein in The Commodore's neck throbbing violently, but he didn't say anything.

Bell End gallantly held up his glass to the Signora in a toast, and Signora's eyes twinkled. She nodded approvingly and smiled. Bell End had a way with the prickliest ladies, that was for sure.

Even though everyone started complaining about how exhausted they were, Sister Regina insisted we explore the nightlife. 'Let's go and have a jig at one of those discothèque thingamees I read about in the travel guide to Florence,' she suggested, nudging Sister Bethlehem to back her up. Sister Bethlehem took a sip of her brandy and smiled serenely. 'Come on, we don't get out much. Don't be such sticks-in-the-mud,' she urged. 'Take pity on us poor nuns and take us out for a jig.'

'But we're underage,' Portia said.

Sister Regina tutted. 'Nonsense child! This is Italy; they don't worry about details like age. Besides, I won't tolerate ageism. We take a very dim view of that at the convent, I can tell you.'

Nuns really are in a special little *pazzo* world. And Bell End was no saner. He fully backed Sister up.

'Champion idea,' he agreed, nudging The Commodore in the ribs. 'What do you say, Commodore, eh? Let's get our dancing shoes on. Show these young ones a few steps on the dance floor, shall we? Eh? Eh? What do you say, Commodore?'

By this stage The Commodore's neck vein looked on the verge of bursting. He spoke to Bell End through gritted teeth. 'My name is Mr Rogers, as you well know,

Oscar. But I'm happy for you to call me Biffy if you'd prefer.'

I know, how sad and funny to know your teacher's first name!

'Can we call you Biffy too, sir?' I blurted, which sent Portia, Jenny and the rest of the team into fits of giggledom. One of the other guys, an épéeist, I think, even stood up and shook my hand.

Biffy didn't respond to my request, but he agreed with Sister and Bell End that a 'bit of light entertainment' might help the team unwind and bond. I suspect he was trying to claw back some authority.

So Bell End, Biffy, the nuns, Fizz Whiz, Portia, Jenny, Billy, myself and the rest of the team (whose names I still didn't know) set off into the late Tuscan evening for a jig. Signora Santospirito had apparently given Sister the skinny on the happening place to go and get down.

'Are you a betting man, Mr Biffy?' Sister Bethlehem asked as we wandered through the cobbled lanes.

'I like the occasional game of bridge, and I take a flutter at Ascot if I have a good tip.'

'What about ten quid on who cut Samson's hair?' she asked Biffy, looking at him with her fluffy little innocent nun face.

Nuns. There's no stopping them.

TWENTY-SEVEN

Discothèque Pazzo

I presumed the discothèque would be full of chubby old mustachioed Italian men in gold chains. I envisioned them swinging their wives around the dance floor to Tony Bennett songs while a tattered old disco ball lolled from the ceiling.

Instead, Cavern was a dark, lively, thumping, strobe-lit extravaganza of hip-hoppity music. The doormen didn't look twice at our *pazzo* crowd of nuns, fencing masters and underage teens. He said something to us in Italian, and I worshipped Portia when she replied.

There was the odd mustachioed man decked out in gold chains on the dance floor, but he was the exception. Mostly the club was packed with fit boys and stunning girls in ooh-la-la outfits, smoking cigarettes and sipping sophisticated drinks.

Billy and the other guys asked the girls what we wanted to drink. Sister Regina asked for two limoncellos for her and the now feverishly excited Sister Bethlehem. I swear she was tapping her little wooden hobnailed shoes to the beat. Most of us went for soft drinks, but Jenny had to show off by asking for an elaborate cocktail. Before we'd left the pensione, I'd clocked her stuffing knickers in her bra. I dreaded where this evening would end if Jenny got drunk and pulled.

I thought Biffy might object to the cocktail but he nodded agreeably and wrote down all our orders on a little pad he produced from his jacket of many pockets. Then he went off to the bar with the boys. He was soooo obviously sucking up.

'Let's check out the loos,' Jenny suggested, a proposal that met with solid approval from her friends. 'I heard they have those squat jobbies in Italy,' she announced, as if this prospect thrilled her. If you want my opinion, I think she'd noticed what the rest of us had already discovered: one of her knickers was peeping out of her top.

'I'll stay here and try to grab a table,' I told them.

There would be time enough for squat toilets later. Right now, someone had to be sensible, and it wasn't going to be Bell End, Biffy or the nuns, that was for sure.

'Oooh, isn't this fun, Mr Wellend? I do hope you'll be putting your name on my dance card,' Sister Regina told him as I looked about for a table. Sister Bethlehem looked as awake as the next person, but I figured that was unlikely to last. When she popped off she'd need a chair at the ready.

'If it isn't Calypso, she who drags men from their duties,' a voice behind me said.

I turned and there he was. Malcolm McHamish's Italian doppelganger. He had an unlit cigarette stuck to his lower lip and a glass of something in his hand. I looked him up and I looked him down and then I looked him up and down again. He was wearing a pair of sunglasses perched on his head, an Italian suit over an open-necked Pucci shirt, but apart from his continental taste in clothes, he was a Malcolm clone. Then my little grey cells got to work and I wondered how this stranger knew my name.

I swear if I hadn't been so shocked I would have fainted. It really was Malcolm!

'As ever, you look the very epitome of style and beauty, Miss Kelly,' he said. 'Did you just get here? It's the damndest thing, don't you know. I've been ringing and ringing you for days. Well, that is to say all day.' A waiter passed by and lit the cigarette dangling from Malcolm's lips. Malcolm thanked him profusely in Italian and gave him a wad of Euros.

'What are you doing here? How's Freddie?' I asked in a rush.

Malcolm took a deep drag on his fag before continuing. 'Ah, you want the latest goss on His Royal Nibs. Sick as a cat, poor devil. Spent the night in the infirmary, which is enough to kill off the best of them.'

'Is he going to be okay?' I asked anxiously. 'I mean, I've tried to call him. I feel awful about what happened.'

Malcolm put his hand on my arm and gave me a comforting rub. 'Why? You've not been tinkering with the cobbles at the edge of the bridge, have you? No, darling Freds is made of tougher stuff than that. They sent him home this morning while the antibiotics work their magic.' I watched as Malcolm exhaled his smoke and blew a series of rings that wafted up to the ceiling. It was probably my feverish imagination, but he seemed bored by the conversation somehow. Which made me want to tap-dance for his attention.

'What are *you* doing here, in Italy, though?' I asked.

He waved his fag around. 'Oh, you know, the usual. Immersing myself in the trough of Florence nightlife. Here, try this Disaronno, I swear it tastes like marzipan. Reminds me of Christmas,' he urged, shoving his glass to my lips.

I took a sip and grimaced. 'Yes, marzipan,' I agreed, pushing the glass away. 'But why aren't you at Eades?'

'Oh that. Yes, well, bit of a last-minute thing. The Film Society took a vote and the ayes had it, I'm afraid.'

'A vote on what?'

'Filming the British team fencing in Florence. Also we thought we might get a bit of that heady Renaissance air into our lungs, touch up our Italian language skills and buy a few trinkets for the old madres back home.'

I shook my head, still convinced he was a mirage. Then I caught Bell End swinging the nuns around the dance floor and knew that all was as it should be in my mad little world.

'Sorry, I seem to be banging on about me,' he said, taking hold of my hand. 'Come and join us for a drink.'

I allowed myself to be led over to where it seemed half the Eades Film Society were sprawled out in a large roped-off VIP booth. All of them were dressed like they'd just come from a magazine shoot for Prada or Versace. They barely acknowledged me until Malcolm chucked an ice cube at Orlando.

'You all know Calypso, the Botticelli angel of Saint Augustine's,' Malcolm announced.

They all smiled or raised their drinks, and then it took about a five full minutes to air-kiss them all. Even then, most of them continued chatting to one another as they brushed my cheeks with their lips. 'Ah, and there is the beautiful Portia,' Malcolm cried out as I was still air-kissing the troupes. He waved to her, and she peeled off from the rest of the fencing group and came over.

Another round of air-kissing commenced. Then Malcolm asked, 'What would you like to drink, Portia? I recommend the Disaronno.'

'I've ordered, thanks, Malcolm. Billy's here with us, you know. What are you doing here?' This last question was directed at Tarquin, but he just held his drink up in a toast and carried on an animated discussion with Orlando.

Malcolm replied. 'Yaah, likes his sabre does our Pyke. No, he's one of the heroes that drew us here. Rather hoping to get some triumphant footage of the boy wonder making mincemeat of the legendary Italian swashbucklers.' Then he turned his attentions back to me. 'Calypso, you'll be wanting your usual.' He shouted out to Orlando,

'Hunte, get a bottle of Veuve, will you? Get two, in fact, three, four – a dozen! In fact, tell them to empty the bar.' Then he flung down a huge pile of Euros on the table.

'Get it yourself, McHamish,' Orlando replied, lazily chucking the notes back at Malcolm. 'I went last time.'

'Honestly, I don't want any champagne,' I told Malcolm.

'Nonsense, you live on the stuff.'

'No, I don't,' I told him truthfully.

'Really?' Malcolm looked shocked. 'Well, why are you always swilling the stuff down, then?'

'I'm not always swilling the stuff,' I said with lashings of indignance. 'I don't even like the taste of it.'

Malcolm wiped a stray lock of his slicked-down hair from his face. 'Excuse me, Calypso, but you are a champagne swiller of the highest order. The first night I met you hanging off the wisteria vine outside my room – vision of loveliness though you were – I thought, Malcolm this is not your usual girl. McHamish, old chap, this is a girl who lives life on the edge. Pissing down with rain it was, long after midnight, and yet there you were climbing vines looking for boys. No stopping this one, I said to myself. And then you accepted my invitation to dry off in my room, draped your lingerie on my radiator and made a beeline for the champagne fridge.'

'I was lost,' I explained, outraged. 'I was looking for Freddie, remember? And you offered me the champagne.'

'Ah, but you knocked it back like it was your mother's own milk, as I recall.'

Portia pulled herself away from her brother Tarquin to say, 'She only drank it because she was trying to be polite. Calypso barely ever drinks.'

Malcolm rolled his eyes and then held up his hand to halt further discussion. 'Campari and soda, it is then,' he announced, disappearing into the throng before I could explain that I couldn't drink on the night before the tournament.

TWENTY-EIGHT

Developing My Aptitude in Matters of La Dolce Vita

The Campari and soda was red. Not that I could drink it, but it contrasted nicely with my green dress, so I swirled it around with my straw, hoping it would make me appear fabulous. Even though I wasn't smoking, I was fairly confident that I looked *molto, molto* sophisticated swirling my elegant drink about with my swizzle stick while all around me *pazzo* reigned supreme.

Sister Bethlehem had obviously been storing up reserves of energy during all her years of napping because she didn't leave the dance floor all night. In fact, Bell End, Sister Regina, Biffy and Fizz Whiz were all tripping the light fantastic.

Malcolm, Billy, Tarquin, Orlando et al. did some fancy dancing too.

'There's no way they'd dance like that in England,'

Portia remarked. 'Look at Tarquin,' she said, pointing to her brother, who was in his own little mad world on the dance floor.

'I agree it does seem against nature's way to see British boys actually moving their feet on a dance floor.'

Then I leaned back in the banquet and inhaled the heady scent of smoke and *la dolce vita* into my lungs. I had been feeling an odd mix of emotions that night; it was wonderful being entertained by so many fit boys. Then again, I felt odd about Malcolm being there and *molto* guilty about Freds being ill. Tarquin assured me as Malcolm had that all Freds had was a nasty chill, but still the guilts are hard to shift once they get a grip.

Then Malcolm came up, and without so much as a by-your-leave, kissed me. Right out of the blue, no warning whatsoever, just like that, he wrapped his lips against mine and got on with it.

Talk about frightening a girl. Admittedly, I rather enjoyed it when he kissed me in Windsor, well up until Freds fell in the Thames, anyway. But that was then, in the context of making Freds jealous. This was now, under the watchful gaze of the British national fencing team, my nuns, Bell End, Biffy and Fizz Whiz – not to mention the Eades Film Society. It was the very apex of mal-ness.

'Hang on a minute,' I told him, disengaging from his clinch. 'What in the name of lip-gloss are you up to?'

'I rather thought I was kissing you.'

'Yes, well, I don't know what the rules are amongst you

Scottish film types, but in the real world you don't just go round kissing girls without a by-your-leave.'

Malcolm didn't look in the least bit chastened. 'What the hell is a by-your-leave, anyway?' he asked.

'Yes, I've always wondered about that,' added Orlando, tapping the ash from his cigarette in the ashtray. 'Is it an old highway code or a Shakespearean whatsit?'

That set the whole table off on an in-depth debate on the linguistic origins of 'by-your-leave.'

'Is that even the point?' I asked the table.

Malcolm, who now had his back to me, turned as if he'd only just noticed I was there. 'What?' he asked.

Well, what's a girl to do? I asked myself. So I stood up to leave. I could see Portia waving at me in the distance. Malcolm had turned back to the debate, which was getting highbrow, with Greek translations flying through the air like croissants at Sunday breakfast. I marched off in a stroppish sort of way to see Portia.

'Seriously, Portia, sometimes I wonder if boys are worth the effort. You won't believe what Malcolm just did.'

'Tell me later. We've got a problem with Jenny. She's totally wasted. Alison is holding her head out of the toilet bowl as we speak. I just walked in and found her there with her head down the loo. I swear I thought she was going to drown. And she's asked specifically for you. Can you take over while I have a quiet word with Bell End. I mean, The Commodore will go spare if he finds out.'

'We can't let Biffy or Bell End know that Jenny's drunk!'

I blurted, and then wondered why. I mean, who was Bell End to judge? I thought as I spotted him at the front of a conga line consisting of a large part of our fencing party, with Biffy taking up the tail end. Talk about letting our side down. Here we were in the capital of style behaving like Basingstoke chavs. It was too *pazzo* for words. 'I don't think he'll be much use,' I added.

'I see what you mean,' Portia agreed, having witnessed what I had. 'Well, come in and help anyway.'

Jenny was, as Portia had warned, head down in the loo, which was not one of those squat jobbies, thank God. She was totally châteaued, mortalled, wasted, bladdered, or to put it more plainly, revoltingly drunk. We may have been sworn enemies, but every girl has a duty to every other girl when it comes to this sort of thing.

'Hi,' I said to Alison. 'I'm Calypso.' They were probably the first words I'd uttered to her, which spoke volumes about my commitment to bonding with my fellow teammates. Still, what better way to bond than sharing the load of sobering up a drunk teammate, I told myself.

'Yeah, I know. You're the girl that's going out with that Prince Freddie. I read about you.'

'Yaah, well, *was* going out with Prince Freddie,' I corrected her, feeling a bit of a lump form in my throat. 'Anyway, let me take over for a bit. We've got to get some water into her.'

'I'll go get that,' Portia said, and left Alison and me to it.

'Good thing tomorrow ain't the tournament. She's going to feel like death.'

I signalled my agreement with a nod as I pulled Jenny's head out of the bowl. Her eyes were closed and her head was lolling. She looked rough. 'Jenny?' I said her name to check if she was conscious. It's a trick I learned from watching old episodes of *Beverly Hills 90210*. Whenever someone was drunk or on drugs, their friends would all repeat their name over and over. Sometimes they even slapped them across the face, an idea I nobly pushed aside.

All Jenny did was moan.

'I don't think she's in a good place,' Alison said as she passed me a wad of wet loo paper.

I wiped Jenny's face and told her, 'You've got to get some water down you, Jenny,' even though she wasn't in any state to understand.

I tried not to show it, but I was actually afraid for her. I mean, people died of alcohol poisoning, didn't they? At least that's what they told us in Special Studies. Jenny looked desperately unwell. The only other people I'd seen drunk were Honey, and Star's dad and his mates, but even they had never been drunk like this. Well, no, that's not true. Tiger was often unconscious.

Portia came in with the water and we managed to get Jenny to drink some. Jenny slurred my name, which I took as a good sign. Italian girls were coming in and out and the word 'mal' was being bandied about with much abandon. I know it sounds shallow, but I was feeling embarrassed about sitting on the floor holding my drunk anti-girlfriend's hair out of her face while her head lolled in the toilet bowl. It didn't paint me in that *la dolce vita* light I was aiming for. Portia had said we were representing our country, and this wasn't how I wanted to represent England or America, or Outer Mongolia for that matter.

'I told Bell End,' Portia said once Jenny had finished drinking the water. 'Well, he's going to find out, isn't he?' she added when she saw the look of horror on my face. 'He's gone off to the pensione. Apparently he's got some sachets of electrolytes there.'

'I don't think we should be giving her *more* drugs,' I whispered sternly.

'They're not drugs,' Alison said helpfully. 'They're sort of like mineral salts. They'll bring her mineral levels back up.'

'We don't want her bringing anything else up, animal, vegetable or mineral,' I said as Jenny put her arms around my neck and told me she loved me. I reluctantly let her nuzzle my face for a bit before allowing her head to droop into my lap. She smelt of toilet water.

Portia and Alison left me alone with her – Alison to tell some Italian boy she'd pulled what was happening, and Portia to get more water. I was left alone with Jenny, who was quite sweet when she was drunk, really. Apart from smelling like toilet water and being cross-eyed. At least she wasn't death staring me.

I stroked her hair and said some nice soothing things,

and then she started to laugh. 'Sucked in!' she cried, sitting up as straight as you like. Then she punched the air triumphantly with her fist.

I stopped my soothing talk and death stared her, but all she did was shrug. 'I just wanted to see how far I could take it. No biggie.'

'Erm, take what, exactly?'

'You and your stuck-up friend. Lady High and Mighty. Think you're all that with your entourage of Eades boys flying out to play with you.'

I was wrong. Jenny was as bad as Honey. Maybe even worse. Not even Honey would stoop to sticking her head in a toilet bowl for attention. Like Delilah cutting off Samson's hair, Honey would get someone else to do it for her.

I stood up as imperiously as I could, walked over to the basin and washed my hands. Then I stepped over Jenny and all her mal-ity and left the loo. Let her deal with Bell End, Portia, Alison and the rest of the team and grown-ups, who were no doubt running themselves into a conga line of feverish madness to save the situation.

I passed Portia as I walked through the club. I took the water from her hands and walked back into the loo and threw it over Jenny. Then I grabbed Portia's hand and led her out, briefly filling her in on our anti-girlfriend's pathetic scheme.

'So what should we do?' Portia asked. 'I mean, Bell End's having kittens. He's charged off back to the pensione for electrolytes and . . .'

'I'll tell you what we'll do. We can leave Jenny to sort out her own drama and enjoy ourselves. I'm going to pull Malcolm and you're going to pull Billy.'

'But we've broken up.'

'Only in England. We're in Italy now, the country of good food, good clothes and good loving.'

Then I walked up to the table where Malcolm et al. were still debating the origins of 'by-your-leave.' And without a by-your-leave or a how's-your-father, I unceremoniously sat on Malcolm's lap and kissed his lips off.

TWENTY-NINE

The City of Amore and Melodramas!

While kissing Malcolm was pure *la dolce vita* and I should have floated home on a cloud of bliss, I couldn't help taking a wicked pleasure in Jenny's downfall. I still stunk of toilet water. I have no idea what Malcolm must have thought, but either he was too polite to say or couldn't smell me over the fog of his own smoke. I was glad I took Portia's advice on spurning that particular vice.

When the fencing team found out about Jenny's prank, there was an unspoken agreement that she must be sent to Coventry. Dear little Sister Regina couldn't get her lovely nunnish head around Jenny's motivation for pretending to be drunk.

'She's more Honeyesque than any of us realised,' I explained to her as we tottered back to the pensione that evening.

'Oh but Calypso dear, what a nasty, mean trick. I'm sure

I just can't understand such wickedness, child,' Sister Regina murmured while fingering her way through her rosary.

Sister Bethlehem was snoring happily, slung over Bell End's shoulder in her now familiar fireman's lift. She didn't contribute to the discussion per se, but I'm sure she'd have been devastated had she been awake. Nuns aren't built for such worldly wickedness.

Portia and I heard Jenny getting told off in the courtyard as we were preparing for bed, and we stuck our heads out the window so we didn't miss the brouhaha. Biffy warned her that 'another stunt like that, Frogmorten, and you'll be off the team. Quick smart!'

Then Bell End had a go at her. 'Yer bloody idiot, Frogmorten. What did want to pull a stunt like that for? Eh? Eh? You're part of the Great British fencing machine, yer big girl's blouse. We're 'ere, in Italy, playing the game of games! And you're fooling around like a bloody toddler with its nappy over its head!'

And then Biffy started off on a four-year rantarama about how he wouldn't tolerate insubordination in his ranks. Portia and I got bored at that point and fell asleep.

The next morning all the grown-ups had hangovers, which was très, très funny. Oh, how we laughed. Especially at Biffy, who, far from being on patrol at six, didn't surface until ten! He even had the nerve to complain to the Signora that her knife made too much noise scraping the butter onto his toast. She gave him a look that would melt any knife.

The nuns weren't up when we left. Bell End thought it best not to disturb them in case they got upset. I sincerely doubted we'd see Sister Bethlehem's eyes open again for the rest of our stay. But anyway it was not *permisso* to have spectators at the pools.

Even though the salle didn't look far away on the map we studied at breakfast, Bell End had a go at Biffy for being disorganised and not arranging transport. But Portia and I were delighted to be exploring the streets of Florence. Apart from having to lug our fencing kit over three million miles.

Bell End roared when Jenny moaned.

'What's the matter with you, yer big girl's blouse? Yer young, you can take a knock.'

I actually think he had a point. I loved strolling through the streets – kit or no kit. It was like being in a museum of beautiful people and designer shops. As we walked across the Ponte Alle Grazie bridge, Portia and I stopped to lean over the Arno River and scream out mad things. I don't know what it is about bridges and mountains. They just seem to have that effect on young minds, don't they? Perhaps it was brought on by the shop-fest on the Ponte Vecchio bridge opposite, where finest designer delights of the world nestled tightly against the river, awaiting the most awesomely sophisticated shoppers outside of Milano.

While we had our heads down, I asked Portia about Billy, hoping for a straight answer. All she did was smile enigmatically, which set us off chortling like mad things again. Billy and some of the boys caught up with us and asked us what was so funny.

'Just the foolish madness of teenage girls,' I told Billy while Portia composed her blushes.

The boys Billy was hanging out with were quite nice for a bunch of shorties. One was an épéeist and the other two were on the boys' sabre team like him.

'That Jenny's a bit of a lunatic?' one of them remarked conversationally, but no one said anything. I, for one, was over Jenny, although she'd already had a go at me at breakfast about using all the hot water. We mostly talked about Bell End and Biffy and argued the merits of their respective levels of madness, and then we mused about what the Italian team would be like. Probably fearsomely brilliant.

I found our developing camaraderie magical.

As we walked along, Billy and Portia paired off, and as I watched them chatting away together and pointing out buildings and fountains to one another, I couldn't help thinking how sweet they looked. Billy blond and fit as all get-out and Portia with her aristocratic features and rich chocolaty tresses – they were a match made in heaven. Well, made in Windsor at least.

The salle was beside a Medici chapel, and something about the decaying beauty of the building made me walk more reverently. The Italian team was already there doing stretches, but that didn't stop the Italian boys from ooh-la-la-ing the English girls' team as we wandered in.

'*Pappagaillo* alert,' Portia whispered to me. 'Parrots,' she explained.

'But what are they saying?'

'The usual.' She shrugged. 'How beautiful we are, what lovely figures we have, that sort of thing.'

'Oh, aren't they sweet!' I squealed.

Portia shook her long brown tresses. 'No!'

But as a freakishly tall blonde with fluffy little horns of hair that won't stick down however much gel, wax or other fixative I use, I take my compliments where I can.

Then my eyes clapped onto our old fencing master, Professor Sullivan; the most sauvé, debonair gentleman in the fencing world. I nudged Portia, and gave Professor Sullivan a little wave. He smiled and nodded, but that was all. He was always very minimal in his gestures, so I didn't take his lack of hoorahs to heart. Still, I wanted to run up to him and gush about how we'd won our place on the British national team and how Star had chucked fencing for her music, but Professor Sullivan wasn't one for idle gushing. From the looks of things, he was coaching the Italian team now, which meant we were the enemy, so I wandered aloofly alongside Portia and reigned in my gushing side.

I figured Bell End would puff himself up and go *mano a mano* with his predecessor, but I think he was too hung-over, because he just slumped on the first bench he came to. Biffy went over, though, and the two shook hands amiably.

The British team members peeled off into their respective changing rooms to get kitted up.

'Okay, now I am nervous,' Portia told me as we opened our assigned lockers. Then she did the most uncharacteristic jig.

'I know, and can you believe Professor Sullivan is here?'

'I used to have the most enormous crush on him,' she confided. 'I'm worried that my nerves will throw my game.'

'Was I the only girl on the fencing team not to have a crush on Professor Sullivan?' I asked, and then for some unfathomable reason we chortled madly until we both felt sick. You had to be there, really.

We stopped our laughing when Jenny walked in. Not just because she sneered at us. She's one of those girls who has the ability to suck the fun out of a room. I know you're probably asking yourself how much fun can there possibly be in a girls' changing room – even in Florence. But you'd be surprised. Changing rooms are where you say all those confidential girlie things and get to check out one another's knickers and bras – not in a pervy way – just so you can check you're *en trend*. Also, it was our first Italian changing room and we were all talking in Italian accents, which sounded feverishly sophisticated. I would have to remember to ask the 'rents if there was any Italian blood in our Kentucky/English lineage – the Kellyisimos, perhaps?

The trick to speaking Italian – or rather sounding like you speak Italian – is to accentuate or add a vowel on the ends of words, like 'telephona' and 'lippo-glosso.' Within about ten minutes of practice, I swear no one would ever know we weren't born and bred in Florence. Which was a bit worrying actually, because I didn't want anyone mixing our teams up. Luckily we had *GBR* emblazoned on our kit.

It was *molto* exciting changing into our GBR fencing gear for our very first international match. Oh yes, before Jenny walked in, the room was packed to the rafters with *la dolce vita.*

'Oh my God, did you see how fitisimo those boys out there were?' Alison said in her newfound Italian accent.

'Italian boys do seem to have a genetically higher fitisimo level than English boys,' I agreed in my own excellent accent. 'But I don't think it lasts,' I added sagely. 'Did you see those chubby old chappos with their medallions at the discothèque last night?'

'I don't mean the Italian boys. I mean those Eades boys out there filming,' she said – completely out of accent.

Jenny groaned. 'You're all so stupid,' she sneered.

'You mean *stupido*,' I corrected her.

'Idiots,' she sneered lamely.

I decided she wasn't worth wasting our accents on.

We all agreed to walk out into the salle together. Portia had braided my hair like a horse's tail, so I did a bit of a trot. All of us looked sleek and groomed. Even Jenny Frogmorton was looking spiffy.

As I pushed open the door to the salle, I walked straight into Malcolm's camera.

'Ow!' I cried, holding my nose.

'Bugger, sorry, darling, sorry.'

But before I could give him a piece of my passionate Italian mind, the Italians all started applauding us. The girls and boys and even Professor Sullivan were all in an orderly line, clapping for us like we were superstars. I knew it was only the team because they didn't allow any spectators at the pools, but still it was flattering and made us feel welcome and loved.

I forgot about my sore nose and gave our fans a little wave as I walked as elegantly as possible onto the piste.

Biffy blew his whistle, and then for no reason at all, Bell End blew his. Officially, Bell End was only here to chaperone Portia and myself, but unofficially I figured he had scores to settle. He usually did.

'On behalf of the Italian National Under Eighteens team, we'd like to welcome our friends from Great Britain,' Professor Sullivan announced, first in English and then in Italian. Then he bowed ever so slightly. Now there was a man who had élan. Not a single loon-cell in his brain. I hoped Bell End was taking notes.

I set about doing my warm-up stretches and tried to ignore Malcolm's lens, which remained fixed on me the entire time. It was *molto, molto* off-putting, I can tell you.

Eventually Biffy and Professor Sullivan called out the names for the pools and directed players to their respective pistes. It was hard not to be aware of Malcolm's camera, glued as it was to moi. So much for his claim that he wanted footage of Billy.

My first opponent's name was Carlotta. She had a slightly androgynous beauty, as if she'd just walked out of a Caravaggio painting. She had perfect raven curls that hung loose around her shoulders and eyelashes so long they could have been weapons in their own right.

'Ciao,' she said, and I ciaoed her back as we each wired the other up and checked that our electrics were working. 'How you say, good luck?' she asked, batting her lashes for Italy.

'Erm, well, good luck, actually! Or bon chance,' I joked. She looked at me like I was *pazzo*.

I was morbidly conscious that I towered over her like some freakish white bird. She was a good foot and a half shorter than me, and I remembered Bell End's barbed remark about Biffy – the bigger the target, the more there is to hit.

Professor Sullivan was presiding over the bout, and so it was his job to call 'play.' Back when he taught us at Saint Augustine's he always spoke French. But now he called us to the *en guard* lines in his sauvé 1930s English accent. I suspected it was a secret code for, 'Good luck, my country-men and women.'

Carlotta and I saluted. My salute was the usual English casual tipping of my blade, but Carlotta actually kissed her blade and slashed it in a feverishly stylish and slightly terrifying way. The noise cut through my soul like ice as the realization hit me – I was representing Great Britain. I wasn't equipped. I didn't have a fancy salute. I wasn't even British!

We masked up and 'Pretes! Allez! Avanti!' was called.

My Caravaggio opponent advanced down the piste like a demon. Her footwork was faultless and even before she lunged I knew I was out of my league. Though I tried to summon the spirit of Jerzy Pawlowski, the greatest sabreur who ever lived, all I heard from the president was '*Priorite a ma droit*,' which means priority to my right. I must 'fess up and tell you there were ever so few '*Priorite a ma gauche*.'

I was *gauche* . . . in more ways than one.

Actually, I was fencing very well. It was just that Carlotta was blindingly good. She was in a league of point and priority grabbing excellence such as I'd never witnessed. At the end of play when she tore off her mask, spraying the sweat from her hair everywhere, all I could do was say, 'Bloody hell, Carlotta, you're good. I mean, *bene*.'

She beamed, not smugly, not grandly. She just looked happy to hear my praise and of course for her win. I beamed back. Not even sweaty hair could dim her Renaissance loveliness. I looked over at Malcolm. His camera was still glued to his face, the lens still fixed on me, but I wondered, was he comparing Carlotta and me? I know I was. Freakishly tall, pale blonde girl versus voluptuous, stunning, glowing brunette.

And then I wondered something else. Was I jealous?

Over the course of the next two hours, I won a few bouts and lost a few more. I barely performed well enough to survive the cull from the pools, but I did survive. That meant I would get to play in the tournament tomorrow. Unlike Jenny, who had been culled.

I know it was shallow of me, but it made me feel that justice existed after all. Sometimes, bad things do happen to mean girls.

Professor Sullivan came over afterwards and asked, 'So how does it feel to be on the national team, Miss Kelly?' – only he asked in French of course.

'Yaah, it's really cool, basically, but these girls are, like . . . Well they're really, really good, aren't they? Do you think I can ever be that good?' I asked in my best approximation of a French accent.

And then he smiled. It was a smile that lit up the entire salle, and then something miraculous happened. He spoke to me in English for the first time ever. 'Most definitely, Calypso. Without a shadow of a doubt, in fact. There is one thing I have always had infinite faith in, and that is your ability to be as good as you want to be.'

THIRTY

He Made It Seem Like the Most Sensible Thing in the World . . .

As we came out of the salle, Malcolm grabbed my hand and pulled me aside.

'Can we talk?'

I looked down at his hand holding mine, but I didn't pull it away. I was feeling high and positive, and actually it felt rather nice, especially when he took my shoulder-biting fencing kit from me and put it on his own shoulder.

'What's up?' I asked, but all he did was pull me behind the old Medici church and kiss me long and hard. I know when boys kiss you you're meant to go off to a dreamy cloudland of magical warmth and loveliness, but I have that sort brain that never switches off. I couldn't help comparing Malcolm's kissing to Freds'. Which was totally wrong and shallow, I know. But Malcolm's pulling style was *molto* passionate.

Kissing Freds was cloudlandy. At the time, I always thought it the apex of loveliness, but it was different to kissing Malcolm. Malcolm took a strand of my wet hair and placed it behind my ear and smiled. I ruffled his red hair and looked into his luminous green eyes and studied his face. Just as I was memorising it, he locked his lips on mine and did that dip thing again.

Suddenly he pulled me up as a priest was walking past. He said hello to the young priest in Italian and they had a short chat. I nodded and smiled and laughed when they laughed, but they may well have been discussing trigonometry.

Eventually Father went off to do a spot of shopping – well, that was my assessment – and Malcolm turned his mega-watt personality back onto me. 'I need your help,' he told me seriously.

I thought he wanted to kiss me again and puckered up.

'No, seriously. I think I've found the perfect subject for the film I came here to make.'

'I thought you came here to film Billy.'

'Did I tell you that?'

'Yes.'

He ran his hands through his hair, and for a moment he reminded me of Freds – an older, strawberry-blond, more eccentric Freds. 'I wonder if that's what I meant to do. Anyway, something happened this morning. I have to show it to you; I want your opinion. It was the maddest thing, really – the way it all came about. I went off this morning to get my nipple pierced and –'

'Wait, why did you get your nipple pierced?' I asked, trying to keep all judgment from my mind as I remembered my own navel-piercing fiasco in Los Angeles last summer.

'Eyebrow piercing is so passé,' he said, as if this should be all the explanation I deserved. Boys! 'And well, only hippies and bikers do their ears or lips, don't they?'

'I suppose,' I replied, quite glad he hadn't said anything about navel piercing being passé.

'And on consideration I'm pretty certain the madre would have an embolism if I pierced my face. I did consider a wrist piercing, but only briefly. The chap who did the deed, nice guy, bit of a freak, but anyway point is, he had his wrist pierced. It was the darndest of darn things. I've never considered piercing my wrist before. But I'm not sure it wouldn't become a bit of a nuisance, you know with cuffs and all that.' Then he started looking at old footage in his video camera.

'But I don't understand why you had to get anything pierced?' I told him.

'What?' he looked up. Clearly he'd completely lost the thread of the conversation.

'Why get anything pierced?'

He appeared to consider this for a while. 'I see what you're saying. I hadn't thought of it that way, but anyway, the point is, look, let me show you –'

I took a step back. 'Take it away. I don't want to see your nipple!' I squealed. I like to think I'm a girl made of strong American fibre, but I was not a studier of fresh nipple piercings – or old ones for that matter. Star, Georgina and I had had our navels pierced last summer. It was a bonding sort of thing. But mine had gone septic, and Sarah had made me take it out after a showdown with the poor guy who'd performed the deed. No, I was off body piercing for life.

Malcolm ruffled my hair and laughed. 'I wasn't going to show you my nipple,' he assured me. 'Besides, I bottled out at the last minute.' Then he grabbed my hand and insisted I come with him to see something 'incredibly cool.'

Incredibly cool, incredibly cool. I kept repeating the phrase to myself as he dragged me through the bright winter streets of Florence. I couldn't stop wondering, what in algebra's name would a boy like Malcolm consider 'incredibly cool'? Not cool, mind you, but *incredibly* cool.

'Is it a really amazing Renaissance painting? I know, we're going to the Uffizi to see the Botticelli room?'

He laughed. 'That's in the other direction. Just wait and see.'

'I know, a vinyl shop? We're going to a vinyl shop so you can buy old eighties recordings of tragic, I mean cool, Italian bands no one else has heard of.' Star told me that boys love obscure indie bands they imagine no one else has heard of. But then Malcolm wasn't most boys.

'No,' he told me firmly. 'Just wait and see.'

And then I saw a cinema in the distance. 'I know, I know. It's an arty Italian movie?' Oh yes, that seemed likely.

'No.' He pulled me along faster. 'Just wait, we're almost there.' We turned down a dark, narrow lane where we passed a shop that sold motor scooter parts and then a shop that did tattoos and body piercing. Malcolm waved to the guy inside, whose entire body was glinting with piercings. I began to hyperventilate, but we didn't stop there, thank goodness.

'I know, you've discovered an amazing crumbling-down old building that a mad dead Medici lived in. Everyone's forgotten about it and stopped searching. But you've found it, all vine-covered, and you alone have realised what it really is, and you've started–'

'You really should become an author, Calypso. Your imagination needs a larger canvas.'

Of course I was madly flattered and started walking on air. Freds had never even noticed my creative spirit. He just thought I was mad. I made a mental note to tell Miss Topler that my mind needs a larger canvas than her class.

'We're here,' Malcolm said, gesturing to a shop front. 'Now you can satisfy your curiosity to your heart's delight.'

We were standing outside a pet shop. I looked at Malcolm's face, but his eyes were fixed on something inside. I mean, I'm as keen on pets as the next girl, but as you can't bring animals into the UK without inserting microchips into their ears and getting them special pet passports. It's not really the sort of shop you'd look out for a souvenir. Well, I don't. I worry I'd fall in love with a kitten or puppy or a hamster, and then it would be an awful wrench, knowing I couldn't take it home with me.

I wasn't wildly keen on going inside and finding something too cute to leave behind, so I said, 'So what, it's just a pet shop. That's hardly incredibly cool. They're everywhere.'

Malcolm jerked me inside. 'Look,' he said, pointing to a large wooden crate that was full of tiny paper boxes that looked a bit like Chinese takeaway boxes. They were all open and empty apart from one box where a tiny little black-speckled duckling was franticly flapping and peeping.

'Oh bless!' I exclaimed.

'When I came in here this morning to contemplate the piercing, every one of these cartons here was full of ducklings. I stood here and filmed as customer after customer came into the shop and bought a duckling. I was here for, oh, I don't know, about an hour.' He then spoke to the pet shop owner in Italian.

The guy replied without looking up from his newspaper.

'Yes, Giuseppe thinks it was a bit over an hour. And in that time, every other duckling was sold. Except for this little chap.'

The tiny duckling had his miniature bill in the air. He appeared to be looking and talking directly at us. '*Peep,*

peep, peep, peep!' Honestly, it was the most adorable sight I had ever seen. Even Dorothy wasn't as cute as the duckling, which made me feel disloyal just to think such a thought.

'Can we hold him?' I asked Giuseppe in my best Italian accent. But Giuseppe didn't seem to understand my wonderful Italianised English.

Malcolm asked the owner in Italian for me, but I could tell the answer was no because of all the head shaking and arm waving that went on.

'Apparently he won't let us because last month someone picked up one of his ducklings and dropped it on the floor and broke its wing,' Malcolm translated.

All the while the little duckling was going '*peep, peep, peep.*'

'But I don't understand. Why didn't anyone buy him? He's adorable.'

'Yaah, I agree,' Malcolm said as he filmed the duckling peeping piteously. 'They don't like his mottled colours, apparently.'

'Oh, that's soooo mean. That's what gives him his character.'

Malcolm was taking some close-up footage as he replied. 'I agree.'

I couldn't bear it. I really couldn't bear it. The duckling wouldn't stop peeping and flapping its stunted little wings. Where was its mother? Where were its friends? Where was its pond to play in? It was horrible and I was powerless to help, so I ran out of the shop and down the lane.

Malcolm caught up with me and hugged me tightly into his chest. 'Sorry, I didn't mean to upset you. See, I'm stuck and need your help. I wanted to do a short of all the customers frantically scooping up their ducks and buying them, but then when no one scooped up Rex – that's what I've named him, by the way – it went from being an art-house documentary to a tragedy.'

'What do you mean?'

I can't show this on Film Night at Eades. Everyone would walk out in despair. No, I need to find a happy ending. Someone has to buy that duckling. I've paid the guy for Rex already and said he can offer him for free. So, hopefully when we come back tomorrow he'll be sold.'

I clung to Malcolm like I clung to the hope that Rex would find his home. I felt so emotional. Not just because I was touched by the plight of Rex, but because I was touched that Malcolm had taken me to the pet shop. I was touched that he wanted to share the whole thing with me. He was not your ordinary boy. I mean, of course I already knew that, but now I could hear Star egging me on. Saying, 'Go for it, Calypso, he's so the one.'

Maybe she was right. Unlike Freds, Malcolm was anything but ordinary.

THIRTY-ONE

The End of the Beginning and the Beginning of the End

That evening was a quiet one. Jenny went to bed in a strop. 'That bloody Italian cheated, and that wanker of a president saw it,' she railed.

'Professor Sullivan sees everything,' Portia told her, her black eyes flashing. 'He's the most upright man you're ever likely to meet.'

Jenny flounced out of the room muttering obscenities. 'I think I almost prefer Honey,' I told Portia later. 'At least she's a worthy combatant.'

'You just think that because Honey's hundreds of miles away, Calypso. It's like in that song, "If you can't be with the one you hate, hate the one you're with."'

Portia can be *molto* wise. Probably all those generations of inbreeding.

We went to bed early, leaving the nuns to play cards

with Bell End and Signora. In the morning we showered and bathed and made ourselves look *molto* gorgeous for the tournament. Except for Jenny, who exuded horribleness. Even though she'd been culled, Biffy was making her attend the tournament to boost team spirit. Spectators were allowed today, so the nuns were up at breakfast, bright-eyed with excitement.

'Signora helped make a banner,' Sister Regina announced proudly as she and Sister Bethlehem held up a white tablecloth.

'But Sisters, there's nothing written on it,' I said, hating to be the one to burst their bubble. Poor mad little things.

The Sisters exchanged a knowing look, at least I think that's what it was. It's hard to tell with those big thick spectacles. Then they turned their cloth around, which took a while because they kept getting twisted up in it. But eventually the reverse side was displayed.

The words GREAT BRITAIN RULES THE PISTE were painted professionally in red and blue paint.

Portia and I gave them a cuddle.

Bell End said, 'That's the spirit, Sisters, we'll show them.' Then he turned to us. 'Right, girlies, today's the day you rend the flesh from the bones of the fascist Italian witches. No backbone, these Italians, see, no front bone for that matter. A bunch of big girls' floral blouses with bows on them. No, Great Britain will wipe the salle with their Italian blood. They can bloody well go home and cry in the bosoms of their mothers.'

'Mr Wellend, I think you'll find this is *their* home. We're what's known as the visiting team,' The Commodore explained, laughing into his walrus moustache.

'Not for long, Biff, not for long. Fencing's not a game, as well you know, my old comrade. It's war! Yesterday we let them think we were a bunch of wets. Well, not today! Not today. If blood must be spilled, better theirs than ours is what I say. To your arms, girls, to your arms!' he yelled – and then he blew his whistle.

'Okay, thank you, Mr Wellend, most colourful,' Biffy responded patronisingly. 'But I think you'll find I'm the manager here, and well, to strike a more instructive note, let's just say, may the best team win.'

God I hated him.

Bell End wasn't going to have Biffy pop his mad balloon, though. 'Have their guts for garters!' he cried, and we all punched the air with our fists and cheered.

Jenny said, 'God, you are soooo stupid.'

'You're the bloody idiot that got knocked out in the pools, yer big girl's blouse,' Bell End reminded her.

The boys from the Eades Film Society were waiting for us at the salle where the beautiful Carlotta and her teammates were ready to rinse us. Malcolm was there filming away, and I gave him a little wave. I put on a brave face, which fortified me a bit, but the calibre of these girls was the alpha and omega of perfection – and I don't just mean their looks.

As we started our stretches, a mighty roar erupted from

the Eades boys, which made me blush. Then they started on a series of chavie football chants.

'Eng-ga-land! Eng-ga-land!'

As play was called for the first match, their cries intensified to include classic hits of the football stadiums.

It was soooo embarrassing. Especially when I lost my bout.

As I saluted my opponent in the next bout, I went into a zanshin – a samurai swordsman state of being. Zanshin is a state of mind of complete action when there is no time to take back or fix a stroke or a stride. Zanshin means going beyond technique, because you can't force your opponent to conform to your moves in the way you want. The angle and force of a strike must be adjusted immediately to the energy of your opponent.

I emptied my mind of the English cheer squad. I emptied my mind of Freds and Malcolm and the duckling and asked for divine guidance.

Professor Sullivan and Bell End had two very different styles. Professor Sullivan was all about speed and efficiency and the physical game of chess. Bell End was more a slam 'em with your blade and rain on their parade sort of guy. I wondered what would happen if I drew on both styles for inspiration. As 'play' was called, I was psyched for an aggressive game of chess.

I scored my first hit with a classic Professor Sullivan manoeuvre: advancing down the piste in a seemingly obvious attack by threatening my opponent with a cut to the head. This provoked her into a parry of quinte. I rotated my blade to score an effortless cut to her flank. The point was mine, and we returned to the *en guard* line. As I'd hoped, my opponent's mind ran along predictable lines, which I used to my advantage throughout the game.

The bout was mine. As I was being wired up for my next bout, I ignored my aching muscles and throbbing bruises and remained totally zanshin. I kept up the game of bluff and double bluff, going in for the aggressive attack only to slay her with an unexpected manoeuvre. Professor Sullivan had always been big on wrist action, and I used the adroit strength of my wrists to full advantage that day.

As I made my way back to the *en guard* line between each point, I was vaguely aware of Bell End blowing his whistle while running up and down the various pistes like a madman. I closed my mind and went back to my zanshin state so that his violent instructions to 'slay the filthy witches' would fall on deaf ears.

I won each bout using the same Professor Sullivan/Bell End combination of tactics. Yet despite my own personal victories, ultimately the Great British team was proclaimed the loser.

I know this probably sounds like I'm not a team player, but actually I didn't feel that bad about losing our first international match, because something extraordinary had happened to me on the Italian piste that day. I had metamorphosed into a totally different sabreur than the one who had left England just two days before. By fusing the finesse of Professor Sullivan with the brutality of Bell End I had developed the ability to deliver a ferocious onslaught on the head of a pin. The speed and ferocity of the Italians had taught me that Bell End was right; you needed a lot of aggression to be a sabreur. But Professor Sullivan was right as well; your aggression had to be tempered with precise manoeuvres and intellectual finesse. The British team had lost this time, but I'd played well. Next time we'd wipe the floor with our opponents.

The Italians shook hands graciously and insisted on taking us out to dinner that night. In the changing rooms afterwards, the girls were *molto* charming and gave us a great deal of help with our Italian accents. Even sentences like 'my hair is soooo sweaty' sounded sexy with an Italian accent. When we returned to Saint Augustine's, everyone would think we were Italian goddesses.

After changing, we all went our separate ways. Billy and Portia were off to the Duomo and to do some shopping on the Vecchio. Malcolm took me behind the Medici chapel for another snog-age.

'You were amazing,' he told me, and then he gave me another soulful kiss. 'What on earth happened to you on the piste today? You were like a storm of avenging angels, darling. You really are unpredictable and full of surprises, Calypso Kelly.'

Freds was always telling me that I was full of surprises too. But when he said it, he made it sound like a bad thing. The way Malcolm said it made me feel interesting, mysterious and jam-packed with undiscovered possibilities.

So I kissed him in a very unpredictable way.

THIRTY-TWO

The Italian Duckling Job

As we burst into the pet shop, Giuseppe put down the paper he'd been reading and shook his head. My prayers to Mary, Saint Francis of Assisi (the patron saint of animals) and every other saint I knew the name of had gone unanswered. Which is challenging to a young girl's faith, I can tell you that now.

We could hear Rex peeping before we even looked in his carton. He was flapping his little useless wings, and I was almost certain I saw tears in his eyes. 'How can Italians, the great people who have given us philosophers and theologians by the lorry load, be so horrible to a helpless duckling?' I asked Malcolm.

'Jerkism is an international affliction,' he said as he commenced filming.

'Well, I don't think the pope will be too pleased when he hears about this,' I muttered, only very, very softly, because

Malcolm might have been an atheist or an agnostic or even a communist for all I knew.

'Oh, Rex,' I sobbed. 'There you are, pathetically flapping away in your pathetic paper carton, and us helpless to help.' I wanted him to know I felt his pain.

Rex was peeping himself sick while Malcolm filmed him. Giuseppe put down his paper and came over. I could tell that underneath his mustachioed bravado beat the heart of a duckling lover, because he indicated with a flick of his hand that I could cuddle Rex after all.

I was very tentative at first, but Rex practically dived out of my cupped hands, so I clutched him more firmly as I brought him up to my face for a kiss. I swear he was the most adorable duckling in the entire world. I'd seen his lucky evenly coloured peers on Malcolm's video, and none of them, not a one, had his pluck and character. Rex, for all his speckled blotchiness, was a king among ducklings.

His frantic peeping didn't let up. If I could have translated Italian duckling speak, I'd swear he was begging me to take him home. His little beak felt like batting eyelids on my neck and cheeks. It was very tickly, actually, and I started to giggle. Not that I wasn't *molto* moved and despairing. I held him away from my face a bit and looked at him, girl to duck. His little eyes were all wet and pleading.

I turned to Malcolm – well, Malcolm's camera lens – and wondered if he was thinking the same thing: This whole situation was rum.

'This is too awful, Malcolm,' I said.

Malcolm looked at me for a moment. Really looked, but instead of agreeing with me, he had another conversation, in real Italian, with Giuseppe. Next minute we were leaving the shop with our new duckling.

As we strode onto the street, Rex peeping excitedly, I was thinking about what an un-Freddie thing to do. A nasty part of me even thought Freds would be more likely to shoot little Rex than rescue him. But I knew that wasn't true. Still, I wondered, would Freds ever do anything as random as stroll out of a Florence pet shop with a duckling, sans valid duck passport and microchip?

'What will we do?' I asked Malcolm as we headed back up the lane. 'I mean, we can't take Rex back to England. That was the maddest decision we could have made.'

'I know, but aren't those the best decisions *to* make?' he replied. As we dashed up the lane, it occurred to me that following his flights of fancy was probably something Malcolm did every day. Turning up in Florence like that was a prime example of his eccentric persona. And actually, I liked that about him. As a filmmaker he was bound to be slightly unrealistic, a mad dreamer.

Which was fine for *him*.

In his eccentric Scottish world of endless trust funds, champagne and independence, I guess he could afford to be a dreamer with no grip on reality. But I couldn't. I wasn't Scottish or minted, and I hated champagne. Plus I could hear Bob's voice in my ears – saying in his sternest *pazzo* voice, "Sometimes, Calypso, you go *too* far."

What if my mad padre was right, though? I mean, even a broken clock is right twice a day.

As we wove our way through the streets of Florence, vespas honking at us furiously as we dashed in their path, tourists gawping, café sophisticates smoking and chatting, Rex kept up his chorus of peeps. There would be no way to hide him once we returned to the pensione, and we were flying out tomorrow, anyway. What was Malcolm thinking? I hope he wasn't planning on plopping our little orphan in the Arno to fend for himself.

Maybe this whole duckling rescue was just a plot device for Malcolm's film?

Maybe all he really cared about was a happy ending for *The Last Duckling*?

Maybe I was just incidental. A pleasant distraction in his creative world of plot device and flights of fancy.

Maybe I'd be better off with a nice sensible boy like Freds after all.

These were the questions going through my mind as I scampered through the streets of Florence with a duckling when really I should have been visiting the Uffizi or shopping on the Ponte Vecchio or something sensible like that. I should be writing witty postcards to the 'rentals about my tournament. As it was I visualised a postcard flopping on the mat of chez Clapham as I ran.

Dear Sarah and Bob,
Florence is bellisimo! My fencing has taken on a spiritual quality – even though we did lose the tournament. Oh, by the way I've acquired a duckling since I left England and shall quite possibly be arrested on my attempt to re-enter England. His name is Rex.
Love, Calypso xxxxxxxxxxxxxxxxxxxxxxxxxxxxxxxxxxxxx

(I went mental with the x's to remind them that I was their loving daughter, so they wouldn't get cross.)
PS: What do ducklings eat?
PPS: What do ducklings drink?

I was really starting to panic about Malcolm's motivations now. Why had Freds dumped me? He was nice and ordinary and at this particular point I was thinking ordinary is good. I would never have been imprisoned for duck smuggling if I'd been with Freds. The cobbled lane was too hard to faint on but lordy, lordy, as my gran would say, I've never needed a good old faint more than I needed one that afternoon.

THIRTY-THREE

Aren't the Maddest Ideas Always the Best?

Malcolm and I had our first row a short time later. I shall treasure the memory forever. It took place in a café on the Piazza Santissima Annunziata over double espressos. As settings for arguments go, I can highly recommend this picturesque and noble square on account of its *molto bellisimo* porticoes and church. Also, there is a rather magnifique statue of some bloke on a horse and two fountains on which monkeys dribble water on a couple of sea slugs. Mad.

In addition to being my first argument with Malcolm, it was also my first real row with a boy. Arguing with Freds had always consisted of long periods of him not taking or responding to my numerous calls, txts and e-mails. Fighting with Malcolm involved proper raised voices and the heated exchange of viewpoints.

The fight was over Rex, poor love. First he was stuck in

a Chinese takeaway carton while his peers were snapped up like this season's latest accessory. Then finally, just when he thought he'd found two people to love and care for him, they start brawling about his future smuggling arrangements. And then there was the issue of where he'd live because the thing was, as sophisticated and worldly as this trip had made me, we were still both schoolkids ill-equipped for duckling management.

'Can't he live with you?' Malcolm asked as he lit his fag.

'Are you *mad*?' I shrieked. 'No, don't answer that, because you clearly are quite the nutty one charging off with ducklings like that.'

'It's only the one duckling, Calypso. I don't exactly make a habit of duckling rescue,' he replied. His tone was poisonous with sarcasm, and I felt a bit upset that he managed to look even fitter and more mature as he made his sarcastic remark.

'No, well, I should think not. It's still very irresponsible,' I told him, realising I was sounding like Bob.

'You were the one throwing the Ophelia in the pet shop, darling,' he added. Only he made the word *darling* sound like a nasty insult.

'Well,' I sulked. 'I can't help being a sensitive, feeling person can I?'

'Rex, you are a tug-of-love duckling,' Malcolm told him as he peeped himself stupid in his swaddling napkin.

Ironically we were facing the Spedale degli Innocenti, which was the first-ever orphanage in Europe. Malcolm tried to feed Rex a few crumbs of his biscotti, which I thought proved how ill-equipped he was for parenthood.

'I don't think you should be feeding him biscuits,' I told him, even though Rex seemed delighted. 'They'll rot his teeth.'

'Fine,' Malcolm replied, chucking the biscotti onto the table. Rex looked at me in a pissed-off sort of way.

'Fine,' I replied back, folding my arms and glaring.

So we sat in silence, sipping our espressos, as the sun went down, other couples canoodled and vespas sped past.

Malcolm frowned but he didn't say anything. Then he took back the biscotti and started dropping little crumbs in Rex's beak. It was actually sweet watching Rex eat. His little beak went berserk.

I watched Malcolm holding our little orphan and feeding him crumbs. I already knew he was eccentric, unpredictable and lacking in judgment. So maybe it was a bit unreasonable of me to expect reason, judgment and sanity from Malcolm? Now if Freds were here, he'd know exactly what to do. Then again if Freds were here I wouldn't be sitting here with an orphaned duckling.

Still, Malcolm was being very sweet to Rex, and looking at him I suddenly wanted to pull him. 'I don't want to argue. I'm just worried about how we'll get him through customs,' I explained more gently.

Malcolm looked up at me and smiled. 'Oh, I quite enjoyed our little *contretemps*. Your lips are quite kissable when you're pouting,' he teased, offering me a piece of biscotti to feed Rex. 'Listen, don't be worried. I'm leaving tonight. It's far better that I take him back to England in my hand luggage,' he insisted as he waved to the waiter for another espresso.

'But you can't. The authorities will spot Rex in their X-ray machine thingamees and the poor thing will end up at the mercy of Italian customs officials! I shall do it.'

'Fair enough,' he agreed without a fight. 'You do it.' Then before I could faint with the horror of what I'd just volunteered to do, he kissed me, and people at surrounding tables clapped.

'See, my lovely sabre-wielding wild child, you have me eating out of the palm of your hand.'

On the way back, I decided that Malcolm was not the boy for me even if he did think I was a wild child. He was far too eccentric, even if it was in a creative way. As amusing as he was to be with, life was not a movie set. I needed a nice, normal boyfriend who didn't complicate my life with ducklings and other imponderables. Because now that I'd won the argument over who was taking Rex back, it began to dawn on me what a pyrrhic victory it actually was. I mean, how was I going to smuggle Rex through customs? What if they discovered me and chucked me in Old Chokey and I had to live on gruel and wander an exercise yard with girls who were wise to the ways of crime and flick knives?

I suppose I'd be used to the food at least.

My soul was heavy with all this pondering when

Malcolm eventually said, 'Shall we see if Rex can swim?' And before I could say something cautionary and sensible, he'd dropped him in the fountain.

Rex took to the fountain like a duck to water, but still. 'How could you be so irresponsible!' I screamed. 'What if he'd drowned?'

Malcolm laughed as he picked me up and chucked me in after Rex.

If I had any doubts about whether Malcolm was actually the boy for me, they were drowned in that pool of deadly bacteria.

'Rex,' I told him later after we had gone to Malcolm's grand palazzo to dry off. 'I'm sorry to have to break it to you, but your parents are splitting up.'

Malcolm was drying my hair with one of the big white towels as I broke this shocking news to our duckling child. Rex seemed to take it well. So did Malcolm, which was probably the most *molto* annoying thing about the whole breakup. I know we hadn't officially been going out, but we had adopted a duckling together, and so technically that made him the first boy I'd officially dumped. Only I don't think Malcolm realised this technicality, which was *molto* annoying. When you dump someone, you want to see a certain amount of disappointment.

'I hope you realise that I meant that,' I told him. 'About the being dumped thing.'

'Really?' he asked as he finished drying my hair off. 'Perhaps you should do it by txt? That will show me.'

'Hah!' I said, grabbing the towel and flicking him with it. 'How dare you mock my tragedy!'

And I chased him round the palazzo until we reached the kitchen, where he grabbed me in a manly hug. 'Fancy something to eat, my gorgeous Botticelli angel?' he asked, trying to kiss me.

'Fine!' I replied, pulling away.

So he set to work and whipped up some eggs Fiorentina, which I hate to admit were divinely delicious. I had two servings and then despite myself I had several more servings of Malcolm's delicious lips. 'Don't think that just because I like kissing you we're un-dumped or anything,' I told him sternly.

'Whatever you say, my cherub,' he teased.

It was after eleven when he finally walked me back to the pensione. I let him put his arm around me, but that was only because I was freezing cold. When he tried to kiss me at the door, I pushed him away and delivered my pre-prepared speech. 'I do like you, Malcolm, but we're not suited. I need a nice, normal boy, not a Scottish nipple-piercing filmmaker. This madness is too much for me. It's been a lovely holiday romance, but the time has come to face –'

'Calypso,' he interrupted.

'What?'

Then he pulled me into his chest and gave me the best snog-age I've ever had.

'You do say the most idiotic things. See you in Windsor

on Saturday,' he told me, dashing off into the night. I was still swooning with the dreamy madness of it all as a vespa sped past and almost knocked me off my feet.

I rang the bell of the pensione and waited in the chill night with my swaddled duckling contemplating the Malcolm-versus-Freddie issue. Eventually I was admitted by the night-watch chap.

In the courtyard, Sister Regina and Sister Bethlehem were sipping some petrol – I think the Italians like to call it grappa – with the Signora.

'I'm disappointed in you, Calypso,' Sister Regina said as I entered the courtyard.

I thought she must be referring to Rex, who was peeping away frantically. The idea that tomorrow I was going to successfully smuggle him into Great Britain was madness of the first order. What on earth had possessed me to insist on sole custody of Rex? As a tall, fit boy, surely Malcolm was much better suited to the rigours of Old Chokey than me?

I placed Rex on the table and fell into Sister's arms and sobbed. 'Oh Sister, I didn't know what to do. No one would buy him and Malcolm was filming him and, well, we bought him, and now I don't know how I'm going to smuggle him through customs, and he won't stop peeping, and I'll end up in Old Chokey, and Bob and Sarah will be –'

'Shush, child,' Sister soothed, stroking my hair while Signora Santospirito and Sister Bethlehem clucked away over Rex. 'What's all this? I was talking about you missing the team dinner.'

'Oh no. I can't believe I missed my first post-international tournament team dinner. Will they throw me off the team, Sister?'

'No one's throwing anyone off anything. Though I daresay Mr Wellend and Mr Biffy will give you a steely look or two, but the main worry is drying up these silly tears.'

She dabbed my face with one of her long sleeves. 'Now what's all this about Old Chokey?' she asked.

'Rex.' I pointed. 'I can't leave him here and I can't take him home.'

'I could take him in my sleeve,' Sister Bethlehem suggested.

I looked at her and smiled. Bless. She was so sweet. Daft as socks, but ever so sweet.

'No one would dare look in a nun's sleeve,' Sister Bethlehem assured me.

'That's right,' Sister Regina agreed. 'Not the lowest swine would dare trespass on a nun's sleeve.'

'But someone will hear him,' I reasoned.

'I'll say it's my joints,' Sister Bethlehem told me, and so it was settled.

THIRTY-FOUR

You're No One Until Someone Wants to Sell Stories about You to the Press

I was a bundle of nerves on the flight home, not just because of our smuggling but because each mile was bringing me closer to Freds, and my feelings about him were more jumbled than ever. Sister Regina forced me to drink some brandy to calm myself, but all it did was make me feel sick. Sister Bethlehem slept the whole way, and I had to keep checking on Rex to make sure she didn't crush him. Fortunately the noise of the flight drowned out his incessant peepings, but I was not full of *joie de vivre* as we touched down at Gatwick.

Customs was not at all what I expected. I don't mean the whole smuggling livestock palaver, because that went off without a hitch – walking through the Nothing to

Declare aisle with two nuns was a breeze. Thank you, Saint Jude – patron saint of lost causes – once more, you've come through.

No, the first voice I heard at the other end of the barrier was Honey screaming, 'That's her! That's her! The tall one with fluffy bits sticking out the top of her head. The one in the chav top.'

And then a blaze of flashlights went off in my face.

Blinded, I groped through the noise of a thousand paps clicking their cameras and drowning all thoughts in my mind. You've heard that saying like a deer caught in headlights? Well, that was me. Scared out of my wits. Bell End was right, I was a big girl's blouse.

People were calling out my name and asking me questions. 'So how's it feel to be called the prince's slapper, luv?'

'Is it true you pushed him in the Thames because he dumped you, Calypso?'

'Bitter was you?'

'Were all those things you said true? Did your parents really torture you as a child?'

'Is it true you pulled his best mate, the Laird of Killmarn?'

'What was your Florence love-nest like? Raunchy was it?'

I felt myself being grabbed and groped and began to lash out. Then I made out the shadowy figures of my parents, Sarah and Bob, as I heard them call out to me above the hubbub. My lovely wonderful, protective, much-maligned parents, Sarah and Bob. They grabbed me and I grabbed them like a drowning girl grabbing two life jackets. Suddenly we were surrounded by four blokes in buzz cuts and sharp suits.

'Right, guys, get us out of here,' Bob said with an authority that shocked me to the core.

'But my fencing gear?' I cried – I know, how materialistic. But seriously, you knock yourself out trying to make the national team of your country. You wouldn't let go of the kit either.

'It's all taken care of, darling,' the madre assured me in the tone she used to use when I was ill and allowed to eat egg and soldiers in bed – we're talking four years old here.

The suits led us to the waiting limo as the paps kept up their relentless barrage of questions and flashes.

It was très, très merde with double algebra bells on.

Finally the door of the stretch was slammed shut and the stadium-strength flashlights of the pap's cameras stopped. I could see again. 'What, in the name of old ladies' knickers, is going on?' I asked.

A few indefatigable paparazzi banged on the roof and windows of the limo as we drove away from the curb. Why do they do that? I mean, did they honestly think that I was going to come out and face their prying lenses and obscene questioning?

I guess they did. Hope is a powerful form of delusion. Believe me, I speak from personal experience.

'We thought it best to keep it all from you while you were in Florence,' Bob explained. 'We wanted you to concentrate on your fencing.'

My eyes were still blurry from the flashes that had been blasting my retinas for the last ten minutes, so I was struggling to focus on the buzz cuts sitting opposite us.

'Oh, and who are these guys?' I asked, pointing to the grumpy suits who were eyeing me up like I was a prime suspect.

'We thought you might need some security for a bit,' Bob explained.

'Just until it all blows over,' Sarah added hastily, giving my knee a comforting squeeze.

'Security from what?' I asked. I couldn't help feeling like this was all a practical joke or maybe payback for The Incident when I was three. I swear, I would not put it past my 'rentals to pull a stunt like that to prove a point. They are from Hollywood after all.

'Erm . . . perhaps you'd better read these, Calypso,' Bob suggested as he placed a pile of newspapers on my lap. 'There's a lot more, but that should give you the gist of the situation.'

'Oh,' I replied as the first headline hit me like a lacrosse ball between the eyes. 'Prince's Slapper Claims Parental Abuse!'

This was going to be worse than The Incident – I just knew it. I flicked through the first dozen or so headlines. I'd been accused of purposefully pushing Freds into the

Thames, pulling his 'best mate, the Laird of Killmarn.' Malcolm hadn't said anything about being a laird – whatever a laird was. Oh, and apparently I was a lush to rival all lushes. There was even a snap of me knocking back a cocktail in a nightclub with Honey, presumably taken last term on the weekend she'd famously vomited in my handbag.

Naturally there were loads of quotes from Honey. She'd given a personal account of how she'd desperately tried to prevent my spiralling downfall. Her piece was titled: 'My Friend The Slut!' – the sub read, '*The Honourable Honey O'Hare, It Girl, Socialite and muse to the stars, has kindly donated her fee for this article to the charity ADIG (Alms for Dilapidated It Girls.)*'

Of course she had, darling!

God, I wished Star was here.

But I couldn't blame Honey. The worst of it was that each piece was littered with quotes from my stupid short-listed essay about my mad 'rentals. Had I really written such vitriolic rubbish? It put Nancy Mitford's thinly disguised book about her own family into perspective. I thought it amusing, but most of her family never spoke to her again. One of her other books, *A Talent to Annoy,* came to mind. Perhaps in years to come I would write a book, *A Talent for Dramarama.*

How was I meant to imagine that an essay on my pathetic personal tragedies could make the short list above essays from orphans and refugees and kids with terminal diseases? There were teens out there who had experienced real tragedy.

Over the past week I'd been so preoccupied with Freds dumping me, The Counter Dump, the fall-out of The Counter Dump, the tournament in Florence, Malcolm, and smuggling ducklings that I had totally forgotten about the essay.

Now I was in the merde. I looked at Sarah and Bob as tears of love, compassion, remorse and fear mingled and ran down my face in a river of shame. 'I didn't mean all those things,' I told them. 'Honestly, I did write lots of lovely things about you too. I promise I did,' I ranted. 'But the entry rules limited me to three thousand words, and it had to be about great traumas. I wish I'd never written the stupid thing. I do love you, though, I do!'

'Oh darling,' Sarah laughed as she clasped me to her while Bob patted my back. 'We know you do. And we couldn't be prouder of you, honestly, darling. The essay is brilliant.'

I was officially the worst daughter in the world. I would buy a slab of granite and carve those words into it as I wandered the streets with it slung around my neck.

I clung to my mother and my father and they clung to me, and in that moment I knew they were weren't a bit bonkeresque. Well, just the tiniest bit, maybe. I would hardly be clinging to maddies, would I? No, I relied on these two forgiving 'rentals for everything. Scenes of uncountable kindnesses, angelic acts and selfless sacrifices

– all for a thankless daughter who hadn't even won her first international fencing tournament – montaged into one another.

My tears wouldn't stop no matter how many times they reassured me how proud they were of me.

Proud of *moi*?

Perhaps they *were* mad? I looked at my mother and then at Bob. They were quite fit for a couple of old folks in their early forties. My mother really needed to get something done with her hair, and Bob, well, his dress sense rivalled the chaviest wannabe hip-hop artist onstage. But with a visit to Saville Row for a few bespoke suit fittings, he really could make something of himself, I decided.

'I honestly didn't want to enter the competition, that part's true. But I did write those things, and now, well, you must hate me. Just a little bit?'

Bob and Sarah threw back their heads and laughed like an entire shop of old women's knickers.

THIRTY-FIVE

In Each Letter, a Heart Beats

I returned to school on Sunday afternoon, and before dinner, every Year Eleven girl had gathered in my room. Some to offer their solidarity, some just out of curiosity. I was the cause celeb à la mode.

'I can't *believe* you'd dare to show your face after all the stories you sold about Calypso!' Star sniped at Honey as she cruised in with her fags.

Honey was equally outraged. 'Moi?' she asked, pointing to herself in shock. 'I was just trying to raise my dearest friend's profile a bit. I thought it only fair that someone tell *her* side of the story. Sorry for caring,' she added, slumping on my pillow.

'You gave them photographs of her drinking alcohol in a bar!' Portia pointed out. 'What sort of profile were you hoping to raise, exactly?'

Honey shrugged. 'Actually I thought it was a très flattering shot, considering I took it with my mobile.'

'How did Bob and Sarah take it?' Indie asked, looking at me with her chocolate brown eyes.

'They were absolutely amazing about everything.'

'What? Even about the essay?' Star probed.

I laughed. 'You know Bob. He thinks it was inevitable that his progeny would be a literary genius, and of course it's only natural that I used artistic licence.'

'I knew they'd support you, whatever you wrote,' Star reminded me, chucking me a Hershey's Kiss.

'I know. I guess I underestimated their capacity to worship all creative endeavours, no matter how rubbish it is.'

'I think you underestimate how much they care about you, actually. You've got the coolest 'rentals out of all of us,' Star insisted.

Everyone seemed to agree – even girls who'd never met Bob and Sarah.

'Listen, a part of me doesn't want to give you this, but, well, you probably should check out what he has to say,' Star told me as she chucked a letter from Freds at me.

It wasn't on palace paper, but I recognised the writing.

'It's from Freds,' I said as I opened it up. I looked at the eager faces of the girls gathered around me in the room. 'I'll read it later,' I said but Honey told everyone apart from my closest friends to leave. Actually, what she said was, 'Ciao, ciao, peasants.' Then she clapped her hands at them as if dispersing hens. Naturally, she stayed on and only about half the crew left, but I read the letter out anyway. I was too desperate to know the contents to hold on and too terrified to read it on my own.

Dear Calypso,

I'm not sure I should even be writing you this letter. Last time I wrote you a letter you went into a huge strop and accused The Palace of writing it. Well, I'm using school-headed paper this time, so unless you believe the dark conspiracy of The Palace extends to Eades, I hope you'll accept this letter is written in my own hand and take it in the spirit in which it's intended.

First up, BIG SORRY for the dumping by txt thing. I was totally out of order. Totally.

Secondly, BIG SORRY if you feel guilty about The Counter Dump thing. Don't! I deserved it. Billy told me about the whole scheme, but don't be too hard on him, he's a bit dopey in matters of love.

Thirdly (is thirdly even a word?) BIG SORRY for falling in the Thames and dragging your name through the mud in yet another media frenzy. See, this is why I didn't think I was right for you. You're mad and wild and well, I'm not. I'd like to be, but every time I do anything remotely out of the ordinary, like fall in the Thames, it's front-page news. That's probably why I'm such a boring git.

I also wanted you to know that I'm really happy that you and McHamish are hanging out. He gets you and I know you get him. It kills me that I will never be able to pull a girl as cool as you again. So I guess I'll have to stay confined to my boring little box and face the fact that I will never be enough for you. I wish I was wilder and cooler and capable of being eccentric and worthy of a girl like you without a media frenzy. But I'm not. You give good txt Calypso and I know I've never laughed as much as when we were hanging out.

Anyway, this letter is getting far too meaningful and pathetic. A sad, tragic part of me even wants to say I hope we can still be friends. (I hope you're not reading this out by the way.)

Instead, let's just leave it as it is,

Laters,

Freds. xxx

I felt tears prickling my eyes as I folded the page up and slipped it carefully back in the envelope. I would *definitely* be hanging on to this letter, however tragic Star thought I was.

'I was wrong,' Star blurted, her eyes tearing up.

'What?'

I couldn't believe it, but her lip was actually wobbling. 'About Freds, I was wrong. You have soooo got to get back with him.'

I shook my head. 'There is no way I am getting back with him. The Counter Dump was the daftest idea ever. I am so not –'

'No. I mean *really* back with him. He loves you. You love him. I thought he was this up-himself boring git, but he's not. He's nice and he's real and he's –'

'She's pulling Malcolm now,' Portia pointed out.

I didn't correct her because I couldn't bear to go through the whole Italian dumping drama – which I was fairly certain hadn't stuck anyway.

'Malcolm's balmy,' Star said, dismissing him with a flick of her strawberry-blonde locks.

'I like him,' I told her, even though my pulse was racing at what Star was saying about being wrong about Freds.

And besides, I *did* like Malcolm. The truth was I was already really missing him even though I was determined that he was too much of a drama for a drama queen like me.

'I like Malcolm too,' Star agreed. 'I like him more than Freds, actually, but that's not the point.'

'I think Calypso's right,' Indie added. 'She's with Malcolm now.'

'Me too,' Portia agreed, lifting her head from her magazine.

'Shame he doesn't play polo, really,' Fenella sighed. Her sister, Perdita, agreed.

'Well, if anyone is interested in *my* opinion,' Honey began, but she was wrestled to the ground and smothered in duvets by the entire room of girls.

Then my phone rang, and it was Malcolm. 'How's Rex?' he asked.

'Oh my God!' I exclaimed. 'I forgot all about Rex!' I said to the room at large.

'Who is Rex?' Star mouthed as everyone all around looked on confused.

'I'll call you back,' I told Malcolm, pressing End.

'I haven't even told you about Rex,' I told the room.

'Does Rex play polo?' Perdita asked, suddenly perking up with interest.

'Yaah, is he really, really fit?' Clemmie asked. 'I haven't pulled a boy for an age, and I think my lips may have atrophied,' she groaned, flopping backwards with the despair of it all.

Are all teenagers' lives as fearfully confusing as mine, I wondered as I began telling my *pazzo* tale of the Last Duckling.

THIRTY-SIX

Pulling the Past in Pullers' Woods

Sisters Regina and Bethlehem had done a wonderful job of settling Rex into the convent. Actually, all the nuns adored Rex, and the feeling was mutual. They had the gardener build a small pond, and there was talk of finding him another little companion. Not that he was ever lonely. It was so adorable the way he followed Sister Regina around everywhere she went. I wondered if I could train Dorothy to do that. It would look soooo cool wandering around Windsor with a little bunny hopping along behind me.

The entire week was disrupted by journalists trying to get a personal account from me. But Sister Constance was by now only too familiar with the ways of the paparazzi, and they were thwarted at every attempt. All trips to Windsor were banned for the next weekend, but no one resented me too much for that, as the weather was so filthy. Also, Sunday night was the Burns Supper with the piping in of the pizza, and Star and Indie's band was performing *my* song, which I hadn't needed to rewrite once Indie attacked it with her thrashing guitar solo.

Malcolm called and sent the odd txt, but he was too busy editing *The Last Duckling* to give me much attention. The film was due to be screened the following Sunday at Eades, and Saint Augustine's was invited. I wondered what the film would be like, and okay, yes, I was also wondering if he'd get the chance to pull me. But mostly I was wondering about Freds – not whether he'd pull me, because his letter had made that pretty clear – but what it would be like to see him again. I had read and reread his letter so many times and agreed with Star that I at least needed to respond. What was the etiquette with royal ex-boyfriends?

I didn't see why it was so pathetic that we stay friends. I mean, we were bound to bump into one another, with our schools being so close and both of us being on our school's sabre teams.

Five drafts of my reply later, I decided to txt him and see if he wanted to meet up in Pullers' Woods for a chat. Pullers' Woods seemed like a good place, with the paps still lurking all over Windsor and outside the perimeter of the razor wire.

Freds replied immediately.

Sun a/noon, by tree that attack dog chased you up? F

I replied:

C U there, C

I tried not to dwell on the fact that we weren't doing x's anymore. I decided to take Rex to meet Freds. I needed the support, and also I thought it might break the ice to have a third party there, and I didn't trust Star not to hiss instructions to me.

It was snowing, so I had to wrap Rex in a rug, which Sister Bethlehem had crocheted five hundred years ago and smelt of mothballs. The smell made me sneeze the whole way through the woods. The snow was falling lightly, but not many flakes were making it through the bare branches of the trees. Everything felt still and magical, and I half expected a lion to wander out and start chatting to me. I was armed with Honey's mace in the event we ran into any attack dogs who might be in the mood to eat ducklings, but none came my way.

I had dressed carefully in jeans and a hoodie so Freds didn't think I was making an effort. I'd also taken special care to only wear lots of lip-gloss and mascara, for that no-makeup look that boys love. Careless and carefree was the note I was hoping to strike.

Freds was already there, by the tree, as arranged. Punctual as ever. His hair wasn't doing that sticky-outy thing I loved so much, although now that I knew about his covert gel usage, I was not as enamoured of his hair as I used to be. He'd had it cut, and he looked vulnerable rather than cool, but, oh my God, he was still heartbreakingly fit. It must be the prince thing.

'H-Hi,' I stuttered awkwardly. 'Erm, this is Rex. I thought you might want to meet him because, well, he's the star of the film Malcolm shot in Florence, and well, you'll be seeing it next Sunday. He's very excited. Rex, I mean. Although Malcolm's obviously feverishly excited too. I mean, it's his film,' I blurted.

Freds laughed. I couldn't tell if he was laughing because I was mad as a drawer of old ladies' knickers or because he thought I was funny.

Freds stroked Rex on the beak and Rex nipped Fred's finger. It was all very touching. Then Freds took him out of his swaddling blanket and placed him on the snow and Rex went bonkeresque. He started nipping the snow and dashing about trying to catch flakes as they fell. His little webbed prints looked soooo adorable in the snow.

Freds and I watched him running about like a mad thing for a bit and then we looked at one another. And then Freds kissed me. First on the forehead and then on the nose.

Then just as I feared (or was it a longing?), he was about to kiss my lips, but he said, 'I'm going to the States in the Easter holidays.'

'Cool. Me too,' I said. I mean, I live in America, and Bob and Sarah were going back with me then. And of course, Freds knew all that. Freds knew everything.

'I'm doing this tour thing with Gran and the 'rents.'

'Fancy that,' I replied. I know, I know! I can't believe I said that. The spirit of my own gran must have inhabited my brain.

Freds didn't seem a bit fazed by my insanity, though. 'Yaah, so, the thing is, I know I said it was pathetic to want to be friends, but well . . . I wondered if I might see you there?'

'Where?' I asked, because I was still mentally kicking myself for saying 'fancy that!'

I closed my eyes to gather my thoughts, and that was when he did it. That was when he really kissed me, on the mouth – with his lips. And while it was most *tranquillo* and *fantastico* and *molto* gorgeous, I pulled away.

Then my phone rang. It was Malcolm, and my heart skipped a beat. Not because Freds had just attempted to pull me, but because I realised that I really wanted to see Malcolm more than anyone else in the world. 'It's Malcolm,' I whispered to Freds, as I pressed Answer.

'Want to meet up in Pullers' Woods in a bit?' Malcolm asked. 'So you can dump me again?'

I giggled. 'Sure, I'll bring Rex for a visit. Call me when you're almost there,' I told him, totally longing to see him.

'I'm almost there, actually,' he said. 'Just through the barbed wire gap now.'

'Well, hurry up, then, I'm already here! So's Freds,' I told him, because I didn't want any subterfuge between us. Apart from not wanting to muck Malcolm around, he was the sort of person I could be honest with and be myself around.

'Cool,' he replied happily. 'See you in a mo.'

Freddie, on the other hand, looked at me with one of his wretched disappointed looks.

I poked out my tongue and then – shock, horror – HRH poked *his* tongue out at me!

'Sorry,' Freds said, rubbing his long, tapered fingers through his hair. 'About the kiss thing earlier. I didn't mean for that to happen.'

'It's okay,' I told him gently, suddenly maddeningly aware of his lemony smell again. 'It's just not right. Not now,' I told him maturely even though my mind was screaming, HAVE ONE LAST KISS! HE'S THE PRINCE, YOU MADDY!

Oh, buggery bollocks, just when I thought I knew what I felt, and whom I felt *it* for.

Princes! You can't live with them, but then again, can you really live without them?

Calypso's fencing terms and English words

FENCING TERMS

attack *au fer*: an attack that is prepared by deflecting an opponent's blade

bout: one single fight, usually lasting around six minutes

disengagement: a way to continue attacking after being parried

en garde: the 'ready' position fencers take before play

épée: another weapon used in fencing

parry: defensive move, a block

piste: a fourteen-metre-long combat area on which a bout is fought

point: the tip of a weapon's blade

pool: a group into which fencers are divided during preliminary rounds to assess ranking

retire: retreat

riposte: an offensive action made immediately after a parry of the opponent's attack

sabre: The only cutting fencing blade. Points are scored both by hits made with the tip of the blade and by cuts made with the blade, but more commonly by cuts. The sabre target is everything above the leg, including the head and arms. For this reason the entire weapon, including the guard, registers hits on an electrical apparatus even though hitting the weapon's guard is not legal. This means the sabreur is totally wired – unlike fencers using the other weapons. Before play begins, the sabreurs must check that all parts of their electric kit are working. This is done by the sabreurs tapping their opponents on the mask, the sabre, the guard and the metal jacket so that all hits will be recorded

salle: fencing hall or club

salute: once formal, now a casual acknowledgement of one's opponent and president at the start of a bout

seeding: the process of eliminating fencers from their pools, based on the results of their bouts

trompement: deception of the parry

ENGLISH WORDS

arse: *derrière.* To make an arse of yourself means to embarrass yourself

ASBO: Anti-Social Behaviour Order; a punishment handed out to youth who graffiti or get drunk or use foul language

blag: to talk your way into or out of something, or to fake something

bless: an affectionate, sweet exclamation, but like all English words, it can be used sarcastically

blank/to be blanked: to not register someone; to look through them

blue: blue paper given to write lines on; a minor punishment

bollocks: literally means testicles but used to mean useless, nonsense, ridiculous

bottle out: chicken out, lose your nerve. 'Bottle' is another word for 'nerve,' so you can also 'lose your bottle'

chav/chavie: A person defined by a common way of behaving or dressing. They have their favourite designer brands and love loads of bling. The opposite of posh or Sloaney

common: slang for vulgar, of low social status, lacking charm or manners. Note: you can be rich and still be common

cut: to ignore someone, to look right through them; see *blank*

Daddy's plastic: parental credit cards

DPGs: Daddy's Plastic Girls; girls who are defined by their limitless credit card privileges

dressing down: telling off

en suite: bathroom attached to bedroom

exeat: weekend at which pupils attending boarding school go home, usually every three weeks

extract the urine: a polite way of saying 'take the piss'

fag: cigarette

fancy (v): to find someone attractive

Febreze: spray used to remove odours from clothes

fit: cute, hot, attractive. Girls and boys both use the word to describe the opposite sex. Note: a girl wouldn't refer to another girl as fit – she'd say 'stunning'

gating: a punishment in which one is not permitted to leave the school grounds on weekends

hoodie: sweatshirt with a hood

house mother or house mistress: female head of a boarding house

It Girl: a society girl of royal extraction with a large media profile

Kiltland: Scotland

kit: equipment and outfit for specific event or activity

knickers: panties

leg it: make a run for it

mad: eccentric, crazy or unreasonable – out there

madly: very, as in 'madly late'

mobile: cell phone

Old Chokey: a prison

pash: pashmina

piss-take/to take the piss: to tease, mimic or to make fun of someone, either maliciously or fondly; a joke (see *extract the urine*, above)

pleb: short for plebeian – a derogatory term suggesting lack of class

plebbie: (adj) for pleb (see above)

point: as in making a point in an argument

prat: idiot, fool

pull: to make out, score, kiss, etc.

public school: exclusive boarding school

rinse: to totally decimate your opponent in sport or debate

rip: to ridicule, tease; equivalent to 'take the piss'

Sloane: posh, snooty girl (named after Sloane Street and Square, an upscale area in London)

snog-age: (rhymes with 'corsage') to tongue kiss

sorted: an expression of approval; 'no problem'

soz: sorry

spliff: marijuana; a joint

tomoz: tomorrow

taking the piss: to tease someone, rip it out of them, see *piss-take*

term: Three terms make up a school year: winter term is before Christmas; spring term is between Christmas and Easter; summer term is between Easter and the summer holiday

toff: snobby aristocrat

tuck: snack foods you are allowed to bring to boarding school; junk food

tuck in: pig out

wardrobe: closet

wind up: to tease either gently or nastily

Year: girls start boarding at age 11 in Year Seven, and the 'Years' go up to Year Eleven (ages 15–16). The final two years are referred to as the Lower Sixth and Upper Sixth (ages 16–17 and 18, respectively)

Acknowledgements

First up, shout outs to the stunning, preternaturally gifted girls of Saint Mary's Ascot, Cheltenham Ladies College, Bennerz and my favourite Etonians, you know, the really, really fit ones! In fact, the entire boarding school community should take a bow! I hope your teachers, masters, matrons, bursars and house mothers applaud you every day because one day you'll be in a position to hand out the blues! Speaking of blue, I would be dismally blue without the friendship of Malcolm William Young. In fact, if he didn't exist, I'd have to make him up.

I totally lucked out having an agent like Laura Dail and an editor like Melanie Cecka at Bloomsbury USA. And I know it! Every day I do a mad little tribute dance in their honour. So far, only my family have seen my mad-dance. They recommend I hold off a few millennia before unleashing it on a wider audience. Until that day, I salute you in Latin, *Salve*!

But the laurels and really, really worshipful words go to the girls who read my books, especially the girls who write in to askcalypso@calypsochronicles.com. Seriously, if you don't grow up and rule the world, and see your names in lights over Times Square, I shall unleash my mad little dance.

TYNE O'CONNELL is the author of several romantic comedies, including novels about the American-born, British-educated Calypso Kelly. She has written for newspapers and magazines such as *Vogue*, *Marie Claire* and *Elle.* She lives in London, England.